ONCE UPON A TREASURE HUNT

LINDA NEEDHAM

BIG SCRUMPY PRESS

ABOUT ONCE UPON A TREASURE HUNT

From *USA Today* Best Selling Author, Linda Needham:
Once Upon a Treasure Hunt
Refreshed and Retitled from the original *The Wedding Night*,
and Ready to set your Heart on Fire!

COERCED BY A DRAGON

When mining baron Lord Jackson Rushford coerces folklorist Mairey Faelyn into using her extensive knowledge to help him search for a map to a legendary deposit of ancient Celtic silver, she has no choice but to agree to the devil's bargain. The beastly man has already abducted her family's research library and installed it on his estate, threatening to hire a rival expert to find the Willowmoon Knot if she refuses. The Knot is the key to finding the treasure, and has been missing from her family's protection for centuries. The vast resources that Rushford offers to Mairey prove as irresistible as they are dangerous to her family's legacy. Trapped into 'helping' him, Mairey plots to lead the dark, thunderous 'dragon' astray at every turn.

But while adventuring together into dusty catacombs, castle towers, cozy country inns, even into the bowels of a coal mine, Mairey soon finds that Rushford has charming chinks in his armor, and guards his heart more strongly than any treasure. As their hunt draws them ever closer to the treasure, Mairey finds herself falling deeply for the man, fearing she'll be forced to betray either Jack or her pledge to her family. Is their love just a fairy tale, or will it last forever?

~

Praise for
Once Upon a Treasure Hunt
(originally *The Wedding Night*)

Nominated "Most Hanky Read" & "Most Luscious Romance" — *All About Romance*

"The love scenes are, shall we say, searing." 4 Hearts — *The Romance Reader*

A Desert Island Keeper: "What a fantastic book!" — *All About Romance*

Pure Magic! – This book was a joy from the first page to the last. It has turned Linda into an auto-buy author for me. The hero, Jack, is just spectacular, arrogant on the surface and so heartrendingly vulnerable inside. The heroine is charming, sweet and as loveable as any I've ever read. Even the minor characters sparkle! I loudly recommend this treat to anyone who needs a great escape! — *AMAZON reader*

This story was just enchanting from page one. – With a "to-die-for" hero and a feisty, sharp as a tack heroine, the author provides no waiting to get these two together and start the sparks flying. Linda Needham was a "sleeper" author for me as a long-time lover of historical romance, and I'm so glad I stumbled upon this book. It has everything: Great story that tracks well, believable controversy between the protagonists, ever building sexual chemistry to its crescendo, wonderful character building and supporting cast members, and truly a charming and wonderful read. You'll do yourself a disservice by not picking up this truly fairytale romance! — *GOODREADS reader*

$\sim$

Praise for LINDA NEEDHAM

Linda Needham has the ability to mix laughter with tears to touch a reader's heart. — *Romantic Times*

Ms. Needham has a knack for drawing her readers from page 1, and not letting go even when the story ends — *New and Used Books*

Linda Needham's novels are sheer delight. — *Lisa Kleypas, NYT bestselling author of Chasing Cassandra: The Ravenals*

ANTHOLOGIES

Baby Shoes:

100 Stories by 100 Authors (Flash in a Flash)

WRITING REFERENCES

Brainstorming Your Novel: From First Spark to Blockbuster

DEDICATION

To Stargazer's Panto Prydwen at Anchor, Winnie, our treasure hunter,
who found her way into our hearts.

ONCE UPON A TREASURE HUNT

ONCE UPON A TREASURE HUNT

CONTENTS

CHAPTER 1

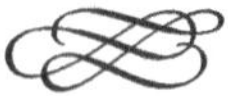

Northwest Lancashire, England
Summer, 1858

"It's an elf bolt, miss! A real and truly one!"

"An actual arrow, made by an elf?" Mairey Faelyn gave a properly astounded gasp, then oooed grandly. The other children scooted in closer to her as she studied the barbed flint arrowhead in little Orrin's coal-begrimed palm. "Amazing!"

"Found it myself, I did!" The boy perched with elfin lightness on a bale of moldering wool sacks in the abandoned fulling mill, a changeling if ever there was one.

He was wearing Mairey's hat—her father's, a tweedy, sagging-brimmed relic of his folklore field-collecting days. Dear and dilapidated, it reminded her of the wonderful years she'd spent following him into hip-narrow caves and weeping catacombs, collecting folktales and marvels from every part of Britain.

"Hey, I found three of 'em, Orrin!" Geordie leaped into the

center of the pack, plucked back an imaginary bow string, and shot an imaginary arrow into the cobweb-draped rafters. "Yep, the sky cracked open one night during a storm and 'n' elf bolts fell right out of the clouds."

"Imagine that!" She'd seen hundreds of such arrow flints; had an extensive collection of her own in her library at Galcliffe College. And although each had been hewn by an ancient human hunter—not by elves and witches—she loved the folk-lore far better than the facts.

Loved the children's tales most of all. "Where did you find this very fine specimen, Orrin?"

"In the barrow field, last winter."

The Daunton Barrow. She was aware of the ancient burial mound, but had never seen it. Daunton was a coal town; the sacred site was probably a slag heap by now, but worth a visit. "Is the barrow far, Orrin? Will you take me there?"

"Oh, no, miss!" Orrin slid off the bale, shaking his head gravely. "We can't go there. It's a dragon's barrow!"

"A dragon! Here in Daunton?" A colliery with its own worm tale? "Does he have a name?"

Orrin glanced warily around at his fellows and their smudged faces, looked beyond them to the open doorway with its afternoon glare, and then blinked back at Mairey and said in a whisper, "Balforge."

The children gasped in delicious dread at the very name, then wrestled each other for a closer spot, primed for a whop-ping good story.

Orrin opened his mouth to continue, but Geordie, the redoubtable showman, thunked a stone onto the floor, startling everyone and missing Mairey's toes by an inch.

"This here's one of his fangs!"

Orrin snorted.

Everyone else oooed, Mairey loudest of all, though Balforge's fang was, in dull, scholarly reality, a primitive flint axe-head. The surprise was that these children called it a dragon's fang. Certainly worth a footnote in the book she was compiling on folk beliefs.

She picked up the axe-head by its blade, and the boys tumbled over each other to get a better look.

"Careful miss! Could be poisoned! Just like his scales!"

"They shoot out of him like quills when he's angry!"

"His wings are as wide as the sky!" Geordie wedged himself and his part of the story into the space beside Mairey. "And when he roars, he scorches the forest—"

"And when he gets hungry," Orrin said, eyeing Geordie and nodding sagely, "he eats virgins."

Mairey bit back a laugh, her fingers itching to write this all down. "Which are …?"

"Oh, very much like onions, my gran told me."

"Ah." Mairey rescued her notebook and stub of a pencil from under the dragon's fang and quickly wrote, *Balforge: fire-breathing, poisoned-scaled, foul-tempered virgin-eater.*

"And he's lived right here, under our village—" Orrin stomped his foot on the planking "—For ten-hundred years, way long before the coal mine came."

Her chest filled so quickly with red-hot anger, her next breath was a billow of steam.

Bloody coal barons and their bloody mines.

The great and terrible Balforge was the product of Daunton's despair. A wicked, relentless beast with a heart as hard and black as the outcropping of coal that had bred its voracious mine.

She wanted to hug Orrin and Geordie and all the other boys gathered around her, but they would find no dignity in her sympathy, and might even run from the nosey lady. It had happened before.

"What do you suppose gave Balforge such a foul temper, Orrin?"

"His treasure, miss," he said, spreading his arms to encompass the whole of the mill. "Was guarding his heap of shiny gold and stolen silver and pirates' jewels and—"

But then Orrin's tale seemed to dry up on his tongue and exited his small chest with a rasping gulp and a whispered "Bleedin' cockles, he's here!"

Suddenly every child went as silent, their gazes fixed with Orrin's on something behind her. Something huge and terrifying, by the wide-eyed, gape-mouthed looks on their little faces.

A niggling fear crept up her spine, its coldness catching at the nape of her neck, a pinpoint of prickling heat between her shoulder blades. She rose slowly from the clinging tangle of boys, then turned and tucked them behind her skirts.

"Balforge," Orrin whispered.

Sweet silver acorns! The towering shape in the timbered doorway could truly have been Daunton's dragon—tall enough by half again as he stepped out of the afternoon sunlight that blazed crimson across his massive shoulders into the colorless shadows of the mill.

"Just a man, Orrin." Though she wasn't altogether sure what sort of man she was looking at. He lacked barbed scales and poisoned fangs, and his wings were only a greatcoat that draped to his calves, but that was surely demon fire dancing in his dark eyes as he swung his gaze across the trembling huddle.

Not a breath stirred, nor a muscle, as each of them, herself included, waited to be roasted and eaten.

The man made a sudden, growling grumble in his throat, sending the children screaming with the shooshing scatter of feet, like frantic wings beating against the bars of a cage.

Then the children were gone, and safe, and the mill tomb-quiet again, leaving Mairey alone to confront their poison-toothed dragon.

A wild-game hunter who had lectured at Galcliffe College once said that when facing down a fierce-eyed tiger in the jungle, it was best to stand stone-still and not to breathe at all. That one should never, *ever* look the slavering beast in the eye, for that signaled a deadly challenge to him.

Well, she'd cut her teeth on dragons and manticores and hoary trolls; had translated the *Bestiary* from its twelfth-century Latin before she was ten. So she understood her monsters from horn to tail. She would easily rid herself of this one—who was surely just the cantankerous landlord, here to banish the children from his mill. Then she'd round up Orrin and the others, finish collecting her stories from them, and be off to the next village.

"You're exceedingly good at frightening children, whoever you are." She swept her father's hat off the tumbled grain cask where Orrin had thrown it and crammed it onto her head. "Have you any idea how long it took me to gain their trust?"

"Have you any idea how long it's taken me to find you, Mairey Faelyn?"

Mairey stared at the shape in the doorway—at the dragon who knew her name. But before she could demand to know why, or who he was, he was bearing down on her in a gait that thundered across the planked floor.

Yet there she stood like a stunned rabbit, a thousand and one questions knotted up inside her brain. She couldn't move at all, and just when it seemed the great beast would overtake her, he shifted his weight and coursed around her in a lingering circle, brimming her lungs with his startling scent of bergamot and saddle-leather, making her think absurdly of Sir Thomas Browne's observation that serpents copulated in slow, sinuous spirals, length against languid length, turning and turning against each other, just as she, herself, was doing with this Balforge-incarnate, countering ever backward until she bumped against a post, forcing her to stare up into his coal-dark eyes.

"Who are you, sir?"

She'd never felt quite so much like a curio, so thoroughly

and keenly appraised as his flinty gaze touched every part of her face: brow and lashes, the edge of her nose, her mouth. Watched in dread as his jaw flexed and his frown deepened.

"Rushford," he said. His hair glistened midnight to his collar, his gaze was darker still. "Viscount Jackson Rushford."

Why would an imperious viscount named Jackson Rushford be looking for *her*? Something to do with Galcliffe College? Surely not one of her father's colleagues; she was quite familiar with most of them. And this man didn't seem the scholarly type. More like a smuggler or a Barbary pirate.

"Begging your pardon, my lord, but I've never heard of you." And yet something about his name seethed in the pit of her stomach, some murky and roiling thing that made her certain she ought to be wary of him. That she ought to run home and shield her family from him. "I've no idea what you would possibly want with me. And I certainly don't appreciate you standing so cl—"

"I 'want,' Miss Faelyn, the Willowmoon Knot." He closed the inches between them, eyes glinting sharply. "And you're going to find it for me."

The Willowmoon!

Her heart stumbled, thudded, and stopped. An alarm bell began clanging so loudly inside her head she could barely think.

Hold fast, Mairey! Hold fast!

But hold fast to what, Papa? He'd told her that no one else knew the Willowmoon Knot existed—no one but the Faelyns! Certainly not this thieving dragon who had curled himself around her and was stealing the air right out of her chest.

She drew in an amazingly poised breath, considering the violent rattling of her heart as it chugged to life again. And, against the big-game hunter's dire warning, she looked up and into the beast's eyes.

Fathomless. Blazing crimson and licking yellow.

He must surely have heard her gulp.

"The Willow ... *which?*" she asked in a little squawk. It was safer to look at the fiercely square line of his jaw and the deadly muscles flexing there than to stray again to his eyes, where the flames had danced so hotly.

He raised her chin with his gloved finger—not sharply, with nary a hint of violence—but causing her heart to rattle around in her chest again all the same.

"The Willow*moon*," he said evenly. That very short, very rumbly 'moon' brushed past her eyelids, made her hitch in a long breath of his exotic scent. "I'm quite sure you're familiar with the piece, Miss Faelyn."

Dear God! She wanted to run for the farthest hills—but running away from a wild beast only made it give chase. And, as Rushford had pinned her between the solid post and his even more solid chest, she wouldn't get any farther than the reach of his powerful arm. Would have to lie through her teeth.

"Sir. Lord Rushford." He still had her chin caught up by his knuckle, was still staring down and deeply into her eyes—a tyrant accustomed to having his own way. His intimidation only raised her hackles and sharpened her senses. "I wish you all the best in finding your Willowy Knotty thing. However—"

"However, Miss Faelyn?" All that earth-rumbling converged inside her chest and settled low in her belly, a provocative terror.

"However, I—" She faltered, but remembered her promise to her father, and stated her unshakable position. "I cannot help you."

There! The simplicity of fact. She couldn't possibly help him find the Willowmoon Knot. No chance in the world.

He only growled, a sound he must have perfected in his underground lair, best suited for shaking mountains. His eyes took on a deadly, narrow gleam even as he straightened and gave her a distant but oddly approving appraisal.

"You are clever, Mairey Faelyn."

She knew better than to take compliments from dragons. "I'm nothing of the sort, sir."

"Oh, yes—and worldly-wise to guard your precious treasure with your life."

"Treasure?" She laughed—"Ha, ha!"—having no other defense at hand. Now the man was talking of treasure! Could he mean silver? Please, God, no! "Sir, I have a train ticket, three pounds ten in odd coins, and a Gladstone full of sticks, stones, and feathers. Hardly treasure—unless you're a rag-and-bone man."

Which he didn't look like at all.

"Now, now, Miss Faelyn." His tsking scratched at her nerves; his smile frightened the life out of her. "You can drop your pretense. Your secret is mine now, and I will guard it as you could never do."

"I have no secrets, sir. Not from the likes of you or from anyone." Her fingertips had gone cold as ice, though all the steamy heat of hell poured off the man, working its way through her jacket, through the too-flimsy linen of her bodice and her camisole, to the cleaving of her breasts.

"You've no secrets from me, certainly. You are Mairey Faelyn of Galcliffe College, daughter and heir to Erasmus Faelyn, and an antiquarian of some note. You have been flitting around the countryside for the last two weeks on some inexplicable mission, collecting—"

"Collecting folktales, sir!"

"Carrying that traveling case and wearing this remarkable hat." He slid his fingers along her jaw and through the hair at her temple until her hat came loose and fell to her shoulder.

She made a feeble grab for it, but he held her pinned and paralyzed as the hat fell to the floor.

"Your father's hat. As I'm told." That dark, unreadable gaze lingered on her face, searching out her secrets. Knowing too much already.

Impossible. Where could Rushford have learned of the Willowmoon? The jumbled legends of the vast deposit of silver rarely surfaced; she'd locked away every page of research in her private library at Galcliffe; held every fact in her head. How had he tracked the Knot to her? And how was she to turn his interest elsewhere? Misdirection, of course!

"You've caught me out, my lord. I am a scholar of Celtic folklore."

Rushford raised a brow but said nothing, sending her careening thoughts into even larger, more dizzying circles.

"And I don't mean to be rude to you, sir, but I often travel alone, collecting my folktales, and as a woman I must be watchful with strangers."

"Indeed." He nodded, an almost gracious tilt of his head, though triumph and a galling amusement shimmered in his eyes.

"Especially strangers who, for no reason at all, seem to know my name." And even more intimate facts about her life.

"I've stated my reason, Miss Faelyn, that you and I have a common interest in the Willowmoon Knot."

"And as a scholar of Celtic art, history, and literature, I can assure you that you've gone to a great deal of effort for nothing." She took a chance and ducked beneath his arm, past the warm, clinging folds of his greatcoat, then slipped behind the post and collected her hat before dodging to her travel case.

"*Nothing*, Miss Faelyn?"

She had escaped his nearness, but not the heat of his gaze, seeping through the wool of her coat as she retrieved her Gladstone from the floor.

"Absolutely nothing, my lord—because I've never in all my studies heard or read of your Willowy Knot. So there, you see, my lord, we have no secrets between us after all. No common interests. Nothing. But I do wish you well on your quest. Now, if you'll excuse me, sir, I need to collect those children you frightened away, before night falls."

Without a whisper of warning, Rushford was behind and above her, closing his hand over hers, the soft leather of his gloves trapping her fingers around the handle of her travel bag.

"Enough of your prevaricating, Miss Faelyn," he said too softly and too close to her ear. "We will discuss the Willowmoon Knot. And we will do it now."

"Please, sir, I have nothing more to say to you." She tried to pull away, but she met Rushford's chest in the curve of her back, her hip against his. Oh, but the underbelly of this poison-barbed dragon was steamy warm, smelled of cedar and smoke.

"Though your dance is charming, my dear, it will not dissuade or distract me. You and I are going to strike a bargain."

"If you do not let go of me, sir, immediately, the only thing I'm going to strike is *you*!"

"And you have underestimated my intentions." Rushford turned her, leaned down until his nose was inches from hers. "I've searched for you these past two weeks, traveling muddied byways and goat paths, through sorry mining towns such as this one—"

"—Chasing your fanciful treasure—"

"Chasing *you*, Miss Faelyn. And a crest of silver knotwork no larger than my palm." He held out his hand between them, a powerful, sinuous scape of dark glove leather, his fingers clutching an imaginary shape so rounded and sultry, that her pulse rose with her imagination and sizzled up her arm. "Ancient, struck in the Celtic form—or so I'm told. But *you* are the Willowmoon scholar, Miss Faelyn. The only person in all the world who can find this treasure for me. And you will."

She'd never felt so exposed, her most sheltered secrets laid bare to this beastly man. Tucking her courage into the deepest part of her heart, she looked up from the broad fist Rushford had made and found him watching her from beneath his savage brow, waiting as a wolf awaits an unwary hare.

Rushford. Why did that name terrify her even more than his knowledge of the Willowmoon? She felt blinded and dizzied, confused, searched her memory for his name.

"Are you an avid collector of Celtic antiquities, Lord Rushford? Is that why you're interested in a fanciful bit of metal work?"

"No." He pulled off his gloves as though planning to stay for tea. The afternoon sun had tracked through the mill's clerestory windows, crossing the oak floor like a druid's clockworks, branding its blazing brightness onto the fine wool cloth of his broad shoulder.

A man who tamed fire.

"Are you an archaeologist, then?" she asked, drawn by his work-bronzed hands, his able fingers as they fisted his gloves. "Are you looking to pillage treasures closer to home, now that Egypt's have been plundered to near extinction?"

"You understand very well the reason I want the Knot, Miss Faelyn." His gloves went into his pocket. "The same reason you want it."

He couldn't possibly. "Then I wish you luck, Lord Rushford."

"I don't need luck, Miss Faelyn." Now he was smiling like a dragon with a belly full of virgins. "I have *you.*"

That simple statement of possession, with its immutably present tense, nearly felled her.

"Sir, if the Knot does exist—if it ever has—and if it should, by some miracle, find its way into your keeping, what could you possibly gain from it?"

His smile broadened. "Silver."

Bright and fraught with peril. In the Glade of the Willowmoon.

Mairey closed her eyes and was standing there among the willows, her village tucked safely below, her sisters playing in the fallen leaves, her father and mother at rest together in the churchyard.

"You must be deep in debt, my lord, if a few ounces of silver can add so very much to your coffers." Though she tried to be glib, her words clung together in her throat. "Melt down your auntie's silver sugar basin and save yourself a lot of trouble. And money."

"I care nothing about the piece itself, Miss Faelyn. Only that the knotwork design on its face is an ancient map that points to a network of silver veins so pure that it glitters from its bed on the forest floor."

Dear God! She suddenly realized, with terrifying clarity, why the man's name had rocked her off balance.

Rushford Mining and Minerals. Tin and copper and coal.

And *silver*!

Jackson Rushford was a mining baron! How could she have forgotten? She knew the man's name as well as she knew the devil's. The Right *Dis*-honorable The Viscount Rushford. A spoiler of fields and meadows, villages and glades of willow. A thief of souls and childhoods.

If it took her last breath on earth, she would fight this dragon in his quest for more treasure. He must never find it— not the Willowmoon Knot or the vein of silver, or her village that nestled in its shadow.

"Mere legend, my lord Rushford," she said evenly, surprised she could look him so plainly in the eye when her world was spinning wildly out of control. "Smoke and shafts of light, shadows, nothing more."

"Where I find smoke and light, Miss Faelyn, I will surely find fire." He was standing too close again, his eyes too dark and smiling. "And when I do, we shall walk through it together."

CHAPTER 2

"My lord Rushford, I wouldn't walk through a slight breeze with you." The brash young woman sniffed at Jack and returned to her battered Gladstone.

He allowed himself a large measure of satisfaction from her angry frown. Though truth be told, he would've preferred prim-faced outrage and eyes that were pinched and bespectacled, as befitted a scholar. In his mind, he'd been searching for a pasty-cheeked, hollow-chested young woman with limp hair pinned tightly to her pointed head, had assumed lank-boned shoulders hunched from a lifetime spent poring over dusty tomes, and an arid wit turned in upon itself.

Instead, from the moment he stepped into the mill, he'd been dancing with the woman in dappled moonlight, reaching for its beams with his fingers, coming away with only the heady scent of peaches and dogwood.

He spent a silent curse on Dean Hayward and the man's shabby college and its inferior university. The blackguard hadn't had warned him that Mairey Faelyn was as breathtaking as she was brazen. That she wore her stubbornness like a shield.

Damnation! His patience for her hedging and petty negotiating was gone. Hayward had given his word. She would carry out the terms to the letter.

"I'll brook no more delays and deceptions, Miss Faelyn. We have struck a deal regarding the Willowmoon Knot. You'll work for me."

"Are you mad, sir?" She pried her Gladstone open, glaring at him all the while. "You and I have made no deal."

"*We* have not, Miss Faelyn." He stepped between her and the doorway, prepared to meet her anger. "However, Dean Hayward and I *have*."

"Hayward?" She paled, all that dusky pink anger washing from her cheeks, leaving her voice unsteady, with a dread that betrayed her fondness for the treasure she had so easily dismissed. "The dean of Galcliffe College? You discussed the Willowmoon Knot with *him*?"

"I'm not a fool, Miss Faelyn. Your secret could not be more safe than it is with me."

"With *you*?" Blushing color returned as bright spots of outrage. "What sort of agreement did Hayward make on my behalf?"

"Your cooperation with me in exchange for a sizeable annual endowment to Galcliffe College."

"Then you're both mad, Rushford. I refuse." She tipped her nose and turned away to stuff a map and a small book of much-abused paper into her case.

Bloody hell! He'd never in his life browbeaten a woman; was trying his damnedest to temper his demands with cold reason. Yet for all his infamous skills at negotiating, Miss Faelyn's open defiance had derailed his plans. He hadn't been able to keep a thought in his head beyond her scent, her softness, the silver-gold of her hair. Though she stood no taller than his chin, she was as sleek as a fallow doe, and could doubtless outdistance him in a sprint.

A dangerous associate for this venture, but he needed her

and her knowledge, her resources, needed to acquire them now, before one of his competitors found her and used her for their own purposes. Whether the Willowmoon Knot turned out to be legend or fact, a map leading to a vast fortune, or a complete waste of his time and money, Mairey Faelyn was the only one who could lead him to the truth.

"Your salary will be paid from an endowment to the college—"

"It already is, sir. The Faelyn Endowment was my father's bequest—"

"Its funds managed by Dean Hayward and the Board of Endowments." An ill-advised, idealistic arrangement on the father's part, but it had provided the perfect opportunity for Rushford Mining and Minerals to step in.

"My father set up the endowment so that I might carry on his folklore research after he was gone. The trustees would never break my father's will. Not unless they've made a deal with ... with—" the young woman's opinion of him had changed from fear and distaste to open loathing in a single breath "—a devil like you. No. I refuse to believe Galcliffe College would do that to me."

"For the opportunity of a limitless endowment?" He drew closer to her furious packing, handing her a bundle of scrawny feathers tied with a grimy string. "A library that rivals the Bodleian, a museum that puts the Ashmolean to shame, an endowment for a Geological Chair? My dear, such a fortune would tempt the angels themselves."

"I'm not a bondswoman, Rushford, or a slave." She snatched the feathers from him and laid them carefully into the Gladstone. "My time is not yours to buy, let alone Dean Hayward's to sell."

He'd been foolish to look for innocence in all that beauty. She was proving devious and resourceful, crafted to the marrow in stubbornness: a formidable adversary.

But she had a price. Everyone did.

"You're to be well-rewarded, Miss Faelyn; your salary plus a substantial royalty for your cooperation."

"A royalty?" She laughed deeply in her throat, as though he had offered her a piece of moldy-green bread. She retrieved a pencil from under a bench, grabbed up the cloud of hair that had loosed itself from its bonds, gave the mass of it a twist, and then stuck the pencil into the resulting nest. "You can sit on your royalties, Rushford, and hope they hatch into fat diamonds for all I care. Let Hayward do whatever he wishes with my father's endowment. I won't help you."

What the devil did she want with a silver mine, this wisp of a girl? Not money, not security; neither had tempted her. Yet, she denied any knowledge of the Willowmoon, as though she'd give her life protecting it. But from what? From whom?

He'd come upon her among the flock of children, had heard their ringing voices and her laughter even before he'd stepped into the mill and found a mother bear and her den of cubs.

What moved this woman to such fierceness: blind loyalty, love, commitment to a cause? Her dreams for this Willowmoon treasure were impossible, whatever they were.

"You're quite foolish, if you think you can keep an entire silver mine for yourself."

"Oh, damn!" She threw up her hands, then fisted them against her slender hips. "You've found me out, my lord," she said, catching him straight on with her glittering gray gaze. "I have a huge, aching need to find the silver before anyone else does. I want it. It belongs to me. I plan to pit-mine it with my bare hands and become grotesquely wealthy beyond all my dreams."

"Absurd."

"Why? Scholars have grand dreams, just as mining barons do."

"Do you own a pick, my dear? A shovel?"

"No." Her stubborn chin went into the air and stayed.

"A cart to carry the silver ore to a smelter?"

"I'll *find* one."

He almost laughed at the image of the tenacious Miss Faelyn hauling a wagon of ore to sell at the local market fair, as she would a load of apples.

"Have you enough capital to buy augers to drill into the earth? For sledges to haul the ore to the surface? For rails to carry the coal to market?"

"I will find enough, too."

"Enough to buy the great steam engines, to house and pay the wages of two thousand workers and their families?"

"Of course I do, Rushford." She stooped to collect a handful of bits and scraps from the floor. "I've at least that much hidden here in my shoe."

"Dammit, woman! How do you expect to turn a profit on your discovery?"

"I have my ways, Rushford." Into her satchel went stones and more feathers, sticks and a string of acorns; detritus he'd have tossed into a hedge. "Whatever I do with my treasure is none of your business."

"The Willowmoon and its silver are now my business, Miss Faelyn." He met her, nose-to-nose, as she stood. "I've a royal warrant from the queen herself, and a grant from Parliament to discover and exploit the mineral wealth of the Commonwealth, which supersedes any claim you might make on anything you find in the ground or above it. You cannot remove a single ounce without my permission."

"Well, then." She crammed her ridiculous hat on her head and raised the brim in a mock salute. "My very best wishes to you in your search, sir. Do write to me, in care of Galcliffe College, Oxford, and tell me of your progress."

She turned a round-bottomed hip to him, hitched her sagging Gladstone over her shoulder, and started away.

"Stop right there." He caught her elbow and turned her. "You and I are associates now, Miss Faelyn."

"We are nothing to each other, my lord. I'm not in the least interested in helping you find your next breath, let alone in wasting my time helping you search the world for a mythical piece of Celtic knotwork." She sighed with great drama and cast her defiance to the timbers above. "Besides, I've got more than enough work to do, including another week of field-collecting."

"A week." Plenty of time to move forward with his plans. "Good. Today is Saturday. I'll expect you to report directly to me on Monday next at ten in the morning, at Drakestone House, Harrow, where you will commence your work."

She blinked up at him, settled on a scowl that winged her brows. "Ah, and just what is it you envision I'll be doing for you at this Drakestone place?"

He knew better than to trust the woman's question as a change of heart. "I expect you to conduct your investigation into the whereabouts of the Willowmoon Knot."

"Ah." She nodded, gave him a cheeky perusal that licked along his every nerve. "How do you expect me to accomplish that, sir?"

The amused bluntness of her question caught him broadside, exposing a weakness in his plan. He hadn't the slightest idea how to begin such an investigation. He opened mines, not museum vaults. Exactly the reason he needed her, damn it all.

"I shall provide whatever you require for your quest. Miss Faelyn."

"What do you mean?" Her question was quick, incisive, cloaking an interest he'd not sensed before.

He could only guess at the needs of an indignant lady antiquarian with sun-silvered hair and luminous eyes. Most antiquaries liked dusty darkness and cubbyholes.

"Say the word and I will provide you with keys that open private vaults and sealed records." The sudden quirk of her brow pleased him, and the bob of her hat brim—telling clues to the workings of the woman's mind. "A simple yes, my dear, and all the resources of the kingdom shall be yours."

Confusion softened her brow and lit her eyes with a flash of possessive anger. Her breathing came more swiftly, raising her chest and parting her rose-damp mouth.

Desire. Hope.

Ah, yes, Mairey Faelyn. There's the chink in your stone-walled defenses. Resources. She needed resources.

She needed *him*.

He caught back his smile for the damage it might do to his credibility, as well as to his strategy, and yet he'd felt that smile —and a long-forgotten rush of happiness—deep in his gut, like hearthfire and a warm brandy.

"Well?" he offered instead, satisfied when her anger flared again with a clear-eyed vengeance.

"No, thank you, sir." She yanked at the brim of her hat, tipping the front upward. "Let Dean Hayward sell my soul to the devil; let the queen issue her royal warrants; let Parliament grant you the moon and all of its cheese, sir—I don't need anyone. And, my dear lord Rushford—" she shook her head "—I certainly don't need you."

Jack watched as the woman dodged her airy way through the bedraggled mill, watched her skirts catch on a rusted gear, before allowing himself his chest-stuffing smile at her grumbled, "Great sizzling toads!" as she yanked them loose.

A moment later, she was gone from his sight—but not from his senses. She was the wild, heady rose in his nostrils, peach down and heavy cream against his skin. Though she couldn't have meant to, she'd left him something of herself: a single, curling strand of her long hair, caught up near his shoulder in the dark nap of his greatcoat.

Pale, precious silver.

"But I need you, Mairey Faelyn."

And you'll soon enough know just how much you need me.

~

"Brimstone-hearted dragon!" Mairey escaped the horrible man, slipping out of the mill into the blazing afternoon sunlight, breathing like a blast furnace, hot nerves, and sizzling anger all caught up in a conflagration that sent her hurrying up the hill toward the village at a near gallop.

Curse the man and bury him in a bog of peat! He'd known everything about her from the moment he walked into the mill. As though he'd searched through her heart while she wasn't looking.

Oh, Papa, just imagine! Unrestricted access to the vaults and catacombs of the British Museum, to the secrets of the Bodleian, the Wren, the Chained Library at Hereford!

The Faelyn Library had been housed at Galcliffe College for the past hundred years. A dear and welcoming place, but small and ill-equipped. Not only home to exotic collections from around the world and shelves teeming with books, but to the arcane history of her family and their ancient pledge to hide and protect the secret location of the Willowmoon Glade. A secret held so closely by her family that every reference to the silver lode had passed into legend more than a millennium ago.

Every reference *except* the troublesome Knot! How she'd like to thump whichever of her misguided Celtic ancestors thought it a good idea to camouflage the treasure, then a craft a map to its heart! Small enough to fit in her palm, more dangerous than a cannonball!

The blasted medallion had somehow slipped from her family's possession in the late 1480s, managed to find its way into the coffers of an Elizabethan antiquarian society, and was last known to be among the inventory of the treasury of Charles I during the war between the Royals and Roundheads, then lost in the chaos that followed.

The Faelyns had been tracing the Knot for the past two hundred-twenty years, scouring scholarly resources, church archives, and museum collections, exhausting their resources, leaving them with little of hope of rescuing it.

But with Rushford threatening to find the Knot—a beast with unlimited resources—finding the bloody thing first had just become her top priority.

All the resources of the kingdom shall be yours.

A beguiling temptation, but easy to resist. Partnering with Rushford was impossible, no matter what doors he could open for her. The Willowmoon and its secrets must remain intact.

For the moment. A skin-prickling thought that sent her flying through the coal-dusted streets of Daunton, past the forlorn-looking train station and down the winding country road. Balforge would have to wait to have his folktale collected from Orrin and his friends; best to be miles from Rushford's threats by sundown.

She would wait to confront Dean Hayward and his gross indiscretion until next week, allow time for her temper to cool. But how dare he sell her services! She was a grown woman and owed nothing to Galcliffe but a token rent for the dismal old chamber that housed her library. She had no intention of interrupting her research trip just to skin Hayward's ears for his arrogance. The sooner she finished, the sooner she could be home in Oxford with her three sisters and Aunt Tattie.

Besides, she'd known Hayward long enough to recognize one of his sentimental but wholly unsubtle attempts to lend a hand to the children of his old friend and colleague.

God save her from such good works.

But if by some horrible chance the trustees *had* stolen her father's endowment, and she needed ready cash to house and feed her sisters, there were plenty of marketable items in the

Faelyn collection of artifacts and oddments. Treasures enough to sell to museums and collectors; all moderately valuable pieces of art, but not in the least sentimental.

Her father would understand and applaud. *For our family, Mairey. For love.*

The ceiling-high shelves in the Faelyn library contained her heart and all her hopes for her sisters, close-packed within its dusty cabinets and crates of curios.

Knowledge. Wisdom. Birthright.

She'd never known just how precious—and how dangerous—a bright bit of knowledge could be until she met Jackson Rushford.

She arrived at the next village just as night fell, dropped into a sagging bed at the Greenleaf Coaching Inn, and slept fitfully through the night, her dreams tangled in the exquisitely amorous coils of a dark-eyed dragon.

CHAPTER 3

Mairey spent the next week coaxing folktales from irascible cotters and reclusive crafters, miners, thrashers, and squads of children, until her Gladstone was brimming with fieldnotes and bits of village folklore.

A blessedly full week with not a sign of Lord Jackson Rushford—curse his blighted soul.

His image trespassed at will, though—that awakening sensation of being surrounded by him in the dim light of the mill. His scent of danger, and the touch of his breath drifting through her hair, his untamed largeness, his fingers tracing the edge of her ear. She'd had no place to run and, she realized now, no real thought to do so.

But she hadn't backed down from her refusal, stood resolute against his threats—and in the end, Rushford hadn't followed.

Which should have reassured her. But the man's conspicuous absence, his biddable acceptance of her final rebuff, only caused her to watch over her shoulder every minute of her travels, guarding against the dragon at the door.

By the time she returned to Oxford, her nerves had been wrung dry and her heart ached from missing her sisters.

The broad, comfortable lawns of Galcliffe College were a ruddy orange in the midsummer sunset. Just ten minutes in her library to unload her Gladstone and sift through her mail, and then she'd return home to her family.

"Miss Faelyn! You, Mairey!"

Dean Hayward. Not now! She wasn't ready to raise her sword and do battle with the foolish man.

But she turned toward his familiar warbling hail and waited as he padded down the gravel path toward her, his polished shoes winking out from beneath his dusty black robes, a cheery smile on his leathery face. Three times her age and twice her weight, Hayward carried all the power and influence of an Oxford dean—and yet the coward had crumbled like a shortbread biscuit the moment Rushford had pressed him.

"Mairey, my dear, dear Mairey!" Hayward beamed at her as though he hadn't a notion that he'd almost ruined her life. "Your travels have pinked your cheeks."

"And I shall tweak yours clean off if you dare betray me again." She dropped her Gladstone at her feet.

"What's this, my dear? What have I done?"

"Rushford, for one!" She focused her glare past his spectacles into the injured hazel of his eyes. "Does the name sound at all familiar?"

"Ah, yes, my girl! Quite an arresting development, eh?" He reached into the pocket of his robe and took out his everpresent flower snips.

"Arresting, sir? You stripped me and my father of our life's work—took the food from my family's table."

"Nonsense, Mairey." Looking away from her, Hayward deadheaded a rose that had bloomed and crinkled to pale brown in the time she'd been away. "I would never do such a thing to you or to your father. I loved Erasmus like a brother—love you like a niece."

"Dean Hayward, you set a barbaric industrialist upon me. That isn't love. That's terror."

Hayward shook his head. "Mairey, Mairey, you misunderstand. Lord Jackson Rushford is a very wealthy man. Your father spent his life and his fortune looking for fanciful things. I could offer Erasmus little help in all the years of our friendship. He wasn't the most companionable of our lecturers. Reclusive, I would say, until he needed something, then he complained to me without end about his lack of resources. I could do little for him; Galcliffe College is not a Merton or a Balliol. Research grants go to more profit-worthy ventures than his: to science and manufacturing, exploration. And after your father died—"

"The lack has fallen to me. But as you see for yourself, my sisters and I are doing just fine with his bequest as it stands. And if the worst should ever happen, I can do without it!"

"Yes, my dear, but the trustees thought it best to, well ..." The flush on Hayward's cheek brightened to well-defined blotches, sending a bolt of fear across her shoulders.

"The trustees thought what?"

"Galcliffe is in a sorry financial state, Mairey. You know that. Rushford's first payment for your services will keep us open for another ten years, at least. Maybe longer!"

"My *services* are not for sale, Dean Hayward. I can't save Galcliffe! I won't work with the man, will leave the college if I must! You can't make–"

"But Rushford is expecting you to—"

"Let him rot." She smiled, finished with the beast for all time, triumphant and at peace with the simplicity of it all. The Willowmoon was safe from his ravaging. She'd never have to see the man again. "Now excuse me, Dean Hayward"—she shouldered the Gladstone and started up the short walk toward the library—"I've been gone three weeks and have a lot to catch up on."

She gripped the door latch, gave a yank, but the handle wouldn't budge.

"Mairey?" Hayward's voice had become wheedling and whiny.

She ignored him and tried the door again. Still nothing, though the entire mechanism looked polished, the plate, the latch.

"Dean Hayward, you can make up for your unforgivable gaffe by planing the door to meet the jamb." She wedged her shoulder against the panel, gave a shove, but came away with an aching arm and a sudden, colossal misgiving.

"Mairey, I couldn't stop him."

"Stop whom?" She didn't like Hayward's ashen pallor any more than she liked the prickling chill that lifted the hair at her nape.

"Rushford."

"You couldn't stop him from *what*?" Yes, Rushford was the misgiving, and the anger that grew hotter at the tips of her ears.

"He wanted—"

"He wanted *what*?" She'd been privy to the power of Rushford's wants but was having difficulty finding sympathy for Hayward's fear of the man.

"Wanted me to give you this." He exhaled and handed her a brassy new key.

She kept back a sailor-blue curse. "He's locked me out of my own library?"

"Well—"

"May the man find adders in his marmalade!" She grabbed the key out of Hayward's icy fingers, crammed it into the lock, and yanked down on the latch. She shoved hard, and the door flew open to a vast, echoing emptiness.

Stunned, she stepped inside, her heart gone hollow.

The orange light of the half-spent evening spilled in from the tall, barren windows, painting soft stripes across a floor stripped of its carpets and the threadbare tracks that she and her father and her grandfather before him had paced into their delicate patterns.

The towering shelves that had once held thousands of books were empty. Gone were the cluttered curio cabinets and the gouged, ink-stained worktables, her father's leather chair with its caressing imprint, and the partner's desk they had shared.

Gone.

A sob filled her chest and clogged her throat. Tears slid down her cheeks.

Rushford.

"He came a week ago, Mairey." Hayward clung to the door handle. "With a half-dozen men and three lorries."

She swabbed away her tears, cursing them as well. "You allowed Jackson Rushford to steal my father's library!"

The Willowmoon!—he'd stolen it all! Every word. Every letter and artifact. Drawings, maps, runes!

"Rushford promised to pay you well, my girl. And he will. We signed a contract." He dipped his chin and shook his head. "I'm looking out for your interests."

You're a fool, Hayward. That wasn't entirely true and would only hurt him more deeply. Hayward wasn't privy to her father's secrets, and would never be to hers. How could he have known the havoc he would cause by negotiating with Rushford? Better that he didn't pry.

"Never mind, Dean Hayward." She slid her palm across the windowsill. Clean. Dusted. Stripped bare. Sterile. The room was cleaner than she'd ever seen it, from ceiling to floor. Not a trace of the Faelyn family remained. "I'll go to Drakestone House, confront the man, and demand he return my library to me!"

"Please don't, Mairey!" He caught her elbow, whispered as though the bare walls could hear, "Surely there's a better way to settle the issue. Rushford is a powerful man! Employs powerful men."

"I don't care who the man is or how many lawyers he employs to do his evil bidding. He's a thief and I will hold him to account." Somehow. She couldn't very well risk bringing in the authorities to make her case against him—too many questions. Too many secrets.

"Please wait, Mairey. Let me meet with the board of endowments."

"And I wish you hadn't put me in this position, Dean Hayward. However, you've given me no choice but to confront him face to face."

To beard the dragon in his lair.

Her temper still red-hot and roaring, Mairey let herself into the little house in Holly Court, wanting nothing more than to see her sisters, to hold them and never let go. But it was nearly ten o'clock, and they would be fast asleep and not expecting her until tomorrow. She could hear Aunt Tattie's nickering snore from abovestairs, her day's work accomplished and her three "baby ducks" snuggled down to their dreams.

How she loved coming home to them. Home, where even the playful shadows and the creaking silence seemed a fond welcome, where the warm smell of tomorrow morning's bread cooling on its rack made her stomach grumble.

Tomorrow.

Tomorrow was Monday. *Rushford's* Monday. Damn the man!

She sat her satchel on the hall chair and was about to make a foray into the kitchen for a cup of tea when she heard familiar whispering curling toward her from abovestairs, looked up to see three ghostly little figures in glimmering flannel on the landing, watched them glide down the steps, their small hands clinging to the rail, but not very well to their giggles.

She knew these errant spirits as she knew her own heart and

loved them as she loved life itself. They were the joy in every-thing she did, her hope for tomorrow, her sacred promise to her parents—and the reason she would defend the secret of the Willowmoon and the glade of silver from predatory men like Rushford.

She stood as still and unnoticed as the spriggy wallpaper, biting hard on her tongue to keep from giggling as her sisters descended the stairs.

First Anna, almost regal at ten, her pale hair veiled by what looked like the sheer lace curtains poached from Mairey's bedroom window.

"Hush your squealing, Caro!" Anna said, none too quietly herself. "Aunt Tattie will hear you."

"Wait for me, Anna!" Caroline whispered, her earnest, ghostly, eight-year-old gait hobbled by a pair of Mairey's boots. Her best and newest!

Followed by little Poppy, dragging Mairey's bed pillow behind her—almost six, but quick to study mischief from her sisters.

Three little whirlwinds—they'd no doubt turned her chamber topsy-turvy again. Poor Aunt Tattie.

The scamps thundered into the dining room and sped toward the kitchen.

Mairey watched the door to the butler's pantry close behind them; waited until she heard voices rising in the kitchen, the clinking of the honey crock, the rattle of the spoon drawer and the plates. She sneaked through the pantry door, then leaned against the kitchen jamb to study them.

"I'll cut," Anna said, the bread knife already halfway through the first inch-thick slice. "Do keep your fingers out of the way, Poppy."

"They're hungry."

"So's this knife. You best hurry and get the butter. And the honey crock, Caro!"

"Uh huh," Caroline said around the finger of honey she'd just stuck into her mouth.

Still hiding unnoticed in the shadows, Mairey flipped her coattails over her head, hunched her back, and stepped into the kitchen, cackling like a wicked old crone.

"Caught you, me tasty little morsels! I'll have me tea with bread and honey, or I'll gobble you all up!"

Three terrified little voices rose up in a single, glass-shattering scream, rattling kettles and pie tins, and setting Professor Martin's old spaniel to barking two houses down. Caro and Anna dove screaming under the table, leaving little Poppy staring up at her, a slice of bread resting in her palm.

"Would you like some honey, too, Mairey?

Mairey laughed. "You're sweet enough, my love!"

"Mairey!" Shrieks of delight pierced the night again and brought on another howl from the dog. Before they tackled her full-on. They fit perfectly into her arms, and she knelt to collect and kiss them all.

"You're home a day early! Hooray!" Caro planted a honey-smeared kiss on the side of Mairey's nose, then danced off in a melody of "hooray, hooray, hoorays."

"You should have told us!" Anna hugged Mairey, her face flushed from her raiding, the lacy window curtain forgotten in a pool beneath the worktable.

"Only a half-day early, my sweet girl." She slid her fingers through Anna's hair, wondering when its baby-fineness had thickened to ropes of silk. "But if pirating is what I'll find when I return, I'd best keep my comings and goings a secret."

"You're going away again, Mairey?" Poppy had fastened her arms like warm shackles around Mairey's neck. "Please, stay! Pleeease!"

No thanks to Rushford, she needed to leave them again in the morning. "I'll be away for only another day, Poppy. I promise."

"Ducks, ducks! My baby ducks! I heard screaming!" Auntie's voice found them well before she came wheeling through the pantry, wielding the poker from her bedroom hearth. "Anna, what is this? What—well!"

The lanky woman stopped at the door and shook her head, sending its white blossoms of cloth-tied curls waving.

"Mairey Faelyn, you're as naughty as your sisters!" Tattie bent down to Mairey and stuck out her cheek to be kissed.

"I taught them all they know!" Mairey gave her aunt a quick peck and laughed as she got to her feet with Caro's sticky-handed help, and Poppy holding on like a cat clinging to a buoy in a raging sea.

Tattie nuzzled Mairey's cheek, and then Poppy's. "Our Mairey didn't say she was comin' in tonight, did she, my Poppet?"

"My plans changed without warning." Radically. Unalterably.

"Changed how, dear?"

She hated to dodge her aunt's question. But Tattie was her mother's sister, as unaware of the Willowmoon and its secrets as anyone else in the world—except a certain dragon. When it came to protecting her nieces, the woman was as possessive as a lioness. Widowed since Waterloo, when she'd lost her handsome young groom, the woman had never had children of her own but had made up for it in the last six years.

"I've a train to catch tomorrow—"

"Can we go with you, Mairey?" Anna gripped Mairey's hand. "Can we please?"

"I love to ride the train!" Caro threw her arms around the lot of them, jumping and making monkey noises. "Please let us go with you!"

Poppy's grip around Mairey's neck tightened, and the girl climbed higher in her arms. "I just want Mairey."

"I'm sorry, my little loves. You can't come with me this time."

"Next time then?" Anna laced her fingers together in girlish prayers, bouncing on her toes, nearly as tall as Mairey.

"Next time, sweet! If it's at all possible. Don't I always keep my promises?" Especially to little girls whose hearts deserved a daily dose of wonder. She tried; oh, how she tried.

Anna kissed her. "You're the best sister in the world, Mairey."

"Another trip to London, Mairey Faelyn?" Tattie had perched her spectacles on the nub end of her nose, great lenses that turned her nondescript hazel eyes into piercing inquisitors.

"To Harrow this time." *A battle to the death with a thieving dragon.* She turned to Anna to avoid Tattie's glare. "Would you put the kettle on for me, Anna, please? I haven't eaten since noon."

"I'll get the honey!" Caro said, dashing after her sister.

Tattie's glare persisted. "To Harrow, by yourself?"

"Yes."

"For how long?" Titania Winther had an unnerving genius for knowing when something was bothering one of her nieces.

"A day." *However long it takes to reclaim her birthright.*

"And a night?"

"Possibly." Unless she ended up in jail for murder or mayhem, or both.

"If I didn't know you better, Mairey Faelyn, I'd swear you were skipping off to see a—" Tattie paused, nodded toward the girls, then mouthed, "A man."

She couldn't help a belly laugh. How simple a bit of sinful cohabitation seemed in the light of Rushford's infamy.

"There's no man in my life, Auntie." *Except a man with a dragon's appetite..* "I'm skipping off after research material." She nuzzled her nose against Poppy's. "Nothing more."

With Anna and Caro clattering dishes and whispering in the pantry, Poppy succumbed to the lure of conspiracy, and flung herself out of Mairey's arms to join them.

"You and your father, Mairey! I don't know what drives you

to wander so. Gone two and three weeks out of every month, from spring till fall."

Mairey sighed, and, as usual, her aunt heard every shade of regret. "I don't wander, Auntie; I collect stories from ordinary people, and publish them in books and magazines. But it seems the girls change overnight. Another year and Anna will be a young lady. Poppy will be as tall as Caro. And Caro will be as wild as a country hare."

Tattie laughed. "An affront to every hare in the county, I think. Oh, dearie, I nearly forgot!" Tattie fingered through her recipe box, past the tattered, food-stained cards, and handed Mairey an elegant, unadulterated envelope. "This came for you. I didn't want to lose it."

The envelope bore a bristling wax shield, emblazoned with an R, and environed in a garland that looked, to her educated eye, like a serpent.

"Rushford," Mairey said, a familiar uneasiness clutching at her heart. "Did he deliver it here himself?"

"What does himself look like?"

"Very tall, very dark, and very, *very—*" she caught herself before she could utter the word *handsome.* He wasn't at all. Not in the standard meaning. He was ... compelling, coercive, insidious. Words that would cause Aunt Tattie to bar the door against her leaving.

"Very ... insistent," she offered, hoping the word was bland enough for her aunt to misinterpret.

Tattie shook her head. "It wasn't 'himself' then. Could have blown this one over with a sneeze. The letter came a week ago today. Sunday."

Her aunt hovered as Mairey stuck her finger into the flap, popped the sealing wax, and fumbled with the contents of the envelope.

Railway tickets from Oxford to Harrow. And a note written in a strong script.

Drakestone House. Monday, ten o'clock. You will be met.

By whom?

"Who is this Rushford fellow, dear? One of your father's antiquarian friends?"

"A collector." Of sorts.

"He's the man you're going to meet?"

"He is."

"Welcome home, Mairey!" Anna stood at the pantry door, flanked by both of her grinning sisters. She held up a tray, its snug landscape complete with a steaming teapot, Mairey's favorite cup and saucer, and a bread plate spilling over its edges with the honey that Caro must have soup-ladled onto the stack of three fat slices of bread.

"A perfect welcome, my dearest loves! Thank you!"

And a poxing curse upon you, Jackson Rushford.

CHAPTER 4

"'*I tell the tale as 'twas told to me.*'"

"I doubt that very much," Jack said to himself as he leafed through one of Mairey Faelyn's many books of untidy scrawlings, making little sense of the words, let alone their meanings. Finding nothing more interesting than a collection of fanciful yarns and exaggerations. Loose sheets and yellowing folios with drawings of stone faces and puzzling diagrams of crumbling ruins, brass rubbings, several photographs of assorted kitchen tools, which caused him to wonder again if he were placing his trust in a crackpot.

Albeit a *stunning* crackpot—one who should have arrived here at Drakestone House hours ago. He shut the lid on the box of random scraps of paper and stacked it on top of its corner-worn twin, could only shake his head at the maze created by the one hundred and forty-three other crates he'd shipped to his estate from that ramshackle library at Galcliffe.

Erasmus Faelyn's name was inscribed in the *ex libris* of every book he'd pulled from the open crate on his desk. Though he'd only had time to skim, he'd found not a hint of the Willow-moon, no mention of a silver mine, or a medallion, a knot.

My very best wishes to you in your search, sir.

Lunatic woman and her accursed hedging. Though he stood amid his own vast private library, he felt blind and extraneous. With its two-storied arched windows overlooking the terraced garden and a mezzanine that ran three sides of the room; books, ladders, high-backed reading chairs, and a hearth that he could stand inside, Miss Faelyn's entire library would fit into one corner of his—roof, windows, battered furniture, and all. Any other scholar in the world would leap at the opportunity he was offering, but he had a strong suspicion that she would not.

He lifted another book from the box, its binding tattered, the pages brittle. Ancient hands had been at work on the wood-bound manuscript, its ownership proclaimed in faded ink and a more florid script than today's fashion. The next book and the next were inscribed with the same name, one Joshua Faelyn.

A very odd legacy of scholarship, a bred-in-the-bone penchant for antiquities. As he sorted through the tomes he found years, ages, of other Faelyns besides the prolific Erasmus and the very unpunctual Mairey.

Even as he thought her name—fully prepared for that hot stirring in his chest whenever she danced across his mind—the marble clock on the library mantel wound itself into a clanging frenzy of gongs. Four of them.

"Devil take the woman!" He shoved another note-box onto the shelf and started for the foyer, only to find his butler stepping through the open doorway.

"Tell me, Sumner," Jack said, tidying up his temper so he wouldn't misuse it on the man's wiry shoulders. "Tell me that you've found Miss Faelyn at the station and that she's waiting in the foyer."

Sumner cleared his throat and shifted his gaze to somewhere beyond Jack's shoulder. "Miss Faelyn wasn't on the 3:38, my lord."

"Great bloody hell! I explicitly instructed the woman to

arrive here this morning by ten. I sent her first-class rail tickets from Oxford to the station at Harrow, with instructions that she would be met—"

"The rail lines vary in their timetables, my lord."

"Damn it, Sumner, you've met every train since before ten o'clock; it's past four now, and not a word from her!"

"Perhaps I missed her, my lord." Jack had known Sumner since they were both pitmen in Labrador, and the man's abiding patience and even-toned voice had always been his most irritating flaw.

"You couldn't have missed her, Sumner. I have cataloged Miss Faelyn's most striking features to you three times before; I needn't again."

"Silver-gold hair, you said, sir. And long, to the waist, if I recall. Gray eyes. Not quite clearing five feet and two inches." Sumner blinked his attention back to Jack, his unsubtle opinion of the situation showing through his usual unflappable butlering. "Shall I try again for the 4:57?"

Silver-gold and *long* was a bland and truncated description of the woman's hair. But he couldn't very well ramble on about how its silky fragrance had roused him like an untried schoolboy, or how the trailing wildness of it had impelled him to wind his fingers through it. He'd be damned if he'd give the man an excuse to go sniffing at Miss Faelyn's hair. Nor did he wish to detail the exact color of gray in her eyes: frosty, with flecks of blue and aqua, lamplight on silver.

"My lord, the 4:57?"

"Yes, all right. But this time I'll go with you."

"Yes, my lord." Sumner gave the stacks of crates and barrels a disdainful arch of his brow, then left the room, no doubt bound for his greenhouse and orchids.

Jack went back to the bristling crate on his desk and shelved more of Mairey Faelyn's books. Requisitioning her library had been a necessary maneuver, though she would denounce him as a thief. Precisely his plan. These books were more than paper and ink and desiccated leaves. They were her memories, all that she had left of her father.

He knew only too well how compelling memories could be. How they could rise up and become indistinguishable from one's hopes.

Mairey Faelyn would come to him. And she would stay. If he hadn't been watching her, if her eyes hadn't been so fascinating and gray-glinted, he might have missed the wonder in them and never have known her heart.

He pried open the lid of another crate, then lifted the bowl end of a pot from the tangle of fine wood shavings.

The neck had broken, bits of the rim falling away as he held it.

"Damn!" This was a hell of a way to embark upon an alliance with the woman. She would think him a careless clod. He rescued the broken piece from the wood shavings and tried to fit it to the ragged edge of the bowl.

Not even close. The next piece fit—sort of.

Perhaps he could glue the bowl back together before Miss Faelyn arrived and set his ears afire. No need to add fuel to the conflagration. He settled the bowl on his desk, picked through the shards until he found a few promising pieces, then sat down on a stool to begin the puzzle.

"Your pardon, my lord."

"Not yet, Sumner. Can't be time yet." He steadied a shard against the broken edge of the bowl, unable to spare the man a glance as he tried still another place. "Oh, and find me a pot of Cement of Pompeii, will you? The kind with a brush in the stopper."

What he needed was a piece that looked like a fish wearing a large bowler.

"She's here, sir."

"Who is?"

"*Me*." The voice was silken and sultry, and fit for one hell of a fight. "I'm here."

Jack looked up from the fractured bowl, across the maze of crates and stacked furniture, and directly into a pair of eyes that leveled him with their clarity.

She *had* come. The formidable Miss Faelyn, framed by the tall, dark, mahogany doorway, and more beautiful than he'd remembered.

Silver-gold. Yes, he'd been right about her hair, though just now its thick plait looked well-used by the wind. She'd dressed with simplicity, clutching her huge, sagging Gladstone in front of her, and glaring at him from beneath the slouching brim of her infamous hat. Outrage sat high and pink upon her cheeks; her chest rose and fell beneath the green wool of her traveling jacket.

"You're late," he said, swallowing hard as he stood up from his desk, unable to think of a single other greeting that wouldn't sound of bluster or relief.

"And you, Rushford, are a bloody thief."

The heat of her glare was a beam of summer sunlight focused through a magnifying glass. If he'd been a dung beetle, she'd have charred him to cinders by now. He heard Sumner clear his throat, saw him vanish through the doorway.

"No, Miss Faelyn, I'm a businessman." Feeling like a shady mountebank, he scooped up the evidence of the broken bowl, set the bundle on the seat of his chair and came round the desk. "The sooner you learn I demand punctuality, the better off you'll be."

"I know all I need to know about your kind of *business*, Rushford. Sack and plunder! Consider yourself lucky you haven't yet unpacked my library. It'll save you time sending the lot back to Oxford by morning. If it's not there by ten o'clock, I promise you, I shall call in the authorities."

"I doubt that, Miss Faelyn." She wouldn't dare, though she

raised her chin against him, eyes sparking with fire as he drew closer.

"You're not above the law, Rushford. You stole my library—"

"Not true. I merely arranged for your books and papers to be packed and shipped here to Drakestone. As per the terms of the covenant between the college and Rushford Mining, the move would have happened eventually, and the result is the same. You are here; your library is here. Your research can begin."

"Of all the arrogant toads!" She dropped her Gladstone with a thunk, stuck her fists against her hips as she stepped closer. "How many times must I tell you, Rushford? I'm not interested in your project. I will *never* be!"

He let her statement boil the air between them, delighting in the anticipation, in the awakening that would come when she learned of the bounty he could put into her hands.

"Have you ever read the *Dirgelion Gofarian*?"

"The—*what*?" Her cheeks paled for an instant before she recovered with an incensed huff. "You're mad, Rushford. We're talking about my *library*, my family's legacy! Not some fanciful—"

"Have you read it?"

Her white teeth worked at her lower lip, sorting her thoughts, deepening the rose hue. All the while charting his eyes, breathing as she might if he'd just kissed her, and she was deciding if she approved.

"I have *not*," she said, spitting with anger, dropping her hat onto a crate, wishing him dead if her scowl meant anything at all. "No one has read the *Dirgelion Gofarian*. No one could read it, because it's the mythical writings of a fourth-century Welsh silversmith-turned-monk. *Mythical*, Rushford. There is no such book."

Not according to his old friend and mentor, Charles Longley, the Bishop of Durham. "Are you so sure, Mairey Faelyn?"

She took another sharp, passion-heavy breath, then laughed,

obviously battling her belief in wonders. "The book is a legend, sir. Not real. Any scholar of the ancient Celts knows that."

She smelled of the outdoors, of the wisteria hedge that clung to the stone walls that bordered the long drive up to Drakestone House. She must have come cross-country from the station, either walking off her outrage or summoning it to its full-blown fury.

He fought the urge to wind a curling strand of hair around his finger and stuck his hand into his jacket pocket instead. "There are many ancient secrets kept from the secular world, my dear—or so I understand."

She crossed her arms over her bosom, tapped her foot. "What has a mythical book to do with you abducting my library?"

"Everything, Miss Faelyn."

"Tell me how, Rushford. Please." She was a tight bundle of indignity: fuming, curious, prepared to deny that the winter sky could be quite blue.

"The *Gofarian,* as you very well know, was at one time a scroll, its pages laced together. Now the pages are pressed flat between wooden covers to preserve it. Locked away in the new Chapter Library at Durham Cathedral."

She blinked, harrumped. "Oh? I suppose you've seen it?" He was close enough to watch her pulse shifting just above the low-buttoned collar of her dark shirtwaist. She feathered a loose spiral of hair into place behind her ear, but a toss of her head shook it free.

"I have. Mildewed and ragged-edged as the book was, the Chapter's conservator assured me I was looking at the *Dirgelion Gofarian.*"

"Don't be absurd. You couldn't have seen the *Gofarian.*" Her eyes sparkled, lit with a bright, beautiful intensity. So protective. So provocative.

I have you, Mairey Faelyn, just where I want you!

"Of course, I couldn't read a word of its Latin, Miss Faelyn. Nor decipher its other inked scratchings." The moment of truth, the core of his campaign to win her cooperation, had arrived. "But *you* can, my dear."

"Can?" Her brows winged with wonder, her mouth glistening. "How do you mean, Rushford?"

"Come."

Mairey didn't know what to think when Rushford smiled and held out his hand to her, his palm broad and bare, dreadfully inviting. A simple invitation that caught her up in a stumbling trance, tempting her to accept, to follow him to a place she dare not explore. Taking a deep breath, she blinked away his charms and found a measure of resistance, balling her fist into her skirts and standing her ground.

"Vaults, Miss Faelyn, museums—just as I promised you." His eyes brightened in his conceit, never shifting from hers as he left her for a small table near the window. He picked up a muslin-wrapped object and held it out to her as though offering her the world on a platter. "My credentials."

Oh, he was very good at conjuring, this mining baron, surprisingly theatrical. Not that he could sway her to his side.

"You're wasting my time, Rushford."

"I doubt that, Miss Faelyn," he said, teasing aside one edge of the cloth, exposing what looked to be the calfskin corner of a book. Doubtless a forgery. "Come, see for yourself."

Even from half way across the room, there was something deeply thrilling about the object cradled in his hands. Something about its weight and slender, boxy size. A book, to be sure. What would it hurt to look more closely?

She snorted at his antics. "Oh, very well."

Setting her resolve against the wicked man, she left her

Gladstone in the middle of the floor and closed the distance between them, prepared for another of his diversions, yet unable to look away from the play of his fingers as he slowly brushed aside the cloth.

And in the next instant, set the room reeling.

The *Dirgelion Gofarian* come to life! The secrets of the Celtic silversmiths. Most antiquarians doubted the book had ever existed. Yet here it was, fragile and fabled, an inch thick, bound between leather-clad panels of wood. And somehow in the possession of this marauding heathen!

"Who did you steal this from?"

"The book arrived yesterday under guard, sent from the Bishop of Durham, at the behest of the queen herself."

"The queen? Impossible!"

"Let me show you, Miss Faelyn." He reached down to touch the leather cover with his bare fingers.

"Please, not that way!" She caught his hand, felt the glance of lightning in his fingers. "A kerchief, please. Or a glove." He frowned as he offered a square of cloth from his breast pocket. She slipped it from him, the silk still warm from nesting against his chest. "Thank you."

Wanting nothing more than to declare the damnable thing an elaborate hoax, she bent down to peer closer at the book still caught in his hands, feeling his glare at the back of her neck.

A most remarkable book. Its sturdy cover was relatively modern, expertly fashioned of calfskin and in-board beech-wood sometime in the last two-hundred years. Even without opening the book she could see that the pages were of very thin, very old, untanned parchment, the edges uneven and sliced, indisputable evidence that each page had earlier been laced together into a long scroll, now secured with silk thread in a Coptic-style binding.

"Your expert opinion, Miss Faelyn?" He stood over her, a thundercloud of heat and impatience.

She looked up into all that arrogance. "First of all, this cover is not the original. Nor is the binding."

"What? It had damn well better be original! How the hell can you tell without even opening the bloody thing?"

Pleased at the man's frustration over his own stunt, she continued as though explaining the process to a school child. "The construction, for a start, sir. Last century's transition between commercial in-board cloth and a conservator's custom binding. A hundred years old. At best."

"From last century?"

"I'm afraid this cover missed the original *Gofarian* by at least a thousand years."

"Damn it all!" The table shook as Rushford lay the book on the table in a crumpled nest of muslin. "The bishop swore to me this book was authentic."

"I didn't say it wasn't." Though, as she opened the cover, her heart was already hammering with hope for a miracle, for proof.

And there it was on the title page: a 9th Century illumination, boldly colored, the words inked in Latin.

The words on the next page chilled her to the bone.

As the Willow shall race the Moon
  On footsteps bright with silver.
  Begetting sorrows,
  Begetting joy.

Tears rushed to her eyes, hot and incriminating if Rushford ever saw them. Here was magic—a priceless sword dangling above her head, held there by a man with the power to destroy her village and the people she loved.

The very same man who could open doors so long closed to her and her family.

"Well?" His voice came rumbling from behind her and

frightened a sob from her chest. The blackguard must have known for a damning fact that she would have crawled on her knees from here to Durham for just a glimpse of the *Gofarian*. And now here it was, trapped inside his library. He was a sorcerer, and she was helpless against his enchantment.

She could almost feel the weight of the Willowmoon Knot in her hand, feel the cool silver turn warm and radiate up her arm into her chest. Still lost, still missing, but feeling as near to her as Jackson Rushford.

"Well, yes," she managed softly, swiping a tear off her lashes "The book is *interesting*." Dangerous evidence of the silver lying at peace in the secret glade, if anyone should decode the poetic images in the text.

"More than interesting. I can see it in your eyes." He was leaning so close, he might have seen right down into her heart.

"A scholarly surprise then, sir."

"Private museums, Miss Faelyn," he said, a wicked crook to his brow. "Gilded invitations into restricted archaeological sites, sacred books, crumbling manuscripts, sealed vaults, tea at Windsor with the queen—they are yours for as long as you associate yourself with my search for the Willowmoon Knot, and the secret of its silver."

Oh, Papa! What should I do?

"We're an impeccable fit, Miss Faelyn." He was impossibly tall. Impossibly dark-eyed and handsome. "Grant your skills to me, and I shall give all this to you. A simple, profitable business relationship."

Not simple. Terrifying. Impossible.

And as tempting as gazing over the side of a cliff and believing with certainty that she could catch his updraft and soar. This man, this predatory beast, was offering her a precious set of wings and inviting her to fly through the mouth of hell.

But he's offering me the Willowmoon.

"But if you're not interested, Miss Faelyn–" he offered his open palms "–I will engage someone else."

His threat was so blatantly idle, she snorted. "Who would that be, I wonder?"

"There was a young man recommended to me. Brawlings, I believe."

"Arthur Brawlings." She knew him well. A despicable charlatan who would boil his own mother's bones in order to salt an ancient barrow with them, if he thought it would bring him an ounce of glory.

Yet Brawlings was also a scholar of the Celts and treasure hungry. With all the resources Rushford was offering, the man would soon be on a trail that would bring sorrow to everyone she loved.

Rushford had thought of everything.

As always, the man was watching her every move, might have seen the teary redness in her eyes and would make the most of her weakness.

"Should you refuse me, Miss Faelyn, I will put these same resources at Brawlings' disposal." He folded the cloth over the *Gofarian*, one corner and then the next, until it was gone from her sight. "I will lose precious months of research while he catches up—a year or two, perhaps. But I'm a patient man, willing to search the world for what I desire. I'll find the Willowmoon Knot, and when I do, its clues will lead me to the silver."

She couldn't risk the chance. Would have to forge a pact with the devil. Yet not on the devil's terms.

The Faelyn family had learned long ago to operate on deception, half-truths, sleight of hand. Let the man believe she was as greedy as he, that they were after the same glittering prize, though the secrets of the Willowmoon rested within her. She would manipulate the truth for her purposes, would blind and deceive him, lie for lie.

"You've left me little choice, Rushford. I want to find the Willowmoon Knot as much as you do. A fortune in silver is difficult to deny." Her heart raw and her mouth dry as dust, she looked up into his eyes and managed the first of many lies. "Very well. I'll join your project."

He raised a dark brow as though surprised he'd won. "Done, then."

"Yes. Done." Feeling flogged and thrown out onto a rock, she righted her hat and squared her shoulders. "Now, sir, if you'll point me to the nearest lodging house, I'll return in the morning to see my library packed and sent back to Oxford, where I can conduct my research."

"No." The word was plain and clipped, but as powerful as a blow. "You work for me now, Miss Faelyn. Your library stays here."

"Impossible! I can't afford to ride the train back and forth to Oxford every morning and evening." She couldn't leave her sisters and her aunt. And if she was to keep Rushford from learning too much from her investigation, she couldn't leave him alone with her findings.

"And I can't afford your time away from me. You'll live here on my estate—"

"I'd rather sleep under a bridge! Good day, sir." She seized her Gladstone and got three steps toward the library door before Rushford grabbed a fist-hold of her skirts.

"Be still, woman!" His momentum propelled him against her before he hauled her backward against his chest.

"I'll not live alone with you, sir!" He was wrapped around her like a winter coat buttoned up against a frosty wind.

"I'm offering you private lodging," he murmured against her ear.

"No."

"I assure you, Miss Faelyn, that if I had improper designs on you, I would be forthright about it."

"What the devil does that mean?" The man was forthright enough with his shimmering heat and the fierce banding of his arms.

"It means that you and I have contracted a business deal, which satisfies both of us in equal measure."

"As I measure it, Rushford, *you* get the bucket and *I* get the hole."

He stood silent and still for the space of a heartbeat, before she heard a rumble and realized that he was laughing, the soft sound coursing through her like another pulse.

"Indeed," he said, freeing her from his grasp but blocking her retreat. "Drakestone is a large estate, several hundred acres, and the lodge is separate, secured behind as many locks as you find comfortable. Come and go as you please, but you will work with me in the main part of the house. My hours are long and unreliable. The sooner we find this Knot and its outcropping of silver, the sooner we'll be quit of each other, and the happier we both will be. Agreed?"

She looked up over his shoulder. His library was enormous, with two full stories of books. A quarter of the shelves on its lower floor stood empty but for a few boxes of fieldnotes lined up together.

Yes! She could build an impregnable fortress against him here.

"Whose desk is this?" She left him and slid her hand just under the edge of the desktop, following the undulations of the mahogany-cabled carving.

"It belongs to me."

"How often do you use it?"

"Never. This is my library. My office is through that connecting door."

"Your hours?"

"They vary, as required by my business concerns."

"The business of your *mines*, I assume." She endured the bitterness, offered him a smile.

"Yes. As well as my forges and smelters, my foundry—"

"So you're busy most days?"

"And most nights."

Busy stripping hillsides of ancient trees and defiling gentle waterfalls with coal slag. Like any busybody dragon, he'd soon tire of sniffing round his new bauble and leave her to the wonders of his lair. Hiding her work from him would be a simple thing if she built her walls of dancing mirrors and distractions.

Oh, Papa, the possibilities.

"May I see the lodge?"

He led her through the clipped shadows of the formal garden, past an afternoon-gilded greenhouse, over a low footbridge and its crystal stream, and into an unspoiled woodland. He was single-minded in his long stride, constantly looking back to make certain she was following.

And when the lodge finally appeared beneath the heavy canopy of oak and hornbeam, Mairey thought they had stumbled upon a storybook house.

It had a thatched roof, thick stone walls, and round-topped windows, three chimneys and a winding path of pearly gravel that seemed to sing as she followed it to the front porch.

"The lodge." Rushford held open the door, and she found herself as charmed by the inside as she had been by the outside. Big, bright rooms freshly furnished, the homey smell of woodsmoke caught up in the timbers. "Do look around."

The girls will love it here! Auntie as well!

"I trust it meets with your approval, Miss Faelyn." He was waiting for her in the wide hall as she came down the stairs.

He'd been almost puritanical in staying below while she explored the bedrooms, this feral-forged man who had thought nothing of pinning her to a post in an abandoned mill and fondling her as though they'd been hungry lovers.

"This house is very unlike you, Rushford."

"An old royal hunting lodge. The first structure on the property, some three hundred years ago. And, as I assured you, a full five-minute walk from the main house, with plenty of locks and a sturdy bar for the door. It's yours to do with whatever you wish."

"Are you married, my lord?" She hadn't meant to ask that question, and never so bluntly, but his marital situation seemed important, if she was going to be tied to the man indefinitely. But she'd seen no sign of a woman's touch in the main house, no portraits, nothing feminine. The question seemed simple enough, but Rushford just stood there looking at her, frowning.

"I only ask, sir, because a wife might object to having another woman living on the estate." Her heart began thrumming under all that glowering. "*I* certainly would."

"You'll have no trouble on that count, Miss Faelyn. I've never had a wife."

Her pulse took a crazy jolt, a little too relieved, a lot too giddy. She hurried the few steps past him into the parlor. "Do you plan to take a wife any time soon?"

"Why?"

Because the idea didn't set well with her. A wife in the offing —a wedding at Drakestone. She couldn't quite look at him, so she inspected the hearth and its damper, rattled the handle and came away with sooty fingers.

"Because, Lord Rushford, although no one hopes to conclude our pact sooner than I do, my father spent his entire professional life looking for the Willowmoon Knot. He was a much more experienced scholar than I am, and after thirty years, he'd made little headway. We can hardly expect success after only a few weeks."

"And?"

She faced him, rubbing the soot off her fingers, glad for the distraction. "And if, sir, three years from now you should find a wife and you and I are still … associated, she would doubtless want me to conduct my research elsewhere than on your estate."

"Would she?"

"I'd demand the same of my husband!"

"Well, then, my dear," he said, leaning too close. "I'll keep that in mind should I ever go looking for a wife."

"You'll warn me if you change your mind?"

"You'll be the first."

That set off more fluttering in her stomach, bubbles of profuse contentment. Absurd—it was the lodge. She liked it too much.

"Good. In the meantime, if I'm to live, as well as work here, I want your assurance that I have the run of the lodge."

He leaned easily against the arch, a dragon who'd trapped his prey. "As long as you don't add on a wing without my permission."

"I won't even paint."

"Paint the place in yellow and orange stripes, if you wish. Raise geese and goats. Just don't go inviting anyone onto the grounds who might threaten the security of our project."

Threaten in what way? Though Caro and Poppy were liable to run wild, given the pond and the stream, and Anna was an unrepentant flower thief, they weren't a risk to Rushford's security. Nor did he ever need to be a part of her private life.

"Of course."

"So, Miss Faelyn. I'm offering you the use of the lodge, a hundred pounds per month in salary, and one-tenth percent royalty on the net profits of the Willowmoon Mineworks in exchange for your cooperation. I can offer no more."

The Willowmoon Mineworks. The words slammed into the backs of her knees and her heart grew cold. She saw thick gray smoke where her village had once nestled against the hillside, and a dark-eyed dragon curled up on a heap of slag and glittering silver.

Remaining close to the beast seemed the safest way to govern him.

Yes, belling the dragon. Heel, Balforge!

"I can hardly turn down such an offer, can I, my lord?"

"Well, then, Miss Faelyn." He offered his hand, and Mairey took it without thinking, never expecting his to so fully enfold her own. It wasn't a handshake, it was a binding. And she could only watch in bewitched anticipation as he lifted her hand to his mouth—so very warm and well-shaped—as he left a grazing kiss in the furrow between her fingers.

"To the Willowmoon, Miss Faelyn."

"Oh, yes." Her breath wobbled out of her chest, leaving her powerless to object, and wondering how his kiss would taste.

"My lord?" Sumner stood in the doorway of the lodge, clearing his throat in short rattling bursts.

"Yes, what, Sumner?" Rushford kept her gaze as steadfastly as he held her hand, his fingers having separated hers to fit between them, as though he believed he had gained possession of her in the bargain and planned to explore her byways.

"There are three gentlemen to see you, sir. I showed them to your office."

"Who?"

"The Messrs. Dodson, Dodson, and Greel."

Rushford straightened, and she thought she saw a despairing confusion soften the flint of his eyes, a weighty sorrow that half-rounded his broad shoulders and drew down the corners of his fine mouth.

"I'll see them now, Sumner. Settle yourself here, Miss Faelyn.

Make a list of what you'll be needing and give it to Sumner. Firewood, food, blankets—"

"My clothes will do for a start."

"Ah." He frowned, distracted, and she felt illogically abandoned by his abruptness. "Send for your things—for anything you might need to get you through this."

She needed Anna and Caro and Poppy, and Aunt Tattie. And a magic potion that would put this disturbing dragon to sleep for the next hundred years.

"I'll send word this very afternoon, sir."

"Yes. Good." Rushford gave an abbreviated bow, then left the lodge as though his coattails were afire.

Oh, how easily she could imagine the stench of sulphur curling toward her as he set off to ravage the countryside. Yet it wasn't brimstone she smelled but the exotic spice of the kiss that he had lingered over, the very same kiss she'd done nothing at all to discourage, that still jangled in her veins.

A dangerous way to build a fortress against the man.

But Rushford had been right about one thing: the lodge was large and self-contained, with a small kitchen, five bedrooms, a dining room, a parlor, and a large sitting room. Five times the size of Holly Court. She explored her new home from the attic to the cellar, noting every cranny and hidey-hole should she ever need to use them in her campaign against her new overlord.

Rushford may be foul-tempered and imperious, but she'd never once felt in physical danger from him. His touch was firm, insistent, but never harsh. Though the girls would be safe anywhere on the estate, she would keep them away from the main house, and Aunt Tattie busy with their schooling and outings.

She smiled as she thought of the terror her sisters would bring down upon Rushford's sensibilities should he ever venture out to the lodge. Anna had become shy in recent months, but Caro and Poppy still had no sense of shame, and thought bath-time was playtime. So the sight of naked little girls squealing down the hallway—their auntie fast on their heels with towels to dry and cover them—was everyday normal in the Faelyn household.

It was a good thing to keep them distant from the staff of Drakestone House. And if things didn't work out here, as much as she would miss them, she could always send the girls home to the sanctuary of their village.

Heaven alone knew how long it would take to find the Willowmoon Knot, or how long Rushford would persist in his search before he gave it up and let her go. The Willowmoon had been missing for two hundred and fifty years; she might be bound to the man forever! The quest stretched out before her as bleak as any prison sentence: Anna and Caro and Poppy grown and moved away, with families of their own. Her own hair gone gray and her heart hollow as Jackson Rushford tore up the countryside looking for the Knot and the glade of silver.

She found a pen, a pot of ink, and a pad of letter paper on the parlor desk.

Dearest Aunt Tattie,

    I have found lodgings near my work and wish you to join me here at Drakestone House as soon as you can pack the girls and all their things ...

And may the dragon beware.

CHAPTER 5

Dodson. Christ, he'd forgotten. Had another June come already? This one had crept up on him, forgotten in his quest to find Miss Faelyn and her bloody silver mine.

No, not altogether forgotten. Never that. The month of June was an everlasting echo in a heart gone hollow.

Jack made a detour into his private office, not yet ready to face Dodson and his partners. This meeting took more and more out of him every year, sapped his strength for days afterward.

It had become a dreaded reckoning, an acrid accounting of his personal failure. He had a file drawer packed with reports and assessments. Eighteen years after the miner's strike had gone so savagely wrong, he was still searching for the family his father had left to him.

Protect them, Jack. The girls, your mother. They need you now, son.

But he hadn't protected them: he'd never seen them again, had lost track of his family even as his father lay dying in his arms.

He'd been sent away that very night, exiled to Canada, with

the law on his heels and a price on his head, had spent his first shilling searching for his family; would gladly spend his last if he had to.

Dodson and his lot had found few traces of them—only rumors and unverified sightings. Eighteen years was a lifetime of waiting, of stark loneliness and phantoms.

And hope was a heavy burden.

He emptied his chest of the pain, of his helpless fury, and dimmed his memories so that they wouldn't flare up and overcome him in the midst of his meeting. He took a steadying breath, then shoved through the adjoining door into his office.

"Your report, gentlemen," he said sharply and without preamble, because he'd found no other way to begin this annual farce. Every year it grew more difficult to speak through a tightening throat. "I haven't time to waste."

The firm of Dodson, Dodson, and Greel, attorneys at law, had been sitting like undertakers around the conference table, and now they scrambled to their feet, all chattering at the same time.

"Well ... sir ... my lord Rushford—" The youngest of the men struggled to right his chair, his fingers creasing an already folded sheaf of stiff documents.

"Speak up, boy!" Jack stood fast at the end of the table, glaring down its cold expanse of mirror-glossed mahogany. "You've had still another year, Dodson. Have you added anything at all to my very thick, but very empty file?"

"No!" the young man said, casting a pleading glance at the elder Dodson. "I mean ..."

"What my son means is that we've found nothing explicitly pointing toward any members of your family." Dodson punctuated his findings with a bow. "I'm sorry."

Sorry. That answer still slashed as deeply through his defenses as ever, made his throat close over and disabled his fury. He turned away to the windows and the green woods beyond the garden, where Mairey Faelyn was settling her brightness into the lodge.

"Detail your report, if you please," he said, hearing the shuffle of papers and the whispering as though their lack of progress was a close-kept secret. A scheme to keep him from his family, to expose his shame.

"Um, sir. We … our operative, that is, he …" It was Dodson's son again, then more whispering.

"Your operative did what?" Jack turned, his anger patched over thickly enough to shield his heart from the blows that would come.

"Our operative searched the usual sources, sir, focusing this time on the parish records in Cornwall and Devonshire."

"You've searched both counties three times before."

Greel wagged a patronizing finger. "But not for years—"

"*Seven* years ago, Greel. I have the report in my own files, compiled by a Mr. Wilfred Rainey." He'd memorized every item, sorted and analyzed, hoping Dodson had overlooked some fact or an idiosyncrasy that only Jack himself would notice. Nothing. "Why do you waste my time looking in places you've already examined?"

Greel lowered his finger. "Mr. Rainey no longer works for Dodson, Dodson, and Greel. We thought that our new operative—"

"Explain to me, Dodson, why I shouldn't fire your firm and find another."

Dodson bristled and blinked. "We are the very best at these issues, sir. We've found many a lost relative, united heirs with fortunes—"

"But what have you done for *me*?" His righteous anger made him feel whole and in control, made him feel as though his mother and sisters were waiting for him at Southampton or at the shore in Brighton, eating frosted cakes, their hands and faces scrubbed clean of coal dust. He need only take the right train.

"The 1842 Devonshire assize, my lord," Greel said quickly, sliding another page out of the report and across the table toward Jack. "As you can see there, a woman named Claire Radforth was fined three shillings for stealing eggs from her employer."

Jack picked up the paper, tasting venom on his tongue. "And I see that the same woman served three months in the Female Penitentiary in Exeter. What has this creature to do with my mother?" Greel's face paled to match his ginger frizzled hair. "Well—we just thought—"

"My mother's name is Claire *Rushford*, not Radforth."

"Yes, of course, sir. But mistakes are often made when the illiterate speak their names to a court official. The name Rush-ford easily becomes Radforth if one—"

"Claire *Rushford*, Mr. Greel." Jack came slowly around the table, grateful that the man was backing well out of his reach, else he might take him by the throat and squeeze too hard. "My mother was a collier's wife, not a street-corner slattern. She taught me and all my sisters to read and to write. She damn well knew how to spell her own name."

"Yes, yes, of course she did, my lord. However—" Greel sat down hard.

"Nor was my mother a thief. You are looking once again in the wrong place."

"There is the graveyard accounting, my lord," Greel said, shuffling wildly through his papers, thrusting one between Jack and himself. "Here." The page crumpled against Jack's chest.

The writing was a blur of swirls and slashes, as it always was at first. That startling fear of finding a name that was too dear, and with it a spiraling pool of emptiness. His hand shook as he went to the open window with the report, where the light was better and the air was sweetened by the wisteria.

"You'll see, sir, that our operative has singled out several possibilities." He could hear the fear and hesitance in Greel's voice; relished it because it matched his own. "Odd spellings and such. Collected in potters' graveyards only because they were connected with relevant dates and locations. The unclaimed body of a woman your mother's age."

A body. He grasped again for his anger and found plenty of the sort bound up in helplessness. It would have to do, was heavy enough to weight him to the spot.

"What else have you to show me, Dodson? I have three sisters: Emma, Clady, and Bryna."

"We know their names, sir."

"They would be twenty-eight, twenty-six, and twenty-one, respectively."

"We know their ages."

"Then why haven't you found them, dammit? I pay your firm thousands of pounds annually, have done so for nearly two decades—long enough for your father to die, Dodson, and your own son here to have grown out of knee breeches and take his bloody place as a partner—and in all that time you have yet to turn up anything of consequence. Not a single word. My family did not vanish from the earth!"

"It isn't easy, my lord," young Dodson said from behind his chair. "Perhaps if you could give us a bit more information."

"I've told you everything I know, Dodson. Year after year." The hottest part of hell was surely reserved for lawyers and their ilk.

"Yes, yes. Without a doubt, sir," the younger man stammered, though Jack had spoken his curse to the senior partner. "Perhaps if you'd tell me again, I'll check our notes."

"Do that. Check your damn notes. I last saw my mother the night my father died. I was on the deck of a smuggling ship that was sailing out of a dark cove off the coast of Furness." Sightless darkness, the sting of salt in his nostrils. A fatherless son, a mother's broken heart. The sea had smelled of desolation and betrayal and untimely farewell ever since. "It was the twentieth day of June, 1840."

Young Dodson's nose was buried in the file, his fingers trailing across the page. "Yes, my lord, as it says right here. And here. When again did you last see your three sisters?"

Jack swallowed the clot in his throat, tossed the report onto the table, and looked up at the enormous map on his wall, the breadth of his domain. Lead, tin, copper, coal. And for what purpose?

"I saw them that morning at breakfast, before they crawled back into the mines for another twelve-hour day of dragging coal sledges to the surface. That was the last I saw of them." But their faces still gleamed each night in his dreams, haloed in golden curls.

"I see. Yes." Young Dodson was still searching his notes. "That was a full two years before Parliament enacted the law prohibiting girls and women from entering the mines. Perhaps your sisters met their ends in an accident. If that were so ... I mean ..."

The young man inhaled sharply and raised his eyes, wary as a mouse cornered by a hungry cat, obviously waiting for him to strike out. But in all the years of searching, Jack had never allowed himself to think of his family lost to a cave-in, or a fall.

Was it time to consider the unthinkable?

Had his family's silence been so immutably real all along? Had he lost them in the beginning, had he been alone in the world all this time? No. He cleared his throat and steadied his hands on the back of his chair, wondering if he would ever be ready to hear that kind of truth.

"I suggest, Mr. Dodson, that if your operative hasn't thought to investigate mining accidents in northern Lancashire between June 1840 and the autumn of '42, perhaps he should do so."

A spark lit the young man's eyes. "Yes, my lord, immediately. I shall oversee the project myself."

He ought to feel grateful for young Dodson's sudden enthusiasm, and for the possibility of this new direction. But a molten hotness pricked the backs of his eyes, the harrowing pain inherent in discovering the truth, his loss made manifest. Lost years, lost lives.

"That will do, gentlemen." He turned away from the stinging heat and found his anger again. "Leave your report on the table, Dodson."

"My lord, we've not finished explaining—"

"One more season," he said, holding open the door to the breezy foyer. "That's all I'm giving you. Then I shall terminate our association."

"But, sir, we—"

"Good evening." Jack waited while the men clucked and eyed each other gravely as they gathered their ruffled dignities and left.

Jack listened to Sumner's balmy tones as the man let the Messrs. Dodson and Greel out into the twilight, wondering if he could ever act upon such a threat. Ending his relationship with Dodson's firm would mean admitting that all hope was lost to him, that he'd abandoned his pledge to his father. A trust betrayed. He wasn't ready for the shame of it; would never be.

More than that, he wasn't ready to be left alone in the world, to reduce his family to phantoms who haunted his dreams, where his parents' small cottage on the edge of the colliery was larger and brighter and warmer than it had ever been. Where his father told stories of his soldiering, and his mother combed the tangle of twig and bramble out of Bryna's hair. Where Emma read the month-old Times aloud and Clady wrapped Jack around her finger, and his heart around hers.

Firing Dodson would mean saying goodbye forever, and he couldn't do that. He'd give Dodson a year, perhaps longer. After all, the man's son seemed to have taken a genuine interest in the case. New blood, new methods. Yes, that's what was needed.

Just as he needed to give Mairey Faelyn free rein to find the Willowmoon Knot. If its design truly was a cryptic map to a vein of silver hidden in some forgotten part of Britain, he would find it as surely as he had found the bright glitter of silver in the depths of her eyes.

Granted, the woman was ill-prepared to conduct a thoroughly competent investigation. Her library had resembled a squirrel's nest and had had just as much security.

If she were to headquarter her work in his library, she'd need a key to the door. And a lecture on his rigid safeguards against petty theft, burglary, and outright robbery.

He unlocked his desk drawer and fished out the extra key. He kept his own deep in his pocket, but for some reason he'd never comprehend, such practical conveniences were never stitched into their garments.

A piece of twine would do nicely.

Relieved to have a head-clearing mission ahead of him, he left the house through the back door, traversed the graveled garden walk to the toolshed. He found plenty of bailing wire—strong, but hardly suited to hanging about a woman's delicate neck. He tried the stable and the laundry, and finally located a thin length of twine in the harvest barn.

Satisfied with his solution, he returned to the library, lit the desk lamp, and noticed the broken pot in its nest of wood shavings, sitting like an indictment in the seat of his chair. A bottle of rubber cement and a small horsehair brush sat in the middle of his blotter.

"Thank you, Sumner," he said to the bottle, "you've just saved my hide." Gluing the bowl back together should take no time, and Miss Faelyn would be none the wiser.

Returning the pot to his desktop, his sat down and quickly found a shard that looked as though it would fit—well, almost—

in the space near the lip of the bowl. He uncorked the cement and was about to dab the sharp-smelling goo against the first piece when the library door flew opened.

"What the devil do you think you're doing, Rushford!" Miss Faelyn was on him in the next blink, a cloud of peach-scented fury as she grabbed the bowl out of his hand and cradled it as though it were a baby chick and he were a slavering wolf.

"It's ... broken," he said, feeling clumsy and foolish as hell for stating the obvious.

"The pot isn't *broken*, sir. It's Pictish!" She held the thing up to the lamp, inspecting the finish as though suspecting he had bruised it.

"Pictish?"

"*And* irreplaceable. What were you trying to do?"

He felt like a child confessing to roughhousing in the parlor. "I was trying to repair the bloody thing."

"Repair it? Sweet blazes!"

She clutched it tighter, abject horror on her face.

This wasn't going well. He'd best confess his error.

"The breakage must have happened in the course of ship-ment from Oxford. See for yourself." He pointed to the shards still tangled in the shavings, prepared to ride out her displeasure and then buy her another pot or two. "Shattered into two dozen pieces."

She obliged him by peering into the box of rubble, then stared up at him as though he'd grown a second nose. An airy, indulgent smile bloomed in her eyes and made them twinkle like the evening star.

"Which is exactly the way my father found it thirty years ago."

Inscrutable woman. She was testing him. There would surely be a lot of that between them; she hadn't come to him gently.

"Your father found the pot shattered?" he asked, willingly

walking into her trap to best learn how she set them, how they could be sprung.

"Yes, shattered. The pieces embedded in clay, in a burial mound near Dundurn in Scotland."

A plausible trap, and utterly absorbing, this antiquarian of his. "Your father kept all these pieces of a broken bowl? Why?"

"Not a bowl, actually. A bevel-rimmed cook pot. Papa kept and cataloged the pieces because he was a scholar of antiquities, just as I am." As thorough and forbearing as a mother lion, Miss Faelyn gathered up all the pieces that Jack had spread out on his desk and replaced them one by one in their nest inside the crate.

"How do you know this cook pot was Pictish and not Wedg-wood?" She smelled too much of the woods and his own roses, too fine to keep him from peering over her shoulder as she continued to resettle the pieces.

"The pot is red slipware, imported by the Romans from the Mediterranean. But the painting is—" she held up the rounded end and drew her finger along a series of black slashes as though she were lecturing to a room full of twelve-year-old boys "—here, Rushford, this raven design is Pictish. Third century AD."

Yes, a fine trap. An even finer fragrance. He sighted down her arm, up the curve of her wrist to her hand. "Ravens are Pictish then?"

"One of their most common designs. The raven was thought by the Picts to give power through omens and sneezing."

"Sneezing?" There were limits to his gullibility. He'd been willing to believe the Picts, the broken pot, the burial mound, and the omens. But sneezing ravens? "Not bloody likely, Miss Faelyn."

"Think what you will, Rushford. But considering your inex-perience in the identification and preservation of antiquities, you'd best leave the rest of the unpacking to me."

Mairey heard Rushford blow a curse from under his breath

and fancied she could feel its warmth on the back of her neck as she dug around in the nearest crate and retrieved a bundle of eighteenth-century guides to county antiquities—one of the first purchases she'd ever made with her own money. She'd been twelve, and proud as a mince pie at Christmas.

"I'm more concerned over the matter of security, Miss Faelyn." He reached into his coat pocket and dragged out a double length of bristly twine. A key dangled from its center.

"Security for what? Hey!" she said as he turned her away from him, then stepped in so close behind that his chest and all that heat met her back like a caress. Before she could protest, he surrounded her with his arms, his broad hands holding out the loop of twine in front of her.

"You'll wear this always, Miss Faelyn." The weight of the key and the twine fell into place over one of her breasts, a buoyant pressure that could have been his touch. But his hands were busy behind her, wrestling with her hair and the knot he was tying.

"So you're trusting me with a key?" She centered the loop between her breasts, trying to sound unperturbed, but the key matched the thrumming of her heart and echoed it in a pulsating swing. "Which of your infamous sealed vaults does this one open?"

He took her by the shoulders and turned her, frowning down into her eyes.

"This is not a game. Nor is it a scholarly grant where you can wile away the hours with your nose so deeply buried in a book that you can't tell midday from midnight. I've made an invest-ment in you—"

"As I have in you."

"Exactly. I am what is known in the world of British finance as a mining baron."

A devil. A dragon. "So I understand."

She hated them all and appreciated his reminder, but not the intensity of his dark gaze and the many shards of crystal she could count there.

"Investors and adventurers watch me closely in everything I do; they follow my viewers when they appraise a coalfield. If my competitors discover that Viscount Jackson Rushford is looking for a silver medallion, every barrow and stone circle, every museum vault and private collection in the country, will be swarming with treasure-seekers. Digging like moles, pilfering, plundering, disrupting my investigation, threatening my medallion. Where would that leave us?"

His medallion. She exhaled, had never imagined his kind of threat to the glade and to her village. The vestiges of the Willowmoon legend were still whispered in the hills of the northern marches. Scavenging scholars like Arthur Brawlings would beat the woods for its mysteries. Rushford might just as well hire a circus parade and reporters from every rag in Fleet Street to tag along behind them.

"If you'd left me in Oxford, sir, where I could have continued my work in secret—"

"In secret, Miss Faelyn? Where this collection of pot shards and rabbit pelts and untold treasure was housed behind a paper-thin door, which was hanging badly on pig-iron hinges and secured by a lock that had rusted open eons ago?"

"The Faelyn Library has never lost so much as a bottle of ink to a thief." Yet she had never given much thought to a burglar.

"Until someone like me, with a large enough wad of bank notes, came along to tempt the impeccably ethical Dean Hayward and his trustees?"

"You are the exception to every rule, my lord."

"Think what you will. If rumors should arise about our little enterprise, everything we touch will become a target for robbery: this library, every cabinet and drawer, bloody hell, this entire estate. We need locks and we need privacy. I'm having a cupboard safe delivered tomorrow." Rushford went to his desk, stripping out of his jacket—a wholly improper action, given the late hour and the fact that they were alone. But her objection never made it past her admiration. The man's shoulders were broad enough when bound by the sturdy seams of his jacket, but they grew massive and straining under the static white of his shirt and the brocade of his pale green waistcoat.

She grabbed a breath. "A cupboard safe, for what?"

"For locking up your notes when you're not with them." He studied her from under his brow as he unlinked his shirt cuffs and pocketed the studs. A thoroughly intimate sight, made of bedchambers and rumpled counterpanes ... his male scent on her pillow, on her breast.

"Rushford!" He'd rolled his sleeves to his elbows, past his corded forearms, and had taken up a pry bar. "What the devil do you think you're going to do with that?"

"Unpacking." He shoved the beveled end of the bar into place under the lid of a crate and yanked downward. The nails came away with a squawk. "I'll open and you can put things away."

Rather than fling herself across the crate and demand that he stop right there, Mairey smiled with as much gratitude as she could muster. "Thank you for the offer, but I'd rather unpack myself."

"And I'd rather help you. Here." He eyed her pointedly and handed her a bristly armful of wood shavings out of a crate marked Desk Drawers. He nodded toward the enormous hearth. "For the firebox."

Erecting a fortress against the man was going to be more difficult than she had imagined. The nosy beast was going to pick through everything she owned. All her notes and private papers from her father, exposed to his questions. She quickly deposited the wad of shavings, returned to find him lifting the top drawer of her desk from the crate, the letterhead and envelopes still in neat stacks.

"I'll take that, Rushford."

"And while you do," he said, handing off the drawer, "you can tell me how your father came to have such an interest in this Willowmoon Knot."

She'd already planned the answer for that most unanswerable of all the questions he would surely ask.

"He just fell into it, I suppose. As scholars sometimes do." She carried the drawer to the empty desk. "He heard about it somewhere and liked the idea of finding a vast treasure of silver. Who wouldn't?"

"Indeed." He lifted two drawers from the crate and frowned at the jumble of pens and knives, rulers, drafting tools.

Knowing with complete certainty that her father would approve of her defaming his character, Mairey shoved the drawer into place on the right side of the desk and noticed that the lock had been pried open with the point of a knife. Her life and her destiny had already been exposed without her permission. Would the man search her laundry as well?

Rushford knelt in front of the desk, muttering as he worked the two ill-fitting drawers into place. She backed up as he stood, as tall as the sky when he looked down his long, slightly crooked nose at her.

Cedar and citrus, she thought absurdly.

"Your father heard about the Willowmoon somewhere?" He narrowed his eyes, said softly, "From his own father, perhaps?"

How could he know that much about the Faelyns? "Possibly. I never really asked." What else could she say? The man was a mind reader!

She slid out from beneath his heady scent and returned to the open crate before Rushford could dig around in it. She hurried back to the desk with another drawer, careful to hide its cache of pocket notebooks her father used in the field. He hadn't been the neatest record-keeper, and she often found a stray note about the Knot in them.

But like a hungry dragon, Rushford was waiting for her at

the desk, and snagged a book before she could slide the drawer safely out of sight.

"What are all these little books?" he asked, fanning the pages hard enough to ruffle the hair off his forehead. "You were writing in one at the Daunton mill."

She knew better than to grab the book from him, though she dearly wanted to. "Fieldnotes," she said, adding an overly nonchalant shrug.

He walked toward the lamp, blessedly distracted. "Yours?" he asked, frowning as he turned the pages. The book so small it looked like a toy in his hands.

"Mostly mine." She used his distraction to carry another drawer to its rightful place in this oh-so-wrong library.

"What the devil is a 'can-wall gorff'?"

A harmless enough question. A chance to practice answering him, if she was going to learn to dodge the man's curiosity without him noticing.

"*Cannwyll gorff*," she said. "A corpse candle." She continued when he raised a questioning brow. "A sourceless light that foretells a death. It's a Welsh term. Also called a fetch-candle in Scotland."

"And Nekha lights by the people of the Mekong River."

She couldn't have been more surprised. "Truly?"

He nodded lightly, looking vastly proud of himself. "Truly."

Nekha lights. Mekong River. The ends of her fingers itched to capture his words. Out of habit, she found a pencil, scribbled Rushford's definition and source onto a shred of packing paper, folded it, and stuffed the piece through the buttons of her blouse into the top of her corset to research and verify later.

She looked up and into Rushford's stark curiosity.

He came toward her, his gaze fixed on the space where she'd tucked the paper. "What's that you've just written?"

She covered her bodice and the gathering heat with her hand. "Why?"

"Show me what you wrote." He seemed immovable, plainly suspicious.

She sighed and turned away briefly, rescued the note, and held it out for him to read. "As I told you—it's what I do when I'm not hunting treasure. I catalog words and capture stories."

He took the note, read it twice, studied the reverse for a long moment, then turned his scrutiny on her. "Delighted to be of service to your folk science, Miss Faelyn."

"Thank you." Feeling thoroughly riffled from chin to stockings, she retrieved the note, her ears aflame. This time, instead of replacing the paper in her bodice—a habit she must break immediately—she hurried to the opposite side of the partner's desk and stuffed it willy-nilly into the top drawer.

When she looked up again, Rushford was leaning against a crate, chewing on a smile. "Now, my dear, why don't you enlighten me about the Willowmoon. Tell me all you know. Everything."

That's never going to happen. "Well—" She would inundate the man with historical accuracies, bore him senseless with facts, drown him in austere lectures. "According to my father, the item of antiquity known as the Willowmoon Knot was first described in an early *Discourse* by an unidentified member of the original Society of Antiquaries."

"Described how?" Rushford came toward her with quiet intensity, planting his palms on the partner's desk. "When? In what form?"

"The discourse was dated 1593, but you needn't worry on that count." She stood fast against his bottled anger, relieved that he remained safely across the desk, praying that he would stay there while she gathered her thoughts. "My fellow antiquaries in Elizabeth's time knew nothing of the silver, nothing of the clue that the knotwork might reveal. As students of ancient history, they were interested only in the Willowmoon's Celtic design."

"You're certain of this?"

"Absolutely." She couldn't very well tell him the full truth: that only one man had known of the silver in the glade at the time—Joshua Faelyn, the first of her family who had tried through the years to rescue the Knot. Unfortunately, Joshua hadn't recognized the significance of the odd knotwork until it was too late to rescue it from the wrath of the king.

Rushford looked unconvinced, but he cleared a spot on the desk and sat down on the edge, closer now and leaning toward her. "Continue."

Which wasn't as simple as it had been when he was across the room, when she could better ignore his eyes and their constant seeking. She reached into a crate and pulled out an armload of note cases, which she began sorting on the shelf behind her desk.

"It was next seen, or rather next described, among an inventory of antiquities confiscated in 1614 by James the First."

"There! The king understood the Knot's value and wanted the silver!"

"No, Rushford. King James knew nothing of the silver in the —" Dear God, she'd almost said *in the glade*! She steadied her thoughts. "In the time of his reign."

"Then what would a king want with a piece of ancient metalwork?"

Her heart was still clanging against her ribs, but Rushford hadn't seemed to notice her near slip. She turned from him and added another notebook to the row on the shelf.

"The king took 'a little mislike' to the Society of Antiquaries, suspecting the group was a political organization conspiring with others to do mischief to his reign." She turned from the shelves to fetch more boxes, but Rushford was suddenly there beside her, his arms loaded to his chin.

"There's a fool for you," he said, setting the boxes on the desk, "to see a threat to his reign among a society of scholars."

Let him spout his prejudices; let him believe she was as ineffectual as her predecessors.

"Exactly, my lord." She slid the boxes one by one next to the others on the shelf. She'd sort them later, build her walls against him while he wasn't looking. "The king ignored the priceless stone axe-heads and bits of bone, but like any right-thinking pirate, he took every item of gold and piece of silver into his personal treasury."

"And then?" Impatient, the man began to pry open the lid of another crate, as though he smelled treasure nearby.

"The Knot next appeared in a royal inventory following the king's death in 1625. It was recorded once again in 1642, when Charles the First went to war against Parliament. It was listed among the treasury items that left Windsor coffered and disguised in various carts, accompanied by a caravan of Cavaliers."

"On its way to where?" He rammed the pry bar under the lid of another crate and gave a rip.

"To Charles's queen, Henrietta, who had already sailed to Holland to arrange the purchase of weapons from the Dutch to use in the war against the Roundheads. But by the time the caravan of the king's treasury arrived at the Aylmouth quay in Northumberland, one of the carts had disappeared. Stolen, or waylaid—history has been absolutely silent on the subject."

"And?"

"We assume the Knot was among the goods in the stolen cart." She sighed sharply, reminded of why she had agreed to Rushford's blackmail—resources. "And that, my lord, is exactly where we start. The question we need to answer before we can take another step."

"What question is that?" He stopped his noisy work and stared at her.

"What happened to the cart? That's the last we know of the Willowmoon Knot."

"The last?" He dropped the pry bar on the crate lid, looking more a pirate scorned than a powerful mining baron. "Hell and damn! Then how the devil do you know the Knot still exists?"

"I don't."

"You—"

"I made that perfectly clear to you from the first, my lord."

"Bleeding hell!"

What a delight to watch the man rake his fingers through his hair in exasperation, to see it curl then fall back into place, a little awry. Good. *Excellent!* With luck, he'd be better inclined to believe anything she told him, to grab on to it with both hands and call it the truth.

Which was exactly what she'd been telling him: the bare, untraceable truth, the facts fully in her control.

"So, this trail of silver goes stone cold all the way back in 1642?"

"Not entirely cold, my lord." His ears pricked, this wily dragon, and his gaze fixed on her as she braved the open crate nearest to him. "Many of the items which were cataloged in that wayward cart have reappeared over the years, returned to their rightful place in the royal treasury, or mentioned in probate inventories. So the Willowmoon Knot is out there somewhere."

"What does this knot thing look like? Was there a woodcut made or an engraving?"

"Not even a sketch." Treading lightly on the facts, she continued, "Only a vague description of the moon's cycle and a knot-work of Celtic tracings." Mountains and a serpentine river, a chevron of geese pointing north, an arrow nocked and aimed directly at the heart of her village. "Meaningless to the modern age."

His eyes were on her, as though he'd discovered some truth of his own that he didn't plan to share. "To anyone but a scholar of the Celts."

She gave a slight shrug. "Hopefully."

"So where do you begin, Miss Faelyn?" He leaned close to her, peering into her eyes. "Which door do you wish me to open first?"

Impossible man—improbable wizard. But oh, the vistas she could see from here beside him!

"Tell me which doors you're offering to open, Rushford, and I'll best know where to begin."

"The *Gofarian*, of course." He nodded to the cloth-wrapped treasure on the worktable.

"I'll start reading through it in the morning."

"And then report back to me."

"That *is* the charter between us, Rushford." But she expected to learn nothing from the miraculous manuscript beyond a hint at the Willowmoon's history. Dear stuff, and heart-singing, but not helpful because it had been written too early, and she already knew it all. "What else can you show me?"

Rushford nodded, unlocked his desk drawer, and pulled out a folder. "Beginning with the most obvious, the Royal Archives at Windsor; the Chapter House at Westminster Palace; the Court of King's Bench at the Lord Chancellor's Office. And, of course, the Public Records Office, which has begun moving a few documents from the Wakefield Tower. Deputy-Lieutenant de Ros and the Keeper of the Records have been notified that I may drop in."

Ah, yes. His commission from the queen. Her father had been a mere scholar, not a mining baron with a title that was probably as old as God's, and pockets as deep as the seas. No wonder he'd gotten nowhere in his search. He wasn't looking close enough.

"What other weapons do you have in your arsenal, my lord?"

He looked up from his list of royal passkeys, dreams of silver plunder alive in his dark eyes. "Far too many to enumerate, and I admit I'm no judge of their significance. So tell me, of all the resources of the Empire, which would you pursue first? What would be your fondest wish?"

To be done with this business! To be free of the burden of the Willowmoon. It had become unbearably heavy in the last days. But here was her chance to find the bloody thing!

"I would like to see the personal papers of Henrietta, Charles's queen."

"Why?"

His directness always startled her, made her stop short and weigh every word before she spoke it. "The queen's personal guards would have supervised the shipment of her treasury under her express instructions."

"Of course. Done. I'll look into the matter in the morning."

Just like that. The Faelyns had spent more than two hundred years knocking on locked doors, and Rushford could open them with a simple wave of his hand.

"What the devil is this thing?" He was staring into a wicker basket he'd pulled from the crate, his nose wrinkled. "Another of your mummified squirrels? Gad, woman, it reeks!"

He stuck the basket and its fusty ripeness under her nose. The offending item was green and withered, and she couldn't help laughing.

"It's a meat pie, my lord. Your cloven-hoofed pixies packed up the lunch I threw away three weeks ago and shipped it here to Drakestone House."

He looked so thoroughly disgusted that she took the basket from him and set it outside the library door.

They worked well into the small hours, stopping only to eat from the tray Sumner had set on Rushford's desk. Like a boy at Christmastide, the blackguard opened every crate himself. She had to run to keep up with him, shoving the books onto the shelves so she could return to the next crate in time to keep him from snooping.

He seemed to be everywhere at once, and always beside her,

steadying her on the wobbling footstool, chiding her for risking her neck, then bearing the task himself.

Her father there beside her, too, in everything she touched. His hand, his script, his philosophies. The Willowmoon and all it had meant to him. His body was buried in the churchyard in her village, on the breast of the hill beside her mother. But he was also here in the library, in her heart, and so very much alive. His fieldnotes rang with his voice, and she couldn't help but turn the pages, remembering their travels through the countryside.

Sometime, in the deepest part of the night, when the shadows clung heaviest to the vaulting mahogany, her yawns became noisy. She flopped in Rushford's desk chair, bone tired but unwilling to leave him alone in the library with all of her research unguarded, prepared to stay till dawn two days hence if the man was so inclined.

"To bed with you, Miss Faelyn." He was studying her from the hearth, the dark of his eyes as old as the earth.

"No, thank you, my lord. Not without you."

Dear God! "I mean—" The string of words had made perfect sense inside her head, but now that she'd launched them into that crackling space between her and Rushford, all she could do was ride out the flush that scorched her from her toes to the ends of her hair.

"A tempting invitation. Miss Faelyn," he whispered, moving toward her, his face planed in the steady flame of his desk lamp. Then he leaned across her shoulder, tipping her backward, and turned down the wick. "But ill-advised, considering—"

"Considering, sir, that I misspoke." She scooted the chair out from under him, stopped when the wheels caught on the carpet fringe. "I meant to say I would stay here in the library and work as long as you were staying. That's what I meant."

"I believe you, Miss Faelyn," he said calmly, letting another lamp gutter out, leaving the library dark but for the gas-lit sconce by the door. "And I applaud your diligence. But the day has been long and we both need sleep. We'll finish this tomorrow. Come, I'll walk with you to the lodge."

"I don't need you to coddle me, Rushford."

"God forbid." The sconce hissed, and the room darkened completely, shadowing him against the pale light from the foyer.

"I've walked the heathlands alone in the dead of winter, sir, and I've rowed myself across the Menai Strait in a coracle that I constructed myself. I can surely find my way alone through the woods."

"Not through mine. Not until you know them better. I have no intention of losing you in the duck pond."

"I can swim."

He laughed broadly. "I'd have bet my last farthing on that, Miss Faelyn, my very last."

She fumed all the way to the lodge, blazing a trail ten feet in front of him.

At the lodge door Rushford lifted her hand, turned it, and kissed her palm. "Sweet dreams, Mairey Faelyn."

But sweet dreams were no longer possible, for a stone-hearted dragon had just overrun her life, and it seemed he planned to stay.

CHAPTER 6

"The Wakefield Tower is an impossible mess at the moment, Lord Rushford." The assistant to the Keeper of the Records offered his apology to Jack as they stood in the inner ward of the Tower of London, but the man's gaze was fixed on Miss Faelyn, who seemed completely oblivious to anything but the stout, stumpy tower rising out of the massive main guard wall.

"I mean to say, sir, what with the Public Record's staff working in there twelve hours every day, sorting and cataloging, preparing for the transfer to Chancery Lane, it's rather like an enormous spring-cleaning."

"No need to explain further, Mr. Walsham," the woman said, dragging her gaze from the tower and cutting Jack a precisely pointed frown. "Lord Rushford and I are very familiar with packing and moving, aren't we, my lord?"

Her hair was drawn off her lovely neck, its pale curls caught in a loose plait and wound beneath the brim of that god-awful hat, which she had to clamp down with her arm to keep it from falling off as she stared up at him with those sparkling eyes.

"Indeed," Jack said at last, refusing to be baited in front of the meddlesome keeper. "Proceed, Mr. Walsham."

Miss Faelyn strode off after the man, her sensible beige skirts flying in her wake, the leather strap of her tapestry satchel slung over her shoulder.

An ordinary woman would have taken Jack's arm and begged his guidance down the grassy slope and around the flotsam of irregular stone blocks and walls that marked the remains of the Tower's ancient, innermost ward. But he was fast learning that there was little about Mairey Faelyn that was ordinary.

Least of all, that she wasn't wearing proper stays beneath her shirtwaist—a fact that had raised a callow sweat and a bullish erection that morning when he found her shelving more books in the library. She wriggled where a proper woman shouldn't, at least not outside the bedchamber. She bobbed. Swayed.

Holy hell, she was a good deal of marvelous.

It had taken two days for him to arrange this visit to the Tower. He'd chafed at the delay, but Miss Faelyn had used the time to nest herself into a corner of his library—a process she declared would take another week. A very long week where he'd been useless to her, to himself, distracted by her every move, every sound, unable to simply read while she was in the same room.

He followed Miss Faelyn and the Keeper's assistant at his own pace, and caught up with them as the woman stopped to admire a vine of just-blooming roses that had affixed itself to a crumbling wall. Walsham cut a flower with his penknife and shyly handed it to her, a schoolboy pink blushing his already sunburned face.

"When was Wakefield Tower built, Mr. Walsham?" The woman brushed the furled petals past her nose and sniffed, a gesture so simple and yet so provocative that Jack felt it like her kiss across his mouth. The shock traveled like a bolt of lightning to his groin.

"Some historians say William Rufus began the Tower back in 1093. But recent theories—my own included—lean toward 1220, about the time Henry Three began redesigning the entire complex." Walsham seemed to be in his element now, guiding a lovely woman on a personal tour of his tiny kingdom. He spread his weedy arms and legs like a stickman, then crossed the distance between the grass-bordered stones and the no longer existent walls. "By the end of Henry's reign, he had rebuilt the Great Hall on this very site."

Miss Faelyn listened to the fatuous little fellow with every part of herself, leaning toward him on her toes, smiling, those clear eyes catching every nuance as though she were committing the entire performance to memory.

Jack recognized a courting dance when he saw it. Walsham's was ridiculous. Misplaced entirely. Miss Faelyn couldn't possibly be interested in the dullard.

"You are a font, Mr. Walsham." She blinked back at Jack. "Isn't he, Lord Rushford?"

She was bobbing, or would certainly be if he could see beneath her jacket to the linen of her blouse. He could only stare, as much a mooncalf as Walsham, who continued his gamboling.

"Henry next connected the hall to the Wakefield Tower, which he then used as his apartments. In fact, the upper floor, where the Public Records are now stored, was his privy chamber."

"How long have the records been kept there?" She was still bright-eyed with interest, still making maddening love to the rose and its copious petals.

"Since the first Edward, we believe. Thirteenth century."

"That's a lot of paper," she said, her brows pinched as she gaze up at the tower.

"And we've so little time." His patience at an end, Jack scooped the woman's fingers through his and fixed them into the crook of his elbow. She scowled at him, but held fast around his arm as Walsham scurried ahead of them to the thick door. He unlocked a massive lock with a key from a crowded ring that must have weighed a full stone.

"Here we are, then." Walsham shoved open the door, and Miss Faelyn followed the shaft of sunlight into the round room as it spilled onto the floor, leaving her rose scent to swirl around Jack's head.

The room was scattered with tables piled high with wooden file crates, loose-sheeted books, and safety lamps. In the middle of the room, a thick post strained under the weight of whatever was pressing down on the floor above.

"Well now, my lord, if you can tell me what record you're looking for, perhaps I can point you in the right direction."

"Royal letters written in the autumn of 1642." Miss Faelyn spared the man a patient smile, but she was already eagerly leafing through the papers in the boxes. "I'm the one who is looking for a particular record, Mr. Walsham. My father's family has always claimed a blood connection to Charles the First, through his queen's second cousin."

Jack nearly laughed at the baldness of the woman's lie.

But Walsham's eyes grew large and his voice conspiratorial. "Ah, and you're looking for proof! Is that it?"

"Indeed." She lowered her thick lashes, then proceeded to unravel her impossible story. "Though I am sure I'll find that proof on the ... well, on the wrong side of the bedclothes."

The man gasped, thoroughly scandalized. "How dreadful!"

"A royal peccadillo, I'm afraid."

Preposterous woman. She was a practiced mountebank, and Walsham was falling for her sleight of hand. Jack would have seen it from twenty paces—at least he hoped he would—but the defenseless little man was beguiled.

"Apparently, the woman in question was the daughter of the king's chamberlain. Once her transgression began to ... show itself—" Miss Faelyn demurely mimed a bulging belly and Jack's heart skipped. The splendor of filling that space with himself struck him like a ball of blue thunder.

"As was done in those days, Mr. Walsham, the poor girl was married off to a Yeoman of the Guard, a man whom, according to family legends, the queen trusted with the secret transfer of the royal treasury whenever the king's army needed weapons. If I could locate the name of that yeoman, then perhaps I could discover where my many-greats grandmother lived after she married, and follow her branch of the family directly to my own."

"How fascinating, Miss Faelyn." Walsham's cheeks blazed crimson.

Jack's head was spinning from lack of air, from watching the woman artfully dance around the truth.

"Indeed, Mr. Walsham. I'm looking for Queen Henrietta's private letters here in the Tower, where I might find mention of the names of her loyal guards."

"Queen Henrietta?" Walsham clicked his tongue and scrubbed at his chin. "Not good. Not good at all."

"Why is that?" She stopped her paper rifling, a ruthless cant to her brow.

"William Prynne, to put a shameful pinpoint on it. One of my predecessors. A staunch Puritan who hated the queen and her papist ways."

"What do you mean, Mr. Walsham? He burned her papers?" She spared Jack a glance of frustration.

"More wretched than that—he purposely neglected them when he took office. 1662, it was. Cromwell's papers were protected to the fullest, but according to Prynne's logbook, he dropped Henrietta's into a barrel and sealed the lot with tar."

"So her papers *are* here?"

"Possibly." Walsham nodded skyward, to the sagging ceiling of the floor above. "Up there," he said. "What's left of them."

He motioned them to follow and disappeared up the curl of stairs.

Miss Faelyn grinned at Jack, obviously pleased, or at least used to this labyrinth of shifting fortunes.

He much preferred looking for outcroppings of coal. He was good at finding those. It was there, or it wasn't.

"Our hunt is going very well, my lord." She stuck her nose into the middle of that damned rose, then whispered, "Thank you."

"You're welcome, princess."

She bobbed a mocking curtsey and hurried up the stairs.

He followed her flounce of skirts and trim ankles and emerged in the darkness of an octagonal room that smelled of damp rags and neglect. The ceiling was vaulted and ribbed, the plaster cracked, its paint long ago flaked off. Weighed down by a rabbit warren of iron-bound chests, crates, and barrels, the floor sagged dangerously, might have collapsed if not supported by the timbered posts below.

And Miss Faelyn looked right at home amid the clutter, smoothing her hands across every surface as though she could read its history with her touch.

She stood in a windowed alcove, staring up at the water-stained ceiling, her hat in her hand, her hair twisted and fastened as always by a pencil. "A very sad place, Mr. Walsham."

"Indeed, Miss Faelyn." Jack had completely forgotten about Walsham until the man lit a sconce lamp on the far side of the room. "It is said that Henry Six was murdered right there where you're standing."

"Here?" Any other woman would have scurried away in fear, but Mairey Faelyn knelt and spread her fingers against the planking. She closed her eyes. "Does he haunt these rooms?"

"I hope not. As soon as all these records are gone, the plans are to fix up the Wakefield to display the crown jewels to the public. Can't have a ghost scaring off paying customers."

"Where do you keep the queen's barrel, Walsham?" Jack asked, done with the man's endless tour.

"A very good question, my lord. This quarter of the chamber to the left of the stairs would be about right for Charles the First. I'm afraid it's all badly labeled, and of course, not all of it's here."

Jack glanced at Miss Faelyn, and his heart gave a sharp thud against his chest. Tears were starring her lashes with bright points, and there was an unsteadiness about her chin. Damn changeable woman.

"Leave us, Walsham." He caught up the man's elbow and turned him toward the stairs.

"But my lord, I was told to be at your service for the entire day. To see that you got whatever you needed—"

"I need you to leave us. Immediately."

"Well, all right. Here's a key which should fit nearly every lock. But do come find me should the lady ask. I'll be at the White Tower."

He listened to the man scurry down the stairs, waited to hear the door close before he turned his attention to this partner of his, who was swabbing tears from her cheeks. Great puddles of sorrow, and he could do nothing about them. Damnation! He'd felt just as helpless whenever his sisters had cried, and even more so when his mother had. He didn't need this from his business associate.

"What the devil's gotten into you?" She snuffled and touched her finger to the softly arching bow of her lip as she looked around at the mass of records. There was a smile there, too, rueful and turned inward.

"Treasure, Rushford. Piles of it. Just as you promised me."

He snorted and handed her a kerchief. "If there's treasure here, Miss Faelyn, you'll have to point it out to me. I see broken-down chests, sprung barrels, and damn me, if I don't smell a … Christ, I don't care to know what that is."

"Sorry, my lord, but I'm a weeper." She stuffed his kerchief and the rose into her satchel and pulled out a leather folio. "Pay me no mind."

Like hell. "So, what now, my dear? Where do we start?"

"I brought a map."

"Of what?"

Her eyes met his, and she paused momentarily before sighing and clearing a space on a worktable. "You remember that several items from the stolen treasury have turned up over the last two hundred years."

"I remember." He held the lamp above as she spread out a map on a chest. "Northumberland? What are these red numbers?"

"That, my lord, is a bejewelled sword pommel known to have belonged to James the First. It was recorded in a will here at Bowton in 1729. And in 1817, the Whitehall Firedog was found hanging over a dartboard in a public house in Thread-horne. Number seven is the churching brooch of Joanna, wife of Llewelyn Fawr. There are at least a dozen other historically significant pieces known to have been among the royal treasury as late as 1641, none of which made it to Holland. Notice how they concentrate here around Donowell?"

"What I do notice, Miss Faelyn, is that you had this map two days ago, and yet told me nothing."

"Because this map was meaningless without our full access to these records."

"In the future, you'll inform me of your plans, thoughts, and assumptions. Everything you know about everything."

She sighed, rolled her eyes at him. "That's exactly what I'm trying to do now, sir. If you'll only listen. My father suspected that whoever waylaid the caravan lived in the area where the booty turned up in the ensuing years. He combed the parish records in each of these towns, and this is all he found. Once we find the name of the guards in the treasury detail, the next step will be to scour the records of Cromwell's Court of Probate."

Every word the woman uttered seemed to be a dodge, a maypole dance with himself as the pole. "Why probate in particular?"

"Because the probate of a will includes the inventory of the deceased's estate, his debts and duns, and also records how those goods were distributed." She settled her satchel on top of the table as though planning to set up shop.

"Yes, yes, I know."

"But few people know that during the Interregnum, Cromwell's probate court had jurisdiction over the entire realm. Nothing was kept in the parish records. Every stick of information was brought to London and stored here." As she spoke, the woman began unbuttoning her high-necked scholarly jacket—one small, round button and then the next, in a long line of gray pearl. "So if the Willowmoon Knot came into the possession of a man in Northumberland—as the other items from the stolen cart seemed to have done—then, when that man died, his last will and testament would have been probated here in London, not in his home parish. Here's where we'll find his name. I hope."

"You hope, Miss Faelyn?" He'd followed her logic, even as he followed the tantalizing progress of her fingers down the front of her coat, wondering how far she planned to go, the bounty awaiting his gaze. "How many men do you suppose died in Northumberland between the years 1642 and 1660?"

"Hundreds at least. Thousands given the war." She finally shrugged out of the jacket, leaving him to stare at her finely pleated shirtwaist. And beneath the white, as he suspected, nothing but a loose-fitting vest of some sort. And all that buoyant swaying. Her breasts were small, barely a handful each, but God bless them, he imagined they would be perfect handfuls.

His palms itched to hold them. He cleared his throat. "Have you looked around you, Miss Faelyn? How do you propose to sift through all these records?"

"Word by word, my lord. It's the only way."

"That could take years."

"It already has." She closed her fingers around his in a startlingly unexpected intimacy, then lifted the forgotten key from between them—a caressing brush, a flash in her eyes—and then she was gone with her map.

Years. Years of clearing a path for the woman, of watching over her shoulder while she deciphered faded documents, as he waited for her to unearth his vein of silver.

Waiting. He'd become too good at that. Had spent the last eighteen years waiting for his life to begin, waiting for joy to replace the ever-present dread, the guilt, the loneliness. The prospect of waiting for his nymphish partner to lead him to a silver mine should have pressed hard upon him, should feel like just another burden. But she had clambered over a chest and disappeared through a thin opening between two iron-strapped wardrobes, and he wanted desperately to follow her.

"Prerogative Court of Canterbury, local to London," she said from somewhere at the back of the room.

"Is that good?" He tried to locate her from the sound of her voice.

"Not particularly. The wrong range of years. But the labels look recent. If I can just move this—" she started shoving at something, which caused a tower of crates to shudder.

"Watch it, woman!" Leaping across the top of a chest, he landed just in time to keep the crates from toppling onto her.

"Oh!" She seemed startled to see him standing so near her in the small well created by the labyrinth, holding an iron trunk above his head. "Thank you, sir. But I've already opened that one."

The exasperating woman gave him a placating smile, then turned away and leaned forward across the top of a chest, apparently trying to read the label on the far side. Her perfectly rounded, wriggling bottom was shaped in spectacular detail beneath the pull of her skirts, which lacked the fashionable, copious crinolines.

No wonder she wore plain, practical clothes and no stays; she was an acrobat. He shouldered the trunk on top of another, thankful for a place to put his hands. They wanted to be up her skirts.

"Prerogative Court records, wrong dates," she said, righting herself so quickly that she would have bounced off his chest if he hadn't caught her around her waist—a two-hand span of warm, curvaceous flesh, hinting at the soft cushion of her breasts, the gentle flare of her hips.

"Have a care." As he must, else he'd soon be ravishing her here in the Wakefield Tower, dashing any chance of a partnership with her. Not that he would ever force a woman into a compromising situation.

"I'll admit, my lord, it's very helpful to have you with me here."

"You're welcome." He did his best to seem indifferent, but in the next moment she used his shoulder for a hand support and hoisted herself to the top of the nearest crate, putting him eye-level with her backside. She rose on her toes, reaching toward a box on top of a locked cabinet, and teetered off center.

He had no other choice, and no better grip, than either side of her hips to steady her. He expected a well-placed kick in the chest for his impropriety, but the woman not only accepted his aid with a "thank you" but used him further to reach even higher, until her skirts fell away from her pale-stockinged calf.

A hot bolt of desire surged through him and lodged itself in his groin.

"Got it!" she said, dragging the box toward her and handing it down to him. She knelt in place, popped the lock, opened the lid and laughed.

"Quills," she said, shutting it with a grin. Her hair was cobwebbed, her shoulders dusty, her cheeks glowing pink with exertion.

Jack could only sweat.

She continued her search, undeterred by dust and dampness and lack of light, accepting his aid when he was near enough to help, and forging on alone when the passages grew cramped and excluded him.

He had accompanied Miss Faelyn to observe her methods, fully expecting to find flaws and inefficiencies, fully prepared to institute changes for the sake of his project. But for the moment, she understood far more about the records and probate business than he did. The place was an inscrutable maze, and all he could do was stand and hold the string while Miss Faelyn searched for their path to freedom.

He was a busy man, wouldn't always be free to escort her in her research. He would make random forays with her, but the job was really hers. Though she spun silk-webbed stories as tightly as a spider in springtime, he would have to trust her investigations—though he would keep guard against her equivocating.

As he would keep guard against the meadowy scent of her skin and the tempting display of her legs.

He spent the next three hours bridling his passion for the eccentric woman, unlocking chests for her and unscrewing parchment presses, while his agile partner passed judgment on the contents. She touched him often in her enthusiasm, a tap on his back, his elbow, his hand, unconscious of its effects on him.

A tedious search that kept him on edge. He was moments

from suggesting they give up for the day, when she burrowed more deeply into a narrowing corridor of chests stacked nearly to the ceiling with a stash of barrels. He heard a gasp of delight and then...

"Henrietta!" she shouted.

Queen Henrietta Maria of France. The label was burned unceremoniously off-center, off-square into the side of the barrel.

"Success."

"Oh! You can't know how much this means to me, my lord." Tears again, huge and streaming.

It seemed the most natural thing in the world when he wrapped himself around her, to fill his arms with the wracking sobs he felt so responsible for. She was much smaller than he'd expected, her fierceness belying her delicate bones. He wasn't at all certain what her tears were all about, but he planned to ride it out with her.

It wasn't until he was pressing his lips against the top of her head, where all that sweet, golden hair grew wild, that he realized he'd been wondering what their children would look like.

CHAPTER 7

"Good God, woman! Sumner told me you were hanging paper in the conservatory. I thought he meant wallpaper!"

Mairey smiled up at Rushford and his familiar scowl, and clothes-pegged another mildewed page of Henrietta's personal letters onto the waist-high maze she'd strung between the table and chairs. He looked every inch the mining baron this morning, in his long black coat and gray trousers. He was Hades in hard male flesh, the giver of riches, the author of this miracle of musty history. A feat that her father could never have wrought.

"Mr. Walsham delivered the barrel himself, first thing this morning."

Rushford snorted and entered the web of twine. "I'm not surprised, Miss Faelyn, the way he flattered you without end."

There was something wildly erotic and inexorable about him as he prowled his way toward her through the maze. "I'm not interested in Mr. Walsham."

"He was very interested in you." Rushford painstakingly followed the rickety, winding path she had laid out, when he could have so easily carved a swath through the forest of chairs and knocked it all down.

"Yes, I know, my lord. I'm not blind." Though she was having some trouble concentrating on her work. "I grew up in a university town, surrounded by randy young men who had but one thing on their minds."

"Not mathematics." His eyes were darker in the morning light, but clearer and questing.

"Definitely biology." She pinned another page to the line, letting its cheerful mustiness flutter away in the warm breeze that blew in from the pair of doors that opened onto the garden.

Rushford finally reached her at the center of the labyrinth, and gazed intently down his long, straight nose at her, nostrils flaring. "Do you have a young man of your own in Oxford?"

She met his frown with one of her own, wondering where his fierceness had come from so quickly. He smelled of bergamot and soap; his hair was still wet from his bath.

"What are you asking, sir? If I've ever succumbed to the sweaty charms of an undergraduate? If my maidenhead is intact?"

All that towering masculinity went crimson, and stammered, "I—I—damn it all, Miss Faelyn, I would never ask that."

Men. So easily threatened by a little honesty from a woman. She was a social scientist. However unmentionable the subject of human sexuality was in polite society, it was the key to human behavior. She'd had many a discussion with her colleagues about fertility rites, sacrificial virgins, ritual circumcision, and polygamy. She wondered what Rushford would think if he knew she kept a collection of carefully cataloged phallic artifacts in a box right here in his library.

"Not that it's your business, sir, but I am *virgo intacta*. Qualified to tame unicorns and tend the Vestal fires should the need arise."

The man was near rattling, his breathing gone ragged. "That

wasn't my question. I only wanted to know if you have a young man in your life."

"I don't."

That made him frown more fiercely. "Well, then," he said, finally. "I've been called to Birmingham today, Miss Faelyn. An emergency at one of my foundries. I'll not be home until very late tonight, possibly not until tomorrow noon."

She searched for relief at the prospect of being free of the man, but found only an alarming disappointment. He'd been almost—well, very charming at the Wakefield Tower, despite his impatience with Walsham, despite the thrill of having his large hands wrapped round her waist a bit too long. They had walked in the garden twice and had taken meals together in the breakfast room. He'd become a perilously agreeable presence in the library, reading *The Times* or studying one of her books on antiquities. She wouldn't miss him—exactly.

"Lord Rushford—" She opened her mouth to tell him that her sisters and aunt would be arriving this afternoon, but the words just wouldn't come. Not a good idea to distract him. "Do have a safe trip."

"Thank you." He left the conservatory with too much arrogant grace.

An emergency. She could just imagine it: his foundry workers striking for safer working conditions, for better pay, for schooling for their children, for food and clean water. A fire, an explosion—Rushford trying to minimize the loss to his profits.

As soon as she finished hanging the queen's musty letters in the conservatory, she returned to the library and set about raising her defenses against the pillaging dragon. She'd already turned the front of her desk to the center of the room to keep him from sneaking up on her and peering over her shoulder. Had mislabeled note-boxes, and created false bottoms inside them, safe places to store evidence she might uncover that could lead him toward the Knot. She kept two sets of journals—one to show him their progress, the other, written in the oghams and runes of the green world, to hide away from his prying.

She even wrote a short report for Rushford, making suggestions for sources and listing items she needed, then put it on the top of his desk in the adjoining office.

By mid-afternoon, with a bit of help from Sumner and his assistants, her father's chair was tucked up against her desk, and two gouged and stained worktables separated her part of the library from Rushford's.

A very small part, indeed. His sumptuous, overly male furniture sprawled across a meadow of woolen carpets, a rival to any library at any college in Oxford.

But so comfortable, scented with the honey warmth of beeswax polish and leather, and the drift of roses from the beautiful windows that opened to the garden.

A lovely place to raise a family.

A family of her own. Children and a husband. A fairy tale of ungainly proportions, but one she longed to have come true. Of course, it could never be. She'd long ago decided never to wed, *could* never. She was already pledged to the Willowmoon, which left little enough room in her life for her sisters, let alone a husband and children of her own.

She shoved away the terrible yearning that seemed to arise out of nowhere; marked it off to the fact that Rushford was, without question, the most compelling man she'd ever met. The compulsion to reproduce was unstoppable; what woman wouldn't want to mix her blood with the very robust Jackson Rushford's?

Biology. That's all it was. Resistible and finite.

Besides, he was her enemy.

"Your pardon, Miss Faelyn." Sumner was standing at the library door, his usually starched exterior wrinkled around the edges. "Three young ladies have arrived and are in the—"

"Mairey!"

Pandemonium broke around Sumner like water raging round a mid-stream boulder. Crinoline and squealing and shouts of joy flowed toward her as Caro and Poppy and then Anna tumbled into the library.

"My loves!" She met them in the midst of the furniture-stuffed room. Poppy launched herself into Mairey's arms and snuggled into an embrace.

"Are you a faerie princess now, Mairey?" Caro asked, squeezing Mairey around the middle.

"Not even a mortal princess, I'm afraid."

Poppy turned Mairey's face with her sweat-sticky palms. "Caro said we shall live in this castle for ever and ever afterward. But how can we, Mairey, if you're not the princess?"

"Is there a kitchen garden, Mairey?" Anna had already purloined one of the yellow roses that grew in profusion along the foundations of the great house .

"Come here, Anna! Look!" Caro had bolted away from Mairey and was standing on a chair at the window, pointing wildly. "A giant's garden!"

"Ah, there you are, Mairey, my girl." Aunt Tattie brushed past Sumner, throwing the stunned butler an irritated glance and handing him a hatbox. "A tad showy, don't you think?"

"You're a brave woman, Auntie. You made it here in one piece with these three little baggages."

"And all our belongings. Which are still outside in the cart." The woman dragged her spectacles to the end of her nose, glared again at Sumner. "What's this all about, Mairey Faelyn? Why did you bring us here?"

"Miss, if I might speak with you a moment?" Sumner was still standing at the door, crooked forward from the waist, apparently fearful of actually entering the library and being drowned.

"Ah, yes. Sumner, this is Mrs. Titania Winther, my aunt"

"Madam." He nodded.

"Mr. Sumner." Tattie sniffed her suspicions.

"The young lady who plundered the rose is my sister Anna." Anna had already found the water cruet, but managed a bobbing curtsey. Not exactly the correct salutation to offer a butler.

"And this is … Caro, sweet, *please* don't rock so hard in Lord Rushford's chair. My sister Caroline." Mairey kissed Poppy's wind-tossed mop of curls. "And this is Persephone. We call her Poppy."

Sumner hadn't moved a muscle, save for the un-Sumner-like slackening of his jaw. She'd seen the same look of disbelief when one of her folk-study subjects was telling her of their first sighting of a commune of fairies cavorting in the midnight mist. The eyes played tricks in the moonlight.

Rushford's reaction would hardly be as guarded.

"Will Mistress Tattie and the young ladies be staying for dinner tonight?"

"I like 'snips," Poppy said, "an' carrots."

"Parsnips," Mairey explained to Sumner.

"And carrots."

The man closed his mouth and nodded. "I shall inform the cook, Miss Poppy."

"Mairey, there's a pond!" Caro rattled the latches and would have thrown open the door if Tattie hadn't grabbed her around the waist. "And ducks!"

"May Caro and I go out to the garden, Mairey?" Anna had poured water from the cruet into Rushford's empty crystal inkstand. "Can we, please?" She dropped the rose into the vessel.

They were home. For good or ill, dragon or no. "Soon," Mairey said, gathering her sisters into her arms.

"Then the children *will* be staying for dinner, Miss Faelyn?"

"Actually, Sumner, my family will be staying with me in the lodge. We'll manage dinner there."

"Through the week's end, miss?"

Through eternity, she wanted to say. "Indefinitely."

"Ah!" Sumner cut a wide-eyed glance toward the foyer, as though Rushford's hearing were superhuman and reached all the way from Cornwall. "Does his lordship know about … your plans?"

"Not yet."

"I see."

She was certain Rushford wouldn't.

But settling her sisters into the lodge proved as difficult as squeezing cider back into an apple. Tattie took command of the lodge kitchen and settled into a bed-sitting-room, while Mairey helped the girls unpack. Anna had her own room for the first time in her life; Caro and Poppy shared the garret next to Anna, just below Mairey's own bedroom. She prayed the ceiling plaster would hold with all their stomping and made them promise not to bounce on the beds.

By the time they returned from exploring the duck pond and the creek and the fairy woods, there wasn't a spot on anyone that wasn't matted with mud, or leaves, or feathers.

And Mairey was as happy as she'd ever been.

Welcome home, my loves.

Jack climbed the wide front stairs to Drakestone in the translucent, blue-gray veil of twilight. He didn't particularly like visiting his foundries; hated the noise and the heat, the bellowing furnaces most of all. And yet, coaxing iron and tin out of bare rock fascinated him; had done so since he was a boy.

He'd arrived at the troublesome foundry at noon, spent two hours moderating the safety issues between his engineers and the men who would run the newly designed forges. He'd worked all sides of the process, from sweating at the furnaces and shoveling coke to engineering better fuel consumption systems. All of which made him aware of whom to invite to the design table when changes were needed. Those university-bred engineers who balked at sitting across from a good furnace man didn't last very long in his employ.

Today had been long, but necessary. He was disappointed not to find the gold-rimmed glow of lamplight spilling from the library. Miss Faelyn had been in the fore of his thoughts all the way home. And no less than a dozen times an hour through the day.

Virgo intacta. She'd ambushed him with that, left his head spinning and his blood sizzling.

He could have stayed the night in Coventry as he often did when he was called away, but tonight he'd wanted to come home to Drakestone House. To Mairey. He had lived so long with no one to come home to that he hadn't recognized the pull until he was halfway back.

He'd imagined finding her sorting through Henrietta's papers, ready with her odd stories and her laughter. Needed no pretense in seeking her out tonight in the lodge; not with a perfect excuse tucked in his coat pocket: an invitation to visit Windsor whenever she liked.

He caught himself whistling as he dropped his attaché case on the desk in his office, scattering the stack of mail.

He picked the top letter off the pile.

Rushford, it read. The writing was familiar, and he touched it to his nose, sniffing the whisper of her scent. Lilac and—he sniffed again—rose. His heart pounded absurdly as he went round the desk, wielding the paperknife like a sword against the seal. He bent his knees, prepared to sit down for a leisurely read.

His bum hit the floor just before he noticed his chair was missing.

"Bloody hell!" He dragged himself, cursing, off the ground and stared at the space behind his desk where his chair ought to be. Where it always was! Designed specifically for him to fit perfectly in the foot-well of his desk! Where the devil—

The library. Miss Faelyn had probably absconded with his chair and was using it for a drying rack.

He unlocked the library door, expecting to dodge the familiar labyrinth of crates. But the packing containers were gone, their contents settled into place as though they'd been so for decades. Miss Faelyn's corner looked particularly stalwart, prepared for a battle.

But his chair was nowhere to be seen.

However, there was a yellow rose plucked from his garden, floating in his inkstand, water dribbled in a ring around his blotter. Next she'd be using his shoes as coal scuttles and his necktie as a lamp wick.

And the door to the garden was standing wide open to the darkness! A blatant breach of security. He grabbed the latch to pull the door closed and came back with a handful of stickiness.

Honey! A great gob of it.

Had the woman gone mad? He washed his hands in the kitchen, then set out into the night for the lodge.

The place was lit like Christmastide, a candle blazing in every window, the front door standing open to the breeze and to every fiend who might pass by.

Damnation! He couldn't have her living here alone. He'd have to convince her to move to the main house. Hell, he'd move her there himself! He should have knocked, but he heard a commotion at the rear of the house—shouting and screaming.

"What the hell?" Fearing the worst, he tore down the hallway toward the sitting room, his heart in his throat.

He threw the door wide, ready to charge in, but, in that moment, time stood by and filled his heart to bursting.

His sisters were playing there in the hazy lamplight, unaware of him, draped in fanciful too-big-for-them gowns, pale-haired and lovely, their little voices chattering like field mice.

Emma, so near young womanhood; Bryna, with her unforgettable smile, and dear Clady, who had loved to ride upon his shoulders.

He'd found them! At last!

The scene blurred and stung his eyes.

"Clady …," he said to the littlest of the ghosts, afraid to take a step into the room for fear of frightening them away.

But three pairs of startlingly clear eyes found him. "Oh, look, Anna! A dragon!"

And then they were screaming in terror, rooting him to the floor.

Emma picked up an apple and heaved it at him. "Away, monster!"

He took one apple in the shoulder, and another to his knee. They didn't understand. Didn't recognize him.

"Maireeeeeey!" Bryna was shouting as she brandished a fire-poker, Clady was throwing pillows.

They came at him in a cloud of nightgowns and streaming hair, still screaming like banshees, and calling for Mairey. Mairey?

He felt warm hands around his waist from behind, and the scent of apples, and then Mairey slid around in front of him, her back warm against his chest, intercepting the attack.

"Anna, stop that right now!"

Anna. Not his Emma, at all. Not Bryna, or Clady. No, of course not. His sisters would be older. Years older.

Mairey was looking up at him, a magnet for the little girls, who'd lunged at her and were tucking themselves into the fullness of her night robe.

"I'm very sorry, sir," she was saying, lifting the one he'd thought was Clady into her arms. "We weren't expecting anyone. You frightened them."

He couldn't find any words, couldn't spare a breath of explanation.

"Is he your dragon, Mairey?"

"No, Poppy." Mairey smoothed her fingers through the little girl's wispy hair, and set a kiss against her temple. "This is Lord Rushford. Our host. You must tell him you're sorry."

"We're sorry!" The chorus of little voices wounded him, made him angry.

"Who are these children?" he bellowed, instantly ashamed to see the little faces fall, their fearful retreat.

Mairey was frowning fiercely at him, as though he were in the wrong. "They are my sisters."

Hers.

"What the devil are they doing here?" He couldn't help staring at the confusion.

"No, Auntie, don't! It's all right." She was shaking her head at someone behind him, waving them off. "And this is our Aunt Tattie."

He turned slightly and caught sight of an older woman wielding a large iron kettle.

"Your lordship." The woman ducked him a curtsey, then took a protective stand beside Miss Faelyn.

They were a wayward sight, the five of them. So out of place and yet so familiar. Hiding from him.

"Come with me to my office, Miss Faelyn." He turned to go, but the children were clinging to her.

"No, Mairey! Don't go! We just got here! A story, Mairey. Please tell us a story." The angel voices rose like a hymn.

"My lord, I believe this matter will wait till morning." Bright smudges of color pinked her cheeks. "I haven't seen my sisters in a long time, and then only briefly. We've missed each other."

"Then we'll talk now, Miss Faelyn. Here."

She must have seen that he meant it. "Tattie, will you please take the girls upstairs—"

"Mairey, nooooo!" The littlest of them clung tighter. He felt a raging rush of guilt when those fawn-brown eyes peeked out at him from under a fine spray of curls.

So like his Clady. His heart lurched, and his stomach roiled with shame and sorrow. And all those memories.

No, they couldn't stay. He couldn't have them living here underfoot. They would get in the way. He had his own family to worry about. The last thing he needed was someone else's.

"I'll be up soon, girls. And you'll each have a story."

"'Little Red Riding Hood'!"

"'Gwynella and the Enchanter'!"

"One each, I said. But only if you go with Auntie." Miss Faelyn helped the older woman funnel their brood up the stairs, to much giggling and pattering footfalls.

"You didn't have to shout at them, Rushford." She held her place at the bottom of the stairs, as though he might storm past her and devour them. "They're only little girls."

"Damn it, woman! You said nothing of this family of yours."

"Did you once think to ask me if I had a family?"

"You should have said."

"And then what? You forced me to live at Drakestone House. Home to me is my family. And here they will stay."

"Not when it means a full-scale invasion of my property."

"They are children, Rushford, not an army of locusts."

"They are a risk to security."

"Ballocks! They are three little girls and a war-widow who would lay down her life for them and me."

"I'm not interested in your family."

"My family, my lord, is the *only* thing I'm interested in. I'm sorry if you can't understand that."

But dear God, he did understand! It was the gaping hole in his heart, wide and lonely, aching for the family he'd abandoned.

"They can't stay."

"Then neither can I, my lord."

A stone thumped against his chest, the empty sound of his heart beating in a hollow drone.

"We've made a bargain. You and I and no one else."

"You knew everything about me, didn't you?" She came toward him, her long hair falling to her waist. "You knew my travel schedule, my library, my desire to find the Knot. How can you possibly have overlooked that I have a family?"

"I would have forbidden them. Drakestone House, the estate is not a place for children."

"Then nothing in the world could have persuaded me to come to live here if I couldn't be with them. I'll keep them away from you, my lord, away from your house. You need never see them."

"Impossible." He remembered his own sisters. As unmanageable as smoke, slipping through his fingers like water to bedevil him and make him laugh.

"Despite what you saw here tonight, sir, my sisters are well behaved and respectful."

A cloud of giggling poured down from above, wrapping his heart in aching wonder. The woman standing guard against him, wearing little more than her robe as armor, glanced fondly at the noise. He recognized the indomitable love in her eyes and envied it in deep, dark waves.

"You won't see them, Rushford; won't hear a peep. I promise to hide them away."

The giggling came again, irrepressible and without guile. And crowded with memories. Dear, soul-flooding memories. He turned away from her, from the mist blurring his vision. He cleared his throat to speak.

"My desk chair is missing."

He felt her relax; knew that she stooped to pick up an apple.

"Ah, well, yes. For that, I must apologize. Caroline noticed it had wheels and tried to use it for a pushcart for our bags. The wheel broke as the chair rolled down your stone steps and is now in the carriage house under repair."

Memories. The wagon he'd made for Bryna, whitewashed with paint he'd stolen from the pit boss. How could he let these children stay and not feel the loss every day?

"Also, there's a rose in my inkstand and water all over the blotter."

"I'm sorry. That was Anna. She loves flowers. I'll take care of it."

His blossoms. *Where are you, Emma? Are you happy? Are you loved?*

"The window latch is sticky with something sweet."

"Poppy. I'm afraid she found the apiary. Loves honey. On everything. Especially her fingers."

"Good Lord! She could have been stung!"

"But she wasn't." The woman's gentle laughter was so forgiving, soothed him when he preferred his anger. She was too close behind him, touching his elbow as if to make him understand what was so very clear to him. "There were no bees involved in the incident, sir. Cook gave her a spoonful from the kitchen crock. I'll clean it all myself. I'm just sorry you don't like children."

What other opinion could she have of him? "I don't like deception."

"That wasn't my intention. They are my sisters, left to my care when our father died. I love them as I love my life. I'll not desert them for you, Lord Rushford, or for the Willowmoon Knot, or for anything in the world. Perhaps you'll understand someday."

He swallowed back the searing shame that had taken hold of his throat. "Just keep them away from me, Miss Faelyn, and the house. Far away."

He started for the door and would have been well gone from

her, but the woman tugged him back with her gentling question.

"Why did you come to the lodge tonight?"

To see you, Mairey Faelyn; to sit with you in the hearth light and tell you of my day.

He was dizzy for lack of breathing, unable to avoid her too-wise gaze. "It will keep till the morning, Miss Faelyn."

He left the lodge and didn't slow his stride until he was well down the wooded path, away from the softly glowing windows, away from the laughter that spilled from the garret.

But not nearly far or fast enough to outpace the ghosts or the dismay in Mairey Faelyn's eyes.

CHAPTER 8

Mairey stood in the open doorway and watched Rushford stalk down the path until his darkness became part of the woods. She ought to be angry with him for breaking down her door, frightening her sisters, and then trying to turn them out into the cold! Anger would have served her best. He might have been bellowing his intolerable demands, but his beastliness bore the unmistakable mark of a raw and painful wound. Its source made him shy away from her and the children, as a lion might with a thorn in its paw.

"Is your dragon gone, Mairey?" Poppy had escaped her aunt and was standing at the bottom of the stairs, a crooked frown creasing her brow.

"That's not your business, Persephone Faelyn. Up to bed with you!" Mairey swept Poppy into her arms, climbed the stairs and tossed her into bed with the other two.

Poppy was asleep long before the wolf had devoured Riding Hood's grandmother; Anna and Caro lasted until Gwynella to refused to marry the prince and ran away with the enchanter.

Tattie was snoring softly in her own room a few moments

later, leaving Mairey to clean up the sitting room where her sisters had pitched their battle against Lord Rushford.

She had arrived in time to see him standing unarmed against the onslaught of apples and Caro's poker. He'd done nothing to defend himself, Goliath allowing Mairey's three little Davids to do their worst against him. If she hadn't stopped them, Heaven only knew what injury they might have inflicted upon the man.

She'd never in her life seen a more vulnerable sight, all that mighty brawn, so achingly disarmed by three little girls.

No wonder he'd demanded they leave. They had already made a mess of his library, had broken his favorite chair, and had nearly disabled him.

The mess in his library would still be there to greet him in the morning, a further reminder of the Faelyn sisters' invasion of his precious privacy—surely a breach of his security, as well. It would be best to clean it right now and not have to face him in the morning.

She dressed and carried a lantern through the woods to the main house, letting herself into the library with the key still strung with twine.

She lit a small fire in the hearth and set the thick desk blotter to dry nearby, washed honey off the window latch and the back of a nearby chair, discovering more of it on a dozen other surfaces Rushford would have bellowed about had he found them. The Faelyns would have to live more lightly on the estate, keep to the lodge, the woods, and the shadows, and out of Rushford's sight.

Waiting for the blotter to dry and finding herself restless, she collected some of Henrietta's papers off the lines in the conservatory and returned to the library. She rolled her father's chair to the fireside, then sorted the still-musty letters by date, setting aside those written after September 1642.

Thinking just to skim over some of the faded passages, she soon found herself caught up in Henrietta's letters. Most were passion-filled missives to her dear Charles, written in the woman's native French, having little to do with the war except for her diatribes against the Roundheads.

Henrietta's personal letters! Doors opened wide to the Tower of London, to all the vaults and collections in the kingdom. She'd sold her soul to Jackson Rushford to gain entrance, but so far the price hadn't been too high.

Some of the ink on Henrietta's letters had washed away, leaving them readable only with a bright light behind the page and a little guesswork. She was holding up a particularly badly faded letter when a latch clicked and the door from the foyer opened to a silhouetted darkness she would have known anywhere.

"My lord."

"What are you doing here, Miss Faelyn?" He was in a fine midnight mood, was her dragon.

"Working," she said, holding up the letter to the fire, hoping that he would leave her to her task.

"Damn it, woman! Is that the way it is between us?" He was on her in the next moment, his wall of heat overwhelming the fire in the hearth as he leaned his weight and his fury so fiercely against the chair arms she rocked backward on its gimbals, making it impossible not to look up into his blazing eyes. "Have I so insulted you and your family that you're burning evidence to spite me?"

"I've burned nothing except wood. It's cold."

He snatched the letter from her, tipping the chair further backward. "Then what is this?" He thrust the paper into the small space between her nose and his.

"It's a letter from Henrietta to her husband. I would never destroy it."

The man growled a curse and straightened to read in the lamplight. Her chair rocked upright abruptly, yet he kept his knee between hers, pressing it against the edge of the seat so she could see nothing but his woolen waistcoat, the gold-fobbed watch chain bridging the line of black pearl buttons that marched down his broad chest to the tapering of his stomach, and the front of his trousers.

Her heart took off on a zithering flight and strung her pulse along behind it. She wanted to reach beneath his coat and shape her palms over his hips. But he was scrutinizing the offending letter as though he suspected it contained the alchemists' secret.

"It's blank," he said, and loomed again, bending her chair backward so that their noses were nearly touching.

"Blank until you hold the page to a backlight." She snatched the letter from between his fingers. "May I rise, sir? Or do you plan some other mischief with me?"

Dear God, he was handsome, and wild-hearted again in his passions.

"The mischief is yours, Miss Faelyn. Yours and your sisters'."

Dew glistened on his hair and across his shoulders; he smelled of the night, of the blueness of the moon.

"Have you been out walking, sir?" Some bit of lunacy made her touch a bead of water clinging to a dark curl at his temple. It slid off his hair and ran down her finger.

"Hunting the moon with my fellow wolves, my dear. Just like the bloody tales of the bloody beasts you tell your sisters." He dipped his head, his breath almost a kiss. "Whatever you think of me, I don't eat grandmothers or little girls."

"Aha!" She pointed her finger between them, amazed at his confession and utterly charmed when she ought to feel spied upon. "You were listening at our window! Why?"

He had the courtesy to look chastened. "I was waiting."

"For?"

"You."

That made her heart leap to all sorts of conclusions it ought to avoid.

"Well, then, sir, if you were at the lodge, you saw me leave there a half hour ago. Why didn't you say something then? Were you lurking?"

He chewed on his lip, straightened and walked to the window, then confessed quietly, "I ..." He glanced back at her, a wryness in his tone. "Fell asleep."

She shouldn't laugh, knew that the slightest whimper in that direction would set the man's pride on end. But even after clapping her hand over her mouth, she couldn't keep the giggling noises from escaping her.

"Thank you, I'm sure."

"Oh, my!" Crispy leaves and bits of loam clung to the back of his coat. She brushed off his sleeve, then handed him a good-sized maple leaf, complete with a winged seed pod attached. "You should have stayed with us, sir. You could have slept on a bed with the other cubs and not in the briars."

He watched her from over his shoulder, his eyes tracking hers like beams of pure sunlight as she continued brushing at the leaves. "Your sisters and aunt can live here," he said quietly. "I won't fight you."

"I wouldn't have stayed."

"I know." There was finality in those two resolute words and a nuance of approval.

Unnerved, she made her way around the brute, almost certain she had no ulterior motives for stroking him repeatedly —quite apart from the luscious feel of his hard-packed brawn. "I'll do my best to keep them away from your house. But I cannot absolutely guarantee that your gardener won't find honey smeared on the greenhouse door latch."

"Drakestone will survive, Miss Faelyn." His voice rumbled against her palm. "I had young sisters of my own, once upon a time."

"Did you?" Ah, then he was used to the changeable fancies of little girls; he would have learned patience under their constant disruptions. "I have just the three, but they often seem like twice that. How many do you have?"

He shook his head and left her for the hearth, giving a dry laugh as he crushed the maple leaf in his hand. "Three. Imagine my surprise when I found *your* sisters in my lodge. I thought for a moment—"

But he stopped there, on the very brink of something that Mairey couldn't see beyond. He seemed altogether tame now. Weary to his soul. And for some unfathomable reason, she longed to wrap her arms around him and put his head against her heart. It pained her immeasurably to think of him asleep outside her window when there had been so much room inside with them.

"Your sisters must be grown and married by now."

He nodded, staring at the flames, but offered nothing more.

"Do you see them often?"

"I haven't for a very long time." He tossed the wadded leaf into the hearth and turned to her. "Look, Miss Faelyn, I ... I waited for you outside the lodge because I didn't want to interrupt the felicitous scene I had leveled with my earlier outburst. I was going to rap on the door as soon as you'd put your sisters to bed. So I listened and waited ...."

"And fell asleep."

He nodded, sighed with the breath he'd been holding. "It was a long day."

She wanted to ask more about his family, but he'd obviously closed the subject. "What was it you wanted of me?"

"This. What I'm trying to say now. That I overreacted and I'm sorry for it. That I won't gobble up your sisters or your aunt should I come upon them in the woods. And that I won't fall upon you in a rage thinking you're destroying evidence as I just now did. That would be absurd, when both of us are chasing the same thing."

"Yes. Well." A little snake turned in Mairey's stomach, cobalt blue and glass-eyed. Deception wasn't the most ennobling skill, even when practiced against one's greatest adversary. "Come, then. I'll show you what I was looking at just now."

She knelt in front of the hearth and added a handful of kindling. The fire brightened and snapped as Rushford joined her on one knee.

She extended the page of washed-out ink toward the flame. "I read at least a hundred letters today. I'd just begun to read this one."

"There's nothing on it."

"So it may seem until you hold the paper just so against a bright—Dear God!" Her heart slammed up against her throat. She brought the page closer, and then back again, so the runny blue coalesced into sharper lines. "Adam Branville! It's him!"

"Who?" He squinted closer and closed his hand over hers to keep the page steady. "Where do you see a name?"

Oh, Papa! Just like that! First Henrietta's papers and now the keeper of the woman's treasury! And here she was, blurting out his name with Rushford looking on, holding her hand, letting her pulse run wild alongside his. She'd grown too comfortable with the man, forgetting to temper her excitement, to shield her successes from him. There was nothing to be done now.

"Here," she said, pointing to the first line in the letter. "Adam Branville, the captain of Henrietta's guards."

"I see blurred blue. And I don't read French. You'll have to read it to me."

Of course! She'd forgotten—another artifice to employ against him. She sniffed away the blink of guilt. It didn't matter that the man was unwavering heat, or that he had fallen asleep under her window, listening to her fairy tales—he was her nemesis. There was no other word for his relationship to her. And no hope for anything better between them.

"It says, 'Dearest husband of my soul, our favorite Branville de Donowell left Windsor this night with ten carts, and under

God's good grace, should make Aylmouth within a fortnight.'" She still couldn't believe their great good fortune, could never have predicted Rushford's part in these miracles.

He handed back the page and studied her face, his eyes dark as coal, flames dancing in their depths. She felt borne upward as he watched her, as though her hair were lighter, and her eyelids kissed.

"You're certain this is Henrietta's infamous shipment of the treasury?"

All that lightness made breathing a little difficult, and whenever she did so, his scent thrilled her. "Of course I can't be entirely certain, but this is Henrietta's hand. Here she writes that the shipment was bound for Holland from the very place where two similar transactions happened during the war. Branville is one of the few men who could have stolen an entire cart from a caravan without a single person suspecting."

He rasped his knuckle along his jawline, across the midnight sheen of his day-old stubble. "There's a Donowell on the coast in Northumberland. It was on your map of items already recovered."

"Yes." She knew the location all too well, was already planning to slip away without him. But not until she found Branville's will, which would only be safe without Rushford constantly snooping over her shoulder, asking his too-precise questions. "The evidence piles up against our Baron de Donowell, doesn't it?"

"So it seems." He was still on one knee, the other bent firmly, his fine leg collecting hearth light along its length, still looking at her. "What next?"

"Next?" How was she supposed to think of ways to outflank the man while he was tangling his fingers in the ends of her hair, an unexpected intimacy that caught her breath in her throat.

"Next."

"Yes, well," she finally managed, "if Branville died during the Interregnum, then his will would have been probated in London and should hopefully be in the Tower. I'll return there tomorrow. And the day after—"

He laughed lightly. "You're quite marvelous, Mairey Faelyn." It was a simple statement made breathtaking when he began to trace the line of her cheekbone with his hand. "Softer than I imagined, for all your sharp edges."

A week ago, she would have scorned him; tonight she dammed up an immodest sigh and braved the alluring pleasure, looked up at him and into those flame-brightened eyes.

"*Do* you imagine such things, Rushford?"

His answer was to touch his fingers to his mouth. "Honey," he said.

She wasn't sure she'd heard him right—surely not an endearment. "What?"

He smiled down on her, catlike, indulgent.

"You have honey on your cheek, Miss Faelyn, and here on your lips—" Because he'd put it there with his fingertip, and now followed briefly after with his mouth and then the tip of his tongue—a grazing of lightning that dazed her, made her take hold of his lapel to keep her balance.

"You taste of honey."

"Do I?" *Are you sure? Please do try again.* Her heart was a scramble of thumps and pauses, made useless by the man's utterly ravenous smile.

"Far sweeter than my imaginings, my dear." He was breathing unsteadily, a sheen of dampness gilding his forehead. "That being so, Miss Faelyn, before I take you back to the safety of the lodge, I'd like to know more of this Princess Gwynella person."

"From the fairy tale?" He was still so close, still tracing her mouth with his fingers, as though he might sample there again.

"Tell me the woman doesn't take up with the prince. He was an ass."

Her heart swelled. He hadn't heard the end of the story. Her impossible dragon must have fallen asleep even before Caro had.

"The Enchanter came back for the princess, my lord. Married her on the spot."

He nodded sagely, satisfied. "Wise man."

"I agree."

"Come, let's get you back to the lodge before I–" he stopped, stood and offered his hand, but said nothing more, letting her imagination run amuck.

A dragon with a taste for honey. Now there was a tale for the ages.

"Steel, Rushford?" Herringham laced his fingers together and settled his hands on top of his briefcase. "I am advising against such an investment."

"Noted, Herringham." Jack slid his gaze along the ridge of stiff-faced men sitting like blackbirds around his conference table. "However, the £8,000 is mine to invest, not yours."

"But sir, Bessemer's invention has yet to be thoroughly tested. British hand-forged iron, replaced by mass-produced steel? Preposterous! What of your own forges? They'll need to be refitted."

"Exactly—and as soon as possible. Here you'll find Stothard's engineering drawings, showing how my factories will be quickly changed over to the new process. We've already begun negotiations to purchase Wright & Sons Tooling. Show them, Stothard."

"Certainly, my lord!" Stothard had spent the entire meeting on his feet, pacing, pointing, commenting. He was Jack's best metallurgical engineer, the very best in the Empire, perpetually charged as if ready to explode. When he did sit, he constructed odd structures out of whatever was at hand. "Rushford Mining and Minerals will not only be the largest foundry to manufacture Bessemer's new steel, we'll also force our competitors to purchase their new machinery from us."

"Refitting the Rushford foundries and factories will cost thousands," Herringham said as he leafed through the report so quickly he couldn't possibly have read let alone understood it. "And what if the process fails?"

"It won't," Jack said, exasperated by the man's dire predictions. Prudence was one thing, but fear of the future would eventually bury the Rushford operation in silt. "I've seen the process myself, from extrusion to finished rails laid down on the roadbed. I've watched rail stock pushed to the limits of speed, with excellent trials and better safety than has ever been possible. Within a few years, every rail-bed in Britain will be replaced with Rushford steel."

"Just as every mining operation will soon employ the new Rushford steam-windings," Stothard said, flipping through the report for Herringham, "as I've shown there on page twelve. This is the refitting design for the Glad Heath Works, already under construction. I'm supervising it myself."

Stothard's excitement soon reached the others around the table: a few investors, two geological engineers, Jack's site-viewers, three factory men, and a Parliamentary official. Near the end of the meeting, even Herringham joined in the discussion, though he looked completely overwhelmed.

Jack leaned back against the bookcase and let Stothard have his due, pleased that Glad Heath would soon be the very safest colliery in all the world, as well as the most efficient. A testament to profitable safety that would bring other mine owners to his side.

He was pleased to his soul that Glad Heath was prospering.

His father would be proud of the changes Jack had accomplished at the mine—the unblemished safety record, revenues that made him the envy of the mining industry, and the choice among investors.

Revenge, Father, he thought with some satisfaction. *A tribute to you, and Mother.*

His guilt pierced more deeply since Miss Faelyn had come into his life, immeasurably so since she'd brought her sisters to live here. He couldn't fault her love for them; he could only stand in awe of her devotion.

She was an ethereal and inconsistent contraption, wore her fragile sentiments on her sleeve. Yet he'd never met a more granite determination. He'd seen little of her and nothing at all of her sisters in the last few days. He'd spent long hours with Stothard, finalizing the engineering designs for the refitting, and by the time he returned home each night, the library was dark and Mairey had retreated to the lodge. She'd accepted his apology for being a great raging boor, but he still sensed a distance between them, a shaft of loneliness through his chest.

Yet, he found himself drifting toward the lodge every evening, his heart as wild as the woodlands in springtime. Sometimes she briefly invited him in, answering his questions in her smoked-silk voice with her hand clutching the door, ready to exclude him from her delicious scents and the sounds of delight just beyond the darkness.

Sometimes she allowed him to sit with her in her little parlor, discussing the Willowmoon Knot or her father's work, but glancing nervously at the ceiling as though she thought her sisters might descend upon them and set him off again.

He wasn't ready to meet the children head-on; he was still wrestling with his own shadows, and frightened as hell of such bliss.

She'd left Drakestone early this morning to continue digging around in the Wakefield Tower again today, searching for

Cromwell's probate records. Tedious stuff, her every move dogged by Walsham and his cow-eyed infatuation. Though the woman denied any interest in the little man, if he ever showed up here with a wad of flowers in his fist, Jack would throw him out on his skinny backside. The thought burned a hole in his gut, made him want nothing more than to end the meeting, and meet Mairey at the Tower.

He'd never taken honey in his tea, but now he ladled it into every cup because it tasted of her, of her perfectly bowed mouth, her sweet tongue. An intimacy that Walsham couldn't ever experience! Ha!

"We've already begun the refitting work at Glad Heath." Stothard was standing in front of the huge map of Britain, which rose nearly twenty feet to the ceiling and spanned the wall from corner to corner. Jack had commissioned it to be painted in the finest geological detail, directly on the wall, behind a set of sliding mahogany panels. His mine works and forges dappled the valleys and ridges, from Bodmin Moor to the River Tyne. An inset map showed the sprawl of his North American holdings. The whole of his empire.

The Willowmoon and its bed of silver were hiding some-where on the map, winking up at the sunlight, waiting for him. A fortune, a quest for the impossible, and one that was leading to places he could never have imagined.

Because he'd never in his life imagined Mairey Faelyn.

"Show them the new outcropping at Ben Alden, Stothard." Jack joined him at the map, and the others rose to surround him.

"Ah, yes," Stothard said, as he climbed the rolling stairs to gesture at Northumberland. "For those of you who don't know, the new coalfield at Ben Alden is here, three-quarters of a mile from the Newcastle and Carlisle Railway. It will be fitted out from the beginning with the very best in steam technology."

"What about a spur line to the colliery, Rushford?" Ahearne

was a steadfast investor, one of his most progressive. "Have you addressed that?"

Jack clapped the man on the back, pointed to the place where Stothard had his finger. "Parliament has approved, the right-of-way for a spur line has been negotiated with the land contracts, and the tracks will be laid—with new *steel* tracks."

"What exactly do all those black spots mean, Lord Rushford?"

The voice came from behind them all, clear and morning-bright. Every man in the room turned in unison, bunching and backing away from Mairey as though she were a magical creature.

An enchantress wearing a small wad of violets in the lapel of her traveling cloak. He felt a blast of molten lead in his chest.

Walsham's flowers! He wanted to scorch them into oblivion.

Jealousy. Pure, but not in the least simple.

"Gentlemen," he managed, though his pulse raged in his ears. "I would like you to meet Miss Mairey Faelyn."

He wanted to lift her out of his office and quiz her about her afternoon at the Tower. He wanted to back her into the library and make love to her. She nodded at the men, then went back to examining the map, the deep wings of her brows canted in scathing disapproval.

"What are the black blotches, Lord Rushford?"

He felt utterly chastened by her interest. He was used to digging in the earth with his bare hands, with shovels and picks and clamoring mine works when necessary. This digging into paper as she was doing, into the distant past, was mind-numbing, made him feel clumsy and unsure. Here on the wall was the extent of his life, painted in brilliant enamels, and suddenly tasting of rust and salt.

And she smelled of Walsham's violets!

"The black blotches, Miss Faelyn, indicate the coalfields owned by Rushford Mining and Minerals."

She took a step closer to the map, craning her neck and touching her fingers to her lovely lips.

"And the red?" she asked, the worry in her eyes deepening.

"My tin mines, Miss Faelyn, and the blue is lead."

The other men were murmuring, approving of the woman, or of the extent of Jack's holdings, or his plans. The why didn't matter. Though he'd always been proud of his success, he felt roundly less than that at the moment, like a braggart who'd been caught in a shameful truth.

She turned her glittering gaze on him. "What of your silver holdings, Lord Rushford? Do you own any silver mines?"

He nearly swallowed his tongue, and came up clearing his throat. What the devil was the woman up to?

"None in England, Miss Faelyn," he said between his teeth.

"Actually, Miss Faelyn," Stothard said, clumping down the ladder to interrupt with his usual enthusiasm, "there are no silver mines in all the British Isles."

"No silver at all?" She still had hold of Jack's gaze. "But what of the work of the ancient Celts?"

"The which?"

Stothard couldn't have known he'd just become a character in one of her fairy stories. Where the hell was she going with this riddle?

"The Celts, Mr. Stothard. Early Britons. I just wondered where their silversmiths had gotten the metal for their artifacts. I'm an antiquarian, and though I see the elegant work of the Celts everywhere, I've not the vaguest idea of where they mined their silver."

"Ah! Well, smelting silver from lead ore is an ancient process. A fleck here, a chunk there, melted out of the rock, just as lead and tin has always been. Silver isn't mined like coal. Not in veins and stockworks. At least not here in Britain."

Jack decided that the woman had caused enough trouble;

God knew where she was leading them all. "What is it you need, Miss Faelyn?"

~

To be free of you, Rushford.

Mairey had never seen Rushford's map before, the grasping hold he had on the riches of the earth. Nor could she have imagined that his holdings so closely ringed the Willowmoon. A chill had come upon her the moment she'd opened the door; it curled around her heart, frightening her to the marrow.

"If you'll excuse me, gentlemen, I'll be right back," Rushford said as he took her hand and slipped it over his arm.

He skidded her through the foyer and into the library, scooping her into his arms and depositing her on top of his desk.

"What the devil was that all about?" he asked fiercely, trapping her with his hands on either side of her legs.

"I only stopped in to tell you I'd returned from the Tower."

"And stayed to ask about silver mining? *Silver*, Miss Faelyn! And the Celts! In public! Are you mad?"

"I was curious." She'd been stunned by the vast scope of his contemptible enterprise, unable to stop her questions.

"You picked a bloody bad time to become curious about silver mining."

The very best time, Rushford. She'd learned splendid news about Branville's will today, but couldn't tell a soul, especially not the reprehensible but dangerously attractive Viscount Rushford. "I'd never seen your map before. Where do you hide it?"

"Damn the map! What do I say when those men stop to wonder who you are, and why you would just wander into my office unannounced? They're sure to ask why I have an astoundingly beautiful young woman living in my house."

"In the lodge." *Beautiful? He thinks I'm beautiful?* Well, and that was the problem, wasn't it—all this crackling attraction between them. She kept forgetting who he was, who she was, needed stark reminders of his threat to everyone she loved, not all this steamy heat clouding her senses. Needed to see his towering map that bled black with his mines to remind her he was her sworn enemy.

"The men are your business associates. They will certainly find out sometime that I live on the estate. Just tell them I am one of those fusty old antiquarians, and that I've engaged your lodge as a place from which to study its history."

"Not bloody likely. You are neither fusty nor old, as every man in that room was patently aware. Not so easily dismissed."

Her ears went instantly crimson at the effort to keep from remembering the graze of his tongue against her lips, the sizzling warmth of his mouth.

"If all goes well, my lord, one day soon we'll find the Willow-moon Knot, and then I'll be gone from your circle and no longer your problem."

Despite all the books and the inch-thick carpets, despite the tapestried drapes, her declaration seemed to echo in the library.

He straightened, a tic dancing along his jaw. He looked angry, frustrated.

"Where did you get these?" He flicked his finger across the sagging violets that her sister had surprised her with that morning.

"From Anna. Why?"

He scrubbed his hand across his mouth, calmed considerably. "They're wilted."

"It's been a long day."

"Made longer by Walsham, I suppose?" He was folding bits of her sleeve between his fingertips, watching her.

"He was … manageable." She hid her amusement; Rushford truly hated the man. She wanted to suspect a heathy dose of jealousy, but that would only rouse too many other suspicions, too many impossibilities.

"Did you find anything of interest today?"

Adam Branville's last will and testament.

"Nothing at all, my lord." Her heart rang hollow as she rattled off her lie.

"Will you go again tomorrow?"

I'll go to Donowell, as soon as I can get away from you, Lord Dragon.

"That depends. There are other clues to follow." While she bided her time.

"My best to Walsham. My worst to him if he should ever touch you wrongly." He lifted her hand in his, pressed a delicious kiss against her fingertips, and then left her to return to his pillaging.

Left her wanting so very much more.

As he'd done every evening over the past week, Jack once again made his way through the twilight toward the lodge, this time carrying a sack of flour. He was running out of excuses for these nocturnal visits, and would have to confess to Miss Faelyn one day soon that he enjoyed her company outside the bounds of their project. Which would sound something like courting. Which brought beads of sweat popping out on his forehead when he realized that—

Bloody hell! He was courting Mairey Faelyn! That explained the gnawing in his stomach and the battering that his heart was giving his rib cage at the moment. Courting?

Hell. No. He merely wanted to talk to the woman about mining. And such. She'd been interested enough a few days ago to interrupt his meeting; he even had a pocket full of drawings and diagrams to help demonstrate the workings. But delivering the flour from the main pantry ... yes, this was the best excuse he'd come up with yet.

Near to whistling, he followed the stream till it widened to a pool, his step lighter than it had been in years.

Courting?

"Shhh!"

He stopped at the oddly hovering voice, unable to locate its source. Then came a tugging at his pant cuff. Miss Faelyn's shadow-pale face peered up at him from behind a fallen tree, her wide eyes bright and blinking.

"Miss Faelyn?" he asked, his voice sounding harsh in the cool night.

"Down, Rushford, you'll scare them away." She tugged again at his trouser cuff, the gentle pressure bringing him to his knees beside her.

"Scare who?" He noticed then that her sisters were sprawled like wood nymphs in the giant roots that had once anchored the old willow to the bankside. The youngest was draped precariously on a drooping branch, her fingers dragging in the water.

"The fair folk are out tonight," Miss Faelyn said, her words dappled in amusement as she nodded toward the pool. "We're watching them."

"Are you?" he asked, aware of little more than the glint of moonlight on her mouth.

"There's another one, Mairey!" The little voice was bright with awe, and far too loud for secrets. "Look! Look! Do you see?"

"I do, Caro. I see four. Anna?"

"Oh, yes, Mairey, I see them, too."

He saw nothing. Only the woman's moon-bright hair. "Fair folk?"

"There." She pointed at the air above the pond. "Carrying lanterns to light the dancing at their revels."

He saw only the phosphorescence given off by decaying matter in the rushes. "Miss Faelyn, those lights are—"

"*Fairies*, my lord," she said, leveling a frown. He could feel her eyes on him, daring him to contradict her. "What do you call them where you come from?"

"These fairies belong to his lordship." The middle child—Caro, if he remembered rightly, the one who had wielded the poker against him—jumped off the tree to hang off Mairey's shoulder, her round little face between theirs, her eyes sparkling with conspiracy. "They're your fairies, aren't they, sir?"

He looked again at the ethereal illuminations, their feathery lightness matching the stars for acrobatic grace. He remembered his family lying like rag dolls under the open skies, for no other reason than the fact that it was huge and magnificent and they loved each other.

"The fairies aren't mine, Caro," he said, swallowing hard to keep his voice steady, "but they do pay rent to live at Drakestone."

"Really, sir?" He heard the soft laughter in Mairey's question, and his ears went hot with pride. "How do they pay you? With acorns?"

"Well, candy." He caught himself smiling at her, and crossed his legs as she was doing and sat fully on the spongy ground.

"Chocolate candy?" The littlest of the girls slid into Mairey's lap and peered into his face, smelling of rose soap and childhood.

The woman was waiting for his answer as readily as her sisters, her eyes sparkling, her mouth dew-damp and stunningly inviting.

"Yes, chocolate," he said, delighting in the grin she gave him, and nearly jumping out of his skin when she patted his hand.

"Poppy's favorite."

"My favorite!" The squeal of laughter would have sent all the fairies in England back into their holes, or wherever the devil they lived.

"What's in the sack, sir?" Caro asked, poking at the bag of flour he'd set beside him.

"Candy for the fairies?" Poppy leaned down to look.

"For us, too, I hope?" The elder, Anna—the flower thief who had pelted him with apples—knelt down beside him, too much the young lady to squeal or poke like the other two.

And still Mairey said nothing, only smiled from behind Poppy's curls and let him blunder around and gain his bearings.

"The sack is only full of flour, I'm afraid."

"Fairy flour to make fairy cakes!" Poppy flung herself out of Miss Faelyn's lap and into his, all pointy elbows and sticky fingers, and was circling like a puppy for a better seat. "I like fairy cakes!"

"Poppy, be careful with Lord Rushford." She looked pained when she saw where the girl was stepping.

"Jack," he said firmly. "My name is Jack. I feel a hundred years old and a thousand miles away when you call me 'Rushford' or 'my lord.'"

"Are you a hundred years old, Lord Jack?" Anna had taken Poppy's place in Miss Faelyn's lap.

"Are you?" the woman asked, smiling.

"Thirty-three." He grunted as Poppy dropped into place and lounged against him, a bare foot kicking the fallen tree.

Caro was now hanging on his shoulder, draped over his back, whispering, "I know how to make fairy cakes."

"With honey, I'll wager."

The little girl's eyes widened. "Then you know, too! Mairey! Can we make fairy cakes tonight? Can we?"

"It's late for cooking cakes, girls," she said, to a chorus of groans. "Aunt Tattie will be asleep."

"We'll be quiet!"

"Yes, I can imagine that happening." She raised a brow at

Jack, inviting him to remember the sounds of a household full of children.,

"Please, Mairey," Anna said, old enough to rally her patience, but ready to spring away like a gazelle.

"All right. But only if you're quiet"

Anna snatched up the bag of flour and dashed down the shadowy path with Caro on her tail.

Miss Faelyn got up, dusting off her skirt "Will you come, my lord?"

He didn't see how he could get away. The realization that he didn't want to came over him in a rush of yearning. Poppy had a hold of his neck, and Mairey had a grip on his heart. Where else would he go?

"I'm no good at all with a cook pot, Miss Faelyn."

"I know." Mairey could well imagine her dragon curled up in her aunt's kitchen, warming his belly on her stove, snoozing after inhaling a plateful of cakes—his mouth sweet with stolen honey. She ought to have sent him back to the main house for safekeeping. But he stood so easily with Poppy in his arms, and the little scamp seemed extraordinarily attached to the giant.

Ah, Poppy. I know the feeling too well.

"I can't stay long," he said, as though he knew her thoughts. "I'm off to Cornwall before daylight."

She felt her face go pale, and hoped that he couldn't see in the near darkness. "Until when?"

"Two days, maybe a little longer."

Long enough for a trip to Donowell without him—a prospect that didn't rest as comfortably as it might have a few weeks ago.

"Come, my lord, we've fairy cakes to make."

"Indeed."

CHAPTER 9

Mairey made Donowell by late afternoon the next day, and found a room in a small inn on the sea cliff, run by a pair of elderly maidens. She was standing in the nave of Holy Martyr's Church a half hour later.

Rushford was safely in Cornwall for the next few days. She had followed him secretly to the station to be sure he was gone, then left an hour later on a different track. Yet still she watched over her shoulder for him, feeling every bit like a sneak-thief. Her dear father had spent all his life plotting out the places where the queen's stolen treasury had been recovered. It had taken Mairey less than two weeks to find Adam Branville, his will, and a list of his possessions:

> *... six gilt knives, bonne-handled; one silv'red disk, anciently orna-mented; one brass ewere ...*

One silv'red disk, anciently ornamented. *The Willowmoon Knot.*

All because of Jackson Rushford. The very man who must

never see the fruit of all his beneficence. She would spend the rest of today and tomorrow following Branville's trail, and then return to Drakestone without him knowing that she had ever come.

The deception made her jaw hurt and her heart ache.

But she would persist. For love and devotion, for her village, for the glade, for her sisters and her father.

She forced the chant into her thoughts, trying to banish the sound of Jack's close and gentle laughter, the disarming way it reached down into her chest, and lifted the breath right out of her. The way the moonlight made his eyes sparkle, made his fine teeth gleam through his so very reluctant smile.

He'd won Poppy with that smile, and had threatened her own composure when her wee sister had slipped her hand into his and dragged him along the path toward the lodge.

Impossible dragon.

Filling up her mind with more productive images of the man's ravaging nature—of slag heaps and gaunt children—she shouldered her bag of foolscap and graphite and went in search of Sir Adam Branville.

Holy Martyr's had once been a priory, its chapel an echo of Canterbury cathedral in miniature. In the long centuries since, it seemed that every family in the parish had commissioned a monumental brass or stone marker to commemorate the loss of a loved one. The walls and floor were nearly paneled with them. She hoped Adam Branville's heirs felt as much dedication to his memory.

She scoured every wall and niche, reading every plaque, walking the length and breadth of the entire sanctuary, deciphering the worn letters in the carved stones embedded in the floor. She checked the Lady Chapel and the transepts, rounded every pillar, and was about to take her search outside into the churchyard when she remembered the tower.

Two winding stories later, on a wall in the middle of the

spiraling steps, just below a narrow arching window, she found the name that made her heart quicken.

Adam Branville. Dates, titles, praise, and prayers for his soul. The thieving devil. *Did your queen ever learn of your duplicity? And was the Willowmoon Knot among the heirlooms you left behind, Sir Branville—the 'silv'red disk, anciently ornamented?'*

Wishing her father were here to share her success, she dropped her hat at her feet, then unrolled a thick piece of parchment and fished around in her bag and retrieved the block of graphite.

She almost wished Jack were here with her, too. Not the rapacious Viscount Rushford of Rushford Mining and Minerals, but the Jack who had helped her make fairy cakes with her sisters. By the time Aunt Tattie had come down the stairs, roused from her bed by the unstoppable merriment, everyone and everything was sprinkled with flour.

Griddle cakes, the man had called them, best eaten slathered in butter and thick maple syrup on a cold Canadian morning. Poppy never left his side; Anna was completely in love; Caro had found a best friend; Aunt Tattie was flirting wildly; and Mairey had wanted to cry. Because the Jack who made cakes with them wasn't real. He was part of her fairy tales. Dragons never won the fair maiden—she had best remember that.

She fit the parchment against the brass plaque, squaring her arm and elbow across the top edge to hold it fast against the wall, then started rubbing the block lightly over the page to capture as much of Branville's memorial as possible. As awkward as it was, there was no better or more accurate way to copy the text. The block hit the rim of the raised crest beneath and bounced out of her fingers. She muttered, "Blazing toads!" She reached for the piece as it rolled two steps down the spiraling stairs—

And up against a pair of expensive boots, dusty and dreadfully familiar.

Rushford!

"Do let me help you, Miss Faelyn."

Possessive beast!

Rushford knelt and picked up the block, his eyes feral and dangerous, and utterly cold.

"How did you—"

"How did I find you?" He stood, trapped her hand against the wall and the parchment with his own, hot-palmed and huge, his fingers invading the cool spaces between hers. His eyes shuttered, as dark as the midnight of his hair gleaming blue black in the evening light spilling from the clerestory window. "Your sisters wanted me to insure you hurried home to them. I agreed."

He was closed down so tightly Mairey couldn't read him at all.

"You told me you'd be in Cornwall," she said, trying to erase his suspicions with a smile that felt as feeble as it must look. "I thought I might …."

"Show me." He held the lump of graphite in the short span between them.

"Show you what?" Branville's will? How did he know she'd found it?

"Show me how to take a rubbing. Isn't that what this method is called, Miss Faelyn?" His question brushed against her ear as he leaned in for a closer look at the lines and shadings.

"A rubbing, yes." Her fingers were cloddish and trembling as she took the block from him. "You begin like this," she said, feeling his gaze shift to her mouth and then to her eyes. "Hold it flat and … and work the edge of the letters first."

Her hair was a curling mess after all her travels, her plait fallen to the front, and in the way of her rubbing. But he'd caught her like a rabbit, unable to shift in any direction without moving against him.

"Is the Knot here in Donowell, Miss Faelyn?" He lifted her

plait off her shoulder and smoothed the curls at her nape. "Is that why you came here?"

"I don't know yet where the Knot is."

"But Branville had it at one time, didn't he?" He shifted his length to the same step as hers, and caught her even closer, his weight and warmth pressing against the back of her skirts, his heat spreading through folds of fabric, and collecting like honey low in her belly.

"Yes. I think so."

"*Think* so, Miss Faelyn?" He tucked his words behind her ear, a whisper that felt more like a lover's caress than the inquisition she knew them to be. "You must have found his will among Cromwell's probate courts."

"I did." Her confession slipped out like an inevitable sigh, leaving her nothing of her own to defend herself with. "I found it among the queen's papers this morning, just after you left."

"So you came straight here."

"I couldn't help myself, my lord." She turned slightly inside his embrace, steeling herself as she looked up into all that glowering. "I'm sure you can understand my excitement. To be this close, after my family's been searching all these centuries—"

"Indeed. Then continue." When he said nothing more, she returned to the rubbing, thanking him for bracing the parchment more firmly against the wall when it would have slipped.

"Done!" she said, her nerves raw and ragged from his nearness, her breath as unsteady as she turned to him with the parchment. "Proof positive that Branville lived and died in Donowell. And, if I'm right, that the Knot was here among his belongings and bequests when he died."

He scowled down at her. "So, where does Branville's will take us next, Miss Faelyn?"

Us. There'd be no putting him off now; he'd be more suspicious than ever. Would follow her like a thunderstorm, would know as much about the progress of the search as she. Her only solace was that she already knew exactly where the treasure lay. Would risk her life to keep it safely hidden from the man whose only desire was to pillage and plunder its beauty.

"We now know that Branville had an heir—a son, John. We need to find the son's will, which could be here in Donowell or in York—"

"Why York?"

"It depends on which prerogative court proved the will after John died. And from there we follow the trail of bequests until it dead-ends. A lot of work. A lot of travel."

"My schedule is clear, Miss Faelyn. Take all the time you need."

Oh, go dig in your coal pit, Rushford!

"It's too late this evening. We'll have to continue in the morning." She rolled up the parchment. "I'm staying at an inn at the edge of town—"

"At the Belle Heather, with the elderly Misses Potterfell. So am I. Come." Without a glance at her, he scooped up her tapestry satchel, took her arm, and started down the stairs.

"What do you mean you're staying at the Belle Heather?" She stopped dead. They said she was lucky, that they'd only her room to let. The other had been full. "There's no room for you."

"But there's always room for romance. I told the ladies that my dear wife and I had a falling out—" A simple tug on her arm and she was hurrying after him.

"Your *wife!*"

"I told them I'd been a damned fool, that I had hoped to make it up to her tonight with flowers and ... well, I let them imagine my apology."

"You didn't!" Stunned to her marrow, she stopped again, and again the brute tugged her along after him until they reaching the bottom of the stairs.

"The ladies seemed quite concerned over the sorry state of our marriage."

"Jackson Rushford, how dare you?" She would have dashed ahead of him, but he brought her close against his length.

"Because I doubt very much that the Misses Potterfell would have approved my sleeping in your room tonight without our having been married these past two months."

"You are not sleeping in my room!"

"Oh, but I *am*, Miss Faelyn." His words steamed heat against her nape. "I'll not be letting you out of my sight, ever again. Not until we've found the Willowmoon Knot and all its precious silver. Maybe not even then."

His last threat frightened her most of all. Not because she wanted to be free of his prison, but because—dear God—she'd grown too fond of it.

~

Everything in the Belle Heather made Jack feel enormous, a fuming, foul-tempered giant in the tree-root home of a pair of ancient, chittering elves—from its low, timbered ceilings, to the small windows, to the diminutive Potterfell sisters themselves. They were fretting over the deliciously cunning Miss Faelyn as though she'd come limping home from Waterloo on crutches, were forcing a biscuit and a cure-all cup of tea into her hands.

"You should have told us of your marital troubles when you first arrived, Lady Rushford. You poor, frightened dear. And so newly married."

Miss Faelyn sniffed up at him. "You'd be surprised, ladies, just how newly married we are!" She was having her hand repeatedly patted by one of the sisters, sending him a blistering, narrow-eyed scowl over the woman's bobbing, blue-gray curls.

The fault was hers alone. She'd gotten herself into this sticky spot. Had run from him at the first opportunity, with a fistful of information that she'd doubtless intended to hide from him. He'd had no choice but to find and keep her.

Keep her? Like keeping a handful of diamond dust from blowing through his fingers. Damn the woman!

"Have you dears any children?" The other Miss Potterfell had toddled over to Jack and was smiling innocently up at him.

"Children?" He'd almost bellowed the nonsensical word, but it had softened in his throat to a breath of air that made him look across the room at the woman, remembering how she'd mimed a belly at the Tower and the stirring it had caused in his chest.

"Too soon," he whispered through a peculiar tightness in his chest, imagining children with Mairey Faelyn. Bright haired and wild, reckless hearted, like she was. And they'd have all those incorrigible aunts to love them.

Anna and Caro and Poppy. And his own sisters. And a doting grandmother who must already have other grandchildren.

He wasn't very good at keeping the people he loved. Love meant trust and devotion. He was careless.

Not like the dragon-hearted woman who, at the moment, looked as though she might castrate him with her bare hands if she could get close enough.

Children? His chest felt huge, and stuffed with hope and fear.

"Sleeping with a robin's egg beneath your pillow helps, or so I've heard," said the first Miss Potterfell.

"Now, now, sister. Children will come in God's own time. You see, my dears, neither of us ever married, but we can well imagine the trials of a young bride and the demands of an older groom."

Older? He was barely past thirty.

He heard a snort, saw Mairey catching back her smile.

"Come, wife," he said, hunching to avoid smacking his head into the ceiling beams—though it might knock some sense into him. "You and I have some important matters to discuss."

The leave-taking was a gauntlet of patting and tsking and

more fertility suggestions, but he finally herded his muttering 'bride' through the Potterfell parlor, up the narrow twist of stairs and into the garret room, before shutting the door and facing the fuming Miss Faelyn.

"Oh, damn you, Rushford! Damn you! *Damn* you!"

"Right to hell, Miss Faelyn. I'm certain of that." He locked the door pointedly behind him, hoping to rouse the anger in himself that he'd felt that noon when he'd returned to Drakestone early, and only because he couldn't stay away. Because even a single night seemed too long without her. "But once a man is past redemption he really hasn't anything to lose, has he? Now, you will show me Adam Branville's will, and then you will tell me why you skulked away as soon as I was gone."

"I don't have his will. And I don't skulk."

"Branville's probate record, then."

"I only have a copy, and I didn't need to bring it with me."

"Liar." He could see that well enough in the side shift of her eyes, a glance that swung back full of self-righteousness.

"I traveled lightly, Rushford. I only meant to be here overnight." She stood like a sentinel in the center of the small room.

"You're a brilliant researcher, Miss Faelyn; you would never have left such an important document behind, would never have relied only on your memory. Let me see the copy."

"I don't have it."

He could play her game of dodge and parry. "Then take off your shirtwaist."

The woman blushed instantly, all the way to her hairline. "What did you say?"

"You heard me clearly. I meant what I said. Now." He took a threatening step toward her, "Take off your shirtwaist."

"I will not! And you, sir, will die trying to take it off me!"

He'd die *of* it, of the sheer pleasure. She'd covered her bosom, her hands and arms crossed like wings against a storm.

"Then so be it." He took another, more menacing step; allowed her to dash behind a chair, deeper into the room. The move gained her nothing, trapped her fully against the window wall and the dying light of the day, and made golden webs of her hair.

"You're a monster, Jackson Rushford." She was breathing as though he'd chased her down a wooded path.

"And you are a charlatan, Mairey Faelyn. A trickster, a cheat."

"How dare you malign my good name!"

"I dare because I've paid good money for Branville's probate record, and I know for a fact that you keep your most precious notes in ... there." He pointed to the woman's bosom, where her outrage pumped and billowed against the wool of her jacket. He hoped to hell his own cheeks weren't flushed as hotly as they felt, because his imagination was suddenly overfilled with plans for her creamy breasts, as it had been since he'd met the woman. And the room was just too close for that kind of imagining. "I've seen you stash your notes in your ... between your ... in your damn shirtwaist!"

Her eyes had grown enormous in her outrage. "You're mad!"

"Perhaps, Miss Faelyn. But if you don't remove your shirt-waist so that I may retrieve the copy of the will from its hiding place, then I shall remove it myself!"

And he would find that place far too enticing. She was too lovely, smelled too fragrant. He'd never had to threaten a woman to remove her clothes, and prayed to God, whose son had once walked the earth as a man, who'd fought all of its temptations, that the foolish woman would cooperate and show him Branville's record without further persuasion. But he would have the record by any means, if only to make a point that he was in charge and would not tolerate secrets between them.

"Very well, Rushford. If you insist. But I am disappointed in you!"

She shrugged off her jacket, revealing tiny pleats of linen, and the ripe, round, unsupported bouncing that entreated his hands like just-picked summer pears. And now the foolish woman was reaching behind her neck for … what? The buttons of her shirtwaist ….

He shouldn't have dared her, and was about to call back his demand when she tugged a silver chain from beneath her crisp collar and slipped it off over her head. A tiny key dangled from the end.

"The copy of Branville's probate record is there, Rushford, in my Gladstone, in an envelope. You're welcome to it. It's nothing more than I told you when you asked."

Swallowing hard, he thunked the Gladstone onto the chest at the foot of the bed and fit the key into the lock on his first try. She stood over him as he fumbled past her silky smallclothes and her stockings before finding the sturdy envelope and the probate records.

"There," she said, her indignant huff riffling the underside of his jaw. "Just as I told you."

It took all his concentration just to read, "'… six gilt knives, bonne-handled; one silv'red disk, anciently ornamented; one brass ewere …'"

"One silv'red disk, anciently ornamented," she repeated, with a grunt, retrieving the note and stuffing it back into the enve-lope, as though that were the end of her obligation to him. "The Willowmoon Knot."

"That's all? You came all this way, made this fuss for a 'sil-v'red disk, anciently ornamented'?"

"It's the Willowmoon Knot, Rushford. What else could it be?"

"A fish plate, a pot lid, a coronation medal. Bloody hell." He dropped onto the bed chest, utterly bewildered and frustrated to the core.

"I'm sorry, my lord, but that is the way and the risk of treasure hunting. Down one trail until it's cold, then up the next. If you find the search too frustrating, then maybe next time you should stay behind and leave it to me. I was right not to wait for you to return from Cornwall."

"You couldn't have been more wrong." He'd partnered himself with a lunatic: a head-spinning, riddle-speaking lunatic, one whom he might be forced to follow to the ends of the earth and back again. "You could damn well have left me a note."

"What would that note have said?" She leaned down to him, her nose an inch from his. "'Found clue to the treasure. Am going to Donowell to pick it up.' You'd have skinned me for breaching your security."

"You're intelligent enough to have been more cryptic than that." He stood up, and she stayed, her chin nearly touching his chest. "Besides which, you're a woman. You shouldn't be traipsing around the countryside without an escort." Without me.

"It's what I have always done."

"No longer. Not while you and I are partners in this project. Do you understand me?"

"So very well, sir." She circled behind him and dumped the contents of her Gladstone into the middle of the bed. "Now, please, go take a long walk. I'm tired, and I would like to wash up and go to bed."

"Not on your life. I'm not going down those stairs without you on my arm. You'll have to trust I'll keep my back turned." He shoved the chair toward the window and dropped himself onto its flower-flouncy cushion.

"Afraid to face the Misses Potterfell and their questions about our troubled 'marriage'?"

"Utterly terrified."

"So am I." He loved her laughter, loved that she was ever free with the rippling rise and fall of it, whether she was angry, wistful, or plainly amused—as she seemed to be at the moment.

He heard the dash of water in the basin, then a rustling of her clothes, apparently believing he'd keep his promise to avert his eyes. Not wishing to disabuse her of the notion, he settled firmly into the chair, enjoying the sounds of her ablutions, enjoying the soft, evening breeze as it blew in off the blue-dark sea, damp and salty.

He still didn't know what to make of the woman's artful trip to Donowell, or of her conveniently discovering Branville's probate records the moment he'd left for Cornwall.

Supposedly, she'd told him all she knew of the Willowmoon's history, and was forever regaling him with her Celtic legends. But, all too often, he felt as though his control over the situation was entirely an illusion, concocted by the woman herself, merely to appease him.

He wanted to believe she was entirely plain-speaking and fiercely honest. Needed only to recall their initial meeting: his demands, her outrage and her refusal. Her absurd declaration that she would mine the silver with a shovel if she found it! No matter her reluctance, his partner was as passionately intent upon the treasure as he was; she had been raised up from child-hood to see its discovery.

But Mairey Faelyn wasn't a fortune hunter. She was crafty, intelligent, and heroically devoted to her family; her clothes were simple, and she seemed to find her greatest pleasure in telling fairy tales to her sisters. He couldn't imagine her sweeping through Paris on a shopping holiday, throwing lavish dinner parties, or buying villas in Spain.

"What do you plan to do with your part of the Willowmoon treasure, Miss Faelyn?"

"Do with it?" She became so silent that he thought she had vanished. He almost turned to see for himself, but then she spoke. "I don't know. I haven't thought that far."

He heard her strike a match, then her corner of the room filled with light. The sea breeze gusted and nudged the window on its hinges, the gentle movement catching her reflection in a single pane.

The glass was old and rippled, making silvery clouds of her nightdress and her hair.

He would have closed his eyes, but there would be no rest for him there.

"Thank you, my lord." He heard the bed creak and turned slightly in the chair, wondering if she'd meant that she was safely tucked beneath the counterpane and that he was free to move from the chair.

"For what?" He stood casually, hoping for the best.

"For keeping your word." She was sitting in the middle of the bed, covered to her waist by a quilt of blue-printed country scenes, bent over one of her books of fieldnotes, already making small notes with a pencil.

"What's that you're writing?"

"'Sleeping with a robin's egg beneath your pillow helps.' Hmmm." She looked up at him and touched the end of her pencil to her mouth. "Do you suppose that Miss Potterfell believes the robin's egg aids in the conception of a child, or that its presence under the pillow acts as an agent to increase passion, thereby bringing the hopeful parents together more fervently?"

He coughed, cleared his throat. This wasn't a subject for idle conversation. He opened his mouth to say as much, but shut it before he could babble a meaningless answer. Righting his thought with a deep breath, he finally managed, "I don't know, Miss Faelyn. But I'll be damned if I'm going to go downstairs and ask the lady."

"I didn't mean for you to ask. I should have done so myself, but I was too furious with you. Tomorrow morning I'll ask where she'd heard the robin's eggs advice, and when she'd first heard it." She was looking around the room, studying every stick of furniture. "Where are you going to sleep?"

"On the floor." He'd decided on that strategy the moment he'd seen the bed.

"That's absurd. There's room here." She patted the pillow and moved to the left side.

There was nothing like confession to clear the boards and point out the threats. "Do you know that I'm mad for you, Miss Faelyn?"

She put her notebook down on her lap. "What do you mean, 'mad'? What have I done now?"

"I mean I feel very much like one of your Oxford swains. Every thought I have in my head right now involves making love to you until dawn."

"Truly?" Damn the woman for not being shocked, appalled, threatened at the very least; for searching his face and then lighting so boldly on the front of his trousers.

"Yes. Truly. So I am trapped here with you, my dear, in a very precipitous state—"

"Hoisted on your own petard." She cocked her head, smiling —actually waiting for him to reply—not in the least embar-rassed over her inexcusable knowledge of the male anatomy. What else did she know? And who the hell did she learn it from?

"If we weren't tucked all the way up in a third-floor garret and if the ocean cliffs weren't a hundred feet below—"

"And if the formidable Potterfell sisters weren't just outside our 'marital' chamber, waiting to hear of our reconciliation and news of our child on the way, you'd take yourself off for a dip in the ocean."

"Exactly." The word came out in a strangled heap.

She leaned over to the bedside table and blew out the light, plunging the room into a milky, moon-on-the-sea darkness, made soft noises into her pillow as she drew up the counterpane, sighs he wanted to feel against his mouth. He was still hard as a rock for her, his fists clenched as firmly as his teeth.

"Sleep wherever you like, my lord. I wouldn't be here with you alone in the dark if I didn't trust you with my reputation, absolutely."

He slept the night on a very uncomfortable rug.

CHAPTER 10

M airey woke to the soft sound of snoring coming from the floor beside her bed.

"Balforge," she murmured, rolling quietly to the edge of the mattress to steal a glance at her snoozing dragon. The provocative sight of all that classical maleness quickened into a blush that heated every inch of her skin.

The brute was dreadfully handsome—even as he lay on his back, sprawl-legged on the blanket, his pillow astray under one knee, his shirttails bunched to his ribs. His stomach was flat, wonderfully rippled, darkly furred against the white edge of his drawers that peaked out of his trousers.

Making love until dawn. Was that even physically possible? What would have happened if she'd confessed a similar madness for him. She'd studied many an artistic rendering of the act of sexual union: Greek statues, Flemish etchings, lovely pastel-hued Oriental paintings, carpets, stoneware vessels, each decorated with couples cavorting together happily, intricately, poetically, the women as ecstatically active as the men.

Clearly, her dragon wasn't the sort who'd allow a lover to 'suffer and be still,' as her friend Sarah Ellis advised reluctant new brides. He was an explorer, a ravisher, a man of tumultuous endeavors. She suspected they would have been ecstatic together. Until dawn.

An overpowering fantasy, the adult part of her fairy tale. But such a stolen interlude was never meant to be. Rushford was her nemesis, a dreadfully evil, dangerously handsome enchanter.

She rolled off the other side of the bed, washed quickly under the tent of her nightgown, and then dressed, all the while listening for the man to stir. He awoke with a roar and shot to his feet, looking as though he'd had a fight with a cyclone.

With hardly a word, she left him to dress on his own and descended the stairs, prepared to do battle with the Potterfell sisters, who were standing at the ready with their questions in the breakfast room.

"How are you, my dear?"

"Did you sleep well?"

"Was the bed comfortable?"

"Work things out, did you?"

She waved off their questions with shy giggles and a genuine blush, and set about rescuing the man from his own petard.

It took nearly an hour of wifely play acting for Mairey to convince the sisters that she and her silent, glowering "husband" were once more happily married. Still another hour to make their way to the clerk's office on the second floor of Donowell's town hall, where the parish records were filed with care and kept in a remarkably temperate room. The registrar had been gracious, helpful, and had left them alone to search the files.

And there it was! The record of John Branville's last will and testament, proved in the parish of Donowell, and duly recorded by the archdeacon in the year 1707. The clerks of Donowell parish could give lessons to the Keeper of the Records at the Tower.

"'In the name of God, Amen,'" Rushford read from the top of Branville's will, one brow slanted and distinctly piratical when he turned to her. "What is this?"

Sitting beside him was much like living in a hut on the side of a volcano. He thumped the table and rumbled out opinions, leaned over her shoulder and caused her heart to tear around inside her. He smelled of the Potterfells' lemon tarts, and his face was shaved so clean that she wanted to smooth her palms over his skin.

"In times past, sir, every will began with a similar divine testament. A sacred trust. An enchantment, if you will, beseeching the Almighty to condemn those who might attempt to scuttle the wishes of the deceased."

Rushford turned the page over and ran his finger down the list of John Branville's chattel as he read off, "'A feather bed, half-dozen trunks, chairs, a pair of spoons ...'"

He stood abruptly. "By God, Miss Faelyn, you were right! It's here in the records!"

The Willowmoon!

Every day another miracle, a step closer to returning the medallion to the safety of the glade. Closer to the end of her ill-fitting alliance with Rushford.

He leaned down from his great height, threaded his fingers through the hair at her nape, and brought her mouth so close to his she thought he was going to kiss her.

"I like this game of yours, Mairey Faelyn." His voice was low and seeking, that possessive rumble she'd come to adore. He touched his lips to her cheek near the corner of her mouth, but went no further—only murmured, "I like it fine."

Her skin on fire for him, she turned her head and caught more of his mouth, stole a half-kiss from him. Didn't dare take more of him.

"Do you, my lord?"

He looked devilishly pleased with himself. "It's like drilling into the earth and bringing up bore after bore of worthless basalt or granite. And then one day, when you're just about to toss in the lot for slag, up comes a shining core glittering with gold, winking at you in the sunlight."

A great hollow opened in her chest, the warning echo of the dragon stirring there.

"It isn't a game, my lord." Grateful for the reminder of the danger, she yanked Branville's will off the table and scooted off to the opposite side of the room, where the light was stronger and the air was less heady. "We're far from finished here."

His frown was quizzical, patient. "Yes, I know."

"John Branville might have had the Knot when he died, but here it says quite clearly that he bequeathed it and 'various pagan artefacts' to the Moorlands School."

"A school? And where would that be?"

"According to Branville's will, it should be somewhere in York."

"York's a large city."

"Not to mention an ancient one. Best we start with the Director of Works at York Minster. An old family friend."

"I might have known. To York then," he said, hooking her elbow and starting toward the stairs.

Which meant another day in the company of Jackson Rushford, and another step closer to the Willowmoon.

The interior of the great, fan-vaulted sanctuary of York Minster had always reminded Jack of a fantastical underground cavern, with its soaring ceiling supported by pillars draped in stalactites, windows throwing watery rainbows across the patterned marble floors. A memory scented with boughs of holly and ivy, of music, and dancing candles. A welcome light in the winter darkness. The last Christmas he'd spent with his family.

And now here he was again, twenty years later, his memories just as sharp, as raw. Tempered only by the woman who'd run ahead of him to throw herself into the arms of the elderly Director of the Works who was waiting on the steps beneath the quire screen, proof that she knew everyone, everywhere.

"But how terrifically good to see you again, child!"

"And you, Mr. Whitstable. Not since my father's funeral."

"What a loss for us all." He frowned and shook his head. "He is missed. And so are you! Now tell me what's brought you here on this flying visit? Another hunt?"

"Of course." She shared a smile with Jack as she introduced them, her eyes flashing with secrets, wild with adventure, as intoxicated by the chase as he was becoming.

"Delighted to meet you, my lord. Now then, how can I help you both?"

"The Moorlands School," Jack said, "are you familiar with the place? Somewhere here in York?"

Whitstable shook his head. "Sorry to disappoint, I've never heard of such a school. Nothing even close."

"I was afraid of that. Just following up on a hunch, is all. A listing in a will dated 1707. I came straight to you because if anyone knew the history of this Moorlands School, it would be you."

"You're your father's girl, right enough. Forever traipsing about the countryside on a hunt for antiquities."

"Hunting, but rarely finding," she said, casting Jack a rueful smile. "Yet, if Father taught me one thing, it's that I should keep asking questions until I ferret out the answer. I know the Chapter's records of bequests to the minster go back centuries."

"Every item logged, described, and dated." Whitstable rolled his eyes. "More comes in weekly. Our vaults are overflowing with the generosity of our parishioners. You've been there, Miss Mairey. Remember the undercrofts. "

"Tidy and organized, but stuffed like a meat pie. But the very place we might find the records describing a bequest from a family named Moorland."

"Ah, yes, I see where you're going!" the man said. "The Moorlands School disbands upon the death of the principal, the estate divided among the family, and the items in their fusty old curiosity cabinet bequeathed to us. Happens all the time."

"Exactly what I was thinking!" Mairey said, dropping a kiss on the man's cheek. "I knew you could help us!"

"Anytime at all, Miss Mairey!" Whitstable plucked his pocket watch from his waistcoat, clicked his tongue. "Good! I've just enough time. Come, I'll let you into the Old Palace."

Mairey hefted her satchel over her shoulder, flashed Jack a triumphant grin, and followed Whitstable through the transept door, out into the sun-dappled garden.

Short minutes later, the man was leading them through the vast library, with its double-storied wall of books, down the stairs into the dimly lit undercroft, then left them to make sense of the expanse of shelves, stacked to the ceiling with boxes and barrels.

"I'd forgotten how much is stored here!" Mairey said, setting her satchel on the worktable nearest the door.

"Well," Jack said, lifting a lantern above their heads, "at least it's more tidy than the Wakefield Tower."

"Let's get to work. Keep in mind, my lord. The Knot is about four inches in diameter—" she demonstrated with her fingers in a circle "—a quarter-inch thick, with serpentine patterns on its face."

"Or so you believe."

She sighed with impatience, her eyes bright with passion for this treasure of hers. Was it incomprehensible for him to wish they burned as brightly, as enduringly, for him?

"Belief is all we have."

She sent him off on his own quest, making him promise to show her anything at all that might be made of metal, reminding him that silver could tarnish to coal black and might be overlooked. Every door and drawer he opened revealed an oddity: stuffed owls, caches of glass beads, or Roman coins.

The woman was in her glory, sharing her discoveries and her laughter with him. She brought life and light to stone statues with her stories of magical springs and great serpents, and gave warmth to the sinuous tracings of brass.

She was singular and impossible and he was falling madly for her.

"What've you got there, Rushford?" she asked, fitting her fingers lightly in the crook of his elbow as he set a wooden box on the worktable.

"'Arrowheads', it says here." He opened the lid. "Flint."

"Elf bolts, my lord." Her smile was teasing, daring him again to protest her facts.

"My name is Jack," he said, turning to her.

"Yes, I know."

"Will you call me by my Christian name? Please?"

Her eyebrows twitched into a tiny frown, the corners of her mouth teasing at a smile. "Why, my lord?"

"Because I'd like very much to call you 'Mairey.'" He felt a telling warmth radiating from his chest "It's who you've become to me when I think of you. And I don't much like having to remember whether I'm talking to you or just thinking about you."

She studied him from beneath those fret-winged brows, her grin fully formed. "Are you so easily confused?"

That was neither the question nor the answer he was looking for. "I'm asking you to call me Jack."

More frowning, as though he'd asked her to bear his children outside of the marriage bed. Then a noncommittal, "I shall try."

"And may I call you Mairey?"

"If it'll help keep your thoughts sorted, I suppose you'd better. Now let's get back to work, my … Jack."

Rascal woman.

The perimeter of the undercroft was more organized and better labeled. Against one wall was a set of wide, flat, glass-windowed drawers. They found blue glassware in one, then a drawer each of tiny stone heads and animal figures. The next two drawers revealed golden Celtic torcs and silvered utensils. The next drawer was unlabeled, its window obscured by a red cloth, causing him to hope that it held something worth concealing from prying eyes.

"Valuable, you think?" he asked.

"Could be sensitive to light or dust." She cast him a hopeful smile and pulled the drawer to its fullest extension, then lifted the cloth away. "Phalluses," she said with a little sigh.

"Excuse me. *What* did you say?"

"Phalluses–carved out of stone. Ah, and here's one of wood. All of them Celtic, I believe. A good sign for us." She picked up a thick stalk of limestone, carved a few thousand years before, looking every inch its fleshly double. "These are penises, Jack. The male member. Surely you recognize—"

"I'm aware of what they are." Two dozen fully erect organs, in various sizes, materials, and conditions. "What I can not fathom, Miss Faelyn, is how you came to understand what … what they, *these* are."

"Call me, 'Mairey'. Please." She laughed lightly, chose another from the box, and studied its tip with exacting care. "The phallus is a fundamental and pervasive symbol in antiquity—as common as flint arrowheads and stone axes. An important symbol of fertility, rebirth, the coming of spring. I have a collection of my own in my library."

"Of arrowheads and stone axes." *Please, God.*

"Of course. And of phallic objects."

"A *collection* of them? Good God! You collect ... male members?"

"My grandmother started the collection, and became quite the expert, in fact." She examined another, holding the perfectly proportioned length of pink-speckled granite to the lamp light, her fingers gripped around its shaft in a gesture so innocently, so dizzingly sensual he thought he might be forced to leave the room. "Definitely post-Roman."

"Your grandmother's collection." *Of course. Why not?* These Faelyns were an eccentric lot.

"My mother enlarged it ... so to speak—" she smiled at her own joke, winked at him "—and now the collection is mine to curate."

He hoped to hell she didn't look carefully at his trousers. "I don't know what to say."

"Are you uncomfortable with the subject, Jack?"

"Hell, yes!" The woman's brows shot into her hairline at his bellow. "No! I'm not *uncomfortable*! What I mean is that—frankly, Miss Faelyn—"

"*Mairey*, Jack. Because you are speaking aloud to me at the moment, not just thinking—"

"Yes, yes, *Mairey*. It's just that I've never in my life had a conversation with a woman while she and I were standing in front of a drawer full of ... of ..." Completely drained of words he could use in public, he flapped his arm in the direction of the drawer.

"Ancient stone phallic objects," she offered.

"Exactly." Not that he was intimidated by the specimens in the drawer, or by the one she was fondling. He would measure up against the lot of them quite nicely, thank you. He nearly said as much, but Mairey had gone back to her minute examination, and he was having trouble breathing. "This isn't a subject to be discussed between a man and a woman."

"My parents did."

"Of course they did." Sweat ran like molten rivers down his back as the woman handled one ancient but hugely virile penis after another.

"In fact, my father presented my mother with a phallus on every one of her birthdays that I can remember."

"Christ, woman! That was their right; they were married to each other!"

"Devoted." She shut the offending drawer and opened the one below it. "Ah, ha! Just as I expected, Jack. You see, the Celts had a great reverence for their women, too. A belly-goddess."

The figure in Mairey's hand was beautiful and lushly primitive, with large, ripe, pink granite breasts at rest on a belly full of child, and a glistening, hand-polished cleft between her kneeling thighs.

He swallowed hard, his pulse dancing madly, his own phallus as alive and yearning, as though it were sheathed within her.

"I suppose your grandmother collected those, too."

"Oh, no," she said, smiling fondly at the figure. "But my grandfather did."

He threw out his hands. "Well, fine. Fascinating. But it's time we get back to looking for that Willow-Knotty thing." *While I can still think.* He broke away to a place where he could adjust his clothes, grateful for the fullness of his greatcoat.

Jackson Rushford, you're a great prude, aren't you?

Mairey never would have credited his bashfulness for an instant. Yet, the man had turned as red as a beet the moment she'd opened the drawer, and redder still with every phallus she'd examined. She wasn't looking to tease him, but he was disarmingly handsome, with streaks of crimson on his cheeks and smudging his brow.

And all that tight-lipped stammering! The blustering! She'd

nearly laughed. But he was a prideful man, and as much as she loathed his business practices, she would never purposely hurt him.

She'd always found the ridges and curves of stone-worked penises elegant and ... well, oddly stirring. Seemed like any other ancient carving to her—until today. With Jack looking on, breathing like a bull, these ordinary objects took on weight and heat, and a vibrancy she'd never noticed before.

Primitive, organic. Yes, and alive.

She flushed to the tips of her toes when she realized that every single, lovely one of them had been Jack's penis! That's where her imagination had gone just now, running wild and naked in the woods! No wonder she'd been light-headed!

She peeked around the corner of the next set of shelves. Jack was rattling through a cabinet of goblets, scrubbing at his hair and muttering, his coat buttoned nearly to his collar.

What the devil was she going to do with the man? With the days and the weeks and the years stretching out before them? She loved being around him, loved his humor, and the way he smelled of sandalwood soap in the morning and woodsmoke in the evenings. His nightly visits to the lodge had become a precious end to the day.

"Excuse me." A library clerk came through the open doorway, a piece of paper fluttering in his hand. "Ah, Lord Rushford! A telegraph message for you."

Jack took the note from the man and read it swiftly.

"What is it? Not the girls?" Mairey ran to his side, fearing news from Drakestone—Caro falling out of a tree or Poppy lost in the woods.

"My God, no. A cave-in at Glad Heath. Christ." He'd gone pale as milk, his great hands shaking, even as his jaw squared and he looked up at the clerk. "Can I send a message back?"

"Certainly."

Jack was already scrawling something on the back of the

telegram, efficient and furious. "Tell them I'm on my way," he said, handing the note to the man.

"I'll see to it, my lord." The clerk left on the run.

"The Willowmoon will have to wait, Mairey. Come." He grabbed her hand and her satchel and started up the stairs, as though she would naturally agree to follow him anywhere.

She twisted out of his grip and drew away. "Where are you taking me?"

"A roof collapsed at Glad Heath Colliery. You're coming with me."

Trouble in your lair, Lord Dragon?

"To one of your mines? Where?"

"Two hours by train. I don't know what I'll find when I get there."

Death, surely. And broken lives. A chill shuddered through her. He couldn't force her to go with him, to follow him into one of his bloody mines.

"I can't help you, Jack."

He slipped his fingers through hers, brought their clasped hands between them, and kissed her knuckles. "And I can't think of anyone who could help me more."

"How?" Her heart was in her throat: a coward's heart that didn't want to know what kind of man she had grown so fond of.

"Bring your fairy tales, Mairey—the children will need them."

CHAPTER 11

Glad Heath seemed a thoroughly devilish place, far from *glad*, and if ever a *heath* existed here, it was long buried beneath its mountain of slag and tailings. A bristling silhouette of infernal machines visible for miles, before the train thundered out of the dark moors and into the brightly lit station that served the spur line into Rushford's colliery.

The platform swarmed with men running alongside the railcar as it steamed to a stop.

"Stay close, Mairey." Jack was on his feet and stepping down from the private compartment before the car came to rest.

She watched from the top step as he was swallowed up for a moment by a surging sea of coal-blackened miners. They pulled at him, shouting, each one vying for his attention, until he finally lifted himself back onto the step beside her.

"One at a time!" he bellowed in a voice that must have carried itself into the very bowels of the mountain, as surely as it stilled the chaos at his feet. "Where is Stothard? I want my engineers here immediately."

He got a hundred answers at once, waved them all quiet, and pointed at a man. "You, Gadrick! Where's your boss?"

"Stothard's below, my lord." The frantic man shoved closer. "He's one of 'em that's trapped inside."

"Oh, Christ" Jack rubbed his temple but recovered an instant later. "Where?"

"The Shalecross, sir. Number Four, at a thousand feet. And the ventilation shaft with it."

"At the new steam-winding? Bloody hell!" Jack slammed hold of the handrail and swabbed his face with his sleeve.

So, the man's investment had gone awry. No wonder he was angry. He was probably already counting up his losses.

"Who else, Gadrick? How many more?"

"Eight men, sir—as far as we know." General agreement murmured across the platform, then all those faces looked up at Jack again, as though he were their savior and not their blood-thirsty master.

"All right. I'll want names, Gadrick." He swept his arm across the crowd, an iniquitous saint dispensing a costly blessing. "And I want the team bosses to meet me in the schoolhouse in ten minutes."

Schoolhouse? A schoolhouse at a colliery? Of course. There would be children here, hiding out from the nightmare and the terror, clinging to each other, lying bleak-eyed and wakeful in their beds.

Eight fathers, brothers, sons, trapped in the earth. All at the mercy of the man who was bellowing orders, dispatching streams of miners into his dangerous mine armed only with picks, to his timber-yard for shoring-stock, to the bank head, sending word to his Strathfield colliery and to London for more engineers and more equipment.

Jackson Rushford was certainly masterful at his disasters, practiced and prepared.

Beyond the rail station, she watched an undulating trail of flickering orange coil up the side of the mountain and disappearing into the darkness. She was trying to make sense of the light and shadows when Jack loomed on the step below her, his eyes shining with intensity.

"Will you visit the families for me?"

She bit back a curse and yanked her hand out of his when he took hold of it. "Which families would that be?"

He sighed, shook his head. "I need someone who can talk with the families of the men who're trapped down there, to let them know what's happening. Be my liaison. Will you do that for me?"

He was asking her to represent his villainy, to explain and excuse it to the grieving widows and fatherless children. Now there was madness.

"You asked me to tell fairy tales, not give excuses."

He seemed surprised, disappointed—a look that made her stomach twist. "Please, Mairey. What I'm asking is leagues outside the bounds of our partnership, but I need you here." He captured her hand and held it this time, unwilling to let it go. "The waiting is utterly hellish for the wives. And so much worse for the children as they wonder if they'll ever see their fathers again."

A shadow crossed his resolute features, lingered within his plea, and made her heart contract

"I'll do it for the children, Jack." She couldn't refuse him or the families in the midst of a catastrophe—not even one of his own making.

He led her swiftly through the crowded, dark lanes of stone block row houses, past windows and the tiny faces peering out of the pale lamplight. People had gathered in the torchlight outside the schoolhouse, reaching out to Jack as he quickly passed them, seeming so grateful for his nod or a clasp of his hands.

Such misbegotten devotion.

The schoolhouse was a surprisingly tidy, whitewashed place, with large windows and a wall heavy with books, reminiscent of

Jack's own library. His team bosses broke into a brawl of opinions and facts as Jack made his way to the front of the mob.

"Austin, you tell me what happened!" he shouted, and order descended in the echo. "What do you know?"

A scruffy-bearded man rocketed to his feet, his hat crushed in his fist. "Stothard took his crew down to inspect a minor roof fall and didn't like the looks of it. Had just ordered new timbers and jacks to be brought down to him, when it happened. We've been digging ever since, five hours now."

"What else do we know?" Jack continued firing questions, writing with fury and huge strokes on a set of maps, making circles and crosses along tunnels and tracks.

Mairey could only wait and watch him conduct his urgent inquest while one of the bosses compiled the list of families for her to visit. In the midst of it all, she helped Jack don a set of leather overtrousers and a jacket; then laced and tied his hobnailed boots as he carried on his meeting.

It felt wrong to be there in the enemy camp, fastening the dragon into his armor while he made plans to minimize his losses. But as the meeting broke up and Jack settled a leather brimmed cap on his head, as he cinched a vicious-looking pick to his work belt, she was struck with a sudden, terrifying realization.

"Where are you going, Jack?"

He was dressed like the other miners, and already had a black streak slashed across his forehead that resembled a fatal bruise. "Into the mine—where else?"

"You can't."

"Can't I?" He gave a small, dry laugh, watching her as he clipped a screened lamp onto his belt.

"Jack, it's dangerous."

"It is *now*. Those are *my* people down there, and I plan to bring each of them up personally—and alive, God willing."

"But—" She'd expected him to stay safely above ground, to

conduct the rescue without creasing his collar, without breaking into a sweat. Without putting his own life at risk.

Now he looked as fragile as the rest of them—made of flesh and blood and crushable bone.

"Dooley has the list of the men who are missing," he told her quietly, with a grave intimacy that drew her unwillingly into his circle. "I'll send someone to you as soon as I know anything."

"And what do I tell these families?" What would she tell Anna and Caro and Poppy if their Lord Jack died inside the mine?

He studied her, his mouth firm. "Tell them I'll do my best for them."

His best against a whole mountain!

He turned to go, but she grabbed his wrist and held him tightly. "Be careful, Jack."

He answered with a half-smile and rakish lift of his devil-dark brow, clamped his cap on tighter, then walked into the swarm of miners and out into the night.

"Godspeed," she whispered, praying that God looked after dragons.

Jack and his team bosses clambered over the rubble, their lanterns and cap lights casting dim, fitful shadows inside the tunnel.

"The roof shouldn't have fallen, sir," Gadrick said, craning his neck toward the ceiling of coal a dozen feet overhead.

"Hellfire," Jack said, sliding his hand along a ridge of glistening coal, newly exposed by the fall.

They were nearly a thousand feet into the incline shaft that had once been the main Shalecross seam, a vein so ancient that it had been opened in the thirteenth century. It had played out centuries ago and now functioned as a faithful friend, holding back the mountain above it to allow the miners to follow the crosscut passageways into other seams. The walls and the roof had been tightly shored up, were minutely and frequently inspected. The shaft was ready for the new steam-winding system that would drag coal trams up the rails to the main passage more quickly and far more safely.

And now faithful old Shalecross had given up a secret stash of coal she'd been hiding just beyond the shell of rock. Odds were that the new vein wasn't large and only needed more shoring. But the fall itself had caused a room-sized collapse into the main tunnel—impossible to predict, impossible to shore against. But the responsibility was his alone, and it made him ill to think of the lives that were at stake.

"Stothard must have suspected it when they were measuring for the new track, sir," Wilson said, leaping out of the way of the brigade of workers who were pulling loose coal and rock away from the fall. "He didn't want anyone but his crew to follow him in here."

Only time and toil would determine how deep this new roof of coal descended along the tunnel. He prayed that Stothard and his men had been far beyond it when it fell in. Even then, without fresh air circulating from the venting system, the coal gas might kill them. There was no time to waste.

"All right, I want every coal tram in the entire colliery on these tracks." Jack tossed a clod of coal into an empty tub. "Then bring everyone you can find into the tunnel. We've no winch, no windings to help us. We'll dig the men out of here the old-fashioned way: loading one tram after the other until the rubble's gone."

He assigned the job to his best team bosses, then rounded up a crew of young men who had more courage than sense and led them with his maps to a shaft that ran two-hundred feet parallel to Shalecross Number Four, before swinging east and diving deeper into the mountain.

"There's twenty feet of solid rock between us and the Shale-cross tunnel, gentleman," Jack said, hanging his lamp on a timberpeg. "We're going to dig a connecting tunnel, and with any luck, we'll be shaking hands with Stothard before noon."

God help them if it took longer. Twelve hours was just about how much clean air the eight men would have to sustain them.

Jack set his muscles and took a satisfying swing at the granite wall with his pick. A fist-sized chunk spin off and smacked him on the knee.

The men were grinning at him. "Pretty good, boss," said the youngest, a strapping lad that reminded Jack of himself a decade ago.

"Not bad for an old man, eh?" He gave another swing, following through with arms and shoulders that had labored too long at a desk. The impact made him grunt. But he worked steadily with the other men, each doing a five-minute shift at a killing speed, then stretching out their kinks as another man took their place.

Two hours later, they had removed less than three feet of stone, and Jack began to despair.

～

"Lord Rushford wishes you to know that he's doing his very best for you."

Mairey repeated Jack's words a hundred times during the interminable night as she went from house to house, offering comfort to the women and children whose husbands and fathers and sons were held hostage by his despicable mine. She'd prayed beside the families, embraced the children as fiercely as if they were her sisters, wept herself, and wiped the tears of others.

She'd sought proof of withered souls in Rushford's colliery. Instead, she had discovered not only unflagging faith and bone-bred courage to carry on, but also a terrifying acceptance of the risks. Disasters were part of Glad Heath's history, and these people blamed no one, especially not Jack Rushford.

"We are blessed to be here in Glad Heath," one woman had said through her tears, clutching her children against her bosom. "He's a fine man. His lordship won't let us down."

"If any man can rescue my husband, it's Jackson Rushford."

"There is no man in the world like our Jack."

Their Jack.

The frightening truth was that he'd also become *her* Jack. And she was petrified for him, couldn't imagine never seeing him again.

She'd received three oral messages from him, delivered each time by a different young man. The messages were brief and impersonal, but she'd clung to them like a lifeline. Proof he was still alive.

Yet he was only as safe as his last message, and that had been hours ago—and her heart leaped to her throat every time she looked toward the mine and saw the bonfires on the hillside.

He was down there in the stench and the steam and the darkness, and she couldn't do a thing to help him but pray.

He'd asked her for fairy tales, and so she gathered the frightened children into the schoolhouse to soothe them with her stories.

And did her best to bring back the light.

Be safe, Jack.

Six hours remaining and at least a dozen feet to go. Jack changed out his crew, bringing on fresh brawn, but he stayed himself, until he was forced to meet the train from his Strathfield works.

He wanted to see Mairey—just see her, because he couldn't

afford more time than that. She'd been sharp tempered and accusing, as though his recklessness had caused the accident.

She'd have to get used to the dangers inherent in mining. He would take the silver from the Willowmoon site in the same way: an open pit as long as it was profitable, then following the individual veins with a shafts-and-tunnel system.

The streets were nearly deserted, almost peaceful. The night wind had picked up a laughing melody in its dance through Glad Heath, and not at all to his surprise, he found Mairey in the schoolhouse.

The lamps were turned low and sleepy, and all the chairs and tables were pushed to the perimeter. The floor was littered with blankets and children, some soundly asleep in their mothers' arms, most looking up at Mairey as she spun one of her stories.

Gwynella and the Enchanter. His favorite. Though, she'd given the Enchanter a different name now: Balforge, the dreadful dragon.

They had come miles since he'd first seen her surrounded by so many captivated children. She'd been the irascible Miss Faelyn then; he'd been boorish. Three weeks, and everything had changed: Mairey had become the reason that he rose in the morning, the reason he came home.

He was about to join her when Gadrick caught his elbow. "Sir, the train from Strathfield will be here in a moment."

It was for the best. He had work to do.

A half hour later he was supervising the addition of more coal tubs onto the lift chain at the shaft, and soon coal was coming out of the Shalecross at an exhausting rate, bringing hope along with it.

But his place was in the rescue passage. So with the better part of four hours remaining, he grabbed up his pick when his shift came and slammed his vengeance into the solid rock, letting the shock of it echo up through his arms, feeling the sting of the blisters breaking on his hands and building again.

He knew the pulse of Glad Heath as he knew the sound of his own heartbeat. He'd been born in a cottage down the lane, had lived there until the night his father died.

That grisly night had come on the heels of a cave-in—one tragedy following another. The mine owner had sent his strike-breakers to make war against Jack's father and the other miners at the Cahill Pit Works, an act that had changed the course of his life forever. In the intervening years, he might have failed his sisters and his mother completely, had betrayed the promise he'd made to his father to protect them; but at least he had avenged the family's memory.

Glad Heath belonged to him.

The irony had been vastly satisfying when he'd returned from Canada with a great fortune and found Cahill bankrupt and the mine on the auction block. He bought the derelict colliery for a song, renamed and rebuilt the complex to his high standards of safety and efficiency. He'd doubled the shoring-timbers, engineered innovative ventilation chambering to keep the air fresh moving, and had installed closed-gear winching and sumps to keep the passages dry. Flame was dangerous, but he'd developed methods that lessened the threat, bringing light and air to the darkness.

He would risk no man's life in the pursuit of profit, so he inspected every tunnel and fissure himself. He employed full-time engineers and the best mechanics, who had been instructed—at the peril of their jobs—to search closely for trouble and to shut down production at the first sign of problems.

He'd learned from his father and from his own bleak years at Cahill's Pit Works that respect for his employees was the key to a man's success. So he sacrificed profits for shorter hours in the tunnels and a living wage for the miners. He took a wild-hearted pride in sharing his profits with the men who worked for him, and he valued those elected to his advisory committees.

His expenses were far greater than any other mining company, but so too were his revenues. His safety record was unparalleled, and he had made enemies of the other owners by hiring any miner who came to him.

And come they did. So many more each year that he had opened whole other tunnels, opened new sites for those who wanted to work honestly and with a mind toward the community. Mairey's Willowmoon silver would be one of those new mines. He hoped she would approve.

Twelve hours gone, plus the five before he'd arrived on the scene. He'd never lost a man yet in his tunnels, but time was against them. He prayed as he lifted his pick, prayed as he sweated and strained and drove its steel point ferociously against the bedrock over and again, laboring through his shift and the next. Until the force of his own pick broke through to the blackness on the other side.

"We're through!" he shouted, his heart ready to burst with joy and fear and exhaustion. Three men crowded around the shilling-sized hole. "Moving air, sir! Feel it?"

The air was moving, but it was rife with coal gas.

"We'll find 'em alive, sir. I'm sure of it."

But Jack wasn't sure at all. Stothard should have heard the sounds of digging long before this; should have been digging from his side to meet them. He hefted the pick again, and took out his fear and fury on the rock until the hole was large enough to crawl through.

"The risk belongs to me from here on; I'll go in myself," he told his men. "You've all done more than enough."

Jack crawled into the blackness, reached back for a Davy lantern, and then started up the narrow incline toward the cave-in.

Please, God, let them be alive.

CHAPTER 12

Just before mid-morning, the colliery whistle began to blow a shrill, nightmarish tune. The schoolhouse emptied in an instant, and Mairey hurried along with the women and children, up the sinuous, neatly tended streets toward the collection of buildings at the mine head, with its towering tangle of wheels and gears and steel-tackled webbing.

Had Jack rescued the men, or was this another horrible cave-in? Rumors had spread throughout the night like a field fire, fanned and flaring and dying, then rising again, until her fear for Jack and the other miners had become nearly unbearable.

Her heart pounded as she and the rest of Glad Heath crowded as close as possible to the head frame building, waiting for the giant wheel to begin turning, to bring up news from under the earth. Anything could have happened down there in all that blackness. How many times had she read of rescuers being killed in the tunnel along with the original victims?

Not Jack. Please God, not Jack. Everyone around her must be praying the same prayer as she for the people they loved.

Loved? No that. Not love. She scrubbed the impossible idea from her thoughts. She couldn't love the man—wouldn't.

The wheel suddenly shuddered to life, the cage began groaning its way up through the center of the iron frame, slowly, inexorably, bearing every heart, every hope in its grip, until it finally jerked to a stop. They all waited while the steel door opened in the dimness, stood together in shocked silence for a breathless moment before a roaring, riotous joy swept the crowd.

The men were safe! All eight of the trapped miners came stumbling out of the mine head into the brightest daylight!

You did it, Jack! He'd rescued his crew, just as he'd promised. Just as all of Glad Heath had believed he would. Her heart swelled with admiration for the man, watched with pride as frantic wives and mothers swarmed around the rescued men and pulled them away from the danger and into their arms.

But as she shared embraces and swabbed tears of happiness from her eyes, she began to search the grimy faces for Jack. But when she couldn't find him among the rescued, a chill of terror swept through her, a fear so fierce she jostled through the crowd into the hoist house where the cage was descending back into the shaft, waited long minutes for the cage to rise again.

As she pushed closer, found a familiar face at the controls—Stothard—the engineer who'd been trapped! She recognized him from Jack's office, though he was altogether inky. She caught his arm, happy to see him safe, but terrified for Jack.

"Have you seen Jack? Is he coming up? Is he all right?"

"Ah, Miss Faelyn, isn't it?" Stothard enveloped her hand and shook it with all the glad vigor of a man recently resurrected, grinning with stark white teeth. "We met at Drakestone."

"Yes, yes. But did you see Jack down there? Is he all right?"

Stothard smiled even wider, pointing over her shoulder to the cage rising again out of the terrible hole. "Looks well enough to me."

Jack! Oh, how she wanted to shout his name and run to him! The lout was safe! And oily black, from the top of his head to his once-crisp white shirttails that now hung out of his stained leather trousers.

And yet her anger burned as brightly as her relief as Jack made his way toward her. Someone shoved her from behind, slamming her against his chest in the tempest of glad-handing and reveling, and he held her tightly, length to length, and grinning.

"We saved them all, Mairey," he whispered, his eyes shot with red. "Thank you."

Thank you? For what? For covering for the sins of Rushford Mining and Minerals, for telling his lies, for praying for him, for his people, during the hellish night?

"'Glad Heath,' Jack? Is that what this valley was before you destroyed it with your coal pits? A misty, heather-scented moorland?"

He frowned down at her, then slid his hand along his cheek as though she had slapped him there. "It was a heath to be sure, Mairey. But long, long before it came to my hands."

"It's ugly here, Jack."

Something unfamiliar and humbling flickered in the clear midnight of his eyes. He set her from him, a distance that seemed lonelier than winter.

"Glad Heath is a colliery, if you haven't noticed. It's not a spit-clean university. It lacks the clipped hedges and the oak-paneled eating halls. It's grimy, stark, and dreary. The work abrades the skin and blackens the lungs—"

"And it crushes people, Jack." Her panic and anger made her reach for him and hold tightly, made his thick, sinewy arms seem all too vulnerable against the force of a mountain bearing down on him. "Can't you see the danger? Couldn't you feel it while you were down there?"

"I have always felt it, Mairey, I know the risk all too well."

She hated that part of him—the cool, mining baron. "I'm sure you do. But the risk is theirs, Lord Rushford, not yours. Their sons and husbands, their fathers."

"And *my* father."

"Oh, and a great risk *he* must have taken every day. Sitting in his fine office in London, worried about his profits, his investment—"

"His *life*. His family." He frowned. "My father had no office in London. I don't know where you get that notion. He labored all his days here at Glad Heath. He died here."

She wasn't sure she had heard him right; she was tired to the marrow and confused by all the celebrating. "Your father died here? How?"

"In a riot during a labor dispute."

"A mining baron, dying at his own mine in a labor dispute? Now there's a switch."

"Mining baron?" He laughed then, throwing his head back to the brightness of the sky, a touch of madness in his laughter. "Bloody hell, Mairey—my father was a pitman."

"A what?"

"A *coal miner*."

"No." He was lying, trying to make some kind of point.

He cocked his head at her, raising a brow that was hardly distinguishable from his coal-begrimed skin. "No?"

"He couldn't have been a coal miner. Then how did you—"

"How did I—the son of a pit man—end up the owner of Glad Heath Colliery, let alone Rushford Mining and Minerals?" He snorted and took the cup of water that a buxom, dazzle-eyed young woman offered to him. He drank it down in a single quaff. "My thanks, Molly."

"And my greatest pleasure, my lord." The brazen woman drew a smile out of him as she sped away with her skirts caught up to her shapely calves.

Mairey felt her face flush crimson as a wave of blatant,

green-tinted jealousy swamped her. A wholly unworthy and out-of-proportion emotion.

"All right, then, Lord Rushford. How *did* you end up with Glad Heath?"

He glared down at her, swabbing his neck with a red kerchief that came away black and dripping with sweat. "I bought it from the estate of the man who killed my father."

Another woman came to Jack, the matronly Mistress Boyd, handing him a chunk of bread and a wet rag, leaving him with a motherly kiss and a pat on his backside. His eyes followed the woman fondly before he turned back to Mairey. He seemed righteously proud of himself and so much at home here.

"My father worked this mine from the time he was eight years old. He formed a union and led a strike against the unsafe conditions, shutting down the mine for a month."

"He was killed for leading a strike? Jack, that's horrible. How could that happen?" Feeling roundly possessive of the man, she took the rag out of his hand as he stuffed the bread into his mouth, and began to scrub the coal off his cheek.

"Cahill set his private, mounted army against a handful of unarmed men and boys."

"How could he?" Horrified, she scrubbed more thoroughly, streaking the black off his neck and forehead, while Jack submitted blissfully.

"Cahill was a bastard who trafficked in human lives. My father was killed right over there." Jack opened an eye and sighted down his inky finger to a lamppost. Its flame burned hotly, even in the blaze of the sun. "He died in my arms."

Her tears blurred his face into a watery gray blotch. "Then you know how dangerous the mines are, Jack. Everything about them, inside and out. How can you, in good conscience send people down there to be killed? They depend upon you, Jack. They trust you."

"And by the grace of God I have earned that trust." He took a step backward and frowned at her. "I've turned blighted squalor into a safe, profitable colliery. One that pays a living wage, provides housing, and health care. Now if you'll excuse me, Miss Faelyn, I have a mine to run."

"Ballocks!"

He had turned away, but now he swung back again, the devil in his eyes. "What?"

"How can you say that your mines are safe, when you've just suffered a cave-in and put all those people in danger?"

"Mairey, some accidents can't be prevented. I would never, ever send anyone down a shaft or into a tunnel that wasn't safe enough for my own father, nor for anyone I loved."

"Ballocks again!"

"I've had enough, woman." He came at her like a bull, head down and charging, and in the next instant he'd thrown her over his shoulder, her backside to the sky, his hand clamped there like a sizzling hasp of iron.

"Put me down. Jack!"

"You've a lesson to learn, Mairey Faelyn." He stomped through the celebrating toward the mine shaft, with its whirling, whining gears and shuddering cables.

"Do you plan to throw me down your mine, Jack Rushford?"

"Tempting, but you'd only gum up the works, woman, and I've just got them working again."

Mairey squirmed just to spite him, knowing he would only tighten his scorching hold around her legs.

As they approached the shaft, its steel cage rose again from the bottomless hole into the towering head-frame, then came to a squealing stop.

"Jack Rushford, where the devil are you taking me?" His answer was to step into the swinging basket. Her courage fled as he finally released her, letting her slide down the length of him as though he enjoyed the contact. "What? No! I don't want to go with you."

"We're partners in a silver mine, my dear. It's time you saw one close up."

Partners—he kept saying that, as though she shared his despicable dreams of silver. They were adversaries.

The lift started down with a shudder. She grabbed his leather coat and hung on for dear life as the cage jiggled down into the darkness.

"Is it supposed to do that?" She was quaking herself, a miserably frightened ninny.

"Do what?"

"That jiggling."

He laughed gently and turned her away from him, so that the layers of rock flew past her nose. "Physics," he said into her ear. "You'll be all right."

She grabbed handfuls of his sleeve where he'd wrapped his arm around her waist. He was warm and breathing steadily, her rock. Her heart was racing, her pulse thrumming against his fingers where his large hand had claimed her shoulder and the rise of her neck.

"It's windy here," she said as a cool breeze blew her hair upwards, a flying, freeing sensation.

"It's supposed to be." He gathered the swirling of her hair into a bundle and held it in his fist. "I've spent a lot of time and money to keep air circulating properly through the ventilation shafts. Engineering the upcast passages, balanced with the downcasts, and the cross headings."

The cage stopped abruptly. Gadrick swung the door open, grinning from ear to ear.

They stepped out of the lift and into a bright chamber, framed like an old Saxon cathedral in tall timbers and crossbeams. A forest on a winter's eve. It had an eerie, underworld beauty. She'd expected stifling heat and the stink of sulphur. But the air was clean, if coal-smelling, cooled by a regular breeze.

"Inspectors here already, my lord?" Gadrick said with a wink at Mairey, and a nod to the handful of equally begrimed men waiting to be sent to the surface.

"A sightseer," Jack said, offering Gadrick a handshake and the others a nod. "Thank you again, men."

"An honor and a pleasure, sir," Gadrick said, clapping him on the shoulder before climbing into the cage with the others and disappearing into the shaft above.

"Come, Mairey. I'll show you the cave-in and where we rescued the men." He settled a cap on her head, a mate to his own, took her hand, and started into one of the tunnels, following a narrow set of iron rails set into the floor.

"Is it safe?"

"It is now."

If she lived through this, if she ever saw the light of day again, she'd at least have a better understanding of her enemy and his lair. The tunnel twisted and rose, then dipped and straightened. She'd expected seeping walls and crumbling terror. But Jack's mine was clean-lined and stout, and as bright as noon. Twice they pressed against the wall, allowing a pair of carts heaped with rubble from the cave-in to pass by them.

He finally stopped at an intersection and slapped his palm against a fat, foot-square timber. "Shoring up the passageways is the key to preventing catastrophes. The more bracing, the better. A great expense, but necessary. I'll take the same care in the Willowmoon tunnels."

You'll never get the chance, Lord Rushford.

"We'll use these same double-screened Davy lamps, an added safety feature developed by my engineers. Explosive gasses aren't the problem with silver mines they are with coal. But light and air are fundamental to a man's spirit, and I'll bring daylight into the darkness of the Willowmoon Mineworks just as I have here."

The Willowmoon Mineworks?

Then light a candle for me while you're there, Jackson Rushford.

Because I'll be dead before I let you riddle my glade with your worm holes.

"Come." He took her hand again and led her deeper into the mine, past a small culvert and a dark pool, under the great air shafts that dropped sunlight-scented air onto them.

It didn't matter that the people of Glad Heath counted Rushford among their saints. And it mattered even less that Mairey herself had seen too much saintliness in the man this past day.

He could pay each of his miners a thousand-pound wage every year; he could build stately town houses for each of their wives; send their sons to Oxford; marry their daughters off to members of the peerage. But he couldn't rebuild the mountain or the woodlands that once flourished here, nor could he restore the streams that had once bubbled up from the springs. And he would never, ever get the chance to do to her village what he and his like had done to Glad Heath.

Agile and sure of himself, Jack moved along the tidy, down-sloping passage with its low ceilings and shadows. He stopped at a short tunnel dug into the stone. It had a hole at the end that emptied into blackness.

"Back there is where we broke through into the Shalecross. We had to cut another, quicker passage. There wouldn't have been enough clean air to last the other way."

"You did all this today?" All the digging and the timbering, as single-minded as ants.

"We did. Took us twelve hours, but we managed." He took the lantern and her hand and led her to the end of the rescue passage.

His palm was torn and rough, and she turned it up to the wavering light. Blisters, broken and bleeding and needing care.

"You helped them dig?"

"When I could. I'm not as young as I used to be, and I'm out of shape."

Hardly. He was huge; had shoulders like a .... Of course! No wonder he was so broadly muscled. "You were a coal miner, too!"

"Like my father." He hung the lantern on a peg above her head. "I started when I was six, holding open the ventilation doors. I was big for my age, so I was picking coal by the time I was eight. I worked Glad Heath until the night my father was killed."

He stood close, so very tall and overwhelming. Her cap pressed against the thick post behind her and the brim lifted off her forehead like a halo, leaving her to stare up into his breathlessly devilish grin.

"Where did you go after that?"

"I emigrated." He stepped closer, still straddling her legs. "I left the country on the next tide, with the law on my tail."

"Jack, why?" The man was a maze of mysteries. The lantern above them planed his features in orange; the coal took the shadows and deepened them. But his eyes were sparkling like diamonds, and made her heart flip.

"Father's strike was illegal, and so was the riot that followed the murders." He threaded his fingers through her hair with tender care, then drew his thumb slowly across her lips, watching all the while, grinning a bit. "I was accused of setting fire to Lord Cahill's offices."

"Did you?"

The corners of his eyes crinkled; his laughter filled up her lungs. "Oh, yes, Mairey. With my father's name on my lips, I did."

Her eyes pooled again with tears, but she snuffled them away. "Good."

"Yes. Good." They stood hip to hip, her belly to his groin. His erection was a wonder. So grandly different from her dusty old collection of stone and wood: hotly independent, compelling her to squirm against him, to do something with it.

"Ah, Mairey." He took forever bending to her mouth,

touching his fingers to her lips. She rose on her toes to be nearer, sooner. It wasn't wise to tempt a dragon, especially when one was deep in his den, miles from the sky and the green trees.

"Beautiful, Mairey."

"Jack, I—" *Oh, bliss. Oh, gracious me.* He covered her mouth with his, possessed her absolutely, sweetly, and then with a hungry, diving groan that shot sparks to the ends of her fingers, to the center of her, where his never-to-be-conceived children slept. Tears gathered in her throat, unshed and aching. His kiss was deep, his lips softly searing.

"Worth waiting for, Mairey." He caught her up in his arms and gathered her against him.

"Yes, Jack." Her head spinning with stolen gladness, she climbed deeper into his embrace, ground her hips against his hardness, wanting more of him, as much as she dared in this dark fairy tale of theirs. She kissed him rampantly, traced the planes of his midnight-bristled jaw, brushed her lips across the soft play of his eyelashes. He tasted of his mine, of danger, and a heart-stopping rescue.

He laughed suddenly, his smile as crooked and mussed as his spiky hair. "I've never in my life kissed a woman in a mine."

She liked that a lot. "You brought me all the way down here just to kiss me?"

"I wanted you alone, Mairey. Need you." Another kiss, slant-ing, slippery, sliding down the front of her bodice, blowing hot through the linen. He shaped his hands beneath her breasts, grazed his thumbs across her nipples, sending a deliciously feverish clenching to the joining of her thighs. "I want you thor-oughly, Mairey. In every way I can imagine."

She didn't know what to say, because she could imagine so very much, all of it ending abruptly in heartbreak, for both of them. He was trembling like the quaking of the earth when he enfolded her in his arms, a caress far more profound than the flesh that still ached for completion.

How simple it would have been to keep on hating him. But he'd taken that from her. He was a man who was doing his best at the only life he knew.

And he did it so admirably, with such easy grace.

She'd survived his horrible mine. He'd kept her safe through it all, just as he'd promised.

What was it he'd said just before scooping her up and taking her spiraling down into his netherworld? That he would send no one into a mine shaft that wasn't safe enough for his own father ....

Or for anyone he loved.

Oh, Jack!

CHAPTER 13

Mairey was still breathless long after his kiss, long after he'd sent her back up into the light.

Glad Heath Colliery was celebrating, and Jack was their hero, though he stayed below, unmindful of the feasting in his name. The community soon put the mine to rights in eager shifts, having beaten back the devil, this time.

And though she looked for Jack all the rest of the day, she didn't find him again until late in the afternoon. He was leaning back against a stack of shoring timbers, seemed to only be standing because his legs were spread wide with his knees locked, his arms fallen heavily to his sides. His head was tipped back and his face glistening a dark amber in the remains of the setting sunlight.

She approached him quietly, thinking at first that he was asleep on his feet. But he coughed suddenly and so violently that he dropped to his knees and bent over, holding himself up on the flat of his hands.

She ran to him, uncertain what to do, wondering if he would want her there or not. She put her hand on his back, soothed his shoulders.

"Ah, Mairey, that feels good," he said, sitting back on his haunches, reeling a little to the right as he cast a sideways, squint-eyed glance at her, "Thank you," he said, with a blink that lasted so long she thought perhaps he'd gone to sleep.

"You're a mess."

"Messy business, this." He smiled up at her as he stood, braced himself against the stack of timber. "But, thankfully, it's done for the moment, the clean-up well on its way. I have to be in London by tomorrow afternoon. And still need to stop at the Strathfield Works this evening."

"Not tonight Jack. What you need is rest."

He waggled a finger at her, nearly cross-eyed with the effort. "There's none for the wicked, as you well know."

The fool launched himself forward, looking drunk as he staggered down the hill.

"Jack! Wait!" She caught him round his waist and nearly tumbled with him in the next step.

"Sorry, sweet," he said, righting them both, leaving them face-to-face as she steadied him with her hands round his waist. "You have a lovely mouth, Miss Faelyn. Mairey. Honeyed. I'd like to taste you again."

She'd like that too. "Not now, Jack. Not now."

He must have read right through her evasion—his teeth showed white against his smile.

"To the train, then." He clamped his arm around her shoulders, as familiar though they'd been together a hundred years. And what lovely, intimate years they would have been.

He stopped a half-dozen times to answer questions and offer suggestions. She finally got him to the train, only to find his well-appointed private car far from private, occupied by a steward, a clerk, two of his engineers and a mound of paper that needed his immediate attention.

"Shall we get to it then, gentlemen?" He roused himself as

though he'd come fresh from his morning ablutions, and became the mining baron once again.

Mairey settled herself into an upholstered chair beside him, fighting sleep with all her might. But it came anyway, benumbed by the rocking motion of the railcar, spellbound in the soothing rhythms of Jack's voice.

She was dreaming of labyrinths and confusion, blackness and starlight. A soothing hand against her cheek. Warm, rugged, a saltiness against her lips.

"Come, Mairey." The voice was very nice, too. As nice as Jack's. "Time to wake yourself."

She found Jack smiling down at her, lifting her hair off her forehead. The car was nearly dark, quiet. "We're at your Strathfield Works?"

She raised up to look out the window. The sun was gone, leaving only an orange burnish to the slate-roofed buildings. She'd been asleep for hours.

"I've already been there, and finished my business." His face was cleaner, but she couldn't tell if those were deeply etched shadows or coal dust.

"Where is here?"

"We're on one of my spur lines just outside Strathfield. Stopping here for the night."

"Sleeping here in your car?" It was very nice, more comfortable than any hotel she'd ever stayed in.

"In my hotel."

"Your hotel?" She stood, bleary-eyed enough to lie down anywhere. "I suppose you own all of Strathfield."

He smiled. "Nearly. Now, come with me."

He had already arranged for two rooms, two steaming baths, and two dinners. Separate, alone.

"Sleep well, Mairey." He leaned toward her in the hallway, holding himself off her with his hands above her head.

His lingering, succulent, goodnight kiss and nuzzling neck-nibbling turned to snoozing into her ear, his chin propped against her shoulder.

"Dear man," she whispered. "To bed with you."

She kissed him lightly, which roused him enough to herd himself to his room through the adjoining door in hers. But not before he gave an overly detailed demonstration of the lock that could only be opened from *her* side of the door.

"Completely safe, Miss Faelyn," he said, blinking. Then he lifted one of his brows and strode through the doorway into his room, rattling the knob in reminder after he'd closed the door.

It was only after she was lying in the tub in the heavenly warm water, that she realized she hadn't turned the key on her side, that he could walk in at any moment—and that he wouldn't. She scrubbed herself clean and washed her hair twice to remove the dinge of coal that had collected in every pore, left the bath only when she caught herself falling asleep.

She tried to ignore the sounds coming from Jack's room while she prepared for bed, but he consumed her senses, her imagination. His firm footfalls and the thunk of what could only have been his shoes—first one, and then, after a very long time, the other. A door opening into the hallway, a stranger's voice and then Jack's, and then a flurry of footfalls and bath-water noises.

She listened to him even as she slipped under the covers, even as sleep tugged at her. She heard the splash of water, then his groan, like a tired mill wheel finally coming to rest after a long career.

A wife would have worked the kinks out of his shoulders, would knead his ropy muscles, and kiss him wherever he needed kissing. Anywhere. Everywhere. Her dreams charted each kiss.

Dreams so vivid she woke sitting up, with a nearby church bell chiming twelve. The doorframe into Jack's room was still limned in bright lamplight, as it had been when she'd fallen asleep three hours before.

Odd. He'd been exhausted, ready to drop.

She padded to the door and put her ear against it, listening for a full minute before deciding to knock quietly.

"Jack?"

Silence. Utter silence. Not even the gentle saw of his snoring.

Perhaps he'd fallen asleep with the lamp still blazing. Or he might have been dragged back to an emergency at Glad Heath—his life in danger again! She opened the door a crack and peered in. A cold fireplace, the four-poster's bedcovers unrumpled, a writing table, a chair. But no sign of the man, no sign that he'd slept in the room, at all.

Her heart pounding in apprehension, she opened the door fully and stepped inside, ready to fetch the proprietor of the inn.

Then she saw him, fast asleep in the longest, largest bathtub she'd ever seen, breathing deeply.

"Oh, Jack."

Her view was straight on and breathtaking. The main's hard-muscled arms hung free of the tub, his legs inside, his knees propped against either edge. The soap was unused and sitting on the side table. He'd cradled his head on his shoulder and the back of the tub, the motion of his chest making soft ripples in the crystal clear, belly-deep water.

He was magnificent. Bewitching. He made her pulse hum in her ears.

"I can't very well leave you like this." He might drown, or freeze to death—he'd been in the water for hours. Even if he awoke and promised to bathe himself, she couldn't trust him not to fall asleep again.

She hurried back to her room and donned a robe for propriety's sake. Then she went downstairs to the kitchen and ordered two pails of hot water from the innkeeper, who frowned at the lateness of the request until Mairey pleaded monthly cramps and an aching back that was keeping her awake.

Wondering where she'd learned to lie so expertly, she went back upstairs, rolled up her sleeves, then stepped into Jack's room to study the problem.

The biggest problem being that Jackson Rushford was a man—in every possible way. Darkly curling hair lay in a fine sheen across his broad chest, and arrowed its way downward to a dark patch. His penis, his ever-so classically endowed penis, was as stunning and heart-stirring at rest as it surely would be fully … engaged.

Was that the word? No. Engorged, a far better word. Her thoughts weren't in the least scholarly at the moment. They were tender and burning and made her hands ache to touch him.

Well, then: washing a large, exceedingly male body couldn't be that much different from washing her own. That wasn't quite correct. He wasn't at all like her, he was rock hard where she was soft, and she selfishly wanted to learn every inch of him. To be tender without him ever knowing—because the man seemed to take tenderness very seriously.

She answered the knock on her door and took the water pails from the sleepy kitchen girl, tipping her a shilling. She waited for the girl's footsteps to pad away from the door before she carried a bucket into Jack's room and poured the hot water slowly into his bath. She watched him for signs of wakefulness, not sure what she'd do if—no, when he woke up.

But he only rubbed at his nose with both fists and then slid an inch deeper into the water, letting his arms come to rest across his hips, just beneath the surface.

Sighing with a shattering longing for her dragon, she added more water until a mist rose off the surface and his skin began to pinken beneath the grime.

Where to begin this purloined venture? He would probably

wake up bellowing about improprieties the moment she touched him. He'd been impossibly incensed about the phallus display, so she lay a towel across his groin, masking all that beautiful masculinity—as much for her own sake as for his delicate sensibilities, then soaped up a cloth and knelt beside him.

His hands, that's where she would start. Tautly sinewed, blistered and cracked from his labors, and outlined in coal, they had taken the worst damage today, and had wrought such miracles in his life, in the lives of everyone in Glad Heath.

He slid his palm across hers, soapy and warm and so very intimate. She caressed the length of his thumb, and he made one of his rumbling sounds deep in his chest.

She was making a careful study of a ragged scar that ran like an extra heart line across the heel of his hand when she noticed his breathing had gone from deep and untroubled to utterly still.

Immediately wary of what she might find at the other end of all that stillness, she lifted her gaze up the long length of him, from the now-floating towel and his narrow waist, over the muscled ridges of his chest, to a pair of dark eyes that glittered dangerously from beneath a thunderous brow.

"Jack. You're awake." Flushed with guilt as much as with desire, she tried to rise and back away, but he captured her hand with a fluid motion and didn't seem the least bit interested in letting go.

He crooked her closer with a flex of his arm. Nose to nose.

"I couldn't possibly be awake. Else there wouldn't be a beautiful woman lounging at my bath side, scrubbing me."

With that, he reached over the side of the tub and hoisted Mairey's backside onto the broad flatness of his hand. Then he lifted her up, over, and into the water.

She landed in his lap.

His very naked, very wet lap!

"Jack!" She finished the blackguard's name and added a curse before he clapped his wet hand over her mouth.

"Shhhh, Mairey. Can't have the proprietor breaking down the door in the middle of my dream. It's far too stimulating, and I'm far too aroused to have my dream interrupted."

Interrupted! "You're not dreaming, blast you!" Her outrage sounding more like *'Burr nuh deenie, ba doo!'*

He tightened his grip and hauled her backward until he'd pinned her shoulders against his chest. The hem of her nightgown billowed with air, then melted into the warm water.

She thrashed and squirmed, tried her best to get away, tried desperately not to laugh, but Jack only clamped his free arm beneath her breasts. He shifted his hips, a great rolling tide, and arranged her higher on his thighs, groaning like a bear just waking from a long winter's night.

"Another of your folk interviews, my dear?" he whispered beside her ear, taking a bit of lobe between his lips and sending maddening shivers down her neck. "A highly unorthodox technique. One I hope you don't use on other men, because I wouldn't like that at all. But let me see, perhaps I can help you. Were you going to ask me what the coal miner's word is for arousal? For that's what you feel against your pretty backside. Me, Mairey, and my aching need for you. Do you feel it?"

Oh, yes! She felt him like a rod of fire against her hip. She nodded immodestly beneath his hand, fascinated when she ought to be outraged and flailing.

"That is my phallus, Mairey. Not an ivory carving, not stone, but my hard flesh—which is all your doing."

Mairey nodded and wriggled against him, thrilled with the sensation, with Jack's words against her ear.

"So full of your science and your fairy tales. Does it feel as you had imagined?"

Better, better, so much better! she wanted to say, but his hand still covered her mouth, though he was drawing his middle finger along the vale of her lips like a kiss. And, oh, all the other places she could suddenly imagine that finger.

"Ah, Mairey, when you wiggle against me like that"—an involuntary shudder seemed to convulse him—"yes, like that, my dear, I'm only roused to want you all the more. Would you like to write that down in your fieldnotes?"

He stirred again, raising her hips with his, setting the swirling hem of her nightgown adrift in his wake. The hand he'd held across her was now gathering up the floating linen, pushing the fabric upward and upward along her thighs toward her hips.

"I'm not made of stone—not like your collection. And I think from your writhing that you're not, either."

She watched in wonder as his dark hand disappeared into the surging folds of linen, in the clear pool where her legs were spread so indelicately, her knees propped wide against his and waiting.

Oh, yes, waiting shamelessly for his magic. She held her breath, disbelieving her anticipation, hopeless with desire for him to do whatever he planned.

His hand swept her curling hair through her drawers, eddies of cool water and then warm, summer sunlight. Sweet anticipation.

Jack couldn't help groaning at the pleasure as he cradled his hand over the wild place between her legs. A riot of wanting, a need to lift her hem and explore further. To take her to heaven, to keep her always.

"Oh, Jack!"

He had freed her mouth to delve there with his finger, to trace her lips and play at her tongue as he might at her cleft. He was so damnably near it!

"Stone doesn't quiver, sweet Mairey. Ivory isn't hot. And it doesn't ache."

"I *do* ache, Jack. For you. I ache like fire."

He thought he just might explode.

She arched against him, his antiquarian clad in her proper Victorian nightdress, her lovely, lean thighs open wide to his hands. She was breathing with hot little sighs and gripping the sides of the tub in a white-knuckled fury.

"Jack, I oh! I—Jack!"

He ached to the depth of his soul to ruck up the hem of her gown and taste her with his fingers. A husband's province, surely. But he wasn't her husband—and that was his dilemma, as her springy curls teased at his palm, her heat coursing up through his fingers.

Had he the right? Had he the will to stop what he shouldn't even have begun without benefit of marriage?

Marriage. The word had meant little to him for so long, and now the very idea plagued his every thought. He measured it against everything she did and said, everything she meant to him.

"You must understand clearly, Miss Faelyn, that you can't just walk into a man's room while he's bathing." He'd awakened stirred to the boiling point, dreaming of her. Dreaming of children, Mairey's and his together. She'd become his life. He couldn't imagine his library stripped of her curios, of her laughter.

"You were sound asleep, Jack" She sighed against his ear.

"You certainly can't bathe him without his waking up, wanting you in the tub with him." He turned her, caught her mouth with his, played at tongues and teasing.

"You were freezing."

"And you can't fondle penises, ancient or otherwise, in front of him without that man—"

"With you, Jack."

"Yes, without *me*—my body reacting to your touch just as yours is now. You feel the ache?"

"In every part of me. Jack," She wriggled her hips, gave a little gasp, and then covered his hand with hers.

Bits of light scattered inside his skull. The linen of her gown rose like a curtain, and he harrowed his fingers through her fleece. "Mairey!"

"Oh, Jack! It's wonderful! I only—" She took a gasping breath as he slid his fingers along her sultry folds and held her, kept her, wary of moving further for the storm it would cause in them both.

"You only what, sweet?"

She had thrown her head back against his shoulder, tilting her pelvis into the cup of his hand as though she would consume him. Her nipples were dark points straining at the wet linen.

"Oh, Jack, I—I didn't want you to drown."

"You're too late, Mairey." He was so drugged with wanting her, he could peel off her gown and take her there in the tub.

But he couldn't—she was made for wedding, for vows, for a marriage bed. Unless he lost his mind completely in the next minute and buried himself inside her.

My God. She was bending toward him, reaching for his scrotum.

"Mairey, please, no!" He caught her by the wrist and she turned in his arms, floated and then settled on him, her nearly bare skin cool against his fire-hot erection.

"What is it, Jack?" Her eyes were wide, and blinking.

"Have you learned nothing from me in the last few minutes?"

"Mmmmm … I've learned far more than I had intended." The minx closed her eyes and took a startlingly precocious pleasure in rolling his penis against the softness of her belly. "I don't know what's gotten into me—"

Let it be me, my love. I want to be inside you, to the hilt.

"I'm not shy of you, Jack." She spread her fingers across his chest, then slid them up his throat to his jaw, her clear gray eyes filled with desire.

"No, you don't appear to be shy at all."

"Though I'm plagued with curiosity—"

"The scholar in you."

"Now I understand the lure of the phallus through the eons. Yours in particular."

"Mairey!" He groaned, pulling her forward in a single wave of water, covering her mouth with his, claiming her with his tongue. Hungry, so hungry for her! He should really stop this. But she made tiny, laughing whimpers in her throat and crawled up the front of him, slipped her arms around his neck, and let him plunder and explore.

Until he realized he was fighting with the third button of her nightgown, that he had breached the opening, was holding a handful of lush breast, his mouth bearing down on a ripely puckered nipple.

Her eyes were wide as she watched him, astonished, as though she wasn't certain this was happening to her.

And it shouldn't. Not now. Not before—

"Sweet Jesus!" He yanked the placket closed, and patted her breast when it was fully covered—out of sight, but never out of mind. Clearly, *he* was out of his mind, deranged! For going this far. For stopping. Hell!

He lifted her hips and stood her up in the well between his bent knees. Her gown was a transparent waterfall, her face flushed, her breasts high and round.

"What, Jack?" She looked incensed in her innocence, fisting her hands against her hips.

Despite the raging fever in his blood, he wasn't fit for a night like this, lacking sleep, lacking any kind of self-control. To continue would be a commitment to something far greater and longer lasting than silver.

"This sort of activity is a marital pursuit, Mairey. And we're not, are we? Married, I mean."

"No. We're not." Her words came out wrapped in a weighty sigh, and the next as horrified as if he'd suggested setting her library on fire. "No!"

Unclear why her eyes should be so filled with terror at the mere mention of a marriage between them, he shelved the subject until a better time, and sent her out of harm's way.

"I think you'd best leave me to my bath, Mairey."

"I will not, Jackson Rushford!" She flipped back her hair, the bottom half wet and clinging, then drizzled her opinions across his chest as she wrung out her hem. "I'm not letting you bathe alone. I found you dead to the world in two feet of water, a bathtub large enough to be a coffin! You're staggering with exhaustion, and I refuse to leave you. Don't move."

He couldn't possibly.

She stepped out of the tub, taking half the bath with her, trailing a stream of water all the way through the open doorway into her room.

"What are you doing in there, woman?" He got to his knees and would have leaped out of the tub and gone for his clothes, but she stuck her head around the panel, her shoulder heedlessly bare.

"Cover yourself with a towel while you finish, Jack. I won't look, I promise. But I will be remain in your room until you're safely out of the water." She disappeared, and he heard the plop of soggy fabric landing on the floor.

She was undressing. The door was half open, and the woman was undressing!

"I've got three little sisters, Jack. I know a lot about the drowsing effects of bathwater on exhausted children. Poppy gets sleepy the moment she sees the bath."

"Clearly, I'm not a child. I don't need your help." He needed time to sort through his thoughts. He needed Mairey.

"And I don't need to find you floating facedown in your bathwater." She came through the door tugging a dressing robe around a fresh nightgown. Her feet were bare, and her hair hung like a drowned siren's around her shoulders.

She swabbed up her watery trail, hung the towel over a chair back, and then sprawled across his bed.

"Wash, Jack. Else I'll fall asleep here."

The woman clearly had understood nothing from his warning, that neither of them were made of stone. But at least she was no longer peering into his bathwater.

So Jack scrubbed himself clean, from his scalp to the soles of his feet. The water went milky gray with soap and grime, the clean fragrance rising into his nostrils like memories of home, of scrubbing his skin to bright pink at his nightly baths in the kitchen after a long day in the mine. Privacy had been a foreign notion then, with the rest of his family at the hearth, just out of his circle of modesty. Emma telling stories, his mother plaiting Bryna's black hair, Clady fast asleep on his father's lap.

God in heaven, he hadn't allowed such memories for years; hadn't dared, for the grief they exposed.

"Jack?"

"Yes?" He was standing in the water, his backside bare to her and dripping with rinse water. He spared a glance at the bed, prepared for the connection of her gaze, for the sharp pang of desire that was becoming as familiar as breathing. But she was tucked up against his pillow, staring at the ceiling, her hands behind her head.

Trust—she was entirely too free with it. To be sure, she kept her secrets from him, rationed her Willowmoon lore as though she were a bank manager suspicious of a borrower requesting a loan. But when it came to the intimate truth between them, Mairey Faelyn was as constant as the coming and going of the sun.

"Jack, I've been wondering about your sisters."

He welcomed the change of subject and stepped out of the tub to dry off. "What is it you want to know about them?"

"You said you hadn't seen them for years."

"I haven't." He pulled on his trousers, having nothing else to wear, and certainly not trusting a towel.

"I confess, that I have assumed you're estranged from them. That ... well, I don't know ... that you had offended them somehow in your magnificence, that you didn't think them your social equal, or that you'd married them off to your business associates for the profits they brought into the family estate." She flopped her arms on the mattress, obviously feeling tied to the bed. "May I look?"

"Hmmmm ... I'd no idea your opinion of me was so *colorful*." He was safely rolling up his shirtsleeve when she sat up and dangled her naked calves over the edge of the bed.

"My opinion of you remains colorful, sir, more so than ever. But the part about your sisters isn't true, is it? You're not estranged, are you? I realize now that you haven't seen them since the night your father was killed."

She was very good at finding things, uncomfortably so. He wasn't sure he wanted to continue. "It was earlier that day. At breakfast. All of us together, as we did every morning."

"The beauty of an ordinary day." When he gave no reply, she allowed a long moment of quiet as he rolled up his other sleeve. "What are their names, Jack?"

Are. Not *were.* Leave it to Mairey to understand the tiny morsels of hope he had tucked away for safekeeping. The bargains he'd made with God. He sat down beside her, gripping the edge of the mattress, staring down at the wooden floor, at the long cracks, the fine grain, and the swirl of the knots. "My mother's name is Claire."

"Claire. Means bright, clear. A lovely name."

"Yes. I hadn't realized until recently that she was my age when I last saw her. Emma was eleven. Bryna was seven. And

Clady had just turned six." He struggled to get his voice past the lump in his throat. "She'd gotten into the honey that morning. I went up to the strike line with a gob of it in my hair."

"Oh, Jack." There it was in her eyes, in the way she turned to him and enfolded his hand in hers. He didn't have to tell her about the hearth shadows and the ghosts at the lodge. Or why he'd fought so hard to banish her own sisters from Drakestone before coming to adore them as he did.

"What happened to them, Jack?" Her voice was a little frantic, echoing the panic whenever he wondered the same. "Where did they go? With your mother, surely?"

Take care of them, Jack, my son. He'd done a hell of a job.

"I don't know. I lost them along the way." He paced to the open door between their rooms, where he could better gain a full head of steam. "I was forced into exile by my own mother. God, how I fought her. I was the man of the family now, entrusted by my dying father in his last breaths to take care of them. But she put me on a ship bound for Canada, afraid that I'd be sent to prison."

"She loved you, Jack. I would do the very same to protect my son if he were in danger."

There was the motherly sort for you. Missing the point entirely.

"I was thousands of miles from home with no idea where my family had gone. When I sold my first nugget of gold, I hired a firm in London to find them, the best team I could afford."

"And in all that time you've heard nothing at all?"

"It's been eighteen years. Nothing."

"That's very odd, Jack. And horribly sad." Her soft brow furrowed. "Has this firm checked the parish registers in Yorkshire?"

"Repeatedly." A cool shiver of guilt rode Jack's neck—a recent memory of Mairey and her expert quest through the Tower, through the ancient records at Donowell, turning over every particle of evidence until she'd found exactly what she expected to find.

Bloody hell, he should have fired Dodson long ago.

"There are so many other places to look, Jack. Have they inspected the emigration manifests? Ships leave every day for America, Australia."

"*Emigration?*" He'd never thought of taking that direction, doubted that Dodson ever had or ever would.

"What sort of firm are you working with, Jack?" She was chewing on her lower lip, her gaze glittering.

"Dodson, Dodson, and Greel. Lawyers." The bastards. One more year and then he'd get rid of them. The decision freed him some.

"Did these same lawyers clear your name, Jack?" She stood suddenly, and her robe loosened like a curtain, completely irresistible. "Or is the constable still looking for you?"

"I am reprieved." *And falling madly for you.* Everlastingly. How could he ever let her go? Quitting breathing would be simpler, or stopping the tides.

She canted her head and smiled. "You bought off the legal system?"

"Absolutely." He laughed at himself, at the grubby coal miner turned peer, and it felt very, very good to see the irony of it all. "I was still in Labrador when I made the New Year's Honors list of 1853—an appreciation of my financial contributions to the Empire, so the letter said." He felt better still when he lifted her into his arms, all seven, delectable stone of her, and started toward her room, and was damned pleased with himself when she nuzzled her chin against his neck.

"So I wrote to the lord chancellor informing him of my regrettable past legal difficulties, and he informed me by return packet, six months later, that my youthful offense had been permanently erased, that I was now Viscount Rushford, and would I be interested in the purchase of old Drakestone House, and three manors in Lincolnshire?"

"Ah, the royal white elephants."

"A whole herd of them." He was quaking again with desire for her, tempted to stay, to join her in her bed, to finish what they'd begun in the bath. But beginnings were precious, delicate; they needed strategies and time to plan them.

She puckered a frown at him as he lowered her into her rumpled covers. "Are you leaving the hotel, Jack?"

"God no. It's two in the morning. I'm going to bed." She pointed at him and gave an ungainly yawn. "But you've got your clothes on."

"Just until I'm back in my room, with the door safely latched between us." He dropped a kiss on her forehead.

"Ah." She was finally blushing, though he couldn't be sure it wasn't a heated flush. "I'm sorry about the bath. I won't do it again."

"Then *I'll* be sorry, Mairey Faelyn. To the end of my days." He closed the door on all that temptation, and listened for the click of the lock that never came.

CHAPTER 14

Dodson, Dodson, and Greel.

Mairey felt another twist of guilt as she stood in front of the tarnished brass plaque that marked the law firm's chambers in a dreary little lane, just off High Holborn.

She should have at least mentioned this visit to Jack beforehand. But he'd been absolutely closed about the subject of his missing family in the week since their return to Drakestone House, so she'd let the matter sink below the surface between them.

The girls had been so delighted to see Jack when he and Mairey had returned, they'd run right past her and flung themselves into his arms, Poppy climbing to his shoulders as if she'd shinnied up his towering trunk every day of her life.

"We took good care of your fairies for you, Lord Jack!" She had the poor man by the ears, bending over to look him in the eye. "The green one's name is Wendell!"

"Wendell? Really?"

"Truly, sir."

If Mairey hadn't been so overwhelmed by the tears that glistened in the dark of Jack's eyes, by his bellowing laughter that rang through the lodge and the smacking kiss he'd put on Poppy's cheek, she might have felt spurned by their desertion. Instead, she was enchanted.

"Sumner helped us plant sweet peas, sir!" Anna waved a seed packet in front of Jack's face, and he'd done his best to follow its bobbing. "And snapdragons!"

"Lookee what I can do!" Caro had come zooming down the banister, on a squealing collision course with the floor. But Jack had plucked her out of the air and stood looking at Mairey helplessly, the giggling girl hanging from his hip like a sack of flour.

"Welcome home, Jack." He was just so very fine.

Her sister's hearts were big, and seemed to know by instinct that he needed their fierce hugs and sticky hand-holdings more than Mairey did. Just as she knew he would lay down his life for them.

As he had done for his own sisters, for his dear mother. How sad that they didn't know how much he loved them, how long he'd stood by their memories. His father would have been so proud of him; his mother must have died inside when she'd sent her son into exile. Perhaps she could help him make progress on his pledge to his father. To forgive himself, which may not happen until he had children of his own.

Our children. Or they might have been, if this sorrowful tale of theirs had been destined to end happily, instead of in grief.

No, she wouldn't think that. It was selfish and dangerous.

Love was sacrifice, and knowing when to let go. Yet, she held more tightly every day to the man. She sought him out every morning, afraid of the stirring in her heart when she caught sight of his dark eyes. His grief and guilt about his lost family were so close to the surface that she wondered how she'd missed them before.

They'd had no more wild embraces, no tumultuous bathtub romps that left her breathless and wanting. And he'd made no more allusions to marriage. That had been a part of the fairy tale: another time, another land, another princess and her dragon.

Yet Jack was persistent, and he stole a kiss from her at least once a day, in the most bewitching way. He would catch her in the green woods, or against her desk in the library, in a carriage where she couldn't escape, or late at night in the lodge when it all felt so right.

The kisses were hardly stolen from her; they were offered, given freely, begged for in her heart, and tucked away for the bleak days when he would be gone from her life.

She could at least do this one kindness for Jack before she found the Willowmoon Knot, investigate her suspicions of the Messrs. Dodson and Greel. If they'd been fleecing him all these years, he might not be prepared to hear the truth. But in any case, she couldn't allow this unforgivable to fraud continue. The dear man had set his heart aside for all those years, waiting to love and be loved again.

"So good of you to come, Miss Faelyn. Please sit down." Dodson senior and junior might have been twins if there hadn't been three decades between them.

"Thank you." She sat down on the edge of the chair and smoothed her hands over the fine linen skirt of the suit Jack had ordered for her. She'd come home to a wardrobe full of new clothes and had argued against them, but she'd fallen to his logic.

For our visits to Windsor, Miss Faelyn. The scoundrel. She'd lost her argument to the softness of the silk, the smoothness. But mostly she'd succumbed to his roguish smile.

I'm starved for you, Mairey, he'd said, before kissing her deeply, sending her off in a great spiral of yearning.

"Now, then, Miss Faelyn, you've come on the recommendation of a Sir Harold Hayward, dean of Galcliffe College?"

"Yes." Hayward's name had been the first to come to her

mind when the lawyer's secretary had asked who had referred her. "Dean Hayward said that you'd done some investigative work for a relative of his. Though I'm afraid I can't recall the man's name. A professor at Oxford."

"Oxford … Oxford? Hmmmm …" The senior Dodson fiddled with the ends of his moustache for a moment and then brightened. "Ah, yes. Blaine, it was. I remember now. A baronet."

Liars from the start! She'd never heard of an Oxford professor named Blaine, and she knew them all.

The younger Dodson scooted his chair closer: a well-turned fellow, classically handsome, but with too-regular edges—nowhere as compelling as the man who let Anna put a flower in his lapel every morning, and took extraordinary care to see that it wasn't crumpled by his day's work.

"How can we help you, Miss Faelyn?"

"What I want to know, gentlemen, is how you would go about finding someone that I have lost."

"Lost?" They were a pair of swivel-necked ravens, nodding at each other.

"It's very sad. You see, for reasons too painful for me to discuss in public, my father emigrated with me to Australia shortly after I was born, leaving my mother behind in England with my three little brothers." A family like Jack's mother and his three sisters, lost about the same time as his.

"A sad turn indeed," the elder Dodson said, leaning back in his chair, weaving his fingers together over his sunken chest.

Warming to her performance, Mairey continued. "Now that my father has passed on, I would like to find my mother and my siblings. They're the only family I have."

"Not even betrothed, Miss Faelyn?" Young Dodson was affecting a rakish brow; God only knew what was going on behind those overly blue eyes.

"Not even a betrothed," she said, patting her smart new reticule. "But I have money enough to retain the services of your firm for as long as you require." She leaned forward and whispered, "How long would that be?"

"Well, Miss Faelyn," the younger said, rising like a judge and striding toward the bookcase, his hands clasped behind him, "the duration of our search depends entirely upon how detailed the information is that you give us."

"What sort of information?"

"Dates of birth, place of birth, wedding, uhm …"

"Emigration records?"

"What?" Obviously a new thought. "Oh, yes, very good."

"What other records do you investigate?"

"Well, uh … many."

"And do you examine these records yourselves?"

"Well … no. Not usually. You see, our firm deals primarily in wills and estates. We have an operative who investigates claims against inheritance."

"And searches for lost relatives when he has the time?"

"Er, yes, but of course he will *make* time for your investigation," the older Dodson assured her hastily.

"And what is your success rate, gentlemen?"

"Good."

"*Excellent*, Miss Faelyn."

Blue ballocks! The Messrs. Dodson, Dodson, and Greel couldn't find their collective hat if it were nailed to their collective wooden heads. Damn them all to the very hottest part of hell for deliberately cheating a fine man like Jackson Rushford. The hero of Glad Heath.

"Thank you, gentlemen." She steadied her outrage and stood, offering her hand, grateful for her deer-skin gloves, which kept Junior Dodson's tainted fingers from touching hers. "You've been most informative."

"We shall await your business with the greatest anticipation, Miss Faelyn. Shall we say next week?"

Say anything you like, you filthy rotter.

"Next week it is." Mairey plunged down the steps and out into High Holborn. She'd never in her life met a more cruel and insensitive pair. "Bastards!"

Her explosion brought a scowl from the cluster of men in frock coats standing nearby. But she was so near the Inns of Court that the sight of a cursing client bowling out of a law chamber was no doubt as regular as the 5:12 from Dover.

Dear Jack, what they've done to you! Her skin was boiling; she wanted to scream and weep. In his innocence, he'd unknowingly hired a company of buffoons who took aim at the most vulnerable chink in his armor and struck gold, filled their coffers with his suffering. The blighters knew nothing about emigration registries, or shipping manifests, or factory lists; and they employed an operative who treated Jack's case no better than a hobby!

May their bones turn to salt! They'd stolen eighteen long and unimaginably lonely years from him. From a man who needed all the family, all the love, he could find.

He was so very easy to love—her sisters had fallen for him immediately, and Tattie.

And me. Dear God! Mairey sat down hard on a bench to await a coach.

I love him. It was true! She loved that he'd engineered the daring rescue at Glad Heath, and that the people there thought him a prince; she loved that honey made him weep; that whenever he looked at her, she imagined suckling his milk-scented babies and sliding her mouth across his lips.

She loved him, plain and simple and as complex as the dance of the stars and the moon.

Impossible.

She wished he'd never come looking for the Willowmoon; wished he had taken no for an answer and gone about his treasure hunting on another hill, in another glade, another heart. Not *hers!*

Try as she might to distract her thoughts away from Jack, they always circled back to him. To his devotion, his love, to the estate he'd created for his family, and so generously opened to hers. To a future with him that could never come to pass.

She owed him his sisters and his mother, those eighteen years of hoping. And she would stand by him, whatever the news she uncovered in her private search. Yet for the sake of his pride and his fragile expectations, she would keep her search a secret from him. To raise his hopes, only to dash them, would cause him more grief and guilt, and he'd had too much of that in his life.

And she knew just where to start. With the heinous Sir Cahill who had owned Glad Heath at the time of the strike, as well as a foundry in Manchester. It was a leap of logic to think that Claire Rushford might have gone there looking for work after her dear husband was killed, but it was a start.

And Jack had waited long enough.

"To the left, Sumner, old man! Paddle to the left!"

"You're in the back, Rushford, sir. You're supposed to be steering!" Sumner missed a frenetic stroke and sheeted pond water back into Jack's face.

"Oh, gad!" Jack swabbed a stringy weed off his face with his shirtsleeves, then went back to paddling.

The girls were squealing at them from the bankside, wriggling like wind-up toys.

"You're wet, Lord Jack!"

"Look! I found a salamander!"

"I can swim good! C'n I show you?"

"Don't you dare, Caro!" Jack shouted from the tiny boat.

The girls were muddy from stem to stern. Mairey might be amused when she returned from London and saw the mess—

she was ever the one to break the rules—but Aunt Tattie was going to skin him alive.

A duck house. Why the devil had he promised to spend his afternoon erecting one in the middle of the pond?

"It's gonna be the bestest duck house in the whole wide world. Lord Jack!"

That was the reason. Those three little hearts cheering them on from the shore. Home and hearth and duck ponds. Bless them all. Hope had always frightened him, made him feel weak and unworthy. Yet here he was, filled with the stuff, and aching to begin a life together with Mairey. Marriage between them was the answer. Had always been.

"Careful, sir! We're tipping." Sumner was paddling furiously.

He really should have called in Stothard to help engineer the structure. "Don't move, Sumner." The little boat was sitting dangerously low in the water, loaded to its gunwales with rocks that would, in a very few nautical yards, become the foundations for Duck Island, the home of the Drakestone drakes.

"We're taking on water, Rushford."

"Jettison the rocks, Sumner!"

Unfortunately, they tossed one of the stone cannonballs from the same side, at the same time.

The boat rocked, listed fatally, and then took on water like a burst dam.

"Lord Jack! You're sinking!" A trio of screams came from the bank.

"Hell," Sumner said.

"Damnation."

The sorry vessel dropped out from under them in a single sucking slurp, and then sank to the bottom fully loaded with rocks, leaving Jack and Sumner treading water and the girls in a shrieking panic.

"Welcome to Duck Island, sir."

"You too, Sumner." Jack laughed and swam the twenty feet to

the bankside, to the little hands that were eager to help but nearly lethal.

"A towel!" Anna was already racing back from the laundry, her arms loaded down with linens. She dumped a load of them into Sumner's lap and gave the rest to Jack along with a kiss on his eye. The other two fell all over him, wanting to help, buffing his hair into a nest.

They discussed what to do next, and the merits of erecting an island on the foundations of the boat.

"Let's ask Mairey," Caro offered.

"An excellent idea. As soon as she comes back," Jack promised, harrowing the last of the tangles from his hair.

"I'm back now," came Mairey's voice from the wooded pathway. "Have I come too soon?"

"Never that." Jack's heart gave a thump, and he dropped the towel on the grassy slope. He would have embraced her and set her mouth on fire, but he was soaking with pond water and surrounded by too many people, and she was laughing.

"Oh, Jack! Sumner! You're all wet!" The woman swiped tears out of her eyes. The others were rolling on the ground, equally demented, echoing their grown-up sister's laughter.

Until they all noticed Aunt Tattie standing at the end of the stone walk, her hands fisted hard against her hips.

"Uh-oh. She's tapping her foot," Sumner whispered loudly, rising on his haunches. "I think I hear Cook calling me."

"You sit right there, Mr. Sumner." Tattie loomed large in the midst of their huddle and took three muddy little hands in one of hers. "Girls, you're coming with me." She kissed Mairey, then raised her spectacles to Jack as he stood there in his dribbling sleeves. "And you, your lordship, ought to know better."

"Yes, ma'am." Jack and Mairey stood silently, hiding from Aunt Tattie in broad daylight, while the others scurried away to their separate corners of the estate.

"It's plain the woman likes you best, Mairey." Jack took her hand and started toward the laundry for a dry shirt, a momentous discussion on his mind.

"The secret is a box of Fry's Chocolate." She ran her fingers through his hair. He had emptied his boots and taken off his socks, but he still squished water out of the soles when he walked.

She stood watching him from the door of the laundry as he exchanged a wet shirt for a dry one, a cat smile on her lips. It was too inviting not to kiss, so he did.

"Ooo, your lips are cool, Jack." Hers were warm and her fingers searing as she buttoned his shirt. He would have to live with wet trousers while he strolled back to the house with her on his arm and her scent in his nostrils, while he formed the perfect proposal of marriage.

"You seemed to enjoy yourself out there, Jack, even when your boat sank. I saw it all."

He was dizzy with happiness, crazy for her smile, and bursting to be alone with her. "You won't tell them, will you? That I'm a sucker for their silly projects?"

"They love you, Jack."

"Ha! They know I'm good for a hobbyhorse ride, or a duck house builder."

"No. Because you love them."

Yes—that was the whirling sensation in his chest. Being needed for himself. Succeeding where it counted. *Ah, Mairey, the joy you've gifted me in a single short month!*

"You had a lot of practice, living with three sisters of your own."

"They were a handful. Stair-stepped in ages and charm, just like Anna and Caro and Poppy."

She seemed distracted from everything but his fingers, opening his hand inside hers and caressing the lines and the hollows. "Time stopped for you that day, didn't it, Jack?"

And started again with you, Mairey.

"Hell, I'm probably an uncle many times over, yet in all my memories, I'm still fifteen and my sisters are still young. They still have the bony little fingers that knew which of my ribs to tickle until I surrendered the sweets I brought them every Saturday."

"The consummate brother."

He snorted. "One who took every opportunity to escape his annoying little siblings. I had discovered women just about then."

"Ah." She raised a brow, the tiniest arc of jealousy.

"The mating instinct, Miss Faelyn. It's very strong in the young human male."

"Yes, I know."

Jack felt the chaotic flush like a fever, borne of this woman and her patience, of the uncommon memories he was making with her.

"And were you successful?"

"At what?" He hadn't the faintest idea what she was talking about, only that she seemed pensive, and intent upon everything he said.

"You and your mating instincts."

"Ah, that." He caught her around the waist and stopped beneath the wisteria arbor.

"I was young and bumbling," he said, remembering too vividly, too quickly, to fend off the image of his first time with a woman—which had taken all of fifteen seconds, and hadn't been accomplished until he was eighteen and the first brothel was built in Chantilly. He never went back to the place; he'd purchased his fleeting pleasure with precious gold that should have gone to finding his family. And in the deepest part of him, he'd understood that the desperate young woman was some-one's sister, a daughter.

"You've grown out of that stage, no longer bumbling."

"I'm glad you think so." Her face was turned up to him, her

mouth the color of Sumner's prized damask rose, now and forever Jack's undisputed favorite.

He cupped her chin, and tasted her lips with his tongue. Very sweet, soft, scented with honey.

"Jack ..." She slipped her fingers into his hair, seemed to choose her words with unusual care. "Jack, I found something today—"

"Tell me you've found the Willowmoon Knot and we can get down to the real business between us–" Marriage. No. *That* would have been a cloddish opening.

"Not the Willowmoon. But I have found something you need to know about."

As a man who had forged a career looking for treasures, Jack knew the stomach-churning thrill of discovery. Yet these were grieving eyes that were watching his face.

"Something that makes you frown?"

"I just don't know how to tell you this, Jack." She looked away from him with her bleakness, and the distance left him starved for air.

"Just tell it straight, Mairey."

She swung her gaze back to him, watery and rimmed in red. "When I first took on the task, it seemed quite the most natural thing for me to do. It comes so easily to me."

"So does your riddling, Mairey. What is it?" A premonition rode him. Was she leaving him? Had Walsham or one of the other men whom she charmed so regularly stolen her fancy?

"I've spent my life looking for lost things, Jack. Digging up burial barrows, capturing folk tales so they won't vanish when all the storytellers are gone."

"Yes, I know. You're very good at spinning a tale." He didn't think he was going to like this one.

"I can't tell you how dearly your search for your family has affected me. I think about it all the time. My parents have passed away, but I was with them both when they died. And I have my sisters, and can love them, hold and kiss them, every day of my life." Tears were rolling down her cheeks, mystifying him completely. "I couldn't imagine never seeing them again. But if something horrible did happen to them, it would be better to know they were at peace in a churchyard, Jack, than simply lost to me."

That hit him like a slap, an insult to the memories he held so dear. "Not better at all, Mairey. I appreciate your empathy, but I would rather let the subject rest."

"It can't."

"It can if I say so."

"Listen to me, Jack. After you told me about your search, I was incensed for you!" She threw her outrage at him, the reflection of his own, though better focused and glaring in its brilliance. "Eighteen years, Jack, and Dodson turned up nothing! That's appalling."

"But it's my business."

"Maybe so. But I couldn't just stand back and not do anything. Not ask questions. And so I—"

He took her arm, sat her down on the stone bench, and knelt in front of her. "You did what?"

She caught her lip with her teeth, lowered her eyes to her fidgeting fingers. "I went to see them. Dodson and his son."

Stunned and wanting to see the truth in her teary eyes, he held her chin. "Why?"

She shook off his touch. "I—"

"Why, damn it?"

"Oh, Jack." She grabbed his hands, forced her fingers between his, and held fast to them. "I had this appalling feeling that Dodson ... that for all these years they had been—"

"Playing me the fool?"

Her face paled. "Worse than that, Jack. I was sure they didn't know what they were doing. Simply wasting your money, your precious time. Worse, that they were wasting your heart. So I asked how they would approach a search for my mother and three brothers. A family much like yours, lost twenty years ago. Oh, Jack, they didn't even know where to begin. They rattled on about their operative who looks through registries *when he has time*! You and your dear sisters were the man's *hobby*, Jack!"

Well, then—his suspicions were confirmed. Nothing more than he had already concluded. He stood, avoiding Mairey's eyes, his heart emptier than before but still whole. He swallowed his outrage so that it wouldn't blaze across the sky.

"Thank you, Mairey." He'd hired Dodson from across the world and had trusted him with his business. He'd been foolish not to look for a new firm once he'd returned to England. "I shall take great pleasure in sacking them tomorrow morning. They aren't my regular staff of legal advisors; I only used Dodson for this single issue."

His anger was burning brightly, but he didn't want to focus too clearly on its meaning. *Treacherous bastards.* He needed to walk for a while, needed air.

"There's more, Jack." She slipped her hand into his.

"More? Did you find them embezzling from me, too? Impossible—I have a whole staff of lawyers and accountants who protect me from theft and incompetence."

She held his face between her soft hands and made him look into her eyes, though they were still streaming with tears.

"Jack ... I found your mother."

His heart went wild and leaping. Heat seared the back of his eyes before Mairey's words settled into the air between them.

"What did you say?" He held fast to her arms, wanted to see and hear her words because she couldn't possibly have said what was ringing inside his head. Sunbursts of hope, star-pinned wonder filled his chest. "My mother? You found her, Mairey? My God, where is she?"

He wondered if he would recognize her after all these years, and why she hadn't come with Mairey.

"Oh, God, Jack, how do I tell you this?" She kissed his palm and held it to her lips, to her damp cheek. "Your mother died, my love, a very long time ago."

"You're mistaken, Mairey." He pulled his hand out of hers, standing stiff and disconnected. That wasn't possible. He'd promised his father he would take care of his mother; he only needed to find her and his sisters and then he could start over. He'd bought this house for them—

"I found the registry of her death, in a parish church just outside Manchester." Her fingers quaked as she handed him a folded sheaf of paper. "I made a copy of it, and a rubbing of her gravestone. Jack, I'm so sorry."

His limbs were numb as he took the bundle, tucked it under his arm, and looked out across his estate, counting all the freshly painted corner posts in the fence that bordered the herb garden. He was waiting for his throat to clear of the volcanic sob seething there, waiting to breathe again without aching.

"When did it happen?" He swallowed back the molten heat, and let it burn its way down his gullet.

"She died in Manchester on the fifteenth of December, 1842."

Eight months after he left Glad Heath. All those years of imagining that his mother was waiting on the porch for him to come home, bread-scented and smiling, holding back the wriggling tide of his sisters. Lost to him completely all those years ago.

"Jack, you have to know this, too." She reached for his hand and took just his fingertips, as though she thought he would lash out at her. "Your mother died in childbirth. And the baby along with her."

That couldn't be! A stunning tide of relief washed over him. He threw the offensive papers on the ground between them, utterly astounded that Mairey would put him through this horror for nothing, without checking her facts.

"You're wrong, Mairey! My mother was not pregnant. She would have told me. Father would have."

Mairey was shaking her head, sternly denying his happiness. "She probably didn't know herself, Jack, not until you were gone. But she was delivered of a full-term, stillborn son."

"No." No. No. No! "It wasn't her, damn you! I will find her!"

"His name was Patrick."

Oh, God! His father's name. An unchecked sob roared out of his chest, became a howl of shame, of loss. Now his brother was a casualty of Jack's neglect, too—his father's request turned to ashes from the first.

"That's where I was today, Jack. In Manchester."

She touched his arm, and his stomach reeled. He shook her off and grabbed up the strewn papers, dry as death, crackling like ancient autumn leaves. "You did all this *today?*"

"In just a little over an hour from the time I arrived at the railway station. I did nothing extraordinary, Jack. The parish register was available; the old vicar pleasant and helpful; your mother's name and the details written quite clearly, and exactly as I would have expected."

He'd always safely entombed his guilt in the knowledge that he had engaged the best agency that money could buy, that Dodson and his lot were as relentless in this quest as he. He'd relied upon men who had made a mockery of his fidelity and a farce of his crusade.

But in the end, that highly polished veneer of diligent pursuit and familial devotion had been stripped away by a single, disposable hour in the life of Mairey Faelyn. He had hired her to find him a silver mine, not to flay open his life and turn it out to the sun so that he had no course but to stare at its ugliness. Would the very capable Miss Faelyn next find his sisters lodged in a whorehouse? "Damn you for meddling."

"Meddling?" She backed away, her eyes flashing silvery hot. "How can you say that, Jack?"

"I didn't ask for you to meddle in my private affairs."

"I know it hurts, that it stings your pride and scrapes your stomach raw. But you've lost eighteen years, Jack; don't lose another day. Let me help you find your sisters."

"No! You've already done enough, Miss Faelyn."

She caught up his sleeve when he turned to leave, bracing her palms against his chest in her angry defense of him. "It wasn't your fault, Jack. None of it. Don't you see that?"

There was the flaw in her logic. So bloody plain he wondered how she could have missed it. "Dodson might well have been using me, Miss Faelyn, but not half as expertly as I was using *him.*"

He left her while he still had breath, before he made a monster of himself and an enemy of the misguided woman that he adored.

CHAPTER 15

Though Mairey spent supper round the kitchen table with her dear family, Aunt Tattie's succulent supper of roasted lamb and potatoes tasted of sorrow and sawdust. The girls fretted, wanting to run free in the woods and search for Jack. He'd been gone since yesterday, God only knew where. He'd ridden from the stable like the madman he'd become in that moment of overpowering grief. A lifetime of loneliness and despair made real.

She'd never seen a man in such anguish. And she was the cause: she'd rammed a spear though the unprotected slit in his spiny armor, found his huge, defenseless heart, and then, because he'd hired her as an expert meddler, she'd given that spear a bloody good twist!

He had cried out in his agony—a soulful lament that had torn open her own heart. But instead of letting her explain her reasons, instead of seeking her comfort, instead of staying to hear her plan to help him find his sisters, his desolation had sent him galloping away from Drakestone, dragging her shredded heart along after him.

"No word from his lordship, love?" Aunt Tattie seemed to be

the only one of the family unaffected by the runaway wobbling of the earth beneath their feet; she seemed happily content with her humming as she padded through the parlor, turning down the lamps.

"I can't very well expect to hear from him." Mairey snuffled back another plague of tears so they wouldn't smear any more of the notes she'd been making in her book. "You see, I told him something he didn't want to hear."

"Ah, men." Tattie sat down on the settle and rubbed Mairey's back in great soothing circles. "Was it something his lordship needed telling?"

That his mother was dead? And that he had a brother he'd never meet? That they'd both been dead for nearly eighteen years, and he could stop looking for her; stop waiting for his life to begin? "Oh, yes, he needed telling."

"Well, then he'll understand."

Tears erupted from Mairey's eyes again, dragging huge sobs from deep in her chest. "I don't think he ever will."

"He doesn't blame you, whatever you've told him. Not really. And certainly not for long. Not the way he loves you."

A whirlwind propelled her off her aunt's shoulder. "He *what?*"

"Don't tell me you haven't noticed, my dear girl. I've never seen the like in a man." Tattie winked and thumbed a tear off Mairey's lip. "Never since my own Perry."

"Jack doesn't love me." He *mustn't!*

"Well, he does. Which is quite the nicest of happenstances, since you love the man to distraction."

"I—" She simply nodded, resigned to the plain, indelible facts. She'd never known a man like Jack. Wise and reckless, compassionate and granite-headed.

And hopefully not angry enough to track down the Messrs. Dodson, Dodson and Greel and beat the daylights out of them. Though if he had, she'd have gladly given her entire collection

of elf bolts just to watch and would have sacrificed her stone
axes to add a punch of her own.

She went to the window and looked out on the moon-blan-
keted woods, cursing this feeling of helplessness.

"Where the devil are you, Jack Rushford?"

Jack leaned up against an elm at the edge of the dark woods.
Mairey's woods. Cricket songs and rilling water, that sweet,
fresh smell of green. The lights of the lodge winked at him,
inviting him to enter.

He'd allowed her family to swarm over the estate willy-nilly,
even encouraged the intrusion; let the household routine
become disrupted; and like a fool, let them all into his heart—
that great big murky chasm, he'd spent years shoring up with
stout timbers, crossbeams and struts. Indeed, heartwood.
Sturdy stuff, impregnable, unbreakable. Best when hollow and
echoing and insulated from ghosts and shadows and unthinkable truths.

Dodson, Dodson, Greel, and *Rushford.* Now *there* was a partnership. Conceived long ago in the conscientious pursuit of his
own lost integrity, dedicated throughout its term to the cherished memory of a valorous father, and executed by all parties
with contempt for both truth and integrity.

Jackson Rushford was a coward. Afraid that if he allowed
anyone, himself included, to search too efficiently for his family,
he would discover that he had done too little and was years too
late. Each of them slipping away from him, falling, drowning,
just beyond the reach of his fingertips.

Fiercely denying Mairey's truth, he'd ridden hell-bent to the
rail station, boarded a crowded train, and had gotten halfway to
Manchester before he had realized where he was going. He had

to see for himself this eighteen-year-old grave. His mother's name. And this other child—his brother ... Patrick.

But as he had stepped down from the darkened platform, he'd realized he didn't know which church, where his mother was buried; he'd been too clumsy, too outraged in his thinking to ask.

He hadn't learned a bloody thing about himself, though Mairey had tried to teach him.

He'd been a damn fool. Blaming her for holding up a mirror to his deficiencies, for loving him; and then tearing away from her like a maniac at the first hint of reality. His pride tasted like metal, chewed like a handful of nails. But he had swallowed it all, and returned home to Drakestone.

He wanted to assure her that he wasn't a lunatic or a brute, that she had courage where he had only bluster, yearned for her wisdom, her help to find his way home. He wanted her to know his heart, all of it. That crowded, madly thumping vessel in the center of his chest, the one that had always seemed so empty but now was full to bursting.

So here he was, lurking outside her house like a lovelorn dolt, holding fast to the monumental decision he'd made this evening on the ride back.

The lodge was now dark, save for a single light high in the garret window. Nine o'clock. The girls would be gone to bed by now, Mairey's bedtime tales tucked under their pillows to sweeten their dreaming. Tonight's tale and last night's would surely have been of fire-breathing dragons and purloined princesses.

And that dragon's name would rightly be Jackson Rushford.

He wondered if the trellis beneath Mairey's window would hold him.

"Look, Poppy! It's Lord Jack! I found him!"

They leaped at him from the understory, flying toward him

in streaks of white gossamer and clouds of giggles and streaming hair.

"Anna Faelyn, what are you doing outside in the middle of the night?" He knelt on one knee to corral them, to hold them close. They fell on him in a clump of arms and legs, landing fairy kisses that would probably leave purple bruises. "Ouch! Caro, does Mairey know you're all out here?"

"No, she'd skin us!"

"Where have you been, you mean old Jack?" Poppy found his neck and clung there, a bare heel in his crotch until he shifted her to his hip.

"We were looking for you."

"Here, in the woods, in the dark?"

"You made Mairey sad when you left." A belly-blow from Anna that had nothing to do with her sharp little elbows.

"I didn't mean to. I made myself sad, too."

"Do you promise never to run away from us again?" Anna had her older sister's persistence and sense of order, and was far too perceptive for her years.

"I promise to do everything I can to make her the happiest woman on earth."

"She'll like that."

"I certainly hope so." This was no place and no time for a conference. "And I don't need to be looked for any longer. You found me; I'm home." At least near it. "Which is where you should all be. Now, be off before Mairey finds you gone, and she skins us all."

But even as he gave the warning, the door to the lodge clicked open and Mairey stepped out onto the wooden porch in her nightgown, a candle held high, searching for something beyond the glow.

"We're in trouble, ladies," Jack whispered, wondering how the hell he had become a confederate to three changelings. He felt himself smiling madly, finding it difficult to hold in the belly laugh that was brewing in his chest.

The four of them became part of the shadowed brambles and the ferns, huddled in a conspiracy of silence as they protected their collective hides and rode out the danger of discovery.

"You should marry her, Lord Jack."

"Shhh!" He clamped his hand over Caro's mouth, felt her silly grin in the middle of his palm.

Marry Mairey? Oh, God, yes! Tomorrow if she'd let him. His heart filled up so fast the tide of it jostled him off balance, and a twig snapped under his knee.

Mairey turned sharply and took a step in their direction, held her candle higher, and leaned forward in her glowing gown and spun-glass hair. She stood for a long time, peering directly at their frozen tableau, before she pinched out the flame and gazed up at the bright moon.

"Come home, Jack." Her whisper or his wish, or a soughing breeze. She was there, and then she was gone. The door closed, and everyone collapsed but Jack.

"Off you go, young ladies! Now! And I mean go straight into the house, or I'll see that Mairey knows you were out here."

"Yes, sir, Lord Jack." Anna was giggling.

"Don't say a word about me, or we'll all be in trouble."

"Cris and cross our hearts!"

Then they were gone, bare feet shushing across the small yard and through the side door of the kitchen.

Not a minute later, their small, smiling faces and waving hands appeared at the garret window.

Ghosts. No, not ghosts—hoarded remembrances, cherished and enduring. Maybe that's all he would ever find of what-might-have-been. His memories. And maybe that would have to be enough.

He let the gouging grief hurt this time, and the lost years; let them sting the back of his throat and fill his eyes to overflowing.

He waved Godspeed to his phantoms and hello to the three little girls who had won over his heart the moment Anna's well-aimed apple had hit him in the shoulder.

He left the woods for his cavernous house, a man with marriage on his mind and Mairey in his heart.

~

Unsure what whimsy had drawn her outside earlier, but suspecting the foolish moon and Jack Rushford, Mairey went back to her restless idling. She dusted the curios on the mantel, read for a time in the parlor, then soaked for an hour in the tub until she was prunish and pink. She made the rounds to the girls' rooms and left kisses on their foreheads, wondering how each of them had gotten bits of twigs and leaves in their hair. Her three dancing princesses.

She tried her best to sleep, but the crickets were in full voice tonight, the breeze that caught at her curtains was too sweet, and soon she was pacing down the stairs in her night rail.

The Willowmoon and its knotwork were on her mind, a maze inside a maze; Jack's life and hers woven together intricately, recklessly. She couldn't leave Drakestone until she'd found the Willowmoon Knot, else he might find it on his own. And yet she couldn't stay for the ache in her heart.

Finding the Knot quickly was the logical solution. The sooner she did, the sooner she could extricate herself and her family.

Which would cause great tides of grief that would drown her every day for the rest of her life. But it couldn't be helped; she had promises to keep. Time to start bringing her work home to the lodge, to separate herself from Jack a little at a time until she could manage perfectly—perfectly wretchedly—

without him. No time like the present, she thought, trying to convince herself of the urgency.

The twenty-volume *Gazetteer of Ecclesiastical Antiquities* had been delivered to Drakestone's library earlier today among the properties that the Royal Family were to give to the new museum at South Kensington, and she hadn't found a single moment to study them. What better time than now?

After donning a long walking-coat over her nightgown and slipping into a pair of garden boots, Mairey left the lodge and made her way toward the main house.

A rustle of guilt stirred the air in her lungs and tainted the sweetness of the night. Not because she had proved Jack's lawyers as devoid of morality as they were of resources; he needed that jolt of truth, whatever it had cost him in agony.

Rather because he was the most honest and trusting man she'd ever met—which left her feeling caddish and hollow. In this partnership between them, she was bound to deceive him, and Jack was her helpless mark. Even if he read his way through all twenty volumes of the *Gazetteer*, even if he memorized every word, he would still be confounded. He needed her to make sense of the passages and to lead him to the Willowmoon Knot, if it still existed.

And that made her great, bellowing dragon vulnerable to her slightest falsehood, the small ones she created every day to keep him off track. The big, sloppy red herrings, she had drawn so easily across his path.

With the weight of the ages pressing on her shoulders, Mairey let herself into the dark library, feeling her way along the familiar textures to her workbench, surprised that Jack's eloquent scent of leather and soap still lingered, strong and evocative, though he'd been gone for more than a day.

She lit the lamp on her worktable, lugged Volume One of the thick gazetteer to her desk and flipped open the cover.

This Volume, intended as a Gazetteer of Minor Collections of

Antiquities, is Respectfully Dedicated to the Most Honorable, the Viscount Norbury, Lord President of the Council of Antiquaries, 1778.

The Willowmoon Knot hadn't been in York; she and Jack had returned to the storage rooms in the minster and had found nothing of Branville's pagan collection, no mention of its ever having been cataloged. It might have been stored there unremarked for decades and then been traded to another parish, or sold to a museum or even to a private collector by one of the minster's deans.

1778. Nearly modern. Here was the most tantalizing resource yet. Inefficiently indexed, and compiled from many sources, it would be a long, hard read. She should have been thrilled at finding the *Gazetteer*, but success had tasted bitter recently.

"If you were to search for my sisters, Mairey, where would you begin?"

"Jack!" Her heart wild with relief, Mairey searched for him in the shadows that stuffed the corners of the library, found him at his desk in the faint glow of her lamp. She'd sensed him in the darkness after all, had heard his breathing like her heartbeat, felt his heat and his scent. She wanted to run to him and hold him through the night—her accidental friend, her inconvenient colleague … and oh, yes, her lover.

"Your sisters, Jack?" she asked instead, trying to assess his mood across the distance between them. "That would depend on what more you could tell me about them."

"Everything, Mairey." His desk chair creaked as he rose. "I would tell you everything. Will give you Dodson's file full of lies and distortions, for all the good it will do you." He teetered in place, caught his hand fast around the back of his chair.

The lout had injured himself, or he'd been drinking. Which didn't seem at all like the Jackson Rushford who planned and controlled the workings of his rigid life to the nearest inch.

"Jack, where have you been?" Concern for his recklessness made her voice far more chafing than she meant.

"Out."

"More than out, Jack. You were gone a night and a whole day." His delicate mood be damned. She carried her lamp to the table beside him, then stood back to examine him as he flinched from the light, squinting down at her.

"Were you worried about me, Mairey?" He looked tattered, tumbled.

"Worried? How about terrified, good sir?"

He smiled sideways, too charmingly bashful for this hour of the night. "I didn't mean to worry you."

His hair stood every which way, finger-combed and drooping damply into his eyes. She reached up and ran her fingers through its silky blackness.

"Your hair is wet."

He was jacketless, collarless, with his sleeves rolled to his elbow. "I took a bath, Mairey. I think I fell asleep again."

"You think?" He looked half-asleep still.

"Could have drowned." He leaned down lazily and pulled her close to whisper in her ear, "I didn't have you there to rescue me."

A very good thing, because she wouldn't have had rescue on her mind.

"Sit here, Jack, before you fall." She wrestled him into the high-back chair. He landed on the upholstered seat with a grunt and a grimace. "Have you been fighting? Did you kill Dodson?"

"Christ, Mairey, I wanted to take on every Dodson and Greel I could get my hands on."

"And did you, Jack? Did you find Dodson and beat him to a pulp?" Hoping he had, Mairey knelt between his spread thighs and took pleasure in the intimate smoothness of his beard against her palms while she turned his jaw to examine him for injuries.

Not a scratch, but for the cut he must have just gotten from his razor.

"I would have, Mairey. But I didn't want you to hate me any more than you do."

"I don't hate you, Jack." Lunatic. She couldn't possibly hate this part of him, the lost boy who was searching for his family. Not when she so wanted to be his family.

He tilted his head, and squinted at her through one wickedly smiling eye. "Not even when I'm an inconsiderate ass?"

"Especially not then, Jack." What the devil had gotten into him on his wild pilgrimage to who knows where? He certainly hadn't been drinking; he smelled of soap and starch.

"I'm exceedingly glad of that, Mairey."

"Well, then, sir. If you were not out looking to bludgeon every Dodson for crimes against you, where did you go?"

"I was hunting for ghosts." He looked quite serious, the way a headmaster might as he was explaining the tidal effects of the moon. "I felt like a damned ghoul last night and all the day long, tramping through every graveyard in Manchester."

"You went to Manchester?" She smiled hugely, relieved that he'd found at least a little hope tucked away in his outrage. "You really hadn't spent the day stalking Dodson."

"Bastard—he's not worth the trouble. I had a more precious mission."

"Your mother." Her heart swelled and grew lighter for him, though it still ached. She bundled his hand between hers. "Oh, Jack, you're wonderful—"

"Don't, Mairey." He brought their clasped hands to his lips and set a kiss on her fingers, his gaze fastened fiercely to hers as it so often was of late. "And don't beam at me like that with your eyes all misty, as though you believe me to be the perfect son and protector. I am not."

He needed sleep—or something. But getting the enormous

man up the stairs and into his bed was going to be a mighty challenge. Leaving him there—alone—might prove impossible.

"Jack, you *are* a perfect son *and* brother. I know of no one who could have been a more exemplary protector, given any circumstances, let alone your own."

"Do not indulge me, Mairey. I've been a damned fool."

Oh, how she could count the ways—and be at the task for weeks! But Jack had never been anything but honorable and courageous in his devotion to his family. He had been their battle-ready champion from the day his father died, and long, long before that, if she knew the boy as well as she knew the man.

"Whatever you say. Jack." He wasn't ready to admit his goodness; battering him with it would only make him more stubborn. She left him and went back to her worktable. "I only meant that I was glad you found your mother's grave."

"Actually, I didn't." He thrust himself out of the chair, stuffing his thumbs into the back of his trousers and pacing the room in his giant's stride. "I couldn't find the bloody thing."

Her spirit sank into the mud; she leaned against the table. "At St. Simon's Chapel?"

"You didn't say which church." He sliced her a self-directed indictment as he paced past her toward the bank of windows. "Or I wasn't listening."

She followed him, feeling guilty. "I'm sorry, Jack, I—"

"Don't you dare, Mairey!" He abruptly turned back to her. She ran into his chest nose first and stayed there to sniff a little of his starchy tang. "The fault was mine—all of it. I should have damn well asked you where my mother was buried before I went storming off. Instead, I raged at you like a feral beast, accused you of ... what was it I accused you of?"

"Nothing that matters, Jack." Nothing mattered but his shamefaced smile and the shadows that planed his jaw. "I understand—"

"You couldn't possibly." He planted himself on the edge of her desk, leaving Mairey standing between his spread knees. "But I am belatedly and enormously grateful for you trying to knock some sense into me, and entirely unworthy of your persistence. And I'm damned sorry for being a jackass, though it won't be the last time. I'm notoriously stone-headed."

"Indeed, you are." But he had a heart of bread pudding, sweet and soft and impossible to refuse. "As for the Dodsons, I would have kissed you if you'd given them both a good wallop."

"Kiss me now, Mairey." His voice was rough, filled with longing, and he tugged her closer. He gazed at her mouth as though he'd been lost in a desert and she was a cool oasis. A kiss wouldn't be wise, not with the way her hands were trembling, the way her heart was pounding. He was leaning forward, had cocooned her nearly completely in his arms as he rested his hands on his knees. His cheek was soft, scented with citrus.

He was whispering soft, feathery things to her. "Home, Mairey. Beautiful Mairey. Forgive me, Mairey."

"I do." If she didn't kiss him soon and be finished with it, the kiss would become outright volcanic. He was so very close, nudging her ever nearer, stealing her pulse and the air between them, until she found his mouth and covered it with hers.

Oh, such a soft and impatient place.

He made a sound like her name, a plea, an exaltation that made her want to sing. Then he was growling low in his chest, his breath shuddering past her lips.

"God, Mairey, I want you." He plowed his fingers through her hair, tilted her face to him, and plundered her mouth. "I want you forever."

Forever? Oh, yes, Jack! She wanted him completely, wanted to stay and stay, wanted children with him and to putter in his garden. But his life was mining, and hers was already claimed by secrets and silver and that blasted village that she loved, and her lovely, sheltered family.

It isn't fair, Papa! But it was the truth. And as dreadful as death. She backed away from him, her arms aching from the need to hold him.

He was shaking, his grip on his knees a white-knuckled clench, and his breathing like a horse after the Derby.

"You're exhausted, Jack Rushford."

He straightened from the desk in all his rumpled, quaking wonder. "I was."

"You need to be in bed." She bolted away from him and ran a few steps up the spiraling iron stairs that led to the mezzanine of books.

"We need to be in bed, Mairey." He stood in the middle of the library grinning up at her, a glint-eyed, unsated dragon looking too pleased for his own good.

Her heart was racing, thrilled when his ringing footfall hit the landing a few steps below her. "That wasn't my meaning, Jack."

"Oh, but it is *mine*, Mairey. I want to make love with you in my bed. *Our* bed—"

"Ours?" What was the man talking about?

"Or in the lodge where you keep your heart." He started up the stairs relentlessly, his eyes fixed on hers, making her pulse thunder against her throat. "Or in the woods, or here in the library."

"You didn't sleep at all last night did you, Jack?" That was the reason for his intimate confessions—not a passion for her. Certainly not love, as Tattie had suggested. He'd said nothing about love.

She'd be lost completely if he ever did.

"I did sleep, Mairey, on the train," he said, closing in on her and her very illogical idea of getting him safely into his bed. "Dreaming always of you and the priceless gifts you've given me."

Odd, but she couldn't remember a single one. "How much

sleep did you get?" She spun away and scooted up the stairs, five steps ahead of him. Then only two.

"I got enough for this."

She stopped on the mezzanine and turned to him. An even greater mistake. "Enough for what?"

He scooped her up in his next stride and started toward his chamber. "Enough to make love with you till next Tuesday."

"Jack!"

"Till Wednesday, then, if you like."

She liked Wednesday too, too much.

"Jack, put me down."

"No."

His chamber door loomed—immense, shiny mahogany, and a fat brass latch that opened too easily to a room bathed in the dim light of slumbering lamps. She saw starry glints of gold and emerald and ruby glittering in the periphery. His bed was as huge as he was, tall, oak framed, and four posted, heaped with pillows and overlain with an undulating sea of autumn-hued counterpane.

Heaven on earth—a place to sprawl, wild-limbed, and collect his kisses wherever he cared to lay them.

"You said you wanted me in my bed, Mairey."

And everywhere else, Jack!

"Well, here it is." He let go of her legs and caught her up against the length of him, so warm and so vibrantly hard in so very many places. "Here *we* are. And damn me, if you're not wearing your nightgown for our pleasure."

His smile was loose and tilting and far too charming; and he was watching her through half-lidded eyes, with a pulse-pounding, possessive hunger she'd *badly* mistaken for exhaustion.

"Jack, I just came to the library to get a book. And I really shouldn't be … oh. Oh, yes." Mairey sighed long and deeply as he trailed his beguiling mouth and then his tongue down the column of her throat; she watched in dizzying expectation as he dipped his splendid fingers past her coat and into the neck of her nightgown, then lifted it aside, exposing the hollow of her throat to his spice-steamed breath and the fevered tracing of his mouth.

"Ah, Mairey, I missed you. Wanted you. Wanted this." His huge and gentle hand cradled the underside of her breast through the linen of her gown. But she might as well have been as naked as the dewy morning for the bliss he was causing with the pad of his thumb, for the exquisite aching between her legs as though his hand was toying there again. She wanted to be free of her coat and her nightgown, to be skin to skin with him.

"Oh, Jack, you ... oh!" Wanted to be possessed by her very own dragon, but it was imminently dangerous to her most secret strategies against him. Baring herself to him like a common jade, delighting in his growls of adoration, taking tiny little gasps inside her throat, grabbing his shirttails and urging his hips and his feral hardness against her belly wouldn't help her cause, either.

He'd get a wholly wrong idea about her intentions.

She was getting a wholly wrong idea about her intentions!

She closed her eyes and banished the voices that warned her to run from him, from the man she loved, who made her laugh, and rented his woods to the fairies. She let her stolen joy and Jack's scent fill her.

He was her phantom kingdom, a sanctuary where dragons were princes, where there was no such thing as the Willowmoon Knot, no silver mine or slag heaps or cave-ins.

"Did you mean it, Jack?"

He backed away a step, leaving an aching confusion of drafts between them. His shirt hung open where she'd freed the buttons, white against rippling bronze.

"Did I mean *what?*" His breath tore out of him, and his thick arms flexed beneath his sleeves, his hands clenching as though he'd been checked in the midst of a fistfight.

"That you wanted to make love with me tonight."

He shook his tousled head slowly, grinning slyly. "I meant *every* night, my love. Until the end of our days."

If only that were possible! "Then make love with me. Jack. Please."

Wasn't that what fairy tales were for?

CHAPTER 16

A bolt of raw, fire-tipped lust jolted through Jack, nearly driving him backward with its power. He'd been fighting to hold on to a mote of common sense while he assembled the right words to propose marriage. Assuring her of his honorable intentions would require careful thought and finesse—and at the moment he was lucky to be thinking at all. His heart was galloping, pumping molten blood through his veins and into his groin, but not a drop was going to his sodden brain.

He'd taken refuge in the library in order to dissuade himself from climbing the trellis into her bedroom in the lodge. Yet somehow he'd managed to conjure her in the library, in her bedclothes, this guileless apparition who had turned his life upside down.

The belt at her waist had come loose, and her coat hung off her shoulders as though it wanted the floor. She was covered to the cleaving of her breasts by her nightgown, and standing in a too-big pair of muddy boots. Boots and bare feet and a plain, plain gown—and still the magic swirled around her.

"God, Mairey, you're beautiful." A diminishment of everything she meant to him, but she laughed kindly.

"This old thing?" Touching that hollow between her perfect breasts, she turned a coy hip and a side-bent knee.

His brain seized up. "Every inch of you, Mairey."

"These too?" She jiggled one boot off and then the other, stood in her bare feet on the carpet.

"Especially those." He was utterly undone, ready to lose himself forever inside her. "But"—he hung onto the shredded remains of his sanity—"I ought to take you back to the lodge while we're still fully dressed and able."

She shook her head as though she didn't want to hear. "No, Jack, please. I want this. I want you. I want tonight to last forever."

Forever. Beginning here and now, my love, not a one-night roundabout. He would peel her of every stitch, find delicate inroads, secret pathways to the treasure she'd become to him.

"Forever it is, then, my love."

She watched him from under her exquisite lashes as she shoved the coat off her shoulders and let it fall to the floor. Her fingers fascinated him as she unfastened the pearly buttons that ran down the front of her pale nightgown to the joining of her thighs—one button and then the next, and then two more, till the gown was hanging off one bare shoulder, teasing him, taunting, till he couldn't stand the wait.

"Let me." He threaded his fingers through the tumble of her hair and made love to her mouth, then stepped back to slide her gown down her arms, to simply stare. He'd watched her breasts tease against her shirtwaist for so long that he knew them intimately, loved them dearly. They were marvelous, creamy, high and lush, rose-tipped and just full enough to cradle in his hands, to crest with his thumbs.

"Oh, Jack, that's sooo—" She inhaled sharply and threw her head back. Her upward motion pressed her closer, allowed him to catch a nipple between his lips. She gasped and impatiently shook off the prison her gown made at her elbows, then clutched the back of his head, tugging him closer. "Yes, there."

"And this too?" He pulled the sweet morsel into his mouth, between his tongue and teeth and set her to mewling, reaching for handfuls of his hair. Her mouth, her breasts, her belly. She writhed and danced against him, and he held her hips to keep them still, then took her mouth again to keep himself from dragging her to the carpet and filling her with his seed, with all his hopes for tomorrow.

Marry me, my love. Be my wife, tonight and always.

"Be closer, Jack." Her gown was still caught up on the fine bones of her pelvis, soft contours of alabaster, the place where he would kneel to worship before the night was over. Even as he loosed the maddening thought, even as he was kneading the span of her waist, she covered his hands with hers and guided him over her hips, pushing the bunched-up linen off the gentle slope to drop to the floor in a puddle.

She was lamplight and ivory, sleek and rounded, dazzle-eyed and blessedly eager, peeling him out of his own shirt, tasting across his shoulders, his collarbone, the hollow of his throat, leaving him breathless and grunting like a boar.

"God, Mairey!" He shrugged out of the other sleeve, then filled his arms with her splendor, lifting her off the ground and against him.

"Ah, much better, Jack. Your chest to mine."

"Your heart and mine."

She wrapped her legs around his waist and held his face between her hands, tracing her mouth across his eyelids and against his lips.

Sweat beaded his forehead and ran down his back while his hands were laced together beneath her bare and quivering flanks, forced by physics into idleness; supporting her when he wanted to be teasing at the seductive cleft pressed so sublimely against his belly. There were still barriers between her heat and his raging urgency, wool and linen and cotton aplenty. But his sense of memory was crystal clear—the exotic fragrance of her on his fingers after their impromptu bath, soft folds and slick heat.

His lot was to just stand there and surrender to her, to count backward from a hundred while she rocked against him and made love to his mouth, murmuring something about secrets and dragons and longings.

He'd been in a nearly perpetual state of arousal since he'd met the woman. He was currently, everlastingly, rock-hard and throbbing, on the verge of some good old prurient thrusting.

"Your trousers, Jack."

Oh, excellent—she was a mind reader. "What about them?"

"They need to come off." She spoke against his ear, with tongue and teeth and no small amount of humid heat.

God in highest heaven, he'd found a treasure. Naked and open and more precious than all the gold in California. He carried her to the edge of the bed, almost mad with need for her. Her fingers were already on top of his, brushing them away from his own buttons.

"Too slow, Jack." She sighed as she smoothed her fingers across the fabric at his groin, which bulged, barely holding back his erection.

He grabbed her wrist, kissed her palm. "Too much exploring, love, if I'm to last long."

"Please, Jack." She was looking up at him, an unclad sprite with deviltry on her mind. "I won't touch until you say I can."

"Hardly a comfort to me, Mairey. I'm already this aroused for you." His unsubtle sprite smiled, and he took in a breath that cleared his head. "You may help."

Her fingers were quick and sped ahead of his down the front placket. She freed the last button. "There!" Then she leaned back on her hands, as though she expected his penis to spring from his trousers and dance for her. She looked perplexed and very impatient.

Before her virginal, but very accomplished hands could find him inside his drawers and work her wiles too quickly, Jack shucked the works: trousers, drawers, socks, and shoes, while she looked on from her backward-sprawling, provocative pose on the edge of the bed, roundly appraising and waiting for him.

Was there ever a man more perfectly formed? Mairey was sure she'd died. And she was in heaven, assigned her very own angel. The man was extraordinary, his skin golden in the soft light from the lamp at his bedside, his smile as husbandly as it was draconian. Hungry and adoring.

His penis had been spectacularly rigid all along, provocative while concealed and now blissfully displayed, thickly veined and pulsing. The grand prize in any collection. Blue ribbon quintessence—and it needed much closer examination.

But he was bearing down on her, bracing himself with one hand beside her hip, and all she could see now was the blazing dark of his eyes.

"Were you looking for the moon at the lodge tonight, Mairey, or for me?" He planted a kiss on her belly.

The moon? His question finally penetrated the cloud of heat surrounding them. He'd been at the lodge tonight; must have seen her on the porch. How lovely! That he'd come to the lodge and the delicious feel of his fingertips gliding upward from her stomach. "That was you? The noise in the underbrush? Why didn't you say something?"

"We—I mean, I was terrified."

"Terrified of—? Oh!" His touch dizzied her, tantalized. So deliciously scandalous and unscholarly, making her nipples crimp and pucker. He teased them, encouraged the spectacular crimping with his fingers, squeezing lightly, licking, lighting a wick deep inside her.

"Terrified of *you*, my love."

"Impossible." He was so large and so tender as he leaned down to kiss her mouth. So maddeningly restrained, leisurely, as though he had a lifetime to spare.

"You are spectacular, Mairey Faelyn." He cradled the back of her head, kissed her ear, then the hollow of her throat, sowing a field of his glittering starlight across her shoulders. "Have I ever told you that?"

"I would have remembered, Jack."

"I plan to make it a habit." He was bedrock, and she was flecks of gold.

Her entire life had been built upon an ancient promise, an often bruising and always desperate promise she'd made to her father—the very same promise that her father had made to his father, that her grandfather had made to his father, and so on, and so on until her head dizzied and she wanted to scream.

She wanted Jack, wanted him forever, but she would have to settle for tonight—despite the ravaging consequences to her heart. She knew where children came from, how to calculating the pertinent dates of her cycle. She couldn't possibly conceive tonight, according to every source she knew, from cotters' wives to modern physicians: she was in the wrong part of her monthlies to conceive a child with Jack. Which made her stomach ache with grief.

But tonight would be her fairy tale, a memory to last a lifetime. There was no one in this mythical kingdom but herself and Jack, her huge, naked-haunched dragon. Bronze above the waist, only a little less below. Thick muscles and compact cords and those appealing whorls of dark hair that she wanted to follow with her tongue to the very root of him.

But she would have to wait her turn while she leaned back on her elbows, her legs spread indelicately, impossibly wide over the side of the bed; while Jack, her extravagant, amazing Jack, braced his weight with one arm against the mattress, nuzzling her throat, making his way toward her breasts and then further downward.

How far down, she didn't dare guess. She felt as ripe as a summer peach, warm and fleshy and ready to burst. His thewy arms were quaking on either side of her hips, and he was breathing like he'd been running cross-country through the woods.

And then he was kneeling between her legs.

"Jack, what are you doing?" She sat upright to see his broad hands slide down her torso to slip round her backside and drag her closer to him. Closer!

"I'm not doing anything yet, my love."

Then why was she nearly fainting from lack of air? Why was her imagination outpacing him? And why was he lifting her ever so slightly off the bed, kissing the inside of her thighs, and then the hollow that joined her leg to her hip?

"But, Jack, you're—"

"I have a tale to tell you, Mairey."

"Now?" When his every word danced across her belly like a steamy, mischievous cloud, to froth against her curls, to drift with his breath and toss about in his storm. And all so very lightly that she thought she would go mad, had gone mad with the wanting.

"Oh, yes, now is the best time to tell my tale, my love. While I have your attention."

"You have just about all of me, Jack!"

"Not yet. Not nearly enough." His dark hair glistened against the paleness of her legs. At the joining of her thighs! Damp curls he shouldn't even be looking at, let alone—oh! Sweet yellow saffron, he kissed her! Lightly, sweetly, and with his tongue, on that vague boundary between her belly and her sex.

"Once upon a time—" The indescribable man was fingering his way further down, sifting through curls, teasing where she was wet and fully awakened. He had held her there once before, and she had felt possessed. But this was—

"Ohhhhh!" She sighed out the breath that had been caught in her throat for the last five minutes. "Soooo wonderful!"

"Ah, the rest of my story is even finer, Mairey." How could anything be finer than this singular intimacy between them? But she was determined to hear his every word, to *feel* his every word!

"Are you taking fieldnotes, Mairey?"

"Oh, yes, Jack. Memorizing everything you say. And everywhere you say it. Please, *please*, go on." And on! "Oh!"

He was parting her with his fingers, seeking something from her, finding the telling hot dampness that had been gathering like a summer storm. Fueling the fire that burned in her belly.

"Once upon a time, my sweet, my tasty Mairey"—he kissed her tenderly, altogether chastely where his fingers played—"there was a fusty, old dragon."

"An irresistible dragon," she said. Another of his intimate kisses, deeper yet probing. An unladylike gasp came whistling out of her chest. "The creature was melancholy, my love."

"Oh, *Jaaack!*" That was the tip of his tongue! His *tongue!* A hot, slick bolt of lightning that wedged itself inside her cleft and then retreated. But just like lightning, its blazing blue artifacts stayed to flare and lick its way into the core of her. She reached blindly for the hand that was kneading her hip, wanting something of him to hold on to, something to keep her from soaring away and losing him.

"Yes?" He grinned as he caught up her hand, kissed her fingers and then the inside of her knee, then led his ravishing tongue along a trail toward still another of his intimacies.

"I doubt this dragon was melancholy, Jack."

"Why is that?" Another kiss.

"Oh, Jack! Because ... Dear God!" His tongue was everywhere, and his fingers, too; sliding and slipping, nuzzling her as though he were kissing her. "Because dragons are usually fierce, yes! Yes, oh, my, yes!"

"Are they, love?" He sounded grandly amused by all her squirming. But she couldn't help herself.

"And they're relentless!" She grabbed the astonishing man by his hair, bringing him closer, and pinned her heels against his shoulders to beg relief from his enchantment, to beg for more of it. "Oh! And big. Jack! Dragons are enorrrrrmous! Oh, Jack!"

He tugged and teased until she was bucking and grinding, ready to explode.

"But still and all, this dragon was sorrowful, my dear—"

Her throat was sore from all her groaning. "Was his name Balforge? It must have been."

"If you'd like it to be."

"Oh, I would!" Balforge was *her* dragon. The one who had coiled himself around her heart, the one whose tongue was laving her as though she were dessert, the one who called her his love.

His love!

He nuzzled her once more, then left that place of startling wonder, left her aching and twisting and unfulfilled, and carried her further backward onto the bed and against the pillows.

"You see, Mairey, my love, this Balforge lived and worked all alone in a drafty old cavern."

She clung to his neck, to his mouth. "Did he have wings?"

"Unfortunately, no." He stretched out above her, kneeling between her thighs, braced on his elbows, looking even more hungry than before he'd sampled her, his stalk dazzlingly large and inviting. "Because if he had, he wouldn't have spent so much time on the train, traveling between his other caverns, and he wouldn't have been so ill-tempered."

She fit her arms around his broad back and kissed him, thoroughly bewitched by her storyteller and his irresistible theatrics. "A very modern sort."

She was about to prompt him for more when he snuggled his penis against the nest he'd so attentively feathered for it.

"There's more, my love."

"Oh, so *much* more!" She raised her hips to collect the thrilling length of him, to slide it here and there. "You are wickedly large, my lord."

"And you are willful." He shook himself like a waterdog, then gulped in a huge breath of air before he focused his eyes on her again with a half-grin. "I meant, my sweet, that my story has a princess."

"I was hoping so." His hips were wonderfully sculpted, his backside carved in shifting marble and just as hard.

"She was beautiful, intelligent, enchanting." He practiced his sorcery with every word, moving his hips and his flesh, pressing her into the mattress as though he couldn't get enough of her.

"And he was handsome, wonderful." She caught his mouth and kissed him thoroughly, memorizing the taste of him, dancing her tongue with his.

"Ah, but, Mairey, the princess turned out to be his downfall."

Guilty tears sprung to her eyes, hot and heart-aching, kissed away by the fine man who loved so fiercely. "I'm sorry for that. Jack."

"Oh, trust me, love—you've taught me about happy endings." He slid his hand down the flat of her belly, followed afterward with his mouth, and just when she thought she'd go mad, he entered her with his finger. "And we will have one."

"Oh, Jack!" She tilted her hips to meet him, gloried in the lush flickering of his tongue, as he delved with two fingers, filling her marvelously but not nearly enough.

She wanted *him*—all of him. Wanted him to hurry with his story, to take her to his place of happily-ever-aftering. "What happened to the princess and her dragon?"

He was maddeningly slow, dazing her with a blinding stroke of his fingers, and then a nibble on her breast, an ardent tugging that made her feel ripe and sun-warmed, spinning his tale with silken strands that tugged her pulse in a thousand and one directions, but ever upward toward a place she couldn't quite reach.

"The uncivilized fellow imprisoned his wanton captive in one of his caverns—"

"She was wanton as well?"

"Mmmmm ..." he hummed huskily against her belly, making her light-headed with his fondling. "Old Balforge was a very lucky dragon, though he didn't know it, and made her work for him day and night."

"His housekeeper?"

"His very own antiquarian. A beautiful collector of folktales, a finder of lost dreams."

"I like your story, Jack, love the way you tell it!" With his tongue and his mouth and—"Oh, yes, finally!" He pressed the broad tip of his penis against her—a star-splintering fit that made her wrap her legs around his hips and coerce him forward with her heels. "There, Jack."

"Not yet, my love. We've much farther to go."

She couldn't imagine surviving another moment of his extravagant torture. Though she opened her legs wider and begged him come, he ignored her graceless hints, though hard-rippling tremors shook him and made him struggle for air.

She wanted to confess that she loved him, that she wanted to stay and stay, but there was too much danger in that. Even here in their very own, private fairy tale where most any magical thing could happen.

Anything.

"I want to touch you. Jack." She reached between their bodies, slid her hand down his lean-muscled trunk, across his flat belly, and closed her fingers around the most brawny shape she'd ever had the pleasure of touching.

"Mairey!—" Jack swallowed a howl and made a grab for her

hand. But she was already there in the steamy hollow between them, her innocent fingers encircling his shaft in faultless, fluting links, her hands making grand forays even as he shot to his knees in pure reflex.

"You're so lovely here, Jack." She was sitting up, fondling the length and breadth of him as she had those others in the drawer. "Warm and hard—and soft, too! Beautiful!" Her words of admiration broke against him, warm and moist and too close.

"Blazes, woman!" He hadn't been prepared for her adventuring; wasn't expecting delicate fingers scribing the details of his anatomy and exalting them, sheathing him thoroughly with her masterful hands, taunting him with that instinctive, pounding, pulsing rhythm and taking him too near the edge before he could stop her. He should have known she would astound him in this, too.

"A kiss, Jack?"

"Almighty God, yes!" But he caught her hands before she could bestow one and drove her back into the pillows, pinning her wrists above her head.

"Why didn't you let me kiss you as you did me?"

"Another time—" Though that promise only hardened him further, if that were possible. Their quintessential parts were heated and poised and throbbing, her legs clutched round him, ready to take him completely. "I'm crazed for you, Mairey. I want to plunge and thrust in you."

"Then do.

Please." She laughed and tucked him closer, expertly now, and harrowed her fingers through his hair.

"I don't want to hurt you."

"You couldn't possibly."

Jack had never in his life waited for anything with such visceral, tethered yearning; he was in her heart and in her eyes; he could see the wonder so plainly, so perfectly. He wanted to be soul-deep inside her, straining with her till the sky fell out from under them. Here was his miracle, making love with him, urging him to pillage her, whispering her silky treasures to him, coiling her hips in wide undulations, taking him against her, pressing and pressing him ever deeper till he met that tender barrier he'd found with his fingers.

Virgo intacta. "You're very tight, love."

"We'll fit together, Jack." She arched her hips and shoved him closer with her heels. "There, do you feel the place?"

"God, yes, Mairey. Stop!" He shuddered with the effort of not plunging forward into all that exquisite heat.

"Then, please, Jack!" His wanton princess had found him again, her eager hand fitting him against the silky wetness he'd drawn from her. "Let me take you inside me. Let me hold you there, Jack."

An irresistible tide urged him. "As deeply as you can bear, my love."

"Then all the way to my heart. Jack." Sighing against his mouth, she tilted her hips and took the tip of him as far as she could, then kissed him. "The rest is for you, my enormous dragon."

"Oh, my love!" Like a man possessed, he thrust fiercely, mindlessly, breaching her swiftly, the pleasure exquisite and propelling as she closed tightly around him, taking him deeper and more fully with each sharp sigh.

"Ohhhhh, Jack, oh, yes! Please, please, do!" Until he was buried to the shank and quaking, and his nymph was stretched languidly beneath him, her eyes streaming with tears and not quite focused, as though she were trying to recognize a beloved scent on a summer breeze.

"I hurt you, my love. I'm sorry." He kissed her eyelids and struggled not to move.

"Oh, no, Jack. I'm restored—filled with *you.*" She wriggled her hips, stunning him with her earthy lust, kissed him hungrily, then began rocking gently, finding the rising rhythm of his heartbeat and hers.

He steadied his breathing and met her deeply measuring strokes, taking leave of her and then returning only when she clutched at his hips and begged, laughing with her as they came together again in ever-ascending fury.

"Whatever happened to Balforge and his princess?"

He paused his weight on his elbows, keeping her close to him and sheltered, just the two of them and their driving need to have union. "Oh, love, he lost his heart to her."

"How fine is that?" She gave him a willowy sigh and a fierce embrace that locked her ankles around his backside, and drove him to the brink with her rocking.

"From the first moment he saw her."

"Oh, my enchanting dragon!" She was breathless beneath him, praising his clever marauding, taking his ravenous kiss as an offering, bestowing her own at his temples and on his mouth, while the tempest rose and raged around them. Exuberance and adoration, and all the swirling forces of nature caught up in a firestorm.

"Tell me your happy ending, Jack. I can't stand the wait."

"Neither can I, my love." He was reeling with restraint and all of it for Mairey, for her pleasure, for her love. He slipped his hand between them where she was wet and ripe for him, where they were fused together and grinding toward the same slivered sunlight, the same everlasting bliss.

A simple touch, a skiff, and then her throaty, "Ohhhh, mmmmy! Jaaack!"

The searing force of her release shattered him, came roaring out of nowhere to overtake him in its whirlwind. But before he succumbed to the fragmenting glory, before he lost himself inside her completely, she needed to know.

"You have my heart, Mairey, my soul."

His heart! Oh, Jack—! Mairey was still soaring from the

splintering, skyrocketing pleasure, still clutching him against her and riding his thermals up and up into the brightness. The crests came and went and came again, catching her up like a gadabout feather, with Jack the wind and her wings.

Her marvelous dragon reared up, nostrils wide and scenting, his sinew and flesh glistening bronze with sweat. He bellowed her name, caught up her bottom into his splayed fingers and then plunged into her, far, far deeper than he had been before, hotter still, and again and again and again. Then, with a convulsive groan, he filled her with a rapturous, spilling heat; his seed, a gift she would cherish always, but forever grieve because it would find no purchase in her womb tonight.

And she wept.

Like a great spent beast falling back to earth, Jack lowered himself to his elbows, snorting air in huge gulps, his muscles still quivering, his hips still pulsing into her. He whispered, "This, Mairey, my delicious love, is what happened to Balforge and his princess."

She kissed his mouth, where he tasted of salt and their own erotic fragrance. "You mean she gave herself to him like a wanton?"

"She did. Repeatedly." He was still inside her, less full now but a tumid congestion that made her want him again. Right now. "They made love through the night—"

"I'd like that, too."

His dark eyes had taken on a brilliant and determined gleam. "And, much to the joy of everyone in their kingdom, they were married the next day."

Her heart ka-thumped, and then somersaulted; terror and joy mingled as sizzling steam.

"Married?" Please God, he can't be thinking that! Wasn't! "A princess can't marry a dragon." She tried to sound scholarly, but he was sliding his huge hand between them to cover her breast, finding her nipple with his fingers. That delicate twist, a husbandly fondness that made her gasp.

"Oh, yes you can, Mairey." He was making slow and devastating love to her ear, to the ridges and the valleys, with his teeth and with his tongue.

"Me, Jack? Why would I marry a dragon?"

His eyes glittered darkly when he turned her chin. "Because you love me as madly as I love you."

Panicked, but slowed by languid limbs and an overwhelming love for him, Mairey tried to scramble out from under his weight, but he was as solid as a mountain, lazing on her like a sun-sated lizard. "I don't like the way this story ends, Jack."

"It's the only possible way." He shifted onto his elbow, his breathing still ragged; still dallying with her nipple, a tether of bliss between them that she couldn't break for the budding pleasure that was stirring her hips to move again. "You couldn't possibly believe I would take your virginity and then leave you?"

"You took nothing from me, Jack; I gave myself to you willingly."

"Brazenly, my dear." She felt a dreadful loss when he shifted his legs and slipped out of her. A plea was on her tongue to call him back, but he replaced his fullness with his inflaming fingers, and she was filled again with the shock of bliss.

"Oh, Jack!"

He laughed gently against her ear. "Another reason that I love you, Mairey."

And, shameless bandit that she was, she took his stroking as she had his shaft, her hips meeting and matching him, crying out his name only a moment later, clinging to him, thrusting against him until she was exhausted and breathless. More in love with him than she could ever imagine.

And sadder than she'd ever been in her life.

"There, sweet. You love me."

"Sexual urges," she managed between close-caught breaths that threatened to be sobs.

"In some, perhaps, but not in you, Mairey—else we would have consummated our heady alliance weeks ago." He nuzzled her neck, her throat, a sated beast toying with a bedazzled mouse. "Under your desk and mine, in the greenhouse and in the broom closet at Windsor. But I would never do that to you, Mairey, and you wouldn't do that to us. Not without love; not without commitment."

"It's impossible, Jack. I can't marry you." She wriggled out from under him and pressed up against the bank of pillows at the headboard, frightened of his certainty and of the vistas he offered. "Please, Jack, don't ask me."

"I already have, my love. And I do again. Marry me. Miss Faelyn."

"No."

He was braced on his elbows, and her legs were spread on either side of his shoulders, knees bent, his face between her thighs and fire blazing in his eyes. Her pulse was still primed for whatever magic he planned, her heart a tattered wreck. But he reached beneath her and the pillows and dragged out a fistful of pristine, white sheet. With indescribable tenderness, he wiped the dampness from her thighs and her belly and the place they had joined.

"We are alloyed, Mairey." The sheet was wet and blood-streaked, the stark evidence of a fairy tale gone terribly awry. He bent his head and kissed her belly; held her with the whole of his hand, his palm pressing against her as though to keep his seed from leaving her. "You and I, and the rest of our lives."

The Willowmoon was her life, apart and separate from Jack. It must always stay that way. She loved him too dearly to hurt him, and that's what would happen in the midst of some distant happiness. They would find the Knot and she would have to leave him, stealing his children and his dreams from him, when all he had wanted from her was love and family.

"I love you, Mairey. We have children to make together. Can't you see that?"

She *could* see it plainly, and it made her weep.

He left his splendorous kiss between her breasts and on her mouth as he rose on his knees and carried her onto his lap. She took him inside her again gladly, let him increase and come and spill himself into her, until he was kissing the tears from her eyes and off her breasts. "There, now. We'll marry tomorrow—"

"No, Jack. I can't!" She shoved at him, taking unfair advantage of his still-fevered embrace to scramble away, across the bed and over the side away from him. "Don't say that! I can't."

He looked so endearingly confused, confessing his love so plainly, his plans for a splendid marriage and even more splendid children.

"Why? Do you have an appointment in the morning?"

"Yes."

Jack could only stare at his love, was thoroughly confounded by her stubborn refusal of his marriage proposal, and vastly in love with the lunatic. She was standing in the middle of the room as gloriously naked as the day she was born, lying to him about some damned appointment that she thought would impede their wedding day.

"Consider it canceled, sweet. You and I are getting married tomorrow morning." He swung out of bed himself and turned up a lamp to better gauge what Mairey was thinking in her addled head.

"No!" She put her hand out and backed away, as though that would stop him. "I can't marry you at all, Jack. Not ever!"

He walked forward toward her. "Why can't you marry me?"

She countered his steps backward, wringing her hands. "Actually, I'm—"

"Already married?"

"No!"

He'd been joking, but was relieved to hear her furious denial. She was a complicated creature; had contrary views on life that few other women would ever entertain. He'd gained three steps on her while she stood fox-frozen in place.

"Then why, Mairey? Are you in love with another man? Sir Dithering Walsham of the Tower, perhaps?" This one made his heart stop as he waited.

"You can't be serious!" The very best answer in the universe; loaded with satisfyingly appalled horror. She bumped up against his tall-winged reading chair, took a backward step up onto the seat, and stuck her heels into the cushion.

"I'm not serious about Walsham, Mairey. But I am certain that you love me."

"I don't."

"You do. And I love you."

"It won't work between us."

"It already has." He was wreathed in her scent.

"No!" She laced her fingers, pleading, her nose so close to his he could feel her exhaling. "We're different people: I'm a scholar and you're a viscount."

"Then wedding me would make you Countess Scholar, I believe." He knelt in the chair, enjoying the view as lamplight played on her bobbing breasts, the sight making him hard again and aching for her. "We'll change the Rushford escutcheon, my love. Add a phallus *rampant* and a willow leaf *environed*."

"This isn't a joking matter, Jack."

"I've never been so damned serious in all my life. You *are* my life."

"What about our search for the Willowmoon Knot?" She closed her arms under her breasts, which only pushed them higher, nearer. "It's ... I've got work to do."

"And so have I." He hadn't expected to have to convince Mairey to be his wife, but he would meet the project head on.

"But the Willowmoon has nothing to do with the two of us marrying and raising up children together."

"But it does, Jack!" That launched her into a full-flight panic. "It has *everything* to do with it!"

He hadn't noticed the fear in her eyes before, couldn't imagine where it was coming from. She wasn't prone to female jitters in any form.

"How does a silver mine have anything to do with us?"

She opened and closed her mouth a few times, before she snorted and threw out a laugh. "I'm your employee."

"You're the woman I want to spend all my days with."

"No! We're partners."

"And friends, I think.."

"I don't love you. I *don't!*"

Protesting too much, my dear?

"Ballocks." She looked small and lost, goose-fleshed and shivering from head to toe. He wasn't sure what was frightening her about his proposal, but he'd be damned if he gave up without a fight. "Tell me why we shouldn't be married. One reasonable reason might satisfy me, though I'm confident that there are none. Debate me with your cons."

"I … I don't have to tell you anything." Her lower lip stuck out in a weepy pout.

"My turn, Mairey. The pros: I am irrevocably in love with you. I am obscenely rich, and well-behaved *most* of the time. I love your Aunt Tattie and your hat, your courage and stubbornness, your almost frightening intellect, and I am mad about your precocious sisters. Who unanimously agree that I should marry you without delay."

She closed her hands over her mouth, her eyes wide in horror. "You discussed our marriage with them?"

"Briefly, but at their instigation. They are wiser than most, those three. And you are my life, Mairey. To the end of my days."

"No, Jack." That faint keening of his name, that plaintive whimper, tugged his heart up into his throat. Then huge tears suddenly pooled in her eyes, soupier than before, spilling over her cheeks in a great wash. She sobbed, her whole sweet face crumpling and working, her shoulders hunched and quaking.

Hellfire! This proposal wasn't going at all well. "I refuse to say that I'm sorry I love you, Mairey. I won't. It's the bloody truth. If you'll just tell me how I offend you—"

"No, Jack, you don't! It's just that—" A hiccoughing belly-sob shook her. "You're ... you're just too ... too—"

"Too what?" He was ready for the worst.

"Too *wonderful*." She was howling again in her inexplicable anguish.

"I'm too—" *Wonderful?* Not greedy or pigheaded, not an unredeemable monster? Wonderful he could work with. Irresistible might take a few days.

"So—" a hiccough. "Soooo—" Another sob. "So, you'd better just forget about meeeee."

Jack tucked her chin over his shoulder and held her close, letting her tears fall while he tried his most *wonderful* to soothe her.

"Ah, Mairey, if I've learned anything in eighteen years of waiting for my life to begin, if I've learned anything from you at all, it's that I must champion my family with my bare hands and that I must love them relentlessly, as I love you."

Which only brought on more weeping, and led finally, blissfully, in the wee hours of the morning, to a fevered bout of lovemaking that set Jack's ears ringing and had Mairey crooning his name in a most encouraging way.

CHAPTER 17

"I won't, damn you! I *can't!*" Mairey stood all alone in the parlor of the lodge, bloody talking to herself, stuffing her most recent notes from the *Gazetteer* into her work-satchel, and snuffling away the tears that seemed to burst forth in floods of biblical proportions whenever she thought about Jackson Rushford.

Which was so *bloody* often she'd not only picked up his infernal cursing but she'd also lost the ability to clear her mind of the man's influence, of his smile, the memory of his kisses, and his so damnably dear proposal of marriage.

Six weeks ago Jack had declared his love and proposed marriage, and since then had led an unflaggingly romantic campaign toward meeting that resolution. Leave it to the impossibly arrogant, pig-headed man to be so dreadfully honorable after deflowering a thoroughly eager virgin.

Marry Jack Rushford? Now, *there* was a cautionary tale to be collected and cataloged as a warning to all women, today and forevermore. Never judge a dragon by the thickness of his armor, for it may be guarding a heart of pure gold.

In those early days, she'd believed the Viscount Jackson

Rushford her greatest enemy, had mounted a fierce battle against him, driving her weapons of lies and deceit into the deepest part of him. Now those very weapons were poised to strike at her own heart, her failing strategy an even greater threat to the Willowmoon than she could ever have imagined.

Even now the man was dogging her every move, eager to accompany her on today's trip into the catacombs of the British Museum, sniffing after the ripening scent of the Willowmoon Knot, no longer confused by the scent of red herrings.

To make matters worse, he was damnably cheery, ruthlessly loving, collected breathlessly willing kisses from her, and paid no attention at all to her rebuffs.

"Please, Jack, I can't possibly marry you. Ever." Which, she had to admit, in recent days had become downright indistinguishable from her encouragements.

She couldn't help it. He was masterfully cunning in his crusade. The girls crowded him with their love, had charmed him out of a pony for each, and he took it all in his stride, like a huge old hound who didn't mind having his ears pulled, but who would tear out the throat of anyone who tried to harm his family.

His family: that's what they all had become to him. No longer a substitute for the one he'd lost so long ago, but a new beginning which, as he so often declared in that charming way of his, he was pursuing relentlessly.

How cruel it would be to deny him a minute of his newfound happiness, would haunt her all her days if she did. Just as he haunted her nights with his heat, his kindness, the low growl of pleasure deep in his throat whenever he kissed her. She hadn't been sleeping well lately, flopping around in her bed until her nightgown was damp with sweat and her head was spinning in circles.

A spinning that sometimes tilted the ground, even in the middle of the day.

Her stomach gave a rolling lurch, breakfast bubbled and squeaked for a moment, and settled only when she sat down and gripped the edge of the table to stop it from whirling.

"He's here, Mairey, dear." Tattie came trilling through the arch, beaming back at whoever was following her—as if Mairey couldn't tell who that was. "His lordship has come for you."

Jack filled up the doorway with his height, and her heart to the very brim with his courting smile. Relentlessly.

"Good morning, my love," he said, as though they were intimately alone and the world belonged just to them, and her aunt wasn't glancing eagerly between the two of them, patting her hands together, ready to applaud, or pray, or both. "You look good enough to eat."

"Lord Rushford, please!" Mairey frowned at him, but flushed to the tips of her breasts, which had become tender and weighty since that night she'd spent in his arms.

His smile grew lazy and wicked as he leaned against the jamb, obviously aware of the crimson blush staining her cheeks —and proud that he'd caused it.

Aunt Tattie only giggled—not a dignified sound from a woman of her age and refinement. "Doesn't our Mairey look pretty today?"

"More lovely every day, Tattie. Have you noticed? She puts the sun and the moon to shame."

More giggling from a woman who had been perfectly sane and a dangerous she-wolf when they'd first arrived. Now Aunt Tattie was Jack's chief promoter.

"Doesn't his lordship look especially fine today, Mairey?" Maybe even a bloody conspirator.

Damn the man for his persistence. And bless him for all the rest. "We'd best get going. It's nearly eight."

"And our Clarence awaits at the house." He proffered a proper elbow. "If you'll allow me the pleasure, my dear?"

"Absolutely not," she said to another of his artfully disguised proposals.

When he only smiled in reply, she sighed and took his arm, treasuring its warmth, painfully aware that she was playing with the most dangerous kind of fire.

Even the Drakestone carriage seemed too small for Jack's lanky frame, his head just inches below the ceiling, the foot-well hardly wide enough for his bent legs. Whether he sat beside her or across from her, riding with him was an intimate affair. Today he lounged in the seat opposite, his knees outside hers, his gaze attentive and too loving.

"I missed you yesterday, Mairey."

I miss you always, Jack.

He'd been in Manchester again, systematically combing the many parish registries and orphanage files for records of his sisters. She'd gone with him the first time, to show him his mother's grave. He left a fistful of flowers that Anna had picked, quiet tears that made her ache for him all the more, and made a stalwart promise to find his sisters.

He had fired Dodson with an amazing amount of restraint.

"If I kill him, Mairey, I'll go to jail," he'd told her. "I'll never find my sisters, and I'll never be able to take you to wife. The bastard isn't worth it."

Then he had taken up his own investigation with all the fervor of a zealot newly come to a demanding God.

He was very good at research, at tracking down a resource, had a memory for names and dates and places that made him even more dangerous. Because, unfortunately, he had trans-ferred this newfound skills to the investigation of the Willow-moon Knot.

"I'm sorry I couldn't go to Manchester with you this time,

Jack. But you found a name that might lead you to Emma." He'd come home to the lodge elated, but wounded by his efforts, and needing a family to share in his joy. Her family. She had slipped into his embrace without thinking and had stayed far too long.

"A slim lead. I still can't believe that it's come to me so quickly." His grin was so natural and hopeful. "I've drafted letters to three manor houses, asking to see their employment records. The letters went out in this morning's post."

"And you did all this without me." She hadn't left him stranded.

"*Because* of you, Mairey." He leaned across the cab and captured her gloved hands in his. "Marry me today. I have the special license my pocket."

A new tactic, this convenient license. "Jack, I can't marry you. I've told you."

"Actually, you've never given me a single reason to refuse me, when I can think of a million reasons for us to share our lives. Starting with the love we feel for each other. Unrestrained and open, passionate, and a hell of a lot of fun. Then there is Anna. Caro. Poppy. Your aunt, and our unborn children. Family. And your damned phallus collection."

"Jack, please." He found her smile and made the most of it, nuzzled her chin and then planted a row of kisses along her jaw.

"Then, my love, there's the prospect of sharing a nightly bath in the same tub. We've more duck houses to build for Poppy and riding lessons for Caro, not to mention fending off the sweaty-palmed young men who will soon be courting Anna in the parlor."

"She's only ten."

"Oh, love, time goes by so quickly." He was so reasonable, so plausible in his dreaming. "And of course, stretching out as far as we can see, is our search for the Willowmoon Knot and all that silver. Partners, remember?"

He might as well have hit her in the stomach. She shoved at

his shoulders and sat upright, banging her head against the little window behind her. She tried not to look his way, tried not to care that she had injured his pride once again.

"All I ask, Mairey, is that you give me one reason we shouldn't be married. Do that and I'll stop asking."

He stared at her, waited for her answer, his eyes so earnest, his gaze so filled with love, she turned away and watched the lorries go by.

I can't marry you, dear Jack, because I love you far too much.

The expansion of the British Museum was only eleven years old, and already its storage vaults were bursting at their seams with new artifacts arriving weekly from Egypt and the Orient, the priceless and the profane crammed into every square inch of space that wasn't used for display in the exhibit halls.

With the aid of clues she'd uncovered among the volumes of the *Gazetteer* and Jack's Moses-like letters of patent that seemed to open any door, they were once again in a cool, airless basement, alone with some of the greatest treasures of civilization.

Knowing Jack's eagerness to join the hunt, she had prepared a false set of notes for him, and had sent him whistling off to a vault around the corner from where she had intended to start searching.

If the astonishing and highly secret theory she'd formed from the *Gazetteer* was correct, that the Knot had somehow made its way from Yorkshire into the possession of the amateur archaeologist Sir Edmund Larkenfield before 1778, then it might well have been donated or sold to the British Museum in 1810, along with the rest of Larkenfield's collection of antiquities, which had remained scattered through the museum's warren of rooms and corridors, virtually unpacked and uncataloged, for nearly fifty years.

As Mairey studied her own encrypted notes, she was struck by a wave of guilt, of deceit that made more of those fat tears form in her eyes, made her stomach pitch again with regret.

Deception. She was an expert at it now, playacting. She could have gone on the stage for all her skill, would have been the talk of London with her sleight of hand.

The only way forward was to let Jack go on believing her lies, that they were working together toward the same goal, to find the Willowmoon Knot. Should that ever come to pass, she would have to steal the Knot and vanish with her family before he even knew she'd found it. Where she would go on living secretly in her village, unmarried, existing on the sweet memories of her handsome dragon. Where Jack would surely go on searching for her and their treasure until his hair grayed and his shoulders stooped, until the light in his eyes had dulled.

Oh, Jack, I'm so sorry! She had only come this close to their treasure because of the excellent man she could hear in the next room, earnestly opening boxes and cabinet doors. She'd never felt so wicked, or so angry at the world. She loved Jack as she loved her life, and all this deception was beginning to drown her.

Deception. Distraction. Sleight-of-hand.

Yet, there was something possibly marvelous lurking within all these convoluted truths, a way forward she'd never considered before today, probably because finding the Knot had never seemed so possible before. The clues were so vivid now, the trail hotter than ever. Which made her wonder what would happen after she had rescued it, after the disk of silver was tucked safely away in the glade?

What then?

A little bell of jangling, implausible joy began to ring faintly in her head. Had she been thinking in all the wrong directions? Plotting against him, when she ought to be plotting his happiness.

What if she *did* find the Knot today, or any day. And what if Jack *wasn't* working beside her at the time? What if he never actually saw it? Then he could never identify the markings, never even know it had been found. Therefore—and this was the glory-cloud miracle and their happy ending—therefore, he could never use the map as the route to the silver.

Oh, yes! A fantastical pantomime was mounting itself in her brain. Magic lamps, mistaken identities, music and dancing. And a pair of lovers whose stars might just become uncrossed.

Let's say that she opened this random drawer in front of her and found the Willowmoon Knot lying there, winking at her, saying, "Good morning, Miss Faelyn. I've been waiting for you." Once she'd picked herself off the floor, all she'd have to do would be to pocket the disk and say nothing to Jack.

The Knot would be gone for good, as simply as that, no longer a threat.

And should she find it, the Knot would burn like molten lead in her satchel, her guilt a shuttered beacon condemning her for a liar. But at the end of that wonderful day, after *pretending* to look for it, after combing through the catacombs with Jack, his partner, his love, the mother of all his unborn children, she would just leave the museum, clinging to his steadfast arm, savoring the weight of the Willowmoon as it jostled against her thigh.

She would feast on the sunlight, as Jack escorted her down the wide stairs and into Great Russell Street. She might even stop him on the steps and kiss the daylights out of him. Yes, she would definitely do that. In fact, she'd make love to him on the way home in the Clarence, and then demand that they be married the very next day.

How the dear man would like that.

Then when Jack went on another of his treks to Manchester or to one of his mines, she would take a quick day-trip to her village, bury the Knot where it would never, ever be found again, then make it home in time to have dinner with her husband.

A fairy tale come true! Why hadn't she thought of it before? Once the Willowmoon Knot was discovered, it merely had to vanish again without a trace. There was nothing in the Faelyn family pledge that demanded she entomb herself with the Knot like one of the pharaoh's servants. She didn't have to hide out like a bandit, because no one would ever know that she'd taken it, especially not Jack. Once she'd rescued it and its map was removed from public memory, then her job was done.

And her life with Jack could begin.

She stood in awe of this pantomime. It was very good.

A flawless plan.

But would only work if Jack never *ever* saw the Willowmoon Knot. That was the trick, the deception that would make all the difference. Whether she found the Knot here at the British Museum or at the Ashmolean or in Queen Victoria's stocking drawer, she could *never* let him know about it.

For that would be the end of everything—her dreams and his. The children that they would never have.

He was as rich as Croesus, contented, titled, and he had no need at all for a silver mine. Once the Knot was safely buried and she was in complete control of its destiny, they could spend years, wonderful decades, looking for it together. A hobby. A family game. The Rushford legacy. How lovely!

Still, she couldn't risk a marriage to him, yet; not until she'd found and hidden the Knot from him. Because if he should ever see it, then she'd be forced to steal away into the night, to disappear with her sisters, and Jack's children—for she could never leave them behind, and retreat to the safety of her village, to vanish from his life as though she'd never existed.

And that would destroy him completely.

There was one path to their happiness, and it was up to her to find the Knot—quickly.

All this heady excitement had winded her. She must remember to breathe more often; she was dizzy again, and not quite right in the stomach.

But she was certainly well enough to rescue her dragon from his lonely cave.

~

Jack tried again to make sense of Mairey's notes. Hellfire, nothing she'd done in the last six weeks had made any sense to him. He asked daily for her hand, confessed his uncompromising, unconditional love for her.

And daily he heard, along with a deluge of weeping, "I love you, Jack, but I can't marry you! I can't! No matter how often you ask."

But then the baffling woman would immediately follow her refusal by throwing her arms around his neck and making love to his mouth.

Only last week she had vehemently refused him and then proceeded to seduce him in the greenhouse. She'd pushed him onto a bench, lifted her skirts, unfastened his trousers, and sat down on him.

Blazes, the memory of her sighing ecstasies still made him hard and quick, even now as he carefully picked through a box of broken pottery. Made him more resolved than ever to marry her. They belonged together, he and Mairey; they deserved a life with the girls and Tattie and all the children that would come from their remarkable union.

This damned Willowmoon Knot seemed to be at the root of all her apprehensions, which made no sense at all. They were after the same thing, surely for the same purpose.

But Mairey's obsession with the Knot had never sat right with him. Disproportional loyalty to her father? A symbol of her independence? Wealth of her own? Pride?

His only course was to find the blasted thing. The truth would be there in its mysterious knotwork. A truth that Mairey would have to unravel for him.

The *Gazetteer* hadn't specifically cataloged a silver crest of pagan design, or anything named Willow or Moon or Willow-crest, or any derivation thereof. Despite all logic to the contrary, his stubborn, faultless mentor with the silver-flecked eyes seemed to think that the Knot might have at least been here in the museum at one time, and stored with a collection of twelfth-century Scottish plate-ware.

He had learned a great deal from Mairey about the fine art of detection. Despite the heady distractions of her rose-scented hair when it slipped out of its prison of pins and pencils, despite her earthy laughter, and his perpetual state of arousal whenever she was within sniffing distance, he was indeed learning to read between the lines of a cryptic text and form a whole image out of its mismatched parts.

Which was why boxes labeled "Larkenfield" had caught his interest when he'd begun searching the vault Mairey had assigned him. The *Gazetteer* listed the man as a collector of ecclesiastical antiquities. The name was memorable to Jack in that Larkenfield had been not only a minor figure in British archaeology during the last century but also a Yorkshireman and a canon of York Minster for fifteen years. Odd that Mairey hadn't noticed the connection. At least she hadn't included it in her notes.

Had Larkenfield been a petty thief? Had he pilfered the minster's storage rooms over the years and assembled a collection of long-forgotten antiquities to grace his mantelpiece? To sell? Barring that intrigue, Larkenfield might even have purchased the pieces from the diocese.

Well! A theory! And he'd devised it all on his own!

Mairey would be quite proud. And best of all, if they found the Knot today she'd have no reason not to marry him.

"God willing, Mairey Faelyn, Sir Larkenfield will bring our family together." Jack tucked Mairey's confusing notes into his jacket pocket and found her where he'd left her, diligently sifting through fat drawers of wood shavings cushioning singular items of Celtic enamel work.

"I have a theory, my love," he said from the doorway.

"Jack!" The eyes that found him were feverish with an elation that seemed to have startled her. Despite the breadth of her grin, her cheeks were chalky and her hands were as damp as though she'd just washed them.

"Have you found the Willowmoon then, Mairey?" He kissed her forehead, fearing that she was ill. "Can we go home and be married?"

"No, Jack! But—" The woman held the rest of her sentence inside her smile, then hooked his neck with both hands and planted a sultry kiss on his mouth, following it with a dozen more all over his face.

"Very nice, my love. Very, *very* nice." Jack just stood there, enjoying her assault, knowing better than to ask where she'd found such happiness.

She finished abruptly and stood back to study him, as though she hadn't seen him in years. She sighed, so blissfully happy that Jack's hopes soared. "You said you have a theory, Jack? Something to do with the Scottish plateware?"

"No. With an archaeologist named Larkenfield."

"Who?" A forlorn hooting, a baby owl lost in the woods. The chalkiness increased to gray. She sat down hard on a tall stool.

"That's it, Mairey. We're going home." He stooped to pick her up. "You're not well."

"No! I have to stay." She twisted out of his embrace and pushed away. "I'm just tired, Jack. Tired of everything." There came the tears again. "I'll rest while you tell me your theory. Go ahead."

"Then sit." Confused, he handed her his kerchief and

watched her carefully as he detailed Larkenfield's many connec-
tions to the Willowmoon Knot, expanding on his earlier theory
that Larkenfield might have been a petty thief, puffing out his
chest because it all sounded as plausible as any theory they'd
followed yet.

His audience listened raptly, sat patiently on the stool, her
fingers white-knuckled and laced in her lap. She wiped at her
brow twice, but by the time he had finished, she looked much
improved and was ready with her questions.

"That's very good, Jack. Where do you plan to look first? In
the Yorkshire registries?"

"I'll start in here with you."

"Why?"

"The name Larkenfield, for one. It's on labels all over these
rooms here."

"Really! I hadn't noticed." She read her way across a shelf of
boxes. "Why, you're right, Jack. Mmm ... to save time, why don't
we each take a room. We'll cover twice as much and be finished
in half the time."

"You'll be all right in here alone?"

"Why wouldn't I be?"

"Because you look like you've seen a ghost." Pale as one, at
least.

"I haven't been sleeping well."

"Neither have I, love. And you know why." He kissed her
cheek again; satisfied that it was cool and dry. Her mouth
was wet and ready for him, and she was tugging him closer,
her fingers making inroads through the buttons of his
waistcoat.

If she was going to run hot today, he was going to make
damn sure she knew he was just as hot. He clamped his hands
over her backside and pressed her belly against his erection.

"Jack, you're—"

He stopped her hand from slipping between them. "Indeed,

my dear." He inhaled cool air through his nostrils. "But this is a museum."

"I love you, Jack."

His heart slammed against his chest. "Marry me then."

Her eyes were awash with those tugging tears again, and he could hardly credit his hearing when she said, "Someday, Jack. With just the right miracle."

"Someday?" He nearly crowed.

She didn't say "no" this time. She said "someday." Someday could be next month or next Tuesday.

Deciding to leave the subject hovering there between them, he tipped her chin to better kiss her, delved deeply, and then left her sighing.

If she wanted a miracle, he'd just have to give her one.

As he opened overstuffed drawers and dangerously stacked cabinets full of close-packed effigies and musical instruments made of dried gourds, and well-endowed wooden icons from some warmer clime, he realized that the Larkenfield collection had never been uncrated because it was nothing more than the busy nest of an eccentric.

Clay whistles and seedpod rattles and feathered headpieces, all of them musty and inscrutably sorted, by alphabet or color, or size, he couldn't tell.

Unwilling to give up on his perfectly good theory, he sorted his way to the bottom of a large trunk, past hefty pieces of stone gargoyles, brass bosses, and—

"Ha!" His heart took a shuddering leap. All these things were Celtic! He had learned that much. Definitely Celtic. The serpentine interlacing on a bowl. The broken hilt of a dagger wrapped in the unsubtle patterns of nature that turned and turned back and forth upon each other.

Mairey had taught him the elements that marked the style; he'd even begun to see them in his sleep.

So there was some sort of order to Larkenfield's collection.

Ecclesiastical *and* Celtic. Exactly the sort of items that might have been lifted from the catacombs of the minster at York.

He picked more carefully through the trunk, looking for Mairey's silver disk. There was knotwork aplenty, but only in wood and stone and ivory. Thoroughly disappointed, and glad that he hadn't called Mairey to come look, he repacked the items, nearly forgetting the flat, ironbound coffer he'd set aside when he'd begun rifling through the trunk.

The coffered rattled when he picked it up, a weighty mass that slid back and forth inside. He popped the little hasp and opened the domed lid. Bird's nests, of all things. Hummingbirds, by the size and shimmer of the feathers still poking from the intricately woven grasses.

He lifted away each of the three nests, expecting more brass bosses or the myriad cloak clasps that littered the halls of antiquity.

Indeed, there were two more gold-encrusted cloak clasps. And below them—

A silver disk, beautifully Celtic. Intricate and undulating with all its asymmetric tendrils, each of which ended in long narrow leaves. The willow. A ridge of chevrons. And the four phases of the moon.

And if all that hadn't convinced Jack, hadn't made his heart race with joy, when he turned over the disk he found a paper label adhered to the back, and on it, in a long-ago hand someone had written,

The Willowmoon Knotte. Source unknowne.

"Mairey!" He shouted her name and whooped, stuffed the precious disk into his jacket pocket, and the clasps and the nests back into the coffer.

"Bloody blazes, woman, come quickly!" She ought to be here with him to see for herself. She ought to have been the one to find it, the first to hold it, to feel its coolness on her palm. The triumph was hers; he was only her grateful, awe-struck apprentice.

"Mairey!" He listened eagerly for the footfalls that should already have come flying into the room. He couldn't wait to see the joy light her face when he reached into his pocket and unfolded the Willowmoon.

Bright silver and unimaginable joy would be the hue of her eyes today. Tonight, they would be the smoky gray of a married woman, or at least a betrothed one.

He stuffed everything back into the trunk so that no one would be the wiser, fighting the forces of nature that had expanded the contents to twice their original size.

The Willowmoon Knot! A step toward finding the old Celtic silver mine. The most important step of all, for it had brought him and Mairey together. A miracle, indeed.

He slid the trunk back into place, then sprinted down the hall toward Mairey, calling her name again and again. He reached the jumbled room at a run, expecting to find her distracted by her notes and her burrowing.

"Mairey!" His heart slid to a stop, then dropped into his gut.

She was lying face up on the floor, her limbs bent like a string puppet's and her face sickly white, an enameled bowl fallen from her hand.

"My God, Mairey!" He scooped her into his arms, raw panic surging through him. He couldn't lose her to some stray illness. Her arms hung limp as a rag while he bent to listen to her heart.

"Thank God!" It thumped solidly against her chest, a blessing from the heavens. He cuddled her against him, brushed her dry lips with his mouth and stayed to feel her warm, strong breath against him.

"Mairey, wake up!" She must have fainted dead away.

But she was already blinking awake, wetting her lips with her delicate pink tongue, and making sighing, good-morning noises in her chest. She yawned broadly and stretched, as contented as a fairy princess roused by her prince's kiss.

"We really shouldn't be making love here, Jack." She reached up and ran her fingers through his forelocks, twirled a hank and pulled him closer with it, whispering, "Not in the basement of the British Museum. Someone will see."

Light-headed with relief, he stood with her in his arms. "We weren't making love, Mairey. You fainted."

"I don't think so. I must have been overcome by your kiss. Snow White in reverse, my prince." She wagged her finger at him. "I know my fairy tales."

Undoubtedly, but at the moment she was in no shape to diagnose her own condition.

"A healthy woman doesn't just faint without reason. You wear no stays, and besides, you've looked ill for a week."

"I feel perfectly fine now, Jack. You can put me down."

"Not on your life." Taking no chances with his lady love, he carried her and her satchel up the stairs and out of the museum. He gladly suffered more of her kisses on the step, but didn't set her down until he had dropped with her into the seat of his carriage, where she seemed intent upon finding a way into his trousers.

"Doctor Timson, in Kensington," he called to his driver. "Quickly!"

Jack listened outside Timson's examination room, his ear stuck blatantly to the panel. Timson's murmuring monotone. Mairey's clear voice, made unintelligible through two inches of oak and the swooshing of blood in his head.

Though he'd known Charles Timson since returning to England, the doctor had steadfastly refused to allow Jack in the room while he was examining Mairey. Certainly he trusted him, one of the few in the British Empire who was both a physician and a surgeon. He'd consulted with him on the destructive health effects of mining, and together they were working on a bill to put through the Commons.

But hell, he'd seen every inch of the woman without her clothes. And she was the least modest woman he'd ever met. He just wanted to know what had been plaguing her and how he could help.

He rapped on the door with his fist. "Hurry up in there!"

Silence. He paced the labyrinthine pattern in the oak floor, glared out the window, studied the roadway of blood vessels on the ghoulish diagram on Timson's wall, then stuck his hands into his pockets.

The Willowmoon Knot! Bloody hell, he'd forgotten! He fished the piece out to study it, but was too wracked with questions and worry, and the symbols were gibberish to him. Mairey would have to translate.

Mairey. He paced some more while he carefully wrapped the Knot in his kerchief and buried it safely in the bottom of his deepest coat pocket. He'd surprise her with it when this was all over. Tonight, after dinner at the lodge, when everyone was asleep, and they were alone in the parlor.

The latch clicked and Timson came through the door, drying his hands on a towel. Jack peered past the man's shoulder, fighting the urge to shove him out of the way. Mairey was sitting on a padded table, her small, straight back to the door. She turned and met his gaze, wide-eyed as a doe in a meadow.

"She'll be out in a minute, Jack." Timson shut the door firmly.

"Damn it, Charles! What's the matter with her? Will she be all right?"

"Eventually." Timson removed the spectacles that hid his gray eyebrows and buffed the lenses with the corner of the towel.

"Eventually! What the hell does that mean?" His stomach reeled with apprehension. Mairey sick, suffering. "Tell me now!"

Timson stuck his spectacles back on and peered owlishly at Jack over the end of his nose, relishing a secret of some sort. "It means, Jack, old man, that you're going to be a father."

"I'm—" The whole blessed world stopped on its axis while he held his breath and waited for the humming of his heart to settle. "What?"

"Miss Faelyn is pregnant."

A father! And a husband. "Ohhhh, yes!"

A surge of joy drove him through the doorway of the sunlit examination room. Mairey was standing in the middle of the room, shoving her arms into her jacket.

"Mairey, my love!" As sylvan and beautiful as the woods she adored, the rhythm of his pulse and the meaning of his life.

"Jack. I'm—" Her eyes were brilliant stars and lit with wonder; her cheeks glowed. "We're going to have a baby."

"Yes, my love, we are." He couldn't help his grin, or his belly laugh as he gathered her into his arms and drew her scent to the center of him. Here was where he wanted to spend his days. He was truly inside of her now, his blood and hers mixed and making everlasting magic. "Ah, Mairey, I love you."

"Jack?"

He held her tightly, not wanting to hear her objections, knowing that they would not stop him from protecting his child, or this woman that he loved. "You'll marry me. Please. Today. Our child will know its father."

"Oh, Jack, I—"

He raised her chin sharply, never so serious in all his life, for his dewy-eyed Mairey and the flower that was budding inside her were everything to him. "I've lost one family to my carelessness, Mairey; I'll not lose another."

Mairey's heart reeled with love for Jack, for the silken thread of miracles that connected them. He wasn't a careless man; he was honorable, principled, and his love, imperishable.

"Well, Mairey?"

I'm sorry, Papa. But the Willowmoon will have to stay hidden for now.

She couldn't risk looking for it now. Not with her husband and their child, their family to protect. The Knot had been safely out of sight for two centuries. And though she was filled with a dark foreboding, it would have to stay put while her children grew, while her marriage bloomed.

"Marry you. Jack?" She put his warm hand on her belly, where their child was sleeping, then slipped her arms around his neck, met his spectacular kiss, and gave him all her dreams. "In a heartbeat, my love."

CHAPTER 18

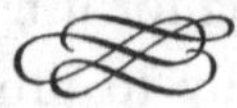

"Are you a princess now, Mairey?"

"Your sister is my *countess*, Caro."

Mairey's intoxicating husband, the vastly handsome Viscount Rushford, looked more like a sagging Christmas tree decorated with squealing little angels than a titled bridegroom freshly home from a hurry-up wedding at the registry office.

Caro was in his arms; Poppy was perched on his shoulders, her arms caught round his head like a mane; and Anna was stuffing a fistful of daisies into every hole in his jacket.

She'd never seen a man so brimming with peace, so alive with happiness. She felt it, too. To her very core. The moment they began sharing their vows, a great calm had swept through her. The driving wind stopped its pestering, and all the voices grew silent. Leading Jack away from the Willowmoon would be critical in the next few years. Of course, he would grumble his frustration, but he would trust her and follow her lead.

And if one day, she did find the Knot at the bottom of some forgotten barrel, her pocket would provide a safe refuge for it until she could take it safely home.

Jack would never know.

Just now he was gazing at her from across the room, his grin lighting his eyes.

Aunt Tattie was beside herself with happiness. "Lord Rushford married your sister, Caro. That makes him your brother-in-law."

"I have a brother!"

"A very *big* brother," Anna said, giving Mairey a bouquet of daisies and a noisy buss on the cheek.

"Just imagine: the pair of you sneaking away today to be married." Tattie dabbed at the corners of her eyes. "Pretending you were off on one of Mairey's trips to the museum, when you might have had a celebration."

"I'm sorry we didn't let you know, Auntie." Mairey gave the woman a guilty hug and looked at Jack across the parlor. "Perhaps we'll have a reception later. You can plan everything."

"I suppose that will do."

"In the meantime, your sister and I will be spending tonight at the main house." Jack's eyes never left Mairey's, even as he let Caro to the ground and disengaged Poppy's arms from around his neck like a grinder and his long-armed monkey. "The rest of you must stay here and pack."

"Are we moving away?" Anna looked stricken.

"Into the main house, of course. If you'd like that." He planted a kiss on top of the girl's head.

That set off a wave of jumping and whooping.

"Now upstairs with you, ladies." Tattie winked at Jack and raised her brows at Mairey, then gave them a little shove toward the door. "You two go along, as well."

Leave-taking took nearly an hour, and included the story of the *Princess and the Pea* in which Mairey was the princess and Jack played the pea and everyone ended up on the floor in a laughing tangle. But as soon as the lodge door closed, and they were safely in the yard, her groom lifted her into his arms.

"I can walk, Jack."

"Yes, my love, but not nearly fast enough." He was already on the wooded path, his shoulder deflecting the overhanging branches while she hung on to his neck.

"Are you in such a hurry then, sir?" She tucked his hair behind his ear to better tease the delicate ridges with her tongue, taking full advantage of his inability to fend off her teasing, which made him sigh and squeeze her closer.

"Indeed. To plow you thoroughly, my countess."

She liked being carried by her husband. And she liked his plow very much. "Your seed is incorrigibly potent, Jack. Probably a boy."

"A son. God bless us, Mairey." He swung off the main path and charged through the understory.

"A shortcut, husband?"

"Privacy. I want to kiss you before I burst."

"An admirable idea." The woods were dewy with the coming night, the highest branches still gilded by the sun and the pale, gentian violet of the sky.

She knew exactly where he was taking her to: the streamside with the enormous, fallen beech along the bank, one side on dry land, the other lying in a few inches of cool water. The thick roots were heavily branched with sinewy twists and tucks. Its smooth gray skin springy with moss.

They'd trysted there twice before. Once at twilight, when the girls were out in the stream catching fairies. A chaste kiss against her cheek, and she'd dreamed about it for the next week. They'd been entirely alone for the second kiss, much longer, deeper, and thoroughly toe-curling.

"Now that we're married, Mairey, I can confess imagining you entirely naked, and waiting for me right here in this very spot. On that very tree."

"Right here?" All that imagination from a man whom she once thought only understood gouging great demonic holes into the earth.

He set her on her feet, bent down, and picked up her stockinged foot. "What happened to your shoes?"

"I lost them down the trail."

He kissed her fully but too briefly and then let her go. "I'll get them. Wait here."

"I'm not going anywhere, husband!" She watched him disappear through the brush, his greatcoat slapping at his calves, off to rescue her shoes. Her very own dragon. Let's see, that would make his child a dragonet.

Though she shouldn't care, she hoped for a boy, a strapping young lad who'd grow up to be his father's reflection. And besides, Jack would indulge a daughter's every whim, and she would grow up hopelessly spoiled.

"Did you really picture me naked here on this tree, Jack?" she called, a bit of wifely mischief catching her imagination.

"Entirely naked," he called back to her from somewhere down the path. "Are you sure you were wearing shoes when we left the lodge?"

"I'm sure!" She grinned and swiftly began working the buttons of her shirtwaist, applauding her husband's inventiveness. Hers was far more risqué and might shock the man to his socks, but she doubted he'd complain.

"What exactly am I doing in this imagination of yours, Jack?" The air was chilly and nipped at her bare breasts. "Just standing there?"

He stopped his brush rattling for a moment. "You are recumbent on the trunk, awaiting my attention."

"Ah!" *Recumbent*, limbs draped like any nymph worth her salt.

She tried not to laugh too loudly as she tossed aside her shirtwaist, stepped out of her skirt, petticoat, camisole and drawers one after the other. She listened carefully to Jack's tramping as she rolled off her stockings and dropped them on the pile of clothes.

She felt wickedly beautiful, a wood nymph awaiting her

satyr. Elfin revels. All the sensuous delights of the late summer forest—dappled shadows and bright water and dancing breezes. Jack's hands, oh, his mouth! Despite the hint of an early autumn, her skin felt as warm as if the sun were playing on her.

"Exactly how would I look as I recumbently awaited you, husband?"

"Lounging exotically, my love, an arm here, a leg there." He was on his way back, all twig-snapping footfalls. "And skin, Mairey—lots of your lovely skin."

"It sounds complicated, Jack. And uncomfortable." She draped herself just so on the fallen tree, lounging her arm exotically along a jaunty root, a leg bent demurely, coyly. Exposing *lots* of skin and other features she was certain Jack would enjoy.

The laurel thrashed and snapped, and suddenly her unsuspecting husband came crashing through the underbrush.

"I found both shoes, Mair—" He came to a full, jolting stop.

"Recumbent like *this*, husband?"

He blinked. Shook his head. Blinked again. And then his eyes grew huge.

"Good God!" Her shoes hit the ground, forgotten. He was with her in a roaring twinkle, straddling the log and her thighs, his greatcoat a glorious tent that trapped his warmth and his spice.

His kisses fell everywhere, expansive and tongue-wet and branding. He coiled her hair in his fist, collected it and scrubbed it over his face with a great sniff. She moaned in her glory as he suckled at her breasts, now so deliciously tender and receptive. He formed his hands like a cradle and murmured against her belly, spoke of precious treasures and miracles.

She opened to him as a moonflower, moaning against his mouth. She was free to be open with him now, truly laughing for the first time in a very long time. His powerful coiling, his wreathing her with his love, hadn't bound her in the least. His love had freed her to love him with all her heart, to be loved by him.

He smelled of a night ride through the forest, his shoulders dusted with bits of moonlight and silver weed. She started working at the buttons on his trouser front, hoping he wouldn't notice. Surprise was the order of this amazing day. Surprise strategies. Surprise babies and weddings.

His buttons were nearly free, and he was bulging against the top of his drawers. So eager. So marvelous. Her hands ached to hold him.

He raised up from where he'd been making love to her breasts, her hungry-eyed husband. "Good God, Mairey, have you any idea what you do to me?"

"I do." The last button, and he sprung free. Aching to explore him to the fullest, she slipped all of that long, velvety thickness between her hands, bent over his hips, and took him directly and firmly into her mouth.

"Ohhhh." Jack thought his brain would burst. He braced his arm on the tree behind him and jammed his heels against the soft ground, which bucked his hips upward and drove him deeper. "Mairey! I want—"

He wanted her to stop—to wait. Until. No!

"Oh, yesssss!" He held his breath and tried to see more than darting stars and Mairey's moonlit hair in his lap. But she had her hand inside his gaping trousers and had scooped up his scrotum; was playing and fondling there while she suckled and tasted and encircled him with her lusty fingers. Oh, the heavens, and the bounteous earth, she'd married him!

"Enough, Mairey."

She sat up and kissed his mouth. "I've been thinking about

this part of you for too long, Jack." Then she went back to her cavorting.

A wife who thinks about his penis! He wanted to hoot, but all he managed was a strangled growl while his wife drove him to lunacy.

"Enough, enough, Mairey!"

He lifted her face between his hands and steadied his breathing while she asked, "Is this what you imagined of me, Jack? Lounging erotically."

"I never, *never* got this far, Mairey. Not nearly!" His commonplace imagination had stopped on the blunt edge of reality, his erotic fantasy arrested by the classical painters of reclining nudes. Lamentable painters with only their art to move them, lacking the smokey fragrance of moss crushed by Mairey's rosy bottom, the silky sleekness of her skin beneath his hands, the feel of her tongue—

"Oh, Jack, I love you!"

And those miraculous declarations of her heart riding on the night wind.

Never had he imagined that he'd find a wife who would tease at his senses in the woods. But that was what came of marrying a nymph.

She had draped her legs over his thighs, leaving her open to him, to cradle his erection and let him tease there, while he made love to her mouth. She unbuttoned his braces at the front and tugged his trousers down his hips.

"Here in the woods, Jack? Should we?" She took him into her hands again, made him growl again and shudder. "To celebrate our marriage?"

"You'll have me baying at the moon, love, and waking everyone up."

She laughed. "Just starters then, and the rest of our wedding night at home, in our bedroom."

A tilt of her hips and she had him poised against all that

luscious slickness, on the brink of thrusting himself into her. He spanned her slender waist with his spread fingers, his arms quaking with restraint.

"Are you happy, my love? You didn't want this marriage."

She caught her lip, and tears sprang to her eyes in the near darkness. "Oh, but I did, Jack. I did with all my heart"

"The child changed your mind?"

"You did. I've never been happier in all my life. Never felt so loved."

"You are."

"Nor quite so naked." She glanced down her length, then up into his eyes.

"You're cold, love. I can see it here." He covered her breast with his palm, hungry for the hard little nipple and its shadowed boundary. He leaned down, drew its twin into his mouth, and warmed it, rolled it.

She sucked air between her teeth and wriggled beneath him, pressing him closer with her enticements.

"Not cold at all, Jack. Just wanting you to come join with me."

"I am astounded, my dear, how our thoughts entwine."

Laughing brightly, her eyes catching all the sparkling grays of the twilight, his unconventional wife laid her hands on top of his and slid them down to fit around the perfect curve of her hips. Then her warm hands disappeared beneath his greatcoat and his shirttails, to seize his bare haunches and give a beckoning shove with her heels.

And she took him just inside her. Just. A suckling pressure around the end of his penis that overwhelmed him and shattered his resolve to take his time.

He hauled her into his arms and propelled himself into her until she sat astride him, her legs hitched up around his waist. He was deeply engulfed, struggling to keep his sanity and his seat while her muscles played him as her fingers had.

"Oh, that's much better." She trembled like the willows that hid them as she gripped his upper arms, rocking on his lap, arching backward and then pitching forward, as though he were a swing and she had plans to soar to the moon.

He wanted this ecstasy to build forever, to fly on the same trajectory as his love, preposterous at first, then undeniable, then absolute and timeless.

"I want your skin against mine, Mairey."

"In our wedding bed." She was clinging to his neck, breathless and sweat-slick, whimpering against his mouth.

"Oh, yes." He found her with his fingers, feverish and damp, her portal filled with his thickness. Her eyes were smokey, her voice sultry and low.

"Oh! Jack! I'm—oh!" She drove against him, arched like the pale crescent moon, her hair streaming silver down her back, her gaze fastened to his. His nymph, his naiad. "I love you so!"

"Ah, wife!" He came unraveled and his release thundered through him along the length of his rod. He thrust deeply, and Mairey took him to the shank. He cocooned her in his arms as he pulsed into her, gushing out his passion.

Mairey felt every long and straining inch of him. Peace came as deeply seated as he was, and all she could do was cling to him, hoarding the last of his shuddering, already feeling the loss that would come when he was no longer inside her.

"The happiest night of my life, Jack."

"And mine." He held her tightly as he kissed her, rocking gently with her in the moonlight, whispering of all the many nights ahead.

She could feel him begin to harden again when something rustled in the brush.

"What was that?" she asked as he closed his coat over her. He pulled out of her and half stood, lifting her up with his arm beneath her backside.

"I am Viscount Rushford, the master here. Come out of hiding, immediately!"

"Blazing toads, Jack! What if it's the girls?" she whispered.

"Impossible—with all their chattering, we'd have heard them a mile away." He pulled a coin out of his pocket and hurled it into the underbrush. "Show yourself!"

A great fluttering and flapping shook the brambles, and a blurring phantom launched itself out of its shadows right at them.

"A hawk owl!"

"Bloody hell!" He clamped his hand over her head and dove to the right, pitching them both into the stream, shifting as he fell to cushion her weight, landing with a growl on his back. She bounced off his chest and then rolled into the calf-deep icy water.

"Heavens, that's cold!" She sat up. "And muddy."

"God, are you all right?" He sputtered, reaching for her as she clambered to her feet in the gravelly bed.

"I'm fine. But you're going to be sore."

"You'll freeze, love. From lack of clothes, from this water— what's so funny?"

She was laughing too hard to reply. He was barely more than a shadow in the pale twilight, and shaking off the water like a hound, hitching up his trousers and fastening them when they wanted to cling to his knees.

He lifted her off her feet and sloshed to the pile of clothes she'd left near the tree. *Their* tree, forever more. "Do you often sport about naked in the woods?" He draped her shoulders with his coat, wet but still warm from his heat.

"Only the occasional bath in a stream when I can't get a room at an inn. Why?"

"I thought as much. Now sit." He found her shoes and stuck

one on her foot. "But no more stream bathing, Lady Rushford, unless you're with me."

"It wouldn't be fun any other way." She stood up when she had both shoes on, stepped into her petticoats and skirt, her hair leaf-strewn and dripping like twisted ropes.

"Then to bed with us both." His grin caught the moonlight as he lifted her into his arms and carried her the rest of the way to the front steps of the main house.

"Welcome to our home, Lady Rushford." He carried her through the door to Drakestone House with pomp, majesty, and a good deal of kissing.

They met Sumner coming down the stairs, frowning at them like a disapproving father. "Good evening, sir."

"You mean good wedding night, Sumner. I'd very much like you to meet the Lady Rushford. We were married today."

"Welcome, my lady." He nodded at Mairey, then wrinkled his nose at their clothes. "I shall have your bathwater drawn."

Mairey soaked up the heat in her bath and scrubbed until her skin was glowing and scented with orange blossoms. Then she tucked herself into their huge bed to await her husband who'd chosen to bathe in the laundry.

"Much quicker," he'd said, with a wink, "and frankly, I welcome the cold water."

His counterpane was silky and lush, the pillows deep. She was warm and sleepy and so contented that she could feel her thoughts drifting.

A dragon lived there in her dreams. A man-shaped one, but with a dragon's heart—as impenetrable as it was predatory. She'd cowered from him at first, afraid he'd tear her family from her. Instead, he held her close, as though he judged her infinitely precious. His eyes were kind, his soul honest. He gave her his child to care for. And when at last the child came, he would be there to soothe her, to call her name—

"Mairey." Mairey, Mairey. He seemed to like her name, liked to whisper it against her mouth, to follow it with his tongue, in the same way he liked to kiss her.

He was big, weighty and warm, like sunlight on a wheat field. And his hands were so able. Oh, yes, able to, *liable* to, do most anything. He could turn a hillside to rubble with a simple gesture, and that still frightened her. But most of all he loved her, loved her family, and gave her children.

Her dream fused seamlessly with her waking, her dragon transformed himself into Jack.

"I love you, Mairey." He was lying beside her, propped on his elbow, claiming her leg with his, tugging at her breast with his lips—little nips, little tugs, and she was making little whimpers to match his rhythm, turned toward him, circling her hips against his astonishing nakedness.

"You are particularly pliant when you're asleep, wife."

"And you are ever-hard, husband. Ever ready."

"Are you?" He found her slickness with his fingers. "Mmmm, you are." He parted her legs with his hands and caressed her until her breasts were ripe and wanting, her hips riding the clouds where his tongue played her, sought her. She rose with his tides, joined in his joyful, raucous surges, until they were both wild and straining against each other and their world was spinning.

Yes, this was life and hope. Jack was her fairy tale come true.

She lost herself in the bliss of their wedding night. Her husband pleasured her for hours and gave her fathomless peace and the whispering of his heart in the quiet that came over them.

It was in the deepest night, while she was cocooned within his arms, where nothing at all could harm her, that Jack suddenly shot up on his elbow, a wild rejoicing in his eyes.

"Bloody hell, Mairey! I forgot!" He kissed her soundly and leaped off the bed. "I can't believe I forgot!"

"Forgot what?"

"Where the devil did I put it?" He took a twice-around tour of their wedding bower, lifting damp clothes and sorting through the mess they had made in their abandon.

"What are you looking for?"

"Ah, yes, I remember now!" A hunter sniffing the air, he stalked toward his dressing room. "My wedding gift to you."

"You're wearing it, Jack." She couldn't help but laugh when he stopped mid-stride and turned a crimson-cheeked grin on her and then on his own half-risen penis.

"That'll have to wait, my love." Though it didn't look as though it was of the same opinion. "Don't move, wife."

"I'm not going anywhere." She fell back against the pillows, deliciously married, profoundly in love, and admiring her husband's backside as he bounded into the dressing room. Hard-shadowed flanks and all that masculine equipage. No wonder it was so difficult to keep her hands off him.

He burst back into the bedroom a moment later, stabbing around in the pockets of his soggy jacket.

"I've had no time to wrap it up in a velvet bag, as it should be."

"Your wet jacket will do—though I can't imagine how you slipped away from me today to find a wedding gift. Unless you divined our baby's intention to bring us together, and planned our wedding for today."

"My hindsight is excellent; I should have seen the signs: my rosy wife and her ripening breasts, her waist just a bit thicker than I remembered."

"I was neither your wife nor amenable to your fondling, if you recall."

"Ha! Not amenable? That's not my recollection."

She blushed to her toes, aching for him, because everything, all her plans had turned out so very right. "What have you there, husband?"

"As you know, in the past my stupendous divination talents have run to coal and lead. And now, with your help—" he pulled a wadded handkerchief out of his pocket, tossed away his jacket, and planted himself in front of her on the bed, a huge, astounded grin on his face.

"Give me your hand, Mairey."

A golden wedding band, perhaps? The absolutely dear man —it must be. Though the object wrapped up in his wet handkerchief wasn't at all wedding-ring shaped … more like a small, thick tea saucer. The gladness drained out of her heart for a moment and flew away in fright, leaving her stomach flipped on edge and her head light. Her palms were damp and fisted into her lap.

The baby again—already making itself known as forcefully as its father, interrupting her every thought.

"Your hand, my sweet wife." He was jubilant, his dark eyes gleaming the brightest she'd ever seen them while he waited impatiently to bestow his gift.

"All right, Jack." She smiled back at her marvelous husband and gave him her hand, trusting him. He took it to his lips, kissed her fingers and her palm, then held it flat against his bare chest where his heart pounded as though it would fly away from her.

"Full circle, Mairey. We were meant to find each other."

She hoped so; prayed that she hadn't stolen this moment of happiness. "I love you, Jack."

"Which makes me the most fortunate man in the world." He put the kerchief and its weighty contents in her palm and closed his hand over the gift.

The odd prickling across her scalp wasn't a manifestation of her pregnancy. It was fear, dark and cringing; an inexplicable foreboding.

"For you, Mairey. For us."

It came again, a great winged terror that swooped over her head and made her flinch, made her clutch her fingers around the round object. No! Not a disk. It couldn't be!

... one silv'red disk, anciently ornamented ...

No! "Jack!"

His eyes were so guileless and proud, so eager to please her with his harrowing secret. "Open it, Mairey."

No, please. Not the Willowmoon. Impossible! Not now. Not yet.

The piece in her hand was unbearably heavy, a murky darkness inside the crumpled linen. Her fingers shook in her dread, though she tried to hold them steady as she peeled back one corner of the linen and then the next, catching the sob in her throat before he could hear it.

"A crest of silver knotwork, Mairey," he breathed. "No larger than my palm."

The cloth fell away like the petals on a spent poppy. It was beautiful and wicked and molten hot in her hand.

The Willowmoon Knot.

She would know it anywhere. Felt it in her soul, like a primal wound. The sweeping spirals of willows and the cycles of the moon. The shale slopes of Nevisfell and the meanderings of the Stoney, the heart of silver and the tiny valley where her innocent village slept. As fine a map as any that Moule could have drawn.

Oh, Papa, what have I done?

"Of course, my love, the achievement is yours." He bent over the Knot, his cheek beside hers, grazing her with his mouth and his day-old whiskers. "You led me right to it with your stories— I merely picked it up. Though I haven't the faintest notion what all those markings mean. Do you know?"

The end of us, Jack. Not an ancient disk of silver, but a lethal arrow, pointed directly at everyone she loved. Aim it anywhere and precious blood would spill. She wrapped the hateful thing in the kerchief and set it on the bed beside her.

"I'll have to study the design myself, Jack."

"But not for days yet, Mairey. We've a marriage to begin. Our lives together. A family to grow and share."

He was such a fine man, immeasurably decent. She grasped at that tiny shred of hope and logic. He loved her. And that being so, wouldn't he, in his enormous capacity to understand, also love what she loved? Wouldn't he see the infamy in scraping away a forest of alder and willow to mine a cold-breasted metal that had no meaning to anyone? Wouldn't he see that not all treasure can be held in the hand?

"When did you find it, Jack?"

He looked sheepish, a scoundrel caught doing a good deed and liking the feeling too much. "This morning, in one of Larkenfield's trunks. Can you imagine my luck?"

Yes—and all of it cruel; ill-timed and far-reaching.

"You've had the Knot since this morning, Jack, and you didn't tell me."

He lifted her chin, studied her eyes. "You fainted, Mairey, if you recall. And then there was a visit to Timson, and our baby–" he spanned her waist with his hands "–and a wedding at the registrar's office. And we've been making love nearly every moment since." His easy smile devastated her. "Priorities."

How easily they fell into place. A daughter's promise to her father, as deeply felt as a son's pledge to his own. Family was all, must ever be so. Had she dared trust her dear husband, he might even have understood the reason she must leave him tonight. But he'd found the Knot too soon, the chink in her own armor and the only way to protect the Willowmoon was to vanish in the night with her sisters.

"I thought you'd be a little more excited, Mairey. After all, I've done a rather miraculous thing."

Her miracle. She couldn't move for the grief bearing down on her. "You've overwhelmed me, Jack."

He feigned injured pride with one of his roguish brows. "I've seen you overwhelmed, my love, and you make a lot more noise than that." He leaned her backward against the pillows and began his tender crusade to steal what little she had left of her heart. "Let me see if I can do better this time."

To embrace him once more, long enough to last a lifetime— through those empty years when she would reach out for him and he would be but her dearest memory.

"I love you, Jack!"

"You are my heart, Lady Rushford, forever more."

She took him into her, and, in the same exquisite moment, she found the Knot beneath her hip, cold and exacting. Furious and already grieving, she shoved it over the side of the bed, unwilling to share her last embrace with its shadows. It landed with a leaden clunk, a sound that echoed through her heart.

He looked up from his nuzzling, a brow cocked. "Not going to sleep with the Willowmoon Knot under your pillow to help you dream about a silver mine?"

Her wayward dragon, who would never learn his own strength, whom she loved more than her own life.

"Oh, Jack, I'd much rather dream of us." She gloried in his touch, wept through every caress, and spent her passion for him through that final release, while the moon in its infallible course crept across the counterpane.

Jack was deep into his untroubled dreams when she slipped from beneath the cover.

Without another breath for fear of collapsing into sobs and slipping back into bed beside him, Mairey retrieved the Willowmoon Knot from the floor and stole out of Jack's life forever.

"**W**ake up, Anna!" Mairey whispered as she gently untucked the covers from beneath the girl's chin, her hands icy cold and shaking badly. "You've got to get up now."

Anna stretched and yawned, then blinked up at her through the dim predawn light of the garret. "Mairey? What's wrong?"

"Nothing, sweetheart. We're leaving." She hadn't shed a tear since arriving at the lodge—couldn't, because there wasn't time, and the girls would panic if they saw her weeping. She needed to get them out before the estate began to stir and Jack discovered her missing from their bed. She feared that most of all. Feared facing the man and his heartbreak.

"Going where?" Anna sat up. "Where's Lord Jack?"

Lost to us, love. "He's sailing away to Canada on the morning tide, to see to an emergency in one of his mines."

Anna scooted out of bed. "Lord Jack went to Canada without us? Without you, Mairey?"

"He wants us to live in the country while he's gone. You remember our old village—the one we used to visit sometimes when Papa was alive. We're to wait for Jack there."

"He'll come and get us?"

Oh, how this wicked knot of silver had tangled their lives in its treachery!

"Of course, he will. He loves us. Come now, sweet. Dress in these." She helped Anna into a pair of knickers and a shirt that were miles too big but would serve as a disguise.

Jack wouldn't be looking for three little boys and a young man in a stableman's hat; he'd be tearing up the world for his wife and his child, for three little girls whom he loved. He'd said it plainly enough: that he'd lost one family to his carelessness; he would never lose another. Because he loved too deeply, and without end.

"Should we wake Aunt Tattie now, Mairey? She takes hours to dress."

"No, Anna." She couldn't risk Tattie's questions. She wasn't a Faelyn; had never heard of the Knot, or the village tucked away in the shade of the Willowmoon glade.

Her heart broken to bits, Mairey fumbled with the buttons on Anna's coat and sniffed back tears that clung to her throat. "Auntie's staying here at Drakestone to look after the lodge while we're gone."

Jack would surely take care of her when he discovered they were missing, would need her support, and she would need his.

"For a whole week, do you think?"

"Maybe a little longer." How long was a lifetime? And how long could a heart grieve? She wound Anna's hair into a knot, then settled a woolen cap onto her head.

"Can I take the book Jack gave me?" Anna slipped the thick volume from under her pillow. "It'll remind me of him while he's away."

Children of the New Forest. The perfect gift from a perfect man. Anna had already read it through twice.

"Of course." They roused Caro, who eagerly wriggled into a linen shirt, a pair of rustic trousers, and a thick coat, before stashing her stick-and-wool pony into a rucksack along with four apples.

Poppy slept on, completely unaware, as Mairey dressed her, wrapped her in her favorite blanket, carried her past Aunt Tattie's dear snoring, and down the stairs. They took little with them beyond their favorite things and just enough food for a long day's ride on the train. They would make the village by sundown tomorrow, and begin a new life without Jack.

Mairey and her three little loves left Drakestone through the quiet woods, following the familiar deer trails, and leaving new, trackless ones as they went, Jack's child and the Willowmoon Knot hidden close against her heart.

I'll love you always, my valiant dragon. My Jack.

~

"Mairey!"

Jack woke in a blind, groping panic, a biting fear gnawing in his gut and his heart trying to tear out of his chest.

He was in his room, *their* room, in their marriage bed. But something was vastly wrong.

Mairey was gone. Her scent, her clothes. He slid his hands over the mattress and into the hollow of her pillow, but even before he'd felt the chill of long-empty sheets, he knew she'd left him hours ago.

For the lodge, surely. Out of habit—to check on her sisters. The girls often rose before the sun to do their mischief. His pulse settled some as he counted up the reasons Mairey would have slipped out of bed on the morning after their unplanned wedding.

To study the Willowmoon Knot was the most probable reason. She had seemed so unaffected by it last night. He'd presented her father's legacy to her on a platter, and all she could do was to stare at it as though it bored her. A testament to the intensity of their love-making, to the newness of their marriage—and their child.

He searched the room for the disk, but it was gone from where it had fallen earlier.

Clearly, that was the answer. Mairey had doubtless awakened with the birds, thrilled at the Knot's reappearance, and ensconced herself in the library, already hard at work deciphering the cryptic symbols. The perfect wedding gift for the both of them. He may have found the Knot, but without Mairey's interpretation of the bewildering glyphs, the disk was meaningless. No more a treasure map to a field of silver than a decorative table trivet.

Amused at his wife's diligence, he pulled on his trousers and a shirt, then left the bedroom for the library mezzanine, intending to entice her back into their bed. He would lock the door this time and never let her go.

"Mairey! Have you unraveled the riddle yet? Have you found our silver mine?"

But there was no answer from the dimness, no movement below as he descended the spiral stairs to the main floor. The library looked exactly as it had for the past few months: a harmonious blend of stuffy mining baron and eccentric antiquarian.

But Mairey wasn't there, nor was she in his office next door.

Sumner hadn't seen her, and neither had the cook or any of the household staff he met as he dashed through the dim hallways. Deciding she must have gone to the lodge after all, he pulled on his overcoat and a pair of boots then set off into woods, trying to ignore the sudden paralyzing fear that had begun settling into his bones the moment he'd found her missing from his bed.

He arrived at the lodge to find the door standing forlornly open and Tattie flying down the stairs in her night-robe and curl rags.

"Tattie, have you seen—"

"Your lordship, my little ducks are *gone!*"

"What do you mean, gone?" Terrified when the woman stammered and burst into tears, Jack raged up the stairs, Tattie on his heels, to find only their empty beds and a terrifying loneliness.

"We have to tell Mairey, sir! She'll know what to do."

Jack caught the woman's shoulders. "You mean Mairey isn't here? You haven't seen her?"

"Not since you took her off to your honeymoon last night."

"Christ, Tattie! Mairey's not with me! I hoped she was with you."

"Then where is she, my lord? It's not like her to take the girls and leave without a word!"

Not like his Mairey at all. "Then they can't be far, can they?"

Desperately wanting to believe he was making too much of their disappearance, Jack tore apart the lodge looking for clues, leaving Tattie to tidy up behind him. He searched through Aunt Tattie's kitchen garden and the greenhouse, the woodland pathways and the pond, all the way to the main house, hoping to discover Mairey and the girls cavorting about on some capricious adventure.

Sumner helped him search the kitchen, the library, his office, every floor, from the cellars to the attics. No sign of them anywhere.

With panic setting in, and fearing they had been abducted in the middle of the night, Jack roused the entire estate to scour the grounds and the woods for evidence of intruders. He led searches of every outbuilding and shed, every niche and hedge and favorite hidey-hole.

His heart in his throat, he enlisted a pair of constables, a team of lawyers, and sent a warning to his account officer at the Bank of England that he may have to withdraw an enormous sum of money at a moment's notice.

"Are you certain your family has been kidnaped, sir?" the banker asked as Jack met him under the *porte cochere*.

"I want to be prepared for the worst, Amberson." He wasn't certain of anything, only that he would spend his entire fortune for their safe return.

Over the next few hours, Drakestone House became the center of a massive search, adding constables, three detectives and a police commissioner to the force, sending the search in ever-widening circles around the estate, and into the surrounding countryside. Leaving Jack to ransack every drawer in Mairey's desk, to check under the blotter, the cubby holes and shelves, to leaf through her books, looking for God knew what clue that might bring her back to him.

Daylight turned to night, his hopes to despair as the search teams returned empty-handed, finding not a single sign of them anywhere.

As though they had vanished into thin air, or had never existed at all. If he hadn't spent the past three months following the intrepid Mairey Faelyn over tottering towers of crates, through miles of musty undercrofts, into caverns of coal, if he hadn't fallen for her and her sisters, he might believe he'd gone mad.

Auntie Tattie was his touch with reality. Her helplessness, her growing fears had become his own. He'd returned to the lodge a dozen times during the day, to comfort her, to buoy his own spirits. To reconnect with Mairey.

"Have the police found anything, my lord?"

"I'm afraid not." He looked around the parlor, as tidy as he'd ever seen it. The chaise too neat, the floor clear of toys and books and blankets. Jackets hung neatly in the vestry, shoes and boots lined up like soldiers against the wall.

"I tidied, my lord. Upstairs too. Their beds are ready for when they ... they ... come home." The last of Aunt Tattie's words fell away into another bout of hiccuping sobs against his chest.

"They'll be home soon, Tattie." He patted the woman's back. "Though I doubt they'll recognize the place. So tidy, you'd never know that three little girls ever lived here."

No sign of the girls at all. A chill rolled down his spine. He ran upstairs to the girls' garret room, hoping.

But as he feared, Poppy's blanket wasn't waiting for her in her small bed. Caro's stick horse wasn't stabled upright against the hearth. Anna's much-loved copy of The Children of the New Forest was missing from under her pillow.

The truth finally found him as he stood in Mairey's room: her father's hat missing, along with her satchel and her Gladstone.

Each of their favorite things, carefully gathered, missing. A blanket, a pony, a book, taken with them when Mairey stole away with everything he loved.

The gut-wrenching truth glittered and danced before his eyes, blinding him with its clarity.

Silver. Of course! The riches of the Willowmoon! That had been her goal all along. The reason she'd refused to help him at first, why she'd reluctantly agreed to help him find the Knot in the end. A brilliant scenario concocted by him, but executed to the finest detail by the treacherously cunning Mairey Faelyn.

Tales of fairies and giants and dragons. Enigmatic riddles. Kings and loyal queens and caravans of jewels. An enchanting pageant she'd created solely to ensnare him, cloaked in scholarly innocence, shimmering with promise and practiced tears. She'd even dangled her little family in front of him—his family, too—long enough to bewitch him, to distract him from suspecting the depth of her artifice.

And, like a fool, he'd believed every part of her tale—because she'd made him love her. When all she loved was the silver at the end of their story.

Damn you, Mairey Faelyn! Hide away in some forgotten corner of the country, decipher the map on the face of the Knot, and try to sell its secrets to the highest bidder. He would find her long before that.

He'd been lost in helpless anger before she'd found him, unwilling to look beyond his own failings. But she'd taught him how to pursue for his heart's desire no matter the pain, to face the truth about his sisters, his mother. The pledge he'd made to his father.

She'd taught him to believe in love again. And would soon discover she'd stolen the one treasure he would search the world to find.

She'd stolen his child.

~

"I've never seen so many trees, Mairey!" Caro launched a great armful of leaves into the air, squealing as they rained down on her head.

Freshly fallen leaves scattered atop last year's fragrant loam, ready handfuls to toss at each other, drawing laughter and more squealing from her sisters.

"I knew you'd love it here, girls.."

Once upon a time, the Glade of the Willowmoon had been Mairey's favorite place in all the world. A meadowy clearing surrounded by a stunning forest, always beautiful in its ever-turning, ever constant seasons. The barren branches of winter, the bright, rich greens of spring that change unnoticed into summer's thick canopy, the high color and brilliant drama of autumn. Alder, ash, and blackthorn, wych elm and elder reaching to the sun, the understory of willow, slender trunks and silvery leaves offering food and shelter to deer and rabbits, baskets and building materials and medicines to her people. Masking the treasure below with its wildness.

Now her refuge of peace felt like a gray-walled prison, with too much sky. Though her sisters frolicked and the sun shone down through the canopy, these three days away from Jack had been bleaker than she could bear.

What a terrible price she'd exacted from the man she loved. Dear God, the mess she'd made of his life and hers. She'd left him not a note nor a hint of where they'd gone, or why. He was a good man and would only suspect she'd betrayed him after he'd exhausted every other motive, denying her faithlessness even as he employed every resource to find her. She was exhausted, weary from running, her energy sapped by the baby's need to make her sleep all the time and by the grief that shaded her heart.

"When is Lord Jack coming back from Canada, Mairey?"

Sweet, Poppy, you'll have to settle for a less dizzying height than our Jack's broad shoulders.

"I don't know, Poppy." Oh, what an unblinking liar she had become.

"I hope he comes here today." Poppy's lower lip stuck out wretchedly as she ambled from tree to tree with her blanket, giving each a hug, as though she believed her beloved Lord Jack would feel her embrace from across the phantom sea.

"I'd like that more than anything."

Here was a fairy tale turned on its head: of the dragon who comes to rescue his princess from the malevolent treasure she was guarding. The world gone topsy-turvy.

"Will he come by Christmas, do you think, Mairey?" Anna had found one of their grandmother's flower presses in the attic of their old house and was collecting an assortment of fallen leaves to start her own specimen book.

"It's a very long way to Canada," Mairey said, lowering herself onto the sinewy trunk of a fallen hornbeam, "and an even longer way across the country."

Some day she'd have to tell the girls that their Jack wasn't coming for them. Would fabricate some agonizing tale about a shipwreck and their beloved hero drowning at sea. What a horrible day that would be! Killing Jack in order to make them forget him, so they wouldn't set out to find him one day when they were old enough. Wicked lies and tender hearts.

She had buried the Willowmoon Knot the morning before; had come here to the glade just before dawn and found a perfect and lasting place to hide it. Had prayed for her father and mother, given thanks for all the devoted Faelyns who'd gone before her, who'd sacrificed so much to spare their village the same fate as Glad Heath.

The Willowmoon and its silver might be safely hidden from the world, but her guardianship had no end. Her life was here now, no chance of returning to Jack to beg his forgiveness and begin their lives together. The risk of him discovering the Faelyn family's ancient secret was too great. The girls in their innocence already knew too much. She must find her joy and contentment in raising Jack's child, and live out her days in the peace of the village, where she would watch her sisters grow to womanhood, and then leave her to seek the wide world. Impossible to consider just now.

"What are you doing, Poppy?"

The girl was spinning like a top, her arms outstretched and her chin lifted to the sun. "I'm wishing for Lord Jack to come home from the sea."

"Wish him home for me, Poppy." *I love you, Jack.*

Her sisters began throwing handfuls of leaves at each other again, stopped to conspire in whispers and then turned the barrage on Mairey, until everyone was squealing and laughing and falling all over each other.

"Not fair, girls! Three against one!" Well, against two, she thought, touching her hand to her belly.

I'll take care of your child, Jack. He'll know what a fine man his father was. No better man in the world.

"My turn!" Mairey stood and scooped up an apronful of leafy ammunition, ready to toss it at her sisters, but they had stopped, frozen in their battle stances, and staring at something in the woods behind her.

Something wonderful by the looks of wide-eyed awe on their little faces. A heron perhaps, pausing in the treetops. A deer.

"Lord Jack! Mairey, it's him!" The girls squealed with glee.

"Jack?" God no! He'd found her, here in the glade! A sob of relief and joy and absolute terror wrenched from her chest; made her turn and stare at him, open her arms and gather her sisters close.

Jack! He'd become her world, her life, the beating of her heart. And now he'd come to destroy her.

He was framed in the gray trunks of the willows, huge in his fury, silent, as flinty as the winter. A man able to rip the trees from the ground with his bare hands. The sharpness of the sun pierced the canopy, dappling his shoulders and his greatcoat in emeralds, turned his black hair to ebony. His eyes gleamed with demon fire, possessive and absolute, and made her heart yearn for him.

He started toward them, a hunger in his gait, a bloodlust that shook the ground, sending silvery leaves falling as he brushed through the understory.

"Stay here, girls." She couldn't allow them run to him, clutched at their arms and hands to hold them back. But like a great tide of happiness they broke free.

"I knew you'd come!"

"Take us home with you, Lord Jack!"

"Don't ever go away again, please!"

She watched them stumble over each other in their headlong dash to meet him. He lifted them into his arms as he walked, took their kisses and their hugs, and returned them fiercely. Yet all the while he was looking at Mairey, the glint of obsidian in his gaze.

"See, Mairey!" Poppy laid her cheek next to his and squeezed him in delight, wrapped her blanket around his neck. "Lord Jack came back when I wished for him! I told you he would."

You wished too hard, Poppy.

He hadn't come to them out of love, but to lay claim to his bloody silver. She'd stolen his treasure, and dragons didn't like that. He was danger and delight. The end and the beginning of her happiness. The father of her child, a man whose duty to family ran as deeply as her own, whose gaze had once wrapped her in splendor and hope.

Now his eyes were searing black, as unrelenting as his long strides that brought him ever closer. She backed up a few steps, seeking a solid place to take her stand against him, where she could better gather her sisters behind her—once she'd disentangled them from him.

"Did you go to Canada already?" Caro was rifling his pockets as she hurried to keep up with him. "Did you see a *bear*? We saw a deer this morning!"

"You didn't go to Canada, did you, Lord Jack?" Anna had captured one of his hands and looked up at him with her heart in her eyes, a lamb taking comfort in the arms of a lion. "It takes more than three days to sail to there and back, doesn't it?"

He stopped two yards from Mairey, a seething beast come to feast upon her heart. Little hands had rumpled him, from his dark hair, to the smudge of dirt on his waistcoat, to the leaves caught up in his trouser cuffs.

"Is that what you told them, Mairey?" His voice came from somewhere deeply distant, filled with bitterness. "That I had sailed to Canada?"

"Jack, I—"

"Kiss him, Mairey!" Caro shoved Mairey gently from behind. "We already did!"

He was waiting for her answer, his chest rising and falling in his unleashed wrath. Nothing she could say would mitigate the situation between them. He would have his silver now, and she would do her best to thwart him in his ravaging. A great storm of destruction was brewing here in the glade; she couldn't allow the girls to suffer its fury.

She drew Anna away from Jack. "Sweetheart, would you take Caro and Poppy to the house and help Mrs. Russell with dinner?"

"Oh, yes! Can we have a picnic in the woods?"

What a fitting tribute before Jack could turn the beauty of the glade into a slag heap. "Of course you may, Anna."

"Oh, goodeeeee!" Poppy scrambled out of Jack's arms and ran after her sisters, their skirts and their laughter flying out behind them, kicking up a flurry of leaves.

Her stomach churned as she watched them disappear down the path that led through the woods, past the winding glint of the Stoney to the slate-roofed cottages of her village.

How long would it take him to befoul its beauty as he had Glad Heath? Resentment sizzled down her spine and she swung around to glare at him.

"How did you find me, Jack?"

"If you thought I wouldn't track you to the ends of the earth, then you misunderstand your worth to me."

"My weight in silver, I'm sure! How flattering."

His jaw tightened. "Damn you, Mairey! I want the Willow-moon Knot. It's mine."

A devastating echo of such a long-ago time—before he'd stolen her heart; before she'd stolen his, and his baby, and all his dreams.

"The Knot? What's that matter now, my lord?" Shamed to her soul that she'd failed her family so completely, she took two steps backward but met with the trunk of a beech, forcing her to look up at him. "You already have everything."

"Everything?" His eyes glittered with molten fury, red-rimmed and haggard. Her coiling dragon, sinuous and unbridled, no sense of propriety to keep him from pressing his hardness against her belly, his mouth against her temple and then the hollow of her neck—an intimacy she craved and met, an unquenchable memory that swept her along with the beating of his heart until he pulled away. "Damn it, Mairey, you've left me nothing."

Their baby, of course. His family.

"I'm sorry, Jack, when you found the Knot, I had no choice."

He reared back, took a breath then bellowed, "No choice but to betray me? Why? Who did you sell it to?"

"Sell *what*?" He was making no sense.

"Enough with your bloody games. Tell me the bastard who has the map!"

"I didn't sell the Knot, Jack." What did he need with the map when he was standing right on top of his bloody treasure? All the silver he could mine, just a few feet under his heels.

"It belongs to me, Mairey. Because you're my wife." He cradled her head with the greatest of care, though his anger shook him, drove his words against her brow. "We married. Whatever was yours now belongs to me. Your books, your collections, and that goddamned Willowmoon Knot."

"Jack, please!" She touched his mouth with her fingertips.

"You remember the Knot, Mairey. I found it in the British Museum, and gave it to you on our wedding night."

"Of course I remember." The sweetest, the dearest night of her life.

"Then why?" His mouth came down roughly on hers, tasting salty from his grief, filling his throat with a desolated moan that made her weep. "You stole my heart, my trust, my family."

"I'm so sorry, Jack. I didn't mean to let you—"

"Let me what? Find you? You don't know me very well, do you? I'll have that bloody, indecipherable map before I leave here. And I'll find that bloody vein of silver without your help."

You'll find it? But you already have, Jack! Her heart thumped around inside her chest, her thoughts flying backward through the last few horrible minutes. The dear man didn't realize they were standing on top of his damnable vein of silver! If he would only give her a moment to think, maybe she could lead him away from the secret, out of the glade and back to Drakestone, where they could be together until the end of time.

Oh, love, we've a chance to be together, after all.

"How did you find me, Jack?"

Jack had wanted nothing more than to hate her, his faithless wife, had determined to shut her out of his heart as easily as she'd shut him out of hers.

Once he'd realized she had stolen everything from him, he expected to follow her glittering path from the lodge to the Savoy, and from there to the fashionable salons of Paris, would find the woman draped in diamonds, and laughing at her success, her newfound riches, at him. The antiquarian who had bested the mining baron at his own game.

But her trail had led him from train station to station, then miles north through a thick, ancient forest of willow and alder, finally, to Mairey herself, standing in this sylvan glade, magnificent in her simplicity, her eyes bright with a pain that echoed like thunder in his heart, leaves and bits of the forest clinging to her hair, harrowing tears wetting her cheeks.

"You taught me too well, wife. I followed a trail of births, marriages, and deaths. Your father is buried in the churchyard below us, in the parish of Lynne, in the North Riding of Yorkshire. Your mother is here, too."

She pushed lightly against his chest. "Please, Jack, don't—"

"And who couldn't follow the trail of three little girls and an overly protective young woman, all of them dressed up as stable hands?" Sweet God, she smelled of the autumn, of smokey resins, spicy and vibrant, caught up in the curls at her temple. "It's difficult to hide such gilded tresses as yours, my dear. They make men think of climbing impossibly tall towers, of slashing through forests of thorns to impress you with their great love for you. Well, I have such a love for you, Mairey."

She was sobbing, clutching her arms around her waist and shaking her head. "I'm sorry, Jack. You can't know how much I love you. I didn't want to hurt you."

"But you have—you've wounded me as no one else in the world could."

"Please!" She twisted out of his arms and he let her move away from him. "Jack, I'm sorry it turned out this way."

"This way? Which way is that, Mairey?" He caught her shoulders and turned her. "That you betrayed me for another man's treasure?"

"There's no other man! How could you even think that of me?"

"For your own treasure, then? Damn it, Mairey. There is nothing right about this whole enterprise. I *know* you. I know your heart in all its splendor. I know its fullness, because I've been there, Mairey. I'm *still* there, inside you. In here." He spread his hand over her belly, his heart aching with the loss of all she'd stolen from them. All their hopes, their happiness. For what? "Tell me why you ran from me."

"I can't, Jack. My mistake was to love you."

"Your mistake? Our child is not a mistake, Mairey. Your sisters. They gave you away."

"The girls?"

"You took too much of yourselves with you when you left. When I thought you'd been kidnapped, I tore apart the estate, the house, the villages, roused heaven and hell searching for you. But in the end, the clues were waiting for me in the lodge. Or rather, they weren't in the lodge. Poppy's blanket, Caro's stick horse—"

"*The Children of the New Forest*. The book you gave Anna."

"You'd not been kidnapped, Mairey, you packed your belongings and vanished with my heart, thought you'd vanished from my life forever–"

"Jack, that's not how it–"

"You said yourself that we belong together. Were you lying to me, then?"

"I wouldn't lie to you, Jack." Her gaze left his and took in the forest all around them, her eyes shimmering with tears as they stood together in this leafy glade, among the willows and the yew, where the sun and its shadows wove a rich tracery into the paleness of her dress. "Not about that."

"About what, then? How could an ancient disk of silver change everything right and good between us?"

"You don't understand."

"Then make me understand, damn it! Tell me why you belong here and not at my side." Was she homesick for this place —for the memory of her father and mother? For her peaceful village far away from him?

That was it, of course! Like a shadow lifting from his eyes, he suddenly understood. Mairey belonged here with the girls, in a nameless village, settled into a cottage, protected by an impenetrable forest.

Remote and wild, hidden from the world, from him. So remote he'd hired a horse that morning from the station master and followed his instincts, guided by an ethereal sense of purpose. He'd crossed the same river three times, followed a trail up a gentle hillside of shale, skirting the edge of a village, and entered these woods, where he'd found Mairey waiting for him, waiting for their lives to begin.

Behind her, above the forest shale hills rose like the dorsals of a serpent into the brilliance of the sky. A geology familiar to him, because at their roots, these ridges would be rich in lead and tin and—

Silver!

The glyphs on the Knot, revealed as clearly as a cartographer's atlas. A thrice winding river, a chevron of hills, a forest of willow, and the full moon at it center. His pulse surged with recognition.

"Christ, Mairey. This is where the face of the Willowmoon led you."

She gasped, paled, and caught hold of a branch. "Don't be absurd, Jack." But she laughed too brightly, falsely. She paced away through the trees, touching the trunks and fingering the yellowing leaves. "I would have engaged an engineer to meet me here, if I suspected there was silver hereabout."

"Like hell you would have." He found a likely spot near an outcropping of shale, then knelt down, yanked away the moss, then dug his hands into the loamy earth.

"What are you doing, Jack?"

"I'm looking for my silver mine." Three inches further, and he was scraping at solid, crumbling rock.

"Stop it, Jack!" She fell to her knees beside him, had a fierce hold of his wrist. "Please don't. If you love me, you'll stop. We can start over again. Away from here."

But he was already pinching a raisin-sized pebble between his fingers, holding its dark, sharp-edged tarnish in front of her. Holy hell! He'd pulled many a nugget from the rivers of Nova Scotia, but none had been as pure as this.

"Silver, Mairey."

He'd never seen a face so filled with defeat. She hung her head, her shoulders drooping. "Yes."

"You knew where to find the silver from the moment I handed you the Knot. While you lay there in our marriage bed. You recognized the river and this hillside of willows."

She said nothing, but rose wearily and turned away from him to look up at the hills. "Think what you will, Jack."

"You made plans to steal the Knot and leave me, and then you made love with me." He stood, wishing for understanding. "For *auld lang syne*, Mairey?"

Her prideful shoulders shook with a sob. "Because I love you, Jackson Rushford. And I would miss you every day of my life."

"Then why leave, Mairey, when we had it all at our fingertips? We'd come so far together." Unless she wanted the silver all for yourself.

Yet something deep inside of him knew that couldn't be the answer. This was Mairey, not some greedy industrialist. She was the clear-hearted woman who loved him, who loved their child and her sisters, her Aunt Tattie.

Who loved the woods, the meadows, the innocent places.

Who'd gone to heroic lengths in her devotion to her family and to her father's memory—

Her father. There was the answer, splendid and bright.

"My God, Mairey. The Willowmoon Knot wasn't a legend to you; it was fact."

"It was."

"You wanted to find the Knot first, before it might lead a mining baron like me to the fortune in silver lying where? Just beneath the ground?"

"Please, Jack, don't spoil my village." The sun lit her face, tears washing down her cheeks. "Don't let this beautiful glade come to be like Glad Heath. Let me keep my promise to my father and to my grandfather."

"And to all the Faelyns who have ever been? Is that it, Mairey?" Christ, his fierce-hearted wife was a champion like none he had ever known. She hadn't stolen the Willowmoon Knot for her own; she'd only returned the artifact to its rightful place, driven by promises far older than his own.

Promises. Family. No wonder she had known his heart so well.

"Please, Jack. I can't stay here to see it happen.

"I don't imagine you could."

Sweet Mairey. She wasn't a deceitful, dishonorable thief, but an indomitable warrior, prepared to sacrifice her own life to protect her family—an incomparable woman who would love him till the end of time.

"Who owns this land, Mairey?"

"The Crown." She stood her ground, her chin firm but her face streaked with tears.

"And the name of your village?"

"It doesn't have one. Our family kept it off the maps that way. An unremarked part of Yorkshire, overlooked for its plainness."

"But loved for its beauty?"

Another shattering sob wracked her, and he loved her for it.

"Please, Jack, don't bring your blight upon my village. Think of Anna and Caro and Poppy, our unborn child—"

"Oh, Mairey, my love." He gathered her into his arms, letting her sob into his waistcoat. "I think of them every minute, as I think of my own sisters. I think of the fortune I would gladly give if I could have them back for just a moment. You see, I always believed that if I increased my fortune, my titles, opened more mines, that one day they might find me. Or I might find them."

"Jack, you can't open this one. Not the Willowmoon—"

"Oh, but I could, love. More simply than I had imagined, if this is indeed Crown land. No greedy peers to include in the royalties—"

She shoved him away, his lady lioness. "If you do, I will fight you. Jack! With every weapon I can find!"

"I'm sure you would, Mairey."

"I'll raise a strike against you—I'll burn you out! I'll speak to the prince consort!"

He didn't dare smile, let alone laugh, though joy bubbled up inside him.

"Speak to Prince Albert if you feel you must, Mairey, but I think I'll speak to the queen myself."

"Throwing your power around as usual?" Her chest rose and fell, her breasts shifting in her outrage.

"Absolutely, my love." Choosing between his wife and a hillside rich with silver was the simplest thing he'd ever done.

Mairey had been breathless with fear since Jack came raging into the glen, became even more alarmed by the sudden change in her husband. He was smiling. No. He was grinning devilishly.

"Tell me, wife, what will you name this village when it belongs to me?"

A heartless question. "I hate you, Jack."

"No, you don't." He was stalking slowly toward her, looking confident and horribly pleased with himself. And why not? He had his mine. She'd handed it to him on a silver tray.

"I'm going to fight you, Jack."

"I doubt that, my love. You'll be too busy raising our children." He lifted her into his arms and kissed her madly. "And I'll be too busy keeping the secret of the Willowmoon for you."

She pushed against his shoulders, misunderstanding his words for the rushing of her pulse against his. "Keeping the secret from your competitors, while you exploit the hillside."

He shook his head. "This is your home, Mairey. I don't need another silver mine, I have you."

Hope made such a clamoring noise in her head she wasn't sure she'd heard him right. "What did you say?"

"I already have two. And if another means losing you, my love, I don't want any part of it."

Alarms changed to joyous bells. Jack's laughter, and the erotic swell of his melody as he made love to her mouth.

"Look, Caro! Mairey is kissing Lord Jack again!"

The girls were at the edge of the woods, coming on fast.

"We're not alone, wife."

"I love you so much, Jack."

"I know." She felt his smile as he closed his mouth over hers; heard the rumble of his laughter. "Does your cottage have a private room, just for the two of us?"

"Oh, yes, my love."

"Excellent. Because I plan a good deal of princess-plundering tonight."

"Come plunder, my dragon. I am yours forever."

EPILOGUE

Drakestone House

Eighteen months later

"You are a darling tyrant, Lady Rushford." Lady Arthur shook Mairey's hand vigorously and started down the front steps of Drakestone House, remarkably agile for a woman of more than sixty.

"We must be relentless, Lady Arthur, if we're going to change the laws to protect the health of miners and their families." Mairey followed the woman to her phaeton, delighted that this afternoon's meeting had gone so smoothly and had been so well attended by the wives of peers and parliamentary ministers. "The mining barons certainly will not spend their own profits on research into coal miner's lung diseases and poor diet and lack of sunshine, unless we force them."

"No, indeed. May the mine owners of Britain beware." She added with a broad wink, "Your own husband included."

"Viscount Rushford is foursquare behind the British Women's Colliery Health Standards Commission." Mairey would defend her husband's honor with her bare hands if necessary. "He's given thousands already!"

"I know, dear." Lady Arthur's grin was filled with affable mischief. "I was referring to the fact that his beautiful wife wraps him so easily around her little finger. Good girl."

Mairey couldn't help her flush or her smile. Her dragon had been wrapped around more than her little finger last night—and early this morning, before their son had awakened for his breakfast.

"My husband does indulge my whims now and then. He would have joined us today, but there was an important meeting he had to attend." Jack's meeting was with little Patrick, an agenda that surely would include rolling the new three-wheeled baby carriage through the woods at top speed, feeding the ducks, collecting a sweet from Aunt Tattie's kitchen in the lodge, and a lot of cuddling and cooing. Hardly a fitting reputation for Britain's most influential mining baron, but a matchless reputation for a father and husband.

"Parade your husband for us next time, dear. He's sinfully handsome, and always quite the gentleman." Lady Arthur waved as her carriage sped away.

Mairey loved her new crusade and was committed to the fullest, but she had missed her son and his father terribly these last three hours. She gathered up her notes from Jack's conference table, and left his office for her desk in the library. A picnic would be a fine way to spend the rest of the day.

The warm afternoon light streamed in through the library windows, scattering rainbows across the room. Her search for father and son ended on the sun-washed carpet. Jack was lying on his back, his head propped on a cushion and his son sprawled loose-limbed across his chest, his long, bronze fingers splayed possessively over Patrick's diaper-thick bottom.

They were both snoozing blissfully.

Mairey felt like weeping for the boundless joy they brought her.

Jack was never far away from her these days. She had assumed that after a chaotic year of negotiating his way past three little girls, a delighted Aunt Tattie, a new wife, and now a son, all of whom adored him, he would have grown immune to his family, weary of their demands. But every day he seemed to draw them even closer.

He encouraged the girls in their pursuits, supported Tattie in her tussles with Sumner, and joined Mairey in her causes.

And now he held her village and the shale peaks from the Crown, a landlord with all the powers of the State behind him. He'd kept his promise to preserve the Glade of the Willowmoon as a secret between them, protected forever under the control of Rushford Mining and Minerals.

"I love you so, Jack," she whispered. Patrick stirred, wriggled his nose and his fingers and his toes, and then settled his little cherub cheek against his father's heart, and Mairey's breasts reacted on cue. He would be bellowing for a snack in a moment, waking his dear father from a much-needed nap.

"Come, my little one." She scooped her baby into her arms, but he slept on, undisturbed even as she settled him into his cradle beside Jack's desk. Jack looked irresistible, too handsome not to kiss while he slept. She knelt to do so, only to feel her husband's familiar hand sifting through her skirts, brushing lightly along the inside of her thigh. She gazed down at his eyes, glistening beneath his dark lashes.

"You were sleeping a moment ago, my dragon."

"Dreaming of you, my love … of this, of your scent." His eyes turned smokey when he found the breach in her drawers, and darkened when she met his questing hand and moaned.

"Oh, Jack! You're incorrigible. And wonderful."

"And you, my love, are delicious." He slipped his free hand

behind her neck and pulled her close to kiss her. "You finally finished with your meeting?"

"Oh, yes." She grew light-headed from his exhilarating caress, but encouraged his exploring. "We voted to petition Parliament for twenty-thousand pounds to establish a visiting medical corps. Oh, my!" She took a sharp breath when he dipped his fingers inside her, and another when he stayed to play.

"And then what, sweet?" The devil.

"We had tea—"

"And?"

"Then I told the ladies how I burned to make love with my husband, shooed them out, and came looking for you."

"And here I am, my love."

"You certainly are!" The rogue knew just how to make her sigh and gasp; and a long, breath-stealing moment later she was thoroughly sated, and tucked against Jack's shoulder.

And their son slept on in his cradle, as Jack described how brilliant Patrick was—and only nine months old, mind you— and Mairey listened with all her heart, until the boy woke up starving and wailing.

~

Jack wondered how happiness could make his heart ache. Stuffed full, he guessed. Even watching Mairey nurse their son was enough to sting the back of his eyes; the feel of the boy's hand wrapped around his finger sent him soaring with pride and filled him with love.

Patrick finished his noisy meal and grinned up at his mother with all the besotted joy that Jack felt.

Could a man be more blessed?

"I was thinking, Jack, of a picnic." Mairey was fastening the two ingenious little openings between the copious pleats in her shirtwaist that allowed modesty while she was nursing.

But Jack was very good at gaining access when his son wasn't busy there. "I was thinking, Mairey, of retiring with you to our bed."

Her smile aroused him in an instant. She stood with Patrick on her hips and offered her hand to Jack, promising a splendid afternoon as soon as they could get the boy to sleep.

But then the library door burst open, and Poppy dashed into the room.

"Michaelmas cakes!" She was carrying a plate of lumpy baked goods. "See!"

They were the oddest cakes he'd ever seen. Plump with whole acorns and crumbling oats, spiced with bits of sea green moss, bristling with golden straw and glistening with honey.

"Are these people cakes, Poppy?" he asked, hoping they weren't, wondering how he would pretend to eat one without injuring her feelings.

Poppy giggled. "For the horses, silly!"

"I see," Jack said, forgiven for his gaff.

"Are the cakes cool enough yet, Poppy?" Caro asked as she came skipping through the door in her riding clothes, older these days, and mad for her new nephew, who seemed to think his young aunt was the funniest thing in the world. She nuzzled his nose with hers. "Hello, my baby duck."

Patrick whirled his fists at her and bounced on Mairey's hip.

"I'm going to jump the pony today!"

Jack's stomach lurched. Mairey shared a look of horror with him, but smoothed her fingers through Caro's hair. "You mind your teacher, Caroline Faelyn."

"Lord Jack!" They heard Anna long before she came clattering through the door in a pair of wooden garden clogs. She would be twelve two months from now, but was fast adding grace to her girlish beauty, and would soon be trailing gangly young men in her wake. Just now, though, she was wearing homespun gardening trousers and a huge, mud-caked shirt.

"For you, Lord Jack." She handed him a thick, battered packet that had suffered far more than her finger smudges.

The mail came to Drakestone twice a day, and company correspondence flowed up and down the drive like ferry boats across the Thames.

This was not that kind of mail.

"What is it, Jack?" Mairey touched his hand, shifting Patrick into her arms.

San Francisco. Addressed in a firm hand to "Jack Rushford, Drakestone House, Harrow." A well-traveled envelope that lodged his heart in his throat.

He had discovered recently that an Emma Rushford had emigrated to America in the spring of 1844, sailing around the Horn to California. His own Emma would have been fourteen, but the manifest hadn't listed ages, so he had sent inquiries to his contacts in San Francisco months ago.

He had learned to hold tightly to his hope.

"Where did you get this, Anna?" he asked.

"I was out at the end of the drive, and a boy came by with it"

"Did he say anything?"

She blushed through her sunburned cheeks. "Not about the mail. I told him I would deliver it to you straightaway."

"Thank you, Anna." His hands shook as he sliced the packet open. He felt Mairey's eyes on him, and absorbed the love that she wrapped him in.

"Were you expecting a letter from San Francisco, Jack?"

Where was the line between expectation and hope?

"Every day, my love." Because Mairey had taught him to love relentlessly.

Dear Mr. Rushford.

He could hardly read for the tears welling in his eyes.

If I am your sister, as your handbill at the San Francisco post office asks, I hope you'll recognize my poor renderings as memories of our shared childhood.

Mairey fit her hand through his arm. The girls crowded in. And all the world stood still.

On the next page was a neat pencil drawing of a cottage perched on the side of a hill, a gable chimney, windows on either side of the door. A man and a woman stood smiling beside each other in front of the cottage, two little girls to the woman's right. On the father's side, a younger man in a miner's cap was gripping the handle of a two-wheeled cart. And sitting inside the cart was a third little girl and a flop-eared dog.

"Who drew the picture, Lord Jack?" Caro asked.

He looked up at Mairey, a huge sob clutching at his heart.

"My sister drew this, Caro. Her name is Emma."

Mairey's eyes were starry with astonished joy, her cheeks streaming with her lovely tears, and her mouth, when she kissed him tasted of all the miracles she'd brought him.

"Happily ever after, Jack." She nuzzled his chin and gazed up at him, while Anna and Caro and Poppy clung to them both, and their son chortled and blew little bubbles between them.

Jack kissed Mairey soundly, his treasure, his dearest heart. "Oh, my sweet love, now and forever after."

THE END

Once Upon a Treasure Hunt by Linda Needham

Dear Reader

Thank you so much for trusting me with your happily ever aftering! I hope you enjoyed Mairey and Jack's hunt for treasure. Theirs was such a fun love story to write!

Once Upon a Treasure Hunt was originally published by Avon Books in 1999 as *The Wedding Night*, my first *Avon Romantic Treasure* imprint. The new, 2023 title is a coincidence, I assure you!

I've always been a huge fan of fairy tales, from The Golden Ass, to Grimm, to the stories at the heart of the Marvel Universe. I can't imagine a world without them.

So my writer's Spidey-Sense began jangling while I was reading the Preface to *The Fairy Faith in Celtic Countries*, a 1910 book of field-evidence gathered by W. Y. Evans-Wentz. The author bemoaned the fact that folklore scholars of the time, as well as their offbeat social science, were shunned by 'serious' academics.

Ah, ha, thought I! The perfect occupation for a feisty, folklorist heroine who struggles to be taken seriously among her cynical colleagues. Add her pledge to protect an ancient family secret, a missing map to the vast silver mine, and a dragon-hearted viscount who coerces her into helping him find the treasure and – voila! *Once Upon a Treasure Hunt* was born!

At the heart of my Once Upon a Time fairy tale is family, love, and loyalty. In the wake of our own unsettled, uncertain times, finding and keeping our loved ones close is more important than ever.

If you're a writer yourself, you might be interested in the examples I used from *Treasure Hunt* in my writing reference, *Brainstorming Your Novel: From First Spark to Blockbuster*.

If you want to keep up with me and my adventures, head on

over to my website at LindaNeedham.com, where you can subscribe to *The Hearth & Heath*, my semi-regular newsletter.

Thanks again and Happy Romancing!

Linda

Please leave a review at your favorite booksellers.

A great way for us to stay in touch is to:

Subscribe to my Newsletter, LindaNeedham.com/subscribe/

ABOUT LINDA

<u>LindaNeedham.com/About</u>

I began my journey on the road to romance writing in 1972 with an overcooked Thanksgiving turkey and my nose buried in a delicious copy of Kathleen Woodiwiss's first novel, *The Flame and the Flower*. Reading had always been one of my favorite obsessions, but Woodiwiss had for the first time fused the sweeping majesty of history with the sensual power of romance, and from that moment the romance novel industry went into high gear and was changed forever. I was desperately hooked on historical romance and soon after began secretly writing my own romance novel. I had a lot to learn!

Nearly 25 years after that fateful Thanksgiving weekend of 1972, my unpublished manuscript, *For My Lady's Kiss* won 1st place in six romance writing competitions, 2nd and 3rd place in six other competitions, and the 1995 Romance Writers of America's Golden Heart for Long Historical. Two months later the book sold, along with a one-line proposal for my second book, *Ever His Bride*, both to Avon Books, and, in February 1997, to my great delight, my first novel—*For My Lady's Kiss* was released! Many more books have followed, with five hitting the *USA Today* Bestseller list.

Of course, like every author, I started writing in early grade school, as soon as I realized that I could put my own words together to make my own stories, just like the authors of my favorite childhood books—*Beautiful Joe, Heidi,* and the *Nancy Drew* mysteries.

My love for storytelling eventually led me to a bachelor's degree in Theatre Arts where I gained a deep understanding of character development, dialogue, scene-shaping and plotting techniques. I'm also a playwright, one of the lucky few who have had full productions of their works—seven full length musicals, four revues and two full-length plays.

I write full-time from my home office near Portland, Oregon. And when I'm not writing, I've been known to direct plays and musicals, garden 'til I drop, spoil my two grandkids, take extended research treks with my hero husband and participate in K9 Nose Work with Winnie, our Portuguese Water Dog.

facebook.com/LindaNeedhamAuthor

instagram.com/authorlindaneedham

pinterest.com/TheLindaNeedham

goodreads.com/Linda_Needham

tiktok.com/@lindaneedham_authorrom